WORMWOOD

SUSAN
WITTIG ALBERT

WORMWOOD

BERKLEY PRIME CRIME, NEW YORK

THE BERKLEY PUBLISHING GROUP
Published by the Penguin Group
Penguin Group (USA) Inc.
375 Hudson Street, New York, New York 10014, USA
Penguin Group (Canada), 90 Eglinton Avenue East, Suite 700, Toronto, Ontario M4P 2Y3, Canada
(a division of Pearson Penguin Canada Inc.)
Penguin Books Ltd., 80 Strand, London WC2R 0RL, England
Penguin Group Ireland, 25 St. Stephen's Green, Dublin 2, Ireland (a division of Penguin Books Ltd.)
Penguin Group (Australia), 250 Camberwell Road, Camberwell, Victoria 3124, Australia
(a division of Pearson Australia Group Pty. Ltd.)
Penguin Books India Pvt. Ltd., 11 Community Centre, Panchsheel Park, New Delhi—110 017, India
Penguin Group (NZ), 67 Apollo Drive, Rosedale, North Shore 0632, New Zealand
(a division of Pearson New Zealand Ltd.)
Penguin Books (South Africa) (Pty.) Ltd., 24 Sturdee Avenue, Rosebank, Johannesburg 2196,
South Africa

Penguin Books Ltd., Registered Offices: 80 Strand, London WC2R 0RL, England

This book is an original publication of The Berkley Publishing Group.

This is a work of fiction. Names, characters, places, and incidents either are the product of the author's imagination or are used fictitiously, and any resemblance to actual persons, living or dead, business establishments, events, or locales is entirely coincidental. The publisher does not have any control over and does not assume any responsibility for author or third-party websites or their content.

PUBLISHER'S NOTE: The recipes contained in this book are to be followed exactly as written. The publisher is not responsible for your specific health or allergy needs that may require medical supervision. The publisher is not responsible for any adverse reactions to the recipes contained in this book.

First edition: April 2009

Library of Congress Cataloging-in-Publication Data

Albert, Susan Wittig.
    Wormwood / Susan Wittig Albert.—1st ed.
        p. cm.
    ISBN 978-0-425-22609-4
    1. Bayles, China (Fictitious character)—Fiction.   2. Herbalists—Fiction.   3. Women private investigators—Fiction.   4. Shakers—Kentucky—Fiction.   5. Murder—Investigation—Fiction.
I. Title.

    PS3551.L2637W67 2009
    813'.54—dc22

                                                                2008053104

PRINTED IN THE UNITED STATES OF AMERICA

10 9 8 7 6 5 4 3 2 1

Author's Note

O Sorrow & joy. Betsy Crossman, Mary Ann Mantle, Amy Reed have finished coloring blue wool, they began the 12th had 105 lb. & more than this, had it all to do over because Maria says we had such poor judgment & got the liquor too strong & too hot I suppose. O Murder, every thing happens this awful year!!!!
                                                        Sister Anna Dodgson
                                                        July 20, 1849

Like many other people, I have been fascinated by the Shakers for more than thirty years, since I first visited the Shaker villages at Pleasant Hill and South Union, Kentucky, and later the villages at Hancock, Canterbury, and Sabbathday Lake. Their self-reliant, communal industry, their interest in herbs, and their meticulous attention to the simplest details of furnishings, architecture, and daily life—all these attracted me. With every visit to a Shaker village, I was more and more drawn to this serene and lovely way of life.

But the more I learned about the Shakers (particularly from their own journals and letters) and the more deeply I explored the histories of individual villages, the more I began to understand the challenging realities beneath the invitingly calm and serene exterior: the infinite contradictions and fallibilities of human nature, as well as the grim realities of social, economic, and technological change with which the Societies were unable to cope. This novel grows out of the uncomfortable awareness that—no matter how deep our longings—nothing is ever as perfect as it seems.

The Shaker community of Mount Zion, Kentucky, the setting for this book, is entirely fictitious, as are the Shaker characters that appear in these chapters. Their letters and diaries, however, are based on published journals and letters, and many of the incidents described in the book actually took place at one or another of the Shaker villages. I am indebted to those who have written about the Shakers (especially the Kentucky Shakers), and who have edited their papers; the work of these scholars has given me a treasury of richly detailed information on which to draw. You'll find a list of the books and websites I have consulted in the Resources section at the end of the novel, together with some interesting Shaker recipes and herbal formulas.

Wormwood is different from other China Bayles Mysteries, in that significant parts of the story are told by the Shakers who lived at Mount Zion in 1912, at a time when the village was under considerable pressure, both from within and without. I chose this narrative form because I wanted to make these characters and their difficult situation as real as possible. China will never meet them, but they have an important role to play in the mystery she has to solve, and I felt that their presence would enrich the narrative.

My thanks go to Sharon Baehr of Diamond Bar, California, who won a character-name raffle and allowed me to use her name in this book. I am once again grateful to Alice LeDuc for her careful botanical reading of the manuscript. As for the herbs mentioned throughout, remember (as always) that medicinal plants can be dangerous if they are misused. If you want to use herbs therapeutically, please do your homework. Rely on current scientific information, not historical records or folklore, and do be careful.

Susan Wittig Albert

Bertram, Texas

WORMWOOD

Chapter One

The Wormwoods . . . belong to the genus *Artemisia*, a group consisting of 180 species, of which we have four growing wild in England, the Common Wormwood, Mugwort, Sea Wormwood and Field Wormwood. In addition, as garden plants, though not native, Tarragon (*A. dracunculus*) claims a place in every herb-garden, and Southernwood (*A. abrotanum*), an old-fashioned favourite, is found in many borders . . . The whole family is remarkable for the extreme bitterness of all parts of the plant.

A Modern Herbal, 1931
Mrs. M. Grieve

"You ought to go," Ruby Wilcox said decidedly. She began stacking the plastic plates at the end of the picnic table. "Really, China, you've been through a lot the past few weeks. You need a break."

"I agree," Cass Wilde chimed in. She put a bowl on the table—cherry tomatoes and mozzarella balls, marinated in her famous tarragon dressing, with toasted Texas pecans added for crunch. "You haven't had any time off since before Christmas. Ruby and I can take care of the shop and the tearoom, and Laurel's available when we need her. So go, China. *Go* already!"

I waved a fly off the plate of fried chicken. "I'm thinking about it," I muttered.

"Good," Sheila Dawson said. "Think hard." She hefted a large picnic jug full of lemonade onto the table, Rambo at her heels. Rambo is the

Rottweiler she recently adopted and is now in training to become Pecan Springs' first K-9 cop. "I agree with Ruby and Cass. You need a break. *We* need a break. You've been down in the dumps and generally snappish for weeks." Her voice softened. "You owe it to yourself, China. Really." Rambo barked and wagged his tail.

They need a break? *I've* been generally snappish? Well, I suppose I haven't been very easy to work with. The past month has been one of the worst in my life. But still—

"I don't see how I can get away," I said flatly. "It's June, and the gardens need work."

"So what else is new?" Cass asked. "The gardens always need work. That's the nature of gardens."

This was true, although this year we'd had a lot of spring rain and the weeds were more enthusiastic than usual. I ignored her. "And it's not like this is slack season at the shops," I went on. "We're busy—thank heavens. I mean, it's nice to have customers, isn't it? Would you prefer the opposite condition?"

"Don't be sarcastic, China," Ruby said gently.

"Well, would you?" I persisted. "And there's the tearoom and the catering service. Oh, and the Farmer's Market." The Pecan Springs Farmer's Market is just getting started, and all the locavores—people who prefer to eat food grown within their local hundred-mile "foodshed"—are loving it. They love locally grown herbs, too, so I'm selling at the market on Saturdays. "Even if I wanted to go to Kentucky, which I don't, there's no way I could."

"Here it comes," McQuaid called, going into his windup. Out on the diamond, my husband was pitching slow balls to my ten-year-old niece, Caitlin. Amy was on first, Kate was hanging out between second and third, and Brian was dancing around in the outfield. Marcia Sellers,

Caitlin's other aunt, was crouched behind the plate with a catcher's mitt. Howard Cosell, McQuaid's elderly basset, was lying flat in the dirt behind Marcia, calling balls and strikes with lazy flicks of his stumpy tail.

Aunt. It's a new word for me. I still haven't quite gotten used to the idea that I am Caitlin's aunt. For that matter, I haven't gotten used to the idea that Caitlin's father—my half brother, Miles Danforth—is dead, murdered. Come to think of it, I've barely gotten used to the idea that I *had* a brother. Until the last few months, my mother and I had imagined that I was my father's only child. Silly us. Silly me.

Swack! Caitlin swung hard and connected. For an instant, she stood there, stunned at having actually hit the ball, until Marcia gave her a push, shouting, "Run, Caitlin! Run, run, run!"

Brian let the ball skitter away from him and lost it in the grass (intentionally, I was sure). Howard Cosell scrambled to his feet, trying to decide whether he should go help Brian locate the ball or chase Caitlin around the bases.

Amy and Kate—Amy is Ruby's daughter and Kate is her live-in partner—were jumping up and down and screaming, "Run, Caitlin, run!" while Rambo, tongue lolling, raced from the sidelines to dance alongside Caitlin.

McQuaid, hands on his hips, was wearing a pretend scowl. "Whose side are you on, anyway?" he demanded of Amy and Kate, as Caitlin scampered around second base, then third. Laughing, Brian finally found the ball between his feet, juggled it, dropped it, then lobbed it home.

But Caitlin and Rambo were already safe at home plate. He jumped up and licked her chin and she sat down with a thump, looking as though she couldn't believe what had just happened. Her first home run. The first of many in her life, I hoped.

Cass and Ruby got up to cheer, and I stood, too. "Way to go, Caitlin!"

I yelled excitedly, whistling around two fingers. "Way to go!" I sat back down on the picnic bench and added, to Cass and Ruby, "And I have to think of Caitlin, too, you know. Marcia's been sick. I don't think it's a good idea to leave just now."

Ruby picked up Baby Grace—Amy's daughter—from her playpen and put her into her high chair. She rolled her eyes. "Oh, for pity's sake, China. You're acting like you're going to *Jupiter*. It's just Kentucky, and it's only ten days. And Marcia says she's feeling better. She looks a lot stronger, don't you think?" She bent over and kissed Grace's nose. "Gwamma's favorite sweetie-kins," she murmured in that doting tone people reserve for babies and new puppies. "Gwamma's precious."

Marcia actually did look stronger, but I wasn't going to admit it. "It's not ten days," I said. "It's fourteen, counting drive time. And I'd have to drive, since Martha Edmond and I would be going together. That's two weeks, Ruby. Two whole weeks. Who'll look after the gardens? And what about the Farmer's Market? We're just getting started there. You can't get along without me."

"Now she thinks she's indispensable," Sheila said sarcastically, over her shoulder. It was her turn to bat, and she was headed for the plate, blond ponytail bouncing, Pecan Springs Police Department cap pulled low over her eyes. "Such arrogance."

Laurel Riley brandished the grilling fork. "We can get along without you just fine, China." Her round cheeks were flushed from standing over the hot dogs and hamburgers. "We do it all the time, don't we?"

"Yes, but that's for just a couple of hours," I pointed out. Laurel fills in for us at the shops, whenever Ruby, Cass, or I have to be gone. "You can't get along without me for two whole weeks."

"You already said that," Cass retorted. "But the rest of us agree that you have become increasingly egotistical, arrogant, and overbearing, and that you need some time off to regain your humility and sweetness of spirit." She smiled sweetly. "What better place to do that than a Shaker village? So just shut up and fetch the pickles, will you? Ruby left them in the car."

Ruby tossed her red hair out of her eyes. "Humility?" she asked with a laugh. "'Sweetness of spirit' I might buy in a pinch, but China Bayles, humble? Not in your wildest dreams!"

I hoisted myself off the picnic bench. "I can see that my talents aren't appreciated here," I said darkly. "I'll get the pickles."

"Bless you," Ruby said, as a cheer went up from the field. Sheila had bounced McQuaid's pitch into Kate's waiting glove, and Amy had tagged her out at first, retiring the side. "Oh, and there's a bag of sliced onions—bring those, too. And please hurry. We're just about ready to eat."

While I am fetching the pickles and onions, I'll take a minute to fill you in on who's who here, in case you don't have a clue. I'm China Bayles—I own an herb shop called Thyme and Seasons, here in Pecan Springs, Texas. I used to be a criminal attorney in Houston, but when life in the fast lane began to taste like leftover mashed potatoes, I cashed out my retirement plan and opted for the small-town life. I won't get rich, but there are plenty of other satisfactions. I love being able to bike around town when I feel like it. I love working with plants, in the shop and in the gardens. And life seems quieter and sweeter here, although appearances often belie the reality. Like other small towns, Pecan Springs is no safe haven from crime, drugs, and family violence. But I'm happy, all things considered. I'm harbored by a loving family and close friends, wonderful friends, like the ones at the picnic today.

Like my friend Ruby, for instance, the tall, skinny redhead in the emerald green top, short green shorts, and outrageous green wedgies, who's cooing at her granddaughter. (Look into her eyes and you'll see that she's wearing green contacts, so her eye color matches her outfit.) Ruby owns the Crystal Cave, Pecan Springs' only New Age shop, in the same building as my herb shop. Along with Cass Wilde, we're partners in a tearoom called Thyme for Tea.

And that's Cass over there, setting out the tray of stuffed mushrooms. Where Ruby is tall and slender as a willow wand, Cass is very well rounded, with lots of luscious curves. "I'm large and I love it," she likes to say, and adds with a wicked grin, "Wanna arm wrestle?" A very fine cook with the credentials to prove it, Cass manages our tearoom. She's also developed a personal catering service called the Thymely Gourmet that's quite a hit in Pecan Springs, especially among the commuting crowd. The three of us, Cass, Ruby, and I, also manage Party Thyme, which caters weddings, reunions, library luncheons, and the like. Ruby calls these three-ring enterprises our "Flying Circus." They do take a lot of time, which makes it hard for me to get away.

But Laurel Riley, the young woman with the plate of hamburgers in her hand and the long brown braid down her back (she's part Cherokee), is a Master Herbalist and a terrific gardener. If there's anybody I'd trust to take over the shop for two weeks, it's Laurel. She'd love it, too, since every customer who comes in the door is a potential client for her newly established consulting practice in herbal medicine and nutrition.

Let's see, who else? Oh, McQuaid, of course, and Brian, who are trotting off the ball field, flushed with victory and the heat of a June afternoon in the Texas Hill Country. I've been married to McQuaid—the tall, dark, blue-eyed, almost-handsome guy with the crooked nose and the burnt orange University of Texas T-shirt—for nearly three years now. A former Houston homicide cop, he teaches part-time in the Criminal Justice department at Central Texas State University. The rest of the time, he works as a private investigator, although we could wish for a few more clients. (If you know of anybody who's got a case that needs solving, you might put in a good word for McQuaid.) Brian, now fifteen and looking more like his dad every day, is our son—well, McQuaid's son. Sally, Brian's mother, shows up occasionally and stays just long enough to make us all wish she'd go away again. We haven't seen her for more than a year now, which probably means that she'll be dropping in soon.

The beautiful blonde with the long, slim legs who just got tagged out at first base is Sheila Dawson, Pecan Springs' police chief—and believe me, she never gets tagged out in real life. Smart Cookie (that's what her friends call her) is our town's answer to the Texas crime wave. Mess with her and you've got trouble. Double trouble, actually, since Rambo, who is a protective hunk of a dog, might just take a chunk out of your leg. The two gals who teamed up to tag Sheila out are Amy—Ruby's wild child and Baby Grace's mother—and her partner, Kate. They've been together for more than a year now, and Kate (who has her own business as an accountant) has been a settling influence on Amy. Or maybe having a baby has settled the both of them down.

Which leaves Caitlin, my niece, and Marcia Sellers, her aunt. Her *other* aunt. This is a terribly sad story, and the sadness is still brutally fresh for all of us. Caitlin—the dark-haired little girl with the pixie haircut, celebrating her home run—lost her mother three years ago and her father three weeks ago. Miles Danforth, Caitlin's dad and my half brother, was killed in a hit-and-run in the parking garage near his firm's law office in downtown Austin. The killer is being held without bond, and the man behind it all has already pled guilty to several lesser charges. Rather than face the wrongful death suit I threatened to file, he's agreed to set up a substantial trust fund for Caitlin. His lawyer and I (I'm the executor of Miles' estate) are still working out the details. The money will never compensate Caitlin for the loss of her father, but at least I can be confident that she will be well taken care of.

And Marcia will certainly see to that. Caitlin's mother's sister, she is now the little girl's court-appointed guardian. Marcia has no children of her own, but she worked as a children's physical therapist and she'll be an ideal mother for Caitlin. Unfortunately, she hasn't been well, although I was happy to see that she seemed better today—more animated, less fragile—than she'd been since Miles' death. It has hit her hard, for she and Miles had been talking of marriage. He's gone now, but she has his child.

As I say, it's a sad story. The past few weeks were exhausting, and I am bone tired and heart sore—and yes, I suppose it's fair to say that I've been snappish, too. Death is always a cataclysmic event in the lives of the left-behind, but murder is worse, much, much worse, and I am still tumbling and whirling in its emotional undertow. There's grief, but there's also anger and bitterness and fear and pain and guilt. My brother offered me the opportunity to know him better, and I didn't take him up on it. I refused, and now I'm sorry. Deeply sorry. There's no way to make amends except to Caitlin, and I'll do whatever I can for her. There's nothing more I can do for Miles.

I sighed. No two ways about it, the last few weeks of my life had been focused on nothing else but the aftermath of Miles' murder—discovering who had killed him and arranging the financial settlement for Caitlin, as well as trying to manage all the details of his extensive and complicated estate. And in that moment, I knew that Ruby and Cass and Sheila were right. I needed to get away. Yes, this was an inconvenient time. And yes, two weeks was too long to leave the shop and the gardens and the Farmer's Market—and Caitlin and Marcia, too.

But going away would give me an opportunity to get some perspective on what had happened, a chance to step out of the situation and deal with my grief and guilt. When I came back, I'd be freshly energized and ready to tackle the tough issues I was facing—the details of Caitlin's settlement, the probate of Miles' estate, the trial of the man who killed him.

And I couldn't have a better excuse for a getaway, actually. Martha Edmond had asked me to go to Kentucky with her. She was offering a couple of one-day workshops on Shaker herbs at Mount Zion Shaker Village, in northern Kentucky. I could help with the workshops (an extra pair of hands is always welcome), enjoy the gardens, relax in the mineral springs, let go, loosen up, unwind. I don't know a lot about the Shakers, but what I do know is intriguing. I'd be glad to learn more about them. And I would certainly be glad to see Martha again. I'd met her when Leatha—my mother—and I were at Jordan's Crossing, my mother's family plantation, when we first found out that Aunt Tullie Coldwell was sick. Martha was now an email buddy, but we hadn't had a chance to get together since—

"Hey, China, the pickles!" Cass yelled.

Oops.

We were halfway through lunch when Ruby brought up the subject again. "We've been telling China she has to go to that Shaker village with Martha Edmond," she said, loudly enough to be heard over the hubbub of conversation around the table. "But she won't listen."

"I listened," I said contritely. "I considered all your arguments, and I've decided—"

"I've been telling her the same thing, Ruby," McQuaid said, sitting next to me. "Brian and I can handle stuff at home. She doesn't need to worry about us. But you know China. Stubborn as an old Texas mule."

"You could leave out the 'old,'" I said.

"I told her, too," Brian put in. His voice is changing, and part of this came out in a squeak. "In fact, I made the mistake of telling her that we'd be glad to have her gone for a few days. It'd be fun for Dad and me to batch it by ourselves. Maybe that's why she won't go."

"Hey!" I protested. "Isn't anybody listening to me? I said I've thought it over and—"

"I just don't understand it, China." On the other side of the table, Cass was shaking her head. "You know, if somebody offered me an all-expenses-paid trip to a mineral spring spa in Kentucky, I'd be all over it like white on rice. Why can't you—"

"I am GOING!" I roared, and slapped the table. "Will you all please listen? I have decided to go to Mount Zion. I will call Martha Edmond tonight and tell her. So everybody can just shut up about it, okay?"

There was a startled silence around the table. Then Ruby broke into a loud cheer. Cass clapped, Sheila whistled, and McQuaid gave me a quick hug. "This is good, baby," he whispered. "You need some time off."

"Yeah, right," I said dryly. "Everybody is obviously eager to get rid of me."

"We're not eager to get rid of you, China!" Ruby cried, distressed. "We just want—"

"We just want you to come back as a kinder, gentler person," Sheila said. She dropped Rambo a bit of chicken and reached for another ear of buttered sweet corn.

"Transformed," Amy said, giving Baby Grace a carrot to chew on. "And totally destressed."

"Rested and relaxed," Laurel added, in an encouraging tone.

"And rarin' to go to work," Cass concluded, waving a drumstick. "Hey, this is really great chicken. Who brought it?"

"I did," I replied, adding carelessly, "I like to cook when I'm feeling snappish. This is my secret recipe. Twelve herbs and spices."

"Hey," Kate said, "that's one better than the Colonel!" She picked up the platter. "Seconds, anybody?"

"Me," McQuaid said, taking another piece. He glanced down at Howard Cosell, soliciting under the table, and tossed him a chunk of dark meat. Howard, no slouch in the chicken department, wolfed it down and nuzzled McQuaid's knee, begging for more. McQuaid grinned at me. "Hey. Howard and I will miss your chicken, babe."

Caitlin, sitting on my left, didn't quite understand that we were all just teasing. "We'll miss *you*, Aunt China," she said in a prim, little-girl voice. "I hope you have a really good time."

"Thanks," I said, and squeezed her hand. *Aunt China.* I could get used to this.

Chapter Two

Elder Aaron Babbitt

May 6–June 2, 1912

The Shakers are their own best historians. We know as much as we do about their life . . . because of what they have told us in their journals and letters, the printed testimonies of their disciples, their monthly publications, and their own literature. This is not by chance. Their Millennial Laws very clearly state that "two family journals should be kept . . . in which all important occurrences or business transactions should be registered."

Shaker Medicinal Herbs
Amy Bess Miller

Documents collected and held in the Mount Zion Shaker Archive, Folder 201, Babbitt, Aaron, Elder.

Document 1.1912.05.15. Text of letter inserted into journal.

Mount Zion, Kentucky
May 15th, 1912

To Priscilla, dear sister in the flesh & Sister-in-Faith, greetings from your brother, Aaron,

These spring days have been filled with work, but the labor has been joyful, as it always is and most especially in the gardens and field. Bro. Alfred and Bro. Charles McBride have been sowing Holly-hock and Sweet Balm seeds, Jerusalem Oak, Poppy, and Penny-royal & Lavender &c. The Sisters peeled White Oak Bark in the woods behind the Ox Pasture and put up 25 pounds of Sage & Thyme in papers for Carter & Co. Others of our family are also plowing and hoeing and doing other much needful work.

I myself have been engaged in reviewing the Dairy accounts and am about to begin on the Herb Department, which I fear will be a vexatious business, as Bro. Charles is not of a methodical mind, altho he has many other great & good gifts, chief among them being a zealous willingness to assume tasks even beyond requirement. He took on the Herb Department after Bro. Joseph was struck and killed by lightning as he worked in the garden (you will recall that unhappy event, some three years ago). It is good to have him, for our numbers are sadly dwindling, and an eager, able-bodied Brother is a great Blessing.

We are under heavy trials here, chiefly having to do with the Mineral Spring. When Bro. Ezekiel Ballard deeded it to us with his land 34 years ago (he being deceased now this past 10 years), we understood that the Spring was his by right of ownership. But recently we have learned that the Spring and its surrounding 40 acres were leased by him, or rather by his father (so it is possible that Bro. Ezekiel himself might not have known this fact) for a term of 50 years. The man who claims to be the true Owner is Will Ayers, a neighbor. He cannot be persuaded to sell the land to us, even if we could somehow find the means to purchase it. Instead, he aims to repossess the land as well as the Cabins we have built on it for the Recuperants who tarry with us while they avail themselves of the Healing Waters. This is the same Will Ayers who caused us so much sorrow three years ago, when he seduced poor Sister Anna White and got her with child. This was the cause of her leaving us, and (as I later learned) of Will Ayers' wife leaving him.

Elder Benjamin of the South Family and I are much afflicted in spirit as to what to do with regard to this Business, for the money brought in by the Spring is greatly needful to us and the most part of our monthly cash income. Without it, I fear that we will not be able to meet the payments on the Bank loan that was so unfortunately executed four years ago by Elder Thomas Evans, who must not have been in full possession of his Faculties when he borrowed money to build the Barn & Dairy, which are much too large for us.

Enough of these burdens. I pray this finds you in good Health, dear Sister. Although troubled in spirit and wishing these vexatious Matters to be resolved, I remain well. Eldress Olive begs to be remembered, and wonders if you have any recent information about the sale of Sarsaparilla Root & whether it is worth our attempting to begin selling it again. She promises to write herself next week and to send the Valerian Root Extract. Please convey my Greetings to our beloved brethren and sisters at Mount Lebanon. Trusting to hear from you soon.

Elder Aaron Babbitt

Excerpts from Elder Aaron Babbitt's East Family Daily Journal, January–December 1912

May 6. Fair skies & moderate. Morning, Bro. Alfred and I hoeing, I sow Horehound, Poppy seeds. Brother Charles and I help Sister Ruth whitewash Drying Shed walls. Afternoon, I take Old Ned to the smith at Bass Corner to be shod. Happen on Will

Ayers, who makes threatening remarks about repossessing the Spring. Elder Benjamin & I have much concern and labor long over the matter, but do not come to any conclusion. Review Dairy accounts and find them up-to-date and accurate.

May 11. Warm, dry. Took up one wagonload of Sage Roots & conveyed them to Henry Wickers for cultivation. He will cut the sage green and bring to us for drying & after it is dried he will have ten cts per lb. dry weight. Bro. Charles got into disagreement with Will Ayers & Blows were struck. Both were bloodied but at least Will Ayers struck first (so say the Witnesses), so Charles cannot be charged with Assault. He has confessed to his sin of Violence and repented, explaining that Ayers exhibited an unacceptable Friendliness toward Sister Ruth, which may possibly explain his Act yet cannot exonerate him.

May 12. Build fire in kiln to dry horseradish root. Sow Sweet Balm. Widow Hannah Chandler and son Seth 12, arrive from Evansville. Hannah a likely woman, professes great Desire to leave the World and become a Believer. Seth removed to the Childrens' Dwelling, under Bro. Joshua's tutelage. Hannah stays with us.

May 18. Rain, cooler. Process 10 lbs. sage. Sr. Lisset and Hannah Chandler (proving herself a willing worker as well as an eager disciple) put up 5 doz. small cans marjoram, Sister Ruth and Charity label. Boys dig dock root, take 65 pounds to Drying Shed. Take dried horseradish and blackberry root to crushing mill. Cut wormwood and southernwood. Eldress Olive reports condition of the 8 Recuperants' cottages, of which our family now has the care (the

North Family having been sadly broken up by illness and departures). Room $1.25 a day board 60 cts. Total income for month from rentals at springs, $451.40. Pray Heaven we may not lose this or we may lose All. Dr. Meacham comes for Sr. Sally Loomis, who is quite ill and ready to go home to Mother. So many elders on the downward march, and lamentably few staunch young Believers to take their places. Hannah asks to come to me for reading & study of Mother's Words. Eldress Olive agrees.

May 27. Hannah is not after all widowed as she has told us (from mistaken concern that she would be rejected), but divorced from her husband Jake Chandler, who appeared here yesterday to fetch Seth. Hannah, being granted Right of Custody of the children by the Magistrate in Louisville, refuses. Much shouting. Many tears. Jake Chandler leaves angry & threatens to return with friends to take the boy.

May 29. Fair, warm. Morning, Bro. Charles and I replace 3 of the posts under the Herb House and do some cleaning in the loft. Girls put up 24 lbs. of herbs (thyme, sage, rosemary) in ¼ lb. packages for Carter & Co. Afternoon, Girls and Sister Ruth go with me and Bro. Charles to the Cliff Pasture to cut elder flowers, gather life everlasting, goldenseal in woodland. Hannah continues daily for reading & study. A studious Scholar, eager to receive the Word.

June 1. Sr. Sally has gone to Mother, full of Years and rich in the Rewards of Labor. Eldress Olive speaks to me of what she observed of Bro. Charles and Sr. Ruth touching in the Blessing Dance. She will speak to Ruth. I will counsel Charles.

June 2. Warm, cloudy. Sow 5 rows of Poppies in West Garden. Put up 25 lbs. fine Elm in papers. Sr. Charity gathers Roses for rose water. I speak to Charles about the Incident of the Dance and he says that the touching was accidental and that there is nothing between himself and Sister Ruth. Family meeting in the evening. Afterward with Hannah, reading & study. Eldress Olive expresses concern regarding this. I reassure her that all is Right & Proper, as it is. John French comes again, asking for readmittance to our Society, but finds no sympathy for his cause, for all suspect that he stole the Hampshire hog from the South Family pig pen.

Chapter Three

Martha Edmond lives in Mississippi's Yazoo River delta, not far from Jordan's Crossing, the Bloodroot River plantation where my mother grew up. Martha was a huge help when Leatha and I were trying to cope with Aunt Tullie, arranging for people to come in and help with the household work and the nursing. Aunt Tullie died not long ago, and Jordan's Crossing was sold, ending the final chapter in the long and bloody saga of the Coldwell family.

On the way to Martha's house, I stopped at the old Coldwell family cemetery. It is well kept and tidy once again, the iron fence painted green, the glazed pottery urns filled with ferns, and the grass mowed around the markers. My cousin Amanda Gleason Aunt Tullie's granddaughter, sees to that. She inherited the defective gene that ended her grandmother's life, but she has not yet begun to exhibit any of the deadly symptoms of what

I've come to think of as the Coldwell curse. Recently, she wrote me that she was going back to Knoxville.

The cemetery contains more Coldwells, Aunt Tullie used to say, than you can shake a stick at. Abner Coldwell, my great-great-grandfather, is buried there with his wife, Samantha, their polished granite marker in the center, the graves of their many Coldwell children and grandchildren laid out around them. And in a far corner, beside a rosemary bush, I saw the flat marker engraved with Ophelia's lovely words: "There's rosemary; that's for remembrance. Pray, love, remember." It's a double marker that spans two graves. Old Aunt Tullie is buried with her young husband, whose murder was one of the darker secrets in our family. I stood for a long while beside their graves, remembering the first time I had seen that marker and thinking about ancestral mysteries and feeling glad that it was all over, at last. Aunt Tullie was at peace, and the pain of the past—most of it, anyway—has died with her.

Before I left Pecan Springs, I had called my old friend Darlene, with whom I had shared some terrifying moments on the Bloodroot River the last time I was here—some moments I would just as soon forget. I wanted to see if Darlene and I could get together for a couple of hours while I was in the area. I'd spent childhood summers at Jordan's Crossing, where Darlene's mother, Queenie, cooked for Aunt Tullie. Darlene is a gifted writer, and she has what it takes to make good on that gift. Her first short-story collection won a major literary prize, and her second book, a novel, had just earned a strong review in the *New York Times*. I was disappointed when all I got was her voice on her answering machine.

I got an update on both Darlene and Amanda from Martha while she was putting our supper on the table in one of those wonderful Southern kitchens with tall white cabinets and ivy-print wallpaper above a white-painted wainscot. Martha reported that Darlene still lives in Queenie's old house, but she's currently on tour with her new book—no wonder she wasn't answering the phone. And Amanda has just landed a full-time job in the Economics Department at the University of Tennessee.

"You and your mother need to get back here to Mississippi more often," Martha told me as we sat down to eat. She had baked her famous tomato-basil pie for me, and now she put a piece on my plate, with a generous helping of salad and a bowl of creamy vegetable bisque.

"I'd like to," I said, meaning it. "But Leatha and Sam have been really busy with that new bed-and-breakfast of theirs. Going great guns, from all reports. And it's pretty hard for me to get away from Pecan Springs."

"Especially now, I'm sure," Martha said sympathetically. "Your mother says you're handling your brother's estate. I was sorry to hear that he died. How did it happen?"

I filled her in on the general outline of what had been going on, not lingering over the awful details. "The most we can hope for," I said at the end, "is that Caitlin can somehow put all this behind her. Thank God for Marcia. If it weren't for her—" I shook my head.

"Losing both parents," Martha said softly. "Such a horrible thing. Given all that's happened in the past month or so, I appreciate your being here even more, China. Thank you for taking the time to go with me to Mount Zion."

"I need to bone up on the Shakers. Mostly, what I know is that they were celibate. And big on herbs."

Martha nodded. "I'll give you an article called 'Hands to Work, Hearts to God.' A good short history. Won't take you long to read." She paused. "Have you visited the Shaker village at Pleasant Hill, Kentucky?"

"No," I replied, "and I hadn't even heard of Mount Zion until you invited me to go there with you." I finished the pie, which Martha makes with thin-sliced tomatoes, layered with basil, onions, and grated cheese, in a bread-crumb crust topped with bacon. "Were Pleasant Hill and Mount Zion settled at the same time?"

Martha tilted her head to one side. She is barely five-two, and her hair is streaked with white. Her skin, brown and wrinkled from long days in her sunny garden, testifies to her seventysomething years. But her blue eyes sparkle, her voice has a cheerful lilt, and an elfin smile gives her the look of a mischievous young girl. At the moment, though, her face was serious.

"Settled at the same time? No. Pleasant Hill was the first of the three Shaker societies in Kentucky. It was established in 1806, and South Union the next year. Mount Zion, the third, was settled around 1825 by a group of people who left Pleasant Hill in a serious dispute over governance."

"A serious dispute?" I raised my eyebrows. "Hey, wait. I thought the Shakers lived a totally serene life, and that they didn't suffer from anger or frustration or lust, like us worldly people. In fact, I read somewhere that a Shaker village was a place where it was 'always Sunday.'"

"Always Sunday." Martha gave a little laugh. "Yes, well, that's the image they wanted to create. It's certainly reinforced when you visit one of the villages today. And since the existing villages are museums, not living settlements, of course, they're serene. But as far as the actual villages were concerned, the reality was different. Yes, the Shakers worked together, lived together, worshipped together. And they tried very hard to get along—harmonious living was their ideal. But they were bound to rub one another the wrong way from time to time. People became Believers, but that didn't mean they underwent a total personality change."

"I suppose that's true of all those nineteenth-century Utopian communities," I said. "Nothing seemed to disturb the peace. But beneath the surface, there was plenty of turbulence." Like Pecan Springs, I thought.

Visit for a day or a week, and it feels like paradise. Hang around for a year, and you get a glimpse of the dark side.

"I'm sure that's true. Anyway, one of the men, Hiram Willard, learned that there was some land for sale around a mineral spring north of Lexington. It looked to him like a good place for a settlement, and since he was unhappy with the way things were going at Pleasant Hill, he pulled out. He took thirty or so of the family with him." She paused, chuckling at my puzzled look. "Ah, I see. You thought Shakers didn't have families."

"Right," I said, pushing my plate away. "Didn't we just say they were celibate?"

"Oh, yes. Celibacy was one of the most important and distinctive teachings of Ann Lee—Mother Ann, they called her. Believers had to live a 'virgin life,' as she put it. Being a Shaker was like being a monk or a nun—you couldn't be completely committed to the spirit if you were committed to a marriage."

"Then how—" I began, by now really mystified.

Martha raised her hand and went on. "But family life was important to them. In fact, it was the principle around which their societies were organized. The families were made up of men and women—ten, twenty, often as many as sixty or seventy unrelated people living together in one big house, with a trustee to manage their business affairs and an elder and eldress to oversee their spiritual lives. At Mount Zion, as in other villages, the families were named for the compass directions—the North Family, South Family, and so on."

"Makes sense," I said thoughtfully, finishing the last of my soup. "Lots of moral support. Makes communication easier, too. No wonder they got so much done."

Martha put down her spoon. "All the families helped out with the general village work, but each one had a specialty craft. At Mount Zion, my great-aunt Mildred lived with the East Family. Her Shaker name was Charity." She smiled. "That's Aunt Charity's vegetable bisque you're eating."

"It's delicious," I said. "Thyme? Savory?"

"Yes to both. The East Family, Aunt Charity's family, was responsible for growing and processing herbs. In later years, when the income from the herb business fell off and the village began to decline, they took over the inn-keeping."

That really surprised me. "The Shakers ran an *inn*? But I thought their villages were off-limits to the public."

"Not exactly. Most villages welcomed visitors. And at Mount Zion, the spring itself was a natural attraction. They offered board and room to the sick folks who came to recuperate and bathe in the springs. By the time the village closed, in the 1920s, it was just about their only income-producing activity." She gestured toward the tomato pie. "Would you like another slice, or shall we go on to dessert?"

I eyed the pie, torn. "What's for dessert?"

Martha stood and collected our plates and bowls. "Raspberry flummery," she said, going to the sink. "It's an old-fashioned milk pudding, made the Shaker way, with rosewater. Another of Aunt Charity's recipes."

"Let's go straight to the dessert," I said with a laugh. "The pie was delicious, though, and so was the bisque." I paused. "How is it that you know so much about the Shakers, Martha? Was it the herbs that got you interested in them?" Martha is an expert in the native plants of Mississippi, many of which were used medicinally by the Choctaw and Chickasaw Indians. It wouldn't surprise me to learn that she works with some of the same plants that the Kentucky Shakers gathered from the wild or grew in their gardens.

Martha took a dessert out of the refrigerator. "Actually, it's the other way around. Aunt Charity was my favorite aunt. After she left Mount Zion and moved to town, she grew herbs and sold them locally. When I came to spend the summers with my grandparents, Aunt Charity used to take me and Allie—my best friend—on 'wild-gathering walks,' as she called them. I got my interest in herbs from her."

I leaned forward and put my elbows on the table. "Your aunt moved back to town? I thought that once you became a Shaker, you were a Shaker for life."

"Oh, heavens, no." Martha chuckled. "There was lots of coming and going. Some people joined the Shakers because they loved the ideal of it, but had to leave because they couldn't handle the discipline. Sometimes people joined because they needed a place to live and something to eat, or because they were hiding out, or even because they wanted to learn a trade—the Shakers were wonderful artisans."

"Why did your aunt leave?"

Martha pursed her lips. "It's odd, China. We—our family, I mean—always wondered about that, because leaving made her desperately unhappy." She spooned pudding into glass dishes and added fresh raspberries. "Whatever happened, it must have been cataclysmic. She mourned the rest of her life."

"Not a clue?"

"Not a clue. Aunt Charity was the most private person I've ever met. She never talked about herself. What little I know came from the journal I found after she died—she lived to a hundred and two, would you believe? Every Shaker was supposed to keep a journal, and hers covered all of the years she lived at Mount Zion. But the journal stops abruptly in 1912. It doesn't shed much light on why she left." She looked up at me. "Now, there's a mystery I'd love you to solve, China. Why did Aunt Charity leave the Shakers, when she loved them so much? I've wondered about it all my life. Everybody in the family has wondered."

"Nobody asked her?"

"Of course they did. But she always refused to say, which only deepened the mystery. I donated her journal to the Mount Zion research library, along with her drawings. If you get a chance, take a look at it. Maybe you'll figure out why she left." She put a sprig of lemon balm on my dish and set it in front of me. "Here. Tell me what you think."

I picked up the spoon and tasted the pudding. "Yum. Light, fruity, not too sweet."

"Aunt Charity said that the Shakers thought it was a perfect dessert for an evening meal." Martha sat down and began to eat. "And of course, they made their own rosewater."

"Growing herbs as they did, I'm sure they must have used plenty of herbs in their cooking."

"No, actually, they didn't. When the Societies were first established, the women who worked in the kitchen had all they could do just to put enough food on the table. The Shakers began growing herbs for sale around 1815, but only medicinal herbs. They didn't sell culinary herbs until 1841, and even then just a few of the basics—marjoram, sage, thyme, summer savory, horseradish."

"No basil? No parsley or mint?" I asked, surprised. "No rosemary?"

"Oh, yes. But they were sold as medicinals, not culinary herbs. They sold parsley root for dropsy, parsley leaves for insect bites, parsley seeds to kill lice. Mint—and ginger, too, of course—soothed stomachs. Basil was used to stop vomiting. And rosemary was brewed into a tea for colds, colic, and nervousness. All according to the best medical recommendations of the day."

I was still thinking of culinary herbs. "But the Shaker recipes I've seen have lots of herbs in them," I objected. "In fact, I sell a Shaker cookbook at the shop. It's full of herbs."

"Later adaptations. As time went on, Shaker women didn't mind borrowing cooking techniques from the World's People. I have a Shaker original you can look at—Sister Mary Whitcher's little book, *The Shaker House-Keeper*. It came out in 1882. The only herbs mentioned are parsley, sage, mustard, and cayenne. When you look at the oldest recipes, you can see that the Shakers were plain cooks, without any gourmet touches. The same was true at Mount Zion. Plain cooking was part of their philosophy."

Which brought us back to the subject. "Mount Zion. Didn't you tell me that you're on the board of trustees there?"

"I am. Lottie Ayers and her husband, Ernest, bought the property in the 1960s, when I was still living in the area. His family had owned land there for many years, and both of them loved the place. Some of the buildings had already been torn down and those that were left were in very bad shape. But that didn't faze Lottie. She and Ernest set up the Mount Zion Foundation as a nonprofit. They put a lot of money into the restoration, including the rebuilding of the guest cabins at the spring."

"Sounds like a project for people with money."

"They had plenty. Ernest raised horses, and Lottie herself came from a wealthy Louisville family. They had the idea of turning Mount Zion into a living museum, a tourist destination, so the ticket money and gift sales would offset the cost of operations. Ernest was the practical one, and Lottie had all the enthusiasm. After he died, about ten years ago, she went on a spending spree and built a conference center, including a research library to house the Shaker documents and journals she'd collected. The library was a wonderful idea, and our curator—Missy Thatcher—is a gem. She manages not only our research library but the conference center, as well. But Lottie expected the conference center to pay for itself, which hasn't happened. We might have to start dipping into the endowment to make the note payment."

"Not a good arrangement," I said. "Sort of like eating your seed corn. It might be necessary in the short term, if you want to stay alive. But it's disastrous in the long haul."

"That's exactly what Allie says," Martha replied ruefully. "She hates the idea."

"Allie?"

"My friend Allie Chatham. She's the director of the financial office at Mount Zion. She—" Martha started to say something else, and then bit her lip.

There was something going on here, but we weren't going to get to it right away. After a moment, I asked, "It was Lottie who invited you to sit on the board?"

Martha nodded. "She was a scrappy old lady who cared deeply about the Shakers. It was easier then, when she was alive. And fun. Lottie always made things fun."

Easier then, and fun. "And now?"

More lip biting. "When Lottie died four years ago, her granddaughter, Rachel Hart, became president of the board. The director of Mount Zion resigned a few months later, and Rachel took on that position, as well."

My, my. "President of the board *and* director of the organization? Some would say that's a little too cozy, not to mention raising serious issues of internal control. Your bylaws permit this?"

"They don't prohibit it." Martha laughed a little. "I don't think it ever occurred to Lottie that such a thing might be likely."

"Has it worked out well?"

Martha looked troubled. "Not very, in my opinion. Rachel has a very distinctive management style, and we don't exactly hit it off. I offered to resign, but she insisted I stay—to represent her grandmother's point of view, she said." She gave me a small smile. "Now, she'd love it if I'd leave, but I won't. There are two more years in my term. I'm staying on the board out of pure stubbornness."

"Actually, it sounds like a natural for you," I observed. "You're an herbalist, you grew up in the area, and you have a Shaker in your family tree. I'd think you'd be an ideal board member."

"Well, maybe," she said slowly. "But I'm not crazy about what Rachel calls our 'new direction.'"

"And that is—?"

"Well, for one thing, she plans to turn the mineral spring into a spa—an upscale spa, at that. Of course, it's still in the planning stage. Maybe it won't happen."

"A spa?" I remembered the recent spa party that Cass and I had given for Ruby at Canyon Lake Spa Resort. The spa itself had been a relaxing experience, although the prices were enough to make me slightly tense. "I thought the Shakers were all about simplicity and frugality. A health resort I could understand. But a spa?"

"My concern exactly," Martha said firmly. "As a trustee, I see the quarterly financial statements. I know we have to attract more visitors, and we have to find a way to pay off the note on the conference center. Allie and I have been arguing that we should go after grants and foundation support, even federal funding. We wanted to apply for a National Historic Landmark status. But with this spa, it looks like Mount Zion is becoming a commercial venture. It's not quite Disneyland yet, but it feels—to me, at least—as if the village is on the verge of losing the Shaker spirit of peace and simplicity. All because we need money." She picked up the iced tea pitcher and refilled my glass.

I wanted to remark that peace and simplicity are usually the first things to go overboard when a financial storm hits, but contented myself with the question, "How many people on the board? How do the others feel about this?"

"There are six board members, plus Rachel. Besides me, there are three women, Rachel's personal friends, recent appointments, and of course, they're in favor of all her ideas. The two men are local—Chamber of Commerce types. Generally speaking, they're gung-ho for anything that might spill more money into the local economy." She paused for a moment, then added, with an apologetic laugh, "If it sounds like I'm being possessive about Mount Zion . . . Well, I suppose I am. Which is silly, of course. Everything changes, with time. But that's how I feel, and it complicates an already tricky situation."

I waited for her to elaborate, but she had fallen silent. Finally I said, "Let me see if I've got this straight. We're going to Mount Zion so that you can lead workshops on wild-gathered herbs at the conference center and attend a board meeting." I finished my flummery and put down my spoon. "I can poke around in the library and learn about Shaker herbs, and we can lollygag in the mineral spring and relax and unwind—'destress,' as one of my friends said. Is that it?"

"That's it," she said, and hesitated. "Mostly."

Mostly. I asked the inevitable question. "So what are you leaving out?"

She hesitated. "It's a little, well . . . troubling, I'm afraid." She raised her eyes to mine. "It's really why I want you to come, China. Oh, I know you'll enjoy Mount Zion. It's a beautiful place with a fascinating history.

But I really want you to talk to Allie. She called a couple of days ago to say that she's turned something up."

"Something? As in—"

"Something having to do with money, something . . . not quite right. I don't know what it is, because she wouldn't talk about it over the phone." She paused. "But it's not just that. Some very odd things have been happening in the village. I'm afraid—" She shook herself and gave a little laugh. "That's silly. I'm not really afraid, of course. I'm just concerned. And uneasy. I'd like to know what's going on. While we're there, I want you to help me do a little . . . well, a little investigating."

Investigating. Poking your nose into things you probably don't want to know about. Sniffing people's dirty laundry. Opening locked closets to see whether somebody's hiding a skeleton or two. It's done all the time in mystery novels, but in real life, it's not fun and games. In fact, it can sometimes get downright dangerous. There are other things I'd rather be doing.

"So what is this thing you're concerned about?" I asked cautiously.

"Well, it's complicated." Martha took a deep breath. "Mount Zion has a gift shop that sells local crafts, Shaker merchandise, that sort of thing." She began folding her napkin, lining up the edges so they exactly matched. "The manager, a very nice young woman named Maxine Sullivan, apparently got into the habit of taking money out of the cash register—to the tune of something like fifteen thousand dollars over a couple of years."

A bad habit, designed to lead the habitué straight to the pokey. "Who uncovered it?"

"Allie. As I said, she's our financial manager. She noticed some irregularities and did a little investigating on her own. When she found out what was happening, she took the information to Rachel."

31

The director and president of the board. "That was smart."

"Yes, but what happened next wasn't. Rachel fired Maxine. But she agreed not to call the police if Maxine would put the money back right away."

"*Not* smart," I said firmly. "Dumb."

Martha pressed her lips together. "Really dumb. Rachel said she wanted to avoid the bad publicity. Maxine agreed. But she'd already spent the money, so she couldn't put it back. She couldn't ask her family for money, either. She killed herself."

A young life lost, over nothing. Almost. "So much for avoiding bad publicity."

Martha's eyes were sad. "I keep thinking that if Rachel had turned the matter over to the police, Maxine might still be alive. She'd be in prison, but she'd at least have the chance to make a new start when she served her sentence."

"And to make matters even worse, Mount Zion took the hit. Your insurance company refused to cover the loss."

Startled, Martha looked up. "How did you know?"

"Because that's how the game is played," I said ruefully. "You can read it in the fine print in your policy, in the paragraph captioned 'Timely Reporting.' You don't report the theft to the cops, the insurance company doesn't pay."

Martha put her folded napkin carefully beside her bowl, lining up the edge with the edge of the table. "We're a small nonprofit, operating on a narrow margin. To us, fifteen thousand dollars is a lot of money."

"It's a lot of money to me, too," I said. "But the theft—that's in the past, right? No more losses?"

"No, not that I know of anyway." She straightened the napkin, realigning it. "But in the past six months, there've been several . . . well, accidents.

Some greenhouse plants were frozen when the heating system didn't turn on the way it was supposed to. The thermostat on the walk-in freezer in the kitchen somehow got turned up, and everything had to be tossed. A couple of weeks ago, one of the village trucks rolled down a hill and smashed into a guest cottage."

I could see where this was going and tried to stave it off. "It's probably just an unfortunate series of accidents, Martha. A run of bad luck."

"That's what we thought, too. Rachel promised to tighten up procedures, and didn't seem too troubled. In fact, she suggested that it might be the Shaker ghosts, playing tricks."

"You're kidding."

Martha smiled slightly. "Well, maybe a little. But the Shakers themselves believed that their spirits would linger at Mount Zion until Judgment Day. And lots of people have seen or heard them over the years. In fact, Lottie collected quite a few reports of Shaker ghosts from the people who worked at the village, particularly during the restoration. She compiled them into a little anthology that we sell in the gift shop."

Ruby calls me a skeptic, and she's right, although I've had a few experiences along those lines myself. "Have you ever seen a ghost there?"

Martha looked uncomfortable. "Well, yes, as a matter of fact, I have. I've seen Brother Joshua, who sometimes appears with a lantern in the middle of the night. The story goes that he's looking for a lost Shaker child." She paused. "As I said, Rachel suggested that maybe we were dealing with a Shaker poltergeist—until a month ago, when the barn burned."

"Uh-oh," I said. "That sounds serious."

"It was. A couple of horses died, and quite a lot of expensive equipment was destroyed. The county fire marshal said it was arson. This time, the insurance company will pay, but that won't cover everything. And it doesn't solve the problem."

"No, it doesn't," I said. "It sounds as if you're right to be worried, Martha. But I don't see what any of this has to do with me. If it's arson, the police will—"

"The sheriff has finished his investigation," Martha put in quietly. "You know what county law enforcement officers are like, China. They can handle traffic accidents and close down meth labs. But give them arson, and they're at a loss."

She had a point. "What about the insurance company?"

"They've already sent their investigator. He hung around for a couple of days and came up empty-handed. No evidence, no clues, not even a lead. Rachel posted a reward, but nobody's come forward with information." She gave me a significant look. "And the other things that have happened—the truck, the greenhouse heater, the freezer—they aren't the kind of problems the police are equipped to handle."

I understood. And agreed. There are plenty of situations where even the best-trained and most well-meaning cops are helpless. But if this was what she wanted me to investigate, I could tell her not to bother. This was a job for a pro, and I knew just the guy.

"You shouldn't be talking to me," I said firmly. "The guy you need is my husband. McQuaid will dig into this situation and find out what's going on, pronto. It won't cost you all that much, either, since you're a nonprofit. I'm sure he'll give you a break." This would give us a break, too. Did I mention that McQuaid could use a few new clients?

"What we need is *you*, China," Martha said with emphasis. "*You* were the one who cleared up those horrible mysteries at Jordan's Crossing. And Leatha told me how you helped uncover your brother's murderer."

"My mother," I said darkly, "has a big mouth."

Martha chuckled. "Your mother is proud of you. She says the police were looking in all the wrong places. They'd never have found the guy who killed your brother. And your father."

I couldn't disagree with that. The killer came from a place too far back in our family's past. The cops would never have gone there, not in a million years. It was something I didn't like to think about.

"Anyway," Martha went on, "if McQuaid came to Mount Zion, he'd look like . . . well, like an investigator. He'd stick out. But you'll fit in. You're an herbalist. You've come to give me a hand with the workshops."

"Ah, so," I said archly. "The truth comes out. I'm supposed to be undercover, am I?"

There was a certain shrewdness behind her pixie grin. "If you want to put it like that, yes, I suppose. In some ways, Mount Zion now is a lot like the original Shaker village. It's a tight-knit community, with a fairly small staff and a team of part-time volunteers. Of course, there are the tourists, but they don't come to the staff areas, and they don't ask questions about the way things operate. If your husband came and started poking around behind the scenes, he'd be immediately obvious, and everybody would be on their guard. But nobody would imagine that *you're* doing an investigation—except for Allie, of course. I'll let her know."

"If this is such a tight-knit community," I said carefully, "whoever is playing these dirty tricks is probably an insider. Somebody you know. Maybe even somebody you like a lot. Correct?"

She sighed. "You always put things so succinctly, China. Yes. I wish it weren't so, but it does seem to me that whoever is doing this must be a member of the staff."

"Has that idea occurred to Rachel Hart?"

She didn't meet my eyes. "I haven't discussed it with her. The politics are—well, a little tricky."

"What about the other trustees? Have you discussed it with them?" She shook her head mutely.

"Is it because you suspect that one of them—"

She gave a horrified gasp. "Oh, no! Of course not! I just . . . Well, I didn't—" Her eyes were wide, and I could see her mentally riffling through a list of people. "Really, China, I can't believe that one of them—"

"In something like this, everybody's a suspect. Everybody. No exceptions. And before you jump into it, you ought to stop and think for a moment. What will you do if the truth turns out to be something really ugly—something you didn't expect and don't want to know?" I paused to give her time to think about what I was saying. "For instance, what if it's a trustee who is behind these dirty tricks? Or Rachel Hart? Or your best friend? Will you press charges? Will you—"

"Stop!" She put her hands over her ears and closed her eyes. There was a long silence. I was sorry to have upset her, but you don't launch an investigation unless you know what you're going to do with the information you dig up. If you can't—or you won't—live with the answers, don't ask the questions.

And there was something else. The events Martha described, the dirty tricks, hadn't injured anyone. I wasn't surprised that Rachel Hart had suggested that they might be the pranks of a Shaker poltergeist. But arson was another matter altogether. And arsonists don't always strike just once. It was entirely possible that there would be another fire, and this one might be deadly. The thought gave me pause. I'd feel pretty awful if I refused to go along with Martha's idea and there was a second fire. A fire in which Martha or someone else was injured. Or died.

Martha opened her eyes and dropped her hands. "It's been difficult, China. I've been frustrated and annoyed. I've come close to resigning from the board more than once. But Mount Zion represents a special dream, an ideal, ordered community where everybody worked together, where all acts were based on love. I want to preserve that. What's more, I'd hate to see Lottie Ayers' efforts go down the drain. And there's Aunt Charity. Mount Zion isn't the same as it was when she was there, but I don't feel right about abandoning it."

"Does that mean you're prepared to deal with whatever turns up?" People aren't, sometimes. When they learn the real truth, they're all of a sudden content to live with a lie.

"Yes, that's what it means." She gave me a steady look. "Something is wrong at Mount Zion, and I need to know what it is, one way or another. I know I should have told you about all this before you drove all the way up here from Texas. But I was afraid you'd say no if I asked you over the phone, or by email." Her voice became intense. "I hope you won't change your mind about going with me, China. I really think you can help."

"But what if I can't?" I persisted. "What if we spend ten days at Mount Zion, and I don't learn a darn thing? That's entirely possible, you know. The petty crimes we're talking about—if they really are crimes, and not just accidents—probably can never be solved."

"That's true. But maybe you'll find something to work with. Or maybe you can set my mind at rest. Maybe these really are just bad luck."

"Maybe," I agreed. I had the feeling they weren't, but that didn't mean I could find out who—or what—was behind them.

"So you'll come?" she asked eagerly.

I couldn't let her do this by herself—it might be dangerous. "I'll come, if you'll promise to let me take some time off to dip into that mineral spring."

"It's a promise," Martha said in a satisfied tone. "In fact, it's an order." She got up from the table. "Come on, China. Let's turn on the computer and take a look at the Mount Zion website. I want to show you the photos. It's a beautiful place, so peaceful. Reminds me of the Garden of Eden."

Chapter Four

"Hands to Work, Hearts to God"
The Shakers: A Brief History

Nine Shakers—"Mother Ann" Lee and eight followers—came to America from England. They arrived in New York in May 1774, on the ship *Mariah*, and after a time traveled north, up the Hudson River, where they bought property near Albany. The land was richly productive and their little settlement flourished. New converts joined them almost daily, drawn by the intense spiritual discipline and the obvious dedication of the Believers, as they were called. (*Shakers* was originally a derogatory word that described the unorthodox worship in dance and movement. It was later adopted by the Believers themselves.) By the end of the eighteenth century, Shaker communities had sprung up in New York, Massachusetts, Connecticut, New Hampshire, and Maine. Over the next few decades, the Shakers joined the Americans moving westward, and by 1810, new societies had been formed in Ohio, Indiana, and Kentucky. Altogether, nineteen societies were established between 1787 and 1836.

In each society, Believers lived a communal life, practicing strict celibacy and worshipping with song and wild, whirling dances. Open to the public and often held outdoors, the worship services were attended by curious "People of the World," who flocked to the bizarre spectacles the way they'd come to a circus. This notoriety, and the Shakers' markedly different way of life, invited persecution. Many Believers were stoned, beaten, and imprisoned; their buildings were burned, their animals stolen or killed. But they held firm to their faith and their numbers grew. At the peak of the movement in the 1840s, some six thousand disciples had declared their allegiance to Mother Ann.

While the World's People mocked the Believers' spiritual practices, the Shaker farms, businesses, and industries were widely admired as models of American productivity. Each of the self-supporting communities produced its own food, tools, furnishings, and clothing, with the various "families" (groups of ten to sixty unrelated women and men living in a single large dwelling) specializing in different areas of production. In addition, each community had its own income-producing industries, manufacturing brooms, baskets, tools, woodenware, mats, shoes, clothing, and fans. Most of the communities also sold plants, shrubs, and trees and carried out a brisk trade in garden seeds, dispatching the brothers on long peddling trips around the countryside in early spring and late summer. They were also known for their quite remarkable architecture—the beautifully symmetrical dwellings, the Round Stone Barn at Hancock Village—and for their stunningly simple furnishings.

But the Shakers were especially known for their herbs. In a time when herbal remedies were the best (often the only) available medicine, the Believers grew, gathered, processed, and sold more than 350 plants, shrubs, and trees, using leaves, roots, bark, flowers, and fruit. In an era of medical quackery, the Believers were trusted to produce clean, unadulterated medicinal herbs picked at the proper time, and carefully stored, processed, packaged, and labeled. Over a period of some fifty years, they annually produced enough meticulously prepared medicinal herbs to make them the largest—and most reliable—supplier to the American pharmaceutical market. The catalogs they published from 1830 to the early 1880s testify to the wide variety of plants they grew or wild-gathered and sold, and to their premier place as purveyors of medicinal herbs. In the Shakers' expert hands, the herb business flourished, as did most of their other enterprises.

But not for long. The Civil War brought distress and lawlessness to the pacifist communities, especially those in Kentucky, and in the era of mechanized industry that followed, the Believers' handmade wares could not compete. When the medical community turned away from plant-based medicines to the newer synthetic drugs, the demand for herbs fell off sharply. The income from these cottage industries was drastically reduced.

The Society's membership was changing, too. The earliest converts were passing on, and the older brothers and sisters were unable to handle the fields and farms. The celibate Shakers had not produced their own "second generation" to carry on the work. Instead, they relied on converts to broaden their ranks and brought in orphaned children who might eventually become productive members of the community. But increasing numbers of middle-aged members, both men and women, had to be expelled for their rebellious spirit or disruptive conduct, and younger people no longer wanted to lead celibate lives in a rural hamlet. In the last quarter of the nineteenth century, the departure of the dissatisfied outnumbered the arrival of the newly converted. Many of the farms had to be rented or sold and the garden and field labor hired out. As the Believers mingled with the World's People who came to the villages to work, their spiritual energies waned and their spiritual purity (as one elder described it) was "sadly polluted."

On top of all this, there were serious financial misdoings. In one of the Kentucky villages, an elder embezzled his family's savings. At others, members got away with horses and wagons and garden produce, or never returned from their seed-selling trips. In one case, a bank employee made off with the entire contents of the community's bank deposit vault, some eighty thousand dollars in banknotes and several lumps of gold. And more than one village had to take on substantial debt because of financial mismanagement by elderly trustees who would have been replaced if younger people had been available.

The situation grew increasingly challenging. Villages began to close, and some—in order to survive—were forced to do things that Mother Ann would not have approved. After the construction of a nearby railroad bridge and station brought more traffic through their village, the entrepreneurial Shakers at Pleasant Hill, Kentucky, converted their Trustees' Office into a boardinghouse and tavern, where they served the licquers and brandies they distilled from their grains and fruits. At the rate of a dollar a day for a room and forty or fifty cents for a meal, marketing their hospitality proved financially profitable but physically and spiritually draining. "Much of the members' time and energy went into taking care of the wants of the guests, who overran the community and disrupted its normal operations," reports Clay Lancaster, in his study of the village's history. The Shakers had turned into innkeepers for the World's People.

But nothing could stave off the inevitable. By 1900, the band of Believers had dwindled to fewer than a thousand souls. By 1931, all but one of the societies had been dissolved, the farms and properties sold, and

the buildings turned to other purposes. Sabbathday Lake, in New Glouc-
ester, Maine (founded in 1794), is the only remaining active society. But
the Shakers' heritage lives on, in their astonishing furniture, their rich
herbal tradition, their self-reliant communal life, and their enduring
spiritual commitment.

Chapter Five

Eldress Olive Manning

June 3, 1912

The name *wormwood* is said to have derived from the story of the Garden of Eden, where the plant sprang up from the track made by the serpent—that giant worm—as it was driven out of the garden. That's why wormwood has such a bitter taste.

When Adam and Eve were expelled as well, the wormwood formed an impenetrable hedge, barring their return and forcing them to live in a cold and unfriendly world outside the garden. This is why wormwood symbolizes the anguished bitterness of repentance and the sad impossibility of ever returning to a state of happy, carefree innocence.

Hands clasped at her waist, Eldress Olive Manning stood at the edge of the graveyard, watching as the Shakers left quietly, the sisters in one single file, the brethren in another. Sister Sally Harmon, whose pine coffin they had just lowered into the ground, had lived at Mount Zion for more than seventy years. As befitted her devout service, Sally had been accorded a public Shaker funeral, held in the Meeting House. Besides the Shakers, a great many black-garbed World's People had been present—most of them Sally's relatives, for she had come from a large family that still lived nearby.

For the Shakers, of course, their sister's funeral was a time for rejoicing. Sally had gone home to Mother, dressed in the spotless white dress and cap she had made herself, testimony to the purity of her life. Olive couldn't rejoice as she should, though. Every funeral—this was the third in two months—was a painful reminder that they were all growing older and their numbers were dwindling, no matter how hard they worked to gather others in.

"I would just like to say thank you for all your kindnesses, Eldress Olive. Aunt Sally often said how much she loved you." It was Sally's niece, Rhoda Edmond, a black veil pulled over her face, in the company of her daughter, Mildred. Mildred was now Sister Charity, having adopted that name when she signed the Covenant. At eighteen, Charity was the youngest of the Mount Zion Believers, and a most welcome one, at that.

"Sister Sally and I were sisters in the faith," Olive reminded Rhoda gently. "And love is the most important thing we have to offer one another."

Charity touched her mother's arm. "I want to say good-bye to Suzanne," she said. "Thank you for coming, Mama." She stood on tiptoes and kissed her mother's cheek. "It is always good to see you."

"Good-bye, Mildred," Rhoda said sadly, and watched Charity make her way through the crowd toward a generously endowed young lady waiting impatiently beside a buggy.

Olive said, "I must tell you, Mrs. Edmond, that we are very glad to have our dear Sister Charity with us. She is a wonderful help, especially in the herb garden. She has a gift for growing things." Olive didn't say so, but Charity's strength was part of her helpfulness. The girl was robust, as muscular as one of the brethren. Give her a hoe and send her to chop weeds, and she'd have the row done before you could blink. And although she was still very young, her devotion to Mother's teachings seemed deeper and stronger than that of sisters twice her age.

"It's good to know my daughter'll have a safe and comfortable life with you," Rhoda said. "Frankly, I gotta admit to not wantin' her to come here in the first place. And to bein' real sorry that she'll not bring me grandchildren. But things weren't right for her at home. And here, she'll escape the sorrows of marriage." She looked around at the orderly gardens and the painted buildings and fences, and her tone became wistful. "To tell the good Lord's truth, Olive, I've oftentimes wished I had a callin' to be a Shaker myself. This is such a peaceful place. No squabblin', no anger. A paradise, like the Garden of Eden in the Bible. It 'ud be good to live here."

"We'd be glad to have you, if you felt the gift," Olive said, speaking truly. Rhoda was still young enough, and strong. They could use her.

Rhoda sighed. "I ain't likely to come, I reckon. Got me too much work at home. And if I did, that husband of mine 'ud just come and fetch me back, 'round about dinnertime. He likes his meals on the table. He weren't happy to see Charity go, neither. Thought she shoulda stayed home and give us a hand."

But pragmatic as Rhoda was, when she said good-bye and walked to her buggy, Olive thought she seemed reluctant to leave.

No squabbling, no anger, like the Garden of Eden. Would that it were so, Olive thought ruefully. It seemed that every year there were more squabbles, more angry arguments. And worse, as more people died, more people left, and the few who came lacked the spirit of willing submission. "Bread and butter Shakers," they were called, "loaf Believers." They joined the Society for what was on the dinner table, rather than for its spiritual nurture. Olive put a brave face on things for the sake of the others, but the present seemed difficult and often dark, and the future did not look much brighter. Sister Sally had gone home to Mother at the right time, while the village might still seem—at least to outsiders—a paradise.

The graveyard was empty now and Olive turned back toward the East Family Dwelling, leaving Sally to rest in the company of other departed brethren and sisters, under a simple white stone marker that bore only her initials. Olive understood Rhoda's wish to find a place of peace, for Charity had said that her father beat her mother when he had had too much to drink—one of the reasons, surely, that the girl had sought refuge with the Shakers.

And one of the reasons, Olive felt sure, that Charity had chosen a celibate life. Of course, these days no one forced a modern young woman to marry. Charity certainly had more choices than Olive had had when she was a young girl. She could move to Lexington or Louisville or even Chicago, where she was sure to find work—which was why there were so few young women at Mount Zion now, and why devout, dedicated young women like Charity were so rare and so welcome. Her budding spiritual dedication to a life of chaste purity was a joy to see, and Olive felt a special affection for her. It would truly be a pleasure to witness and guide her blossoming in the faith.

Olive herself had never married. Orphaned at eight when her parents were killed in a railroad accident, she had come to Mount Zion at the beginning of the Civil War, some fifty years before, and had signed the Covenant as soon as she was permitted. Like Sally, Olive had been one of the lucky ones, arriving when Mount Zion was still full of robust, spirit-filled Shakers, its herb business was prospering, and Mother Ann's blessings were too many to count. She had been a kitchen sister for many years, then an East Family trustee, responsible for organizing and conducting the family's business with the World. Finally, she had become an eldress, responsible for the family's spiritual well-being.

Throughout her half century at Mount Zion, life in the secluded haven had been rich, full, and happy, protected from the buffeting storms of the outside world but never entirely cut off from it. Olive had always liked the fact that the Society didn't wall itself off from every contact with Unbelievers. While the Shakers coveted their separation—"Come out from among them and be ye separate," saith the Lord—they had always offered the fruits of their labors to the World, selling the products of their gardens and farms and shops, creating mail-order catalogs of their herbs, and sending Shaker brothers to peddle their wares throughout the countryside. They even welcomed the World's People to visit their communities and witness their worship, hoping that some, when they were introduced to the simple joys of Shaker life, would be led to accept Mother Ann's teachings. Conversions had always been important—how else were they to grow?—but they became more and more crucial as the years went on. Given that reality, the gathering of a strong, willing young person into the fold was a welcome event.

Like Hannah Chandler, who had arrived in a hired buggy a few weeks earlier with her young son, Seth. An uncommonly beautiful young woman, with dark eyes, gypsy eyes, and flowing dark hair, she had been in great distress—and in great fear, Olive had thought then, although it wasn't clear what the young woman was afraid of.

But it was clear now, and Olive felt a deep misgiving as she thought of it. Hannah had told them at first that she was a widow, that her husband had been killed in a shooting accident, and they had had no reason not to believe her. She had been so happy to join them, so obviously relieved to find a refuge from the World.

In the old days, when there had been many new converts, there had been a Gathering Order at Mount Zion, and a separate Gathering House where newly arrived women and men were tutored in Mother's teachings until they were ready to sign the Covenant and join an established family. Now there weren't enough new folks to justify a separate dwelling, and they were simply welcomed into one of the families. That was why Hannah had been taken in by the East Family. Loving and compassionate, they had accepted her as a recent widow still grieving her husband's death.

But Hannah had been forced to tell them the truth the day Jake Chandler appeared on the doorstep of the East Family Dwelling, shouting that he had come to take his son away. Thankfully, Seth—who had gone to live in the Children's Dwelling—had not witnessed the wrathful scene. At Elder Aaron's request, Hannah had produced the paper that proved her legal divorce and her right of custody of her son, officially granted by the judge in Louisville. Elder Aaron and several of the brethren had then escorted Jake Chandler out of the village, thankfully without physical violence, although Chandler shouted and struggled and made a great many loud threats.

It had been an awful business, Olive thought, as she walked beside the herb garden, noticing that several of the rows hadn't been hoed recently. Green weeds were beginning to crowd the basil, newly set from the cold frame. Intrusions like that of Jake Chandler were upsetting for everyone, but not all that rare, unfortunately. Often, the spouse who had been abandoned when the new Believer left the World vented his or her violent anger on the Society, especially when children were involved. Jake Chandler had threatened to come back, and Olive had the anxious feeling that he'd make good on his threat. They would need to be vigilant.

Jake Chandler wasn't the only reason for being uneasy about Hannah, however. In the beginning, Olive had rejoiced with Elder Aaron over the young woman's fervently expressed wish to become a Believer. She had accepted Hannah with a happy heart, especially when she saw what a good hand she was at work—even the most menial work—and how eager she was to do her share. Too eager, sometimes, for her willingness often ran several steps ahead of her ability, like the morning she failed to follow Sister Pearl's recipe, and the biscuits were like hardtack and had to be softened in milk before they could be eaten. And Olive could wish for a more disciplined appearance, for Hannah's thick dark curls often spilled out from under her white cotton cap, and her carelessly crossed modesty kerchief did not always conceal the generous fullness of her bosom.

Olive had reached the foot of the garden, where the foxglove and larkspur bloomed in a glorious exuberance and June's red roses tumbled over the white-painted picket fence. The early Shakers rejected superfluous adornments and held plainness and simplicity as important virtues. In fact, the Ministry's Orders and Rules—the Millennial Laws that governed behavior—specifically prohibited the gathering of flowers for use in a bouquet. Olive herself had been trained as a child to ignore the delicate, almost exotic beauties of foxglove and larkspur and focus on their uses. Foxglove was cultivated for the treatment of dropsy and asthma, and larkspur was a narcotic and emetic, and that was that. Beauty was a snare and a delusion, and must be set aside.

But now, older, wiser, and more deeply grounded in her faith, Olive felt that beauty was a sweet and special blessing of its own, and larkspur and foxglove were graces sent by Heaven to be cherished and loved for their lovely selves, not just for what they could do. Slowing a little to enjoy the sight of the flowers, she turned to take the path that led toward the Sisters' Shop and beyond that, to the East Family Dwelling. She thought again of Hannah, so beautiful of face, so graceful of form—a blessing in its own right, surely. And her lack of discipline and impulsiveness were small matters, not unusual in a novice, and Hannah would no doubt learn to control herself in time.

But what did trouble Olive was Hannah's request for private instruction from Elder Aaron, in preparation for signing the Covenant. And she was even more troubled—distressed, really—by his ready agreement to the unusual arrangement. This was not the way things ought to be done. It was Olive's responsibility to teach the women, and she took Hannah's request, and Elder Aaron's assent, as a personal affront.

There. Olive felt better for having admitted it, if only to herself. She valued her work as a spiritual guide, and she was deeply vexed at Hannah for asking Elder Aaron to be her teacher and even more vexed at him for consenting. If it had been any other than Aaron, who was nearly sixty and unwavering in the faith, she might have been concerned in a different way. As time had gone on, the Shakers had somewhat relaxed the rule against private conversations between men and women, especially where work was concerned, but the arrangement was unusual enough to cause comment, if it became widely known.

Of course, there was no need to be concerned about temptations to lust where Aaron was concerned, Olive reminded herself. She had worked with him on a daily basis for the past five years—elders and eldresses were permitted private meetings—and never once had she detected anything improper. He was the soul of perfect rectitude. But elders and eldresses were supposed to set an example for all, and in this case, Aaron was electing to set a bad example.

And Hannah's beauty was already causing complications. A day or two before, Olive had noticed Brother Alfred's gaze lingering on the young woman while the two of them worked in the garden. Hannah had rewarded his interest with a sideways glance—almost flirtatious, Olive would have said—and a smile. Olive had drawn Hannah apart and had spoken to her, and she had been so immediately contrite that Olive agreed that there was no need for her to confess her wrong to the family. She had mentioned the episode to Elder Aaron, and he had spoken with Brother Alfred, who (although he was nearing fifty) was young in the faith. Alfred had signed the Covenant only two years ago and might not yet have the spiritual fortitude to withstand temptation.

And while Olive herself had never been tempted beyond endurance, she knew that temptation lay in wait, and all must constantly guard against adventures and lusts of the flesh. And that was why Olive had found it unpleasantly necessary to speak to Sister Ruth about what she had seen during the worship dance on the previous Sabbath. Ruth was only twenty-two, a good worker but impressionable and vulnerable. Brother Charles was older and had lived in the World until five or six years ago, when he'd come to them as a Recuperant. A thoughtful, quiet man of forceful personality, he had become well and strong with them and now managed the Herb Department. Elder Aaron, who had also witnessed what transpired, had spoken to him, although Olive had not yet heard how Brother Charles responded.

Just at that moment, as if the thought had conjured her, Olive glimpsed Ruth through the window of the Sisters' Shop. Her back turned to the window, she was making an adjustment to the loom, preparing to return to her weaving. The Shakers no longer wove their own cloth, contenting themselves with purchased machine stuff for their clothing. It was more profitable to sell the sisters' weaving and put the money toward the repayment of the disastrous loan old Elder Thomas had taken out to build the South Family's huge barn. Olive hated the thought of owing money to the bank and feared what would happen if they could not make the payments. It was like a black cloud hanging constantly over the horizon.

As Olive watched, Ruth sat down at her loom and picked up the shuttle. Olive smiled approvingly. *Hands to work, hearts to God,* Mother Ann taught, for work was worship; work was prayer. Most of the Shakers moved from the kitchen to the garden, the dairy, and the fields, according to an assigned schedule of rotations. But Sister Ruth's weaving—and dyeing, too, for that matter—was of the highest quality and exquisitely beautiful. Her work commanded a very good price in the market, so she had become a weaving sister, permanently assigned to cloth production, with a few hours every week to be spent on other chores, or in the garden or the woods, gathering herbs in the sunshine.

The sisters and brethren had been granted the hour following the funeral as a private time for prayer and reflection, and Ruth was not obliged to come back to the shop. Olive went on her way, pleased to know that the young woman was spending her hour of prayer in sweet labor—a sign of penitence, she thought, for that slight transgression with Brother Charles. Or perhaps no transgression at all. The touching had been brief, perhaps quite unintentional. Ruth herself had insisted that she hadn't even felt it.

Olive was wrong, on both counts. Ruth had lied: Charles' touch was both willful and wildly exciting. And she was not spending her hour of prayer in sweet labor—at least, not in the kind of occupation that Eldress Olive, and certainly not Mother Ann, would have approved. A moment after Olive had passed on her way, Charles McBride appeared in the doorway, smiled gently, and beckoned. Ruth rose from her loom and the two went together into the smaller, windowless storeroom where the carded fiber was kept, and shut the door silently behind them. Olive would have been aghast at what passed between them, the whispers, the kisses, the touches, the eager, greedy passion.

But Olive, serenely unenlightened, had already gone on her way, her thoughts turning from Sister Ruth to that wretched situation with the mineral spring. It now appeared that their spring, Zion's Spring, had never truly belonged to the Believers, after all. What could be done if Will

Ayers made good on his promise to repossess it? Without the room-and-board payments from the people who came to recuperate from illness and bathe in the spring, they could not make the note payments at the bank. They would surely lose the Outer Farm, which meant that they could no longer raise the grain that made their bread and the hay that carried their cows through the winter—although now that they had to hire so much of the farm work out, none of this was a very profitable enterprise. They might be better off to buy hay for the cows and flour for the bread, although that was not the Shaker way.

The Shaker way? Olive shook her head sadly. So many changes, so many little fallings-away from the teachings of Mother Ann. It seemed to her that, in these latter days, nothing was done in the Shaker way.

Chapter Six

'Tis a gift to be simple, 'tis a gift to be free
'Tis a gift to come down where we ought to be.
And when we find ourselves in the place just right
'T will be in the garden of love and delight.

Shaker hymn

A garden was the primitive prison, till man with Promethean felicity and boldness, luckily sinned himself out of it.

Charles Lamb, 1830

It was late in the afternoon on Thursday when I parked my white Toyota under a leafy maple in the parking lot behind the large building that had once been the Trustees' Office at Mount Zion, and still bore that name. About five miles off a main north-south highway and surrounded on all sides by untamed Kentucky wilderness, the village was even prettier than the pictures on its website. The buildings were arranged in a balanced, symmetrical order on both sides of a maple-lined brick street known as New Harmony Lane. The large dwellings were built of rectangular blocks of gray-white Kentucky limestone, their multipaned windows framed by neat green shutters. The fences and other frame structures were painted a glistening white, the grass was a clipped and velvety green, and tidy gardens bordered with bright flowers were laid out around the buildings. Everything was aligned, orderly, neat, a serene enclave wrested from the wilds of what must have seemed, to the early Shakers, a terrifyingly impenetrable forest, full of wild animals. Once built, Mount Zion would have been a heaven on earth.

If there were any wild animals here now, they were staying well out of sight. Today was Monday, and several dozen tourists armed with cameras, sunglasses, and plastic bottles of water were strolling along New Harmony Lane, accompanied by twice that many frolicking children. The sun was shining and the temperature was in the eighties, and men, women, and kids were dressed in unisex T-shirts, crop tops, shorts, and sandals. The Shaker reenactors—interpreters, Martha called them—were a sharp contrast. The sisters were dressed in dark, ankle-length dresses, blue and burgundy, with white aprons and plain white caps. The brothers wore homespun britches, white shirts, blue cotton vests, and straw hats.

Several sisters were standing in the doors of the buildings, greeting the tourists as they entered. Brothers walked down the street carrying baskets, or worked in the gardens, or painted a fence. And from a wooden farm stand, under a sign announcing FRESH SHAKER VEGETABLES, a brother was selling tomatoes, cucumbers, and ears of fresh sweet corn. A pair of gleaming brown horses pulled a buggy filled with photo-snapping tourists down the brick street, hooves clip-clopping. Altogether, the village looked busy and prosperous, hardly a place where somebody might indulge in some surreptitious skullduggery.

Martha seemed serious about this "investigation," as she called it, and as we drove north from Mississippi, she told me more about the village and its history. At its peak population in the early 1850s, Mount Zion had been home to some three hundred industrious souls, not counting those who came to visit or seek a temporary refuge. There were plenty of those, apparently, including slaves fleeing their masters, women running from violent husbands, men running from the law. Later, during the Civil

War, it wasn't unusual for the Kentucky Shakers to feed several thousand men at a time, both the Blue and the Gray—not together, of course. The Believers were pacifists, but that didn't mean they could tell the troops to go somewhere else for lunch.

She also showed me a map of the village as it had been in its heyday. There had been five large, identical three-story family dwellings, each housing up to seventy men and women: the Center Family Dwelling, and dwellings for the East, West, North, and South families. Behind each house and adjacent to it, the family had built whatever sheds and barns and gardens were needed to carry out its work.

There were other buildings. The two-story stone Trustees' Office, where visitors and guests were housed and the village business was carried out. The white-frame Meeting House, large enough to accommodate the whole community. The Children's Dwelling, next to a white-frame schoolhouse. Most of these buildings had at least two entrances, one for the brothers and one for the sisters, for men and women were strictly segregated. Scattered across the area were smaller communal shops and outbuildings: the post office, a smithy, a bath house, the laundry, a spinning and dyeing shed, and several buildings connected with the herb business—the herb house, the drying shed, and buildings that housed the pressing and grinding equipment.

Many of the original structures were gone now, fallen victim to fire, vandalism, and the ravages of time. The family dwellings had been much too large to convert to private residences and the property too remote—some fifteen miles from Georgetown and sixty miles from Lexington, on bad roads—to be an attractive investment possibility. The village had suffered four decades of neglect between 1923, when the Mount Zion Society officially closed, and the early 1960s, when a new highway made for easier access. That was when Lottie and Ernest Ayers purchased the village, the mineral spring, and the surrounding three hundred acres and began the long process of turning it into a living museum and educational center.

The Ayers had restored, redecorated, and furnished the two family houses that remained—the East Family and the South Family. The South Family Dwelling was open to the public, but the East Family house had been converted to an inn, where Martha and I would be staying. The Trustees' Office housed the restaurant; the Schoolhouse had been turned into a gift shop and bookstore; and the Children's Dwelling had been converted to offices and administration. Spinning and weaving demonstrations were given in the Sisters' Shop. A blacksmith worked at his forge in the smithy, and cobblers and harness makers plied their crafts in the Brothers' Shop, where dough bowls were also made for sale in the gift shop. The conference center was the new building at the edge of the woodland, past the picnic ground, and there was an orchard along the hedge-lined lane to the mineral spring and its cluster of guest cabins, out of sight beyond the trees. There had been a large horse barn back there, too, but it was gone, compliments of the as-yet-unidentified arsonist.

Martha had our itinerary all planned. This afternoon, we'd drop in at the main office and say hello to Rachel Hart and the administrative staff, which included Jane Gillette, the assistant director, and Sharon Baehr, the events coordinator. We would also see Allie Chatham, Martha's girlhood friend, who was in charge of the financial office, and Missy Thatcher, the archivist and manager of the conference center. In the evening, we'd have dinner in the restaurant and Martha would introduce me to the kitchen and serving staff. There was a trustees' meeting scheduled for the next week, so I would meet the other five members of the board then. Martha is an organizer, and she'd already figured out how to introduce me so people wouldn't suspect I was there to give them all a careful going-over, which of course I was. She had my investigation all planned out, down to the last suspect.

To tell the truth, I already felt a little silly about the whole thing. I was glad to help Martha out, yes, and I shared her concern that something strange was going on at Mount Zion. I've done my share of digging into malicious mischief over the years, and I've been lucky enough to find out a few things that people were trying to hide. But if Martha wanted a real investigation, she should have hired a real investigator, somebody who knew what he—or she—was doing. And although she seemed to have the whole thing planned, she couldn't plan for surprises.

My experience, limited as it might be, has taught me that something unexpected always happens.

Always.

And after that, all the plans go right out the nearest window.

THE restored Children's Dwelling had the lovely Shaker interiors I'd seen in so many photos—the immaculate plaster walls, tall windows and high ceilings, woodwork painted in shades of gray and blue, gleaming wooden floors. There was a display of Shaker furnishings and crafts: stacks of oval wooden boxes, ladder-back chairs with woven rush seats, a delicate Shaker rocking chair beside a perfectly proportioned candle stand, a superb tall trustee's desk, baskets and sieves, palm-leaf bonnets and straw hats, even a collection of brightly labeled Shaker herb tins and boxes. Martha confided that this had been Lottie's antique collection. It had been appraised for nearly a quarter of a million dollars.

I looked around curiously, trying to spot the security cameras. I didn't see any. I hadn't noticed much in the way of locks on the doors, either. Now wasn't the time to say so, but I made a mental note to tell Martha that it wouldn't take a Houdini to get into this building and make off with this fabulous Shaker loot. Given all the things that had happened in the past few months, it behooved the trustees to do something about it. Pronto.

Our first stop, Rachel Hart's office. It was a large room with white walls and a red braided rug on the wooden floor, where we found Ms. Hart seated at the Shaker table that served as her desk, with a computer on a smaller table at right angles to it. One wall was filled with framed drawings and photographs of Shakers engaged in all sorts of crafts—more of Lottie's collection, I assumed. The opposite wall was hung with several odd, brightly colored drawings, exuberant images and abstractions, wildly imaginative, with ornamental symbols, geometric forms, and strange calligraphy. These unexpected pictures immediately drew me to them.

But before I could take a closer look, Rachel Hart was stubbing out a cigarette and rising to her feet, smiling. She was younger than I had expected, not yet forty, with a fine-boned, carefully made-up face, large dark eyes, feathery brows, and dark hair pulled back into a sleek, shining chignon. She was too thin to be attractive, and there was a kind of nervous brittleness about her. But she carried herself with a definite flair, and her dress—an oatmeal-colored linen sheath—was chic and understated. A coffee-colored silk scarf was draped elegantly across one shoulder and fastened with a gold pin set with diamonds. Real? There was no way to tell.

She was effusively glad to see Martha. "How *are* you, my dear, *dear* Martha? So wonderful that you could be with us for the trustees' meeting!" She came around the desk and aimed an air kiss at Martha's cheek. "I can't tell you how delighted I am that you could offer those popular herb workshops again! You are the biggest hit of our summer, you know!

All of your sessions are already full!" Each of these superlatives was delivered in a honeyed drawl, not quite Southern, but definitely not Northern, laced with nervous exclamation points.

Rachel turned to me, offering an extended hand and an artificial, actressy smile. "And this must be your friend China Bayles! So good to meet you at last, China. Martha has been telling us all about that sweet little shop of yours. Some day I simply must get in the car and zip down to Texas to see it. Although we are always *so* busy here, it's almost impossible to get away." She turned back to Martha. "We have a new nature program for the children, Martha, and of course next month is our annual crafts fair. And while you're here, I hope you'll attend our Shaker songfest. It's being presented by a choir from Georgetown. It should be an absolutely splendid occasion." This long litany gave me the impression of someone who likes to control the flow of conversation.

"I'm sure we'll enjoy everything," Martha said coolly. "Has the sheriff learned anything more about the barn burning?"

Rachel turned away, not happy that somebody else had changed the subject and clearly uneasy with the topic. "Not yet. But the insurance company has agreed to release the funds for the building and the equipment. We didn't get the full replacement value, of course—it was an old barn—but the money will certainly help. The item is on the trustees' agenda."

"And the spa?" Martha's question was pointed.

"Oh, that." Rachel fluttered her hand. "Well, I realize it's not your favorite subject of conversation. But as I'll be reporting at our trustees' meeting, the construction committee has had some preliminary drawings and cost estimates made, so we're ready to—"

"Construction committee?" Martha sounded surprised. "Somehow I missed that. Who's chairing the committee?"

Rachel looked away. "Karen Sanders."

"Ah," Martha replied, with a might-have-guessed glance at me. She had told me that Karen Sanders, one of the trustees, was Rachel Hart's closest friend. "So you already have the drawings? I suppose you consulted with one or two other trustees before you went ahead."

The comment was clearly baited, but Rachel didn't bite. Instead, she gestured toward a set of rolled-up architectural drawings in the corner. "Yes. The drawings are here. I have the estimates, too, if you'd like to look them over before the board meeting." Quickly, she turned back to me, reclaiming control of the conversation. "I do hope you'll enjoy your visit with us, China. We're all so very proud of Mount Zion and eager to preserve all its fine Shaker traditions. If you have any questions about the village, please let me know. I'll do my best to answer them."

If I'd been looking for something to jump out at me, some sort of clue that would tell me whether Rachel Hart was somehow involved in any of the things that had recently happened, I would certainly have been disappointed. But as a lawyer, I've had to learn the trick of seeing through the facade that people erect to hide real feelings, and a couple of things had jumped out at me: Rachel liked to be in charge. And Martha Edmond made her very uneasy.

Well, that was understandable, wasn't it? Martha had made it plain that she wasn't in favor of the latest construction project, among other things. I couldn't help wondering why Rachel had insisted that Martha remain on the board. I would have thought she'd want to get rid of her the minute she became president. But that wasn't a question I was going to ask—yet.

I nodded at the framed drawings on the wall, which had caught my eye when we first came in. "Those are really unusual. Shaker art?"

Rachel laughed lightly. "Oh, no—at least, not art in the usual sense.

The Shakers didn't approve of the decorative arts, you see. They wanted everything to be utterly plain, very simple." She gave a little wave of her hand. "In fact, I'm violating a Shaker rule by displaying these on the wall."

"Not just a Shaker rule," Martha said quietly. "I thought we had agreed that they were to be placed in the museum, where they can at least be displayed properly. The light in this room will fade them."

"Of course you're right, Martha," Rachel said in a conciliatory tone. "I've made arrangements for Missy Thatcher to take them." Turning back to me, she said, "They really are quite astonishing, aren't they? They are gift drawings. Most of them were made by Sister Nora, who lived at Mount Zion from the 1870s until it closed. I can never get enough of looking at them. I always see something new every time I study them."

"Gift drawings?"

"Sometimes they're called spirit drawings. The Shakers believed that seeing through the veil of the material world was a special gift, you see. A gift from the spirits."

"Ah." Ruby would understand that.

"The Shakers were often visited by spirits," Rachel went on. "Sometimes Mother Ann, sometimes Jesus Christ or the angels, or even people like George Washington or an Indian chief. The spirits manifested themselves through Believers called 'visionists,' who received them in trance, or in song or dance, or in messages written in strange tongues."

I snapped my fingers. "Like channeling." I know about channeling, because it's something Ruby does from time to time. She is always reminding me that logic and rationality cannot explain everything in this amazing world.

"Exactly like channeling," Rachel said enthusiastically. This was clearly a subject she enjoyed. "The women who drew these were usually in a trance state, and the spirits communicated through these draw-ings." She stood back, looking at them. "I think they're simply beautiful. And so amazingly rich, in contrast to the rest of the Shakers' art."

Martha stepped forward, pointing to the most intricate and elabo-rate of the drawings, filled with angels with harps, Shaker brothers and sisters with various implements, a large, all-seeing eye, and various bits of script, too small to be easily read. "My aunt Charity drew that one," she told me. "She took it with her when she left the village and moved into town. It was stored for years in a trunk in my mother's attic, along with Aunt Charity's journal and some old letters."

Smiling, Rachel put her arm around Martha's shoulders in what was supposed to be a friendly hug. "And Martha, *dear* Martha has donated these wonderful things to our museum! How *can* we thank you, Mar-tha?"

It sounded incredibly phony. And it wasn't quite the right question to ask.

"You can thank me by letting Missy put these drawings in a safe place," Martha said evenly, pulling away. "Actually, I'm rather tired, Rachel. It was a long drive. Jane has the key to our rooms?"

"Oh, yes, yes, she does." Rachel was nettled by the rejection and trying not to show it. "And of course, your usual room is ready for you—Sister Charity's room. We've put China right across the hall, in Sister Hannah's room." To me, she added, "Whenever we've been able to learn the names of the Shakers who lived in the rooms, we've put their names on the doors, and Missy is writing short biographies. We're hoping that this little effort will give our guests a more personal experience of Shaker life."

I wasn't sure that a "short biography" would do the trick, at least for some people. Maybe they could arrange something a little more dra-matic. An angel bearing a gift? A Shaker ghost?

Martha turned to go. "China and I are having dinner at the restaurant this evening, Rachel. If you'd like to come along, feel free."

It wasn't exactly a cordial invitation, but if Rachel was offended, she didn't show it. She made a dramatically disappointed moue. "Oh, dear, I am so, so sorry, Martha. Bruce is here, and he's asked me to join him." She flicked the corner of her scarf. "But do let me know if you need anything, anything at all."

"Just the drawings," Martha said. "In the museum. Please."

JANE Gillette was Mount Zion's assistant director. Her office, down the hall, was much more utilitarian than Rachel Hart's. Jane was a small, thin, narrow-faced woman, middle-aged, wearing a red-and-white-print blouse, navy blue skirt, and stiff brown curls that looked as if they had been tacked in place with three layers of hair spray—or maybe it was a wig. Without getting up from her desk, she greeted Martha briskly, acknowledged my introduction, checked off our names on a list, and handed over the keys to our rooms.

Jane's office gave the impression of total organization. There were stacks of paper beside the computer on her desk, her bulletin board was plastered with notices and memos, and a big, write-on wall calendar was filled with postings. Beside it was an aerial color photograph of the village complex, showing the orderly arrangement of buildings, gardens, lanes, and paths. In some of the empty spaces, I could see the ghostly outlines of the foundations of long-ago buildings. Surrounding the village was the vast, unruly wilderness.

"Jane oversees the guest rooms, the restaurant, and the buildings and grounds," Martha said, by way of introduction. "In fact, she's the one who keeps this place running."

Pleased but not wanting to show it, Jane gave her a faint smile. "I do my best."

"Sounds like you have a lot of responsibility," I observed admiringly. "Just the inn alone would be a full-time job. How many guests can you accommodate?"

Jane's voice was crisp. "Mrs. Ayers converted the East Family Dwelling to an inn some twenty years ago. Thirty-one rooms are currently in use, ten singles, twenty-one doubles. There are also ten cottages at the mineral spring, although they're not open for guests this summer. The cottages will be replaced, I understand, when the construction of the spa begins." Her eyebrows had pulled together. She wasn't bothering to disguise her displeasure.

"The spring is here, China," Martha said, pointing with a pencil to the top of the aerial photo. "You can't see much from this point of view, though. The pool—Zion's Pool—is hidden by that rocky outcropping and surrounded by trees. These roofs"—she tapped her pencil on the photo—"are the guest cottages." To Jane, she said, "Ms. Hart just told us that she already has preliminary drawings and cost estimates for the new spa and cottages."

I turned from the photograph just in time to see Jane's face darkening. "We have no business getting into a project like that," she muttered, and then pressed her lips together, as if she had said more than she meant to say—at least to us.

Martha gave her a sympathetic look. "Personally, I confess to sharing that feeling. But I'm afraid that you and I are in the minority."

Jane's reply was almost fierce. "I'm sure I shouldn't be telling you this, Ms. Edmond, but we are *not* in the minority. Almost everyone on the staff thinks this expansion is a terrible idea. And I've looked at the cost estimates myself. Given the increased staffing requirements and additional maintenance, I fail to see how the project is going to make any money. In fact, we'll be lucky if it breaks even."

"Have you brought this to Ms. Hart's attention?" Martha asked, frowning.

"Have I—" Jane was indignant. "Of course I have! I got my own estimates together—the projected housekeeping costs, supplies, maintenance, all that sort of thing—and made a formal presentation, right there in her office. But she hardly listened. She's already decided what she wants to do and she's plowing full steam ahead, like some . . . some *bulldozer.*"

"But it's not Ms. Hart who will make the ultimate decision," Martha pointed out gently. "It's the trustees. The majority of the trustees. And whether we like it or not, the majority rules." She took a breath and puffed it out. "I hope you and the rest of the staff will support any decision that's made."

That last sentence was exactly the sort of thing a true-blue board member should say to a discontented employee, I thought. But it was clear that Jane didn't agree. In fact, she might have returned a sharp retort if I hadn't been in the room. But I was company, and she didn't want to hang all the village's dirty laundry on the line in front of me.

Mindful of that, she took a deep breath and said, in a sadly resigned voice, "Sometimes I just wish I could close my eyes and go back to the village the way it was a hundred years ago. Everything was so much simpler then."

"That's what we like to think, anyway," Martha said with a little smile. "You should talk to Missy. She's writing a history of the village and telling me all about the unrest and intrigue she's turned up in her research.

Apparently, Mount Zion never was the enclave of peace and serenity it may have seemed." She sighed regretfully. "A pity."

I turned to Jane. "Speaking of unrest and intrigue, I understand that you had a fire here a few weeks ago. The barn, wasn't it?"

The question seemed to catch Jane off guard. "That's right," she said shortly.

"One of the restored buildings?"

"No, just an old barn where we used to keep rental horses. Not much of a loss."

Martha turned back to the aerial photo and pointed. "This is the barn, China. In better days."

I saw a large rectangular building with a dark roof, next to a fenced corral. "Some animals were killed, though, Martha told me," I said, still speaking to Jane. "That's too bad."

"Two of Mr. Hart's horses," Jane said. Pointedly, she glanced at the clock on the wall. It was four thirty. "Sharon Baehr would like you to stop by her office, Ms. Edmond. She wants to give you the list of people who have signed up for your workshops." She sat down again and pointedly picked up a sheaf of papers. Without looking up, she said, "It was nice to meet you, Ms. Bayles. I hope you enjoy your stay with us."

"THAT was abrupt, don't you think?" I asked Martha, when we were out in the hall. "It felt like she was booting us out."

"Jane used to be friendlier, until what happened to Maxine. Since then, she's been pretty distant. Not just to me, but to everybody."

"Maxine?" I frowned. "Oh, right. The young woman who took fifteen thousand dollars and then killed herself."

Martha flinched. "Yes. Maxine was Jane's niece."

I stopped in midstep. "You've got to be kidding."

"No, of course I'm not kidding." She stopped, too, and looked at me. "Why?"

"Well, think about it, Martha."

She thought. "Oh. She might bear a grudge?"

"Right. And listening between the lines, it didn't sound to me as if Jane is a fan of Rachel Hart, or a supporter of her projects."

"That's a fair statement," Martha said wryly. "She and Rachel never got along, even before what happened to Maxine. But I really don't think—" She stopped. "You're not suggesting that Jane might be behind the barn burning or—"

She stopped again, giving a definitive shake of her head. "No, China. Don't even think it. Jane has been here for more than fifteen years. She's indispensable. She would never—"

"Indispensable employees have been known to burn down warehouses and cook the books and do all kinds of interesting things," I retorted. "I'm not saying that she's done any of this, of course. I'm just saying that it warrants consideration."

There was a silence. Finally, Martha said, "She did seem a little reluctant to talk about the barn."

That was an understatement. But there was something else I wanted to know. "Mr. Hart, the one with the horses. Rachel Hart's husband?"

"Rachel isn't married. Bruce is her brother."

"Oh, yes, the one she's seeing tonight." I pulled my brows together. "He works here?"

Martha looked surprised. "Oh, dear, no. He's a real-estate broker in Lexington—quite well-known, does lots of office and condominium developments. He drives up every so often, mostly to ride, although I don't think Rachel likes his coming here. They're not on the best of terms, although I don't think it's entirely his fault. Lottie could be incredibly fussy, and her grandson must have done something that she didn't approve of. She left him out of her will."

"That's drastic."

"She made it clear that he wasn't to be involved in the management of the foundation, either. Such a shame, seems to me. Bruce obviously has a good head for business—better than Rachel, if you ask me. Mount Zion could certainly use somebody with his savvy. What's more, he's always seemed so helpful, not nearly as abrasive as his sister." Martha paused, pursing her lips and frowning. "I didn't know those were his horses. That's too bad."

"The barn—it was really old?"

"Well, yes, although it's been kept in fairly good shape. There are equestrian trails through the woods and fields, you see. In Lottie's day, people could rent horses and go riding. We stopped doing that a few years ago—it didn't turn a profit, and there was the liability. But until the barn burned, guests at the inn were permitted to bring their horses so they could ride the trails." She smiled at my raised eyebrow. "You're in horse country, China."

"As if I hadn't noticed." The farther north we'd driven, the more horse farms we had seen, lovely horses grazing in wide green fields enclosed by white-painted fences. I grinned. "Sort of a Shaker dude ranch, huh?"

It was a bad joke, and I was glad when she pretended not to hear me. "Lottie always hoped Mount Zion would attract guests who would bring their families and stay for several days or a week. But then, of course, there has to be something for them to do while they're here. That's why we had horses."

"I suppose there's a limit to the number of hours you can soak in a mineral spring," I acknowledged. "Or tour Shaker dwellings."

"Of course, we have lots of other activities—art workshops, weaving and spinning and dyeing classes, Elder Hostel programs—"

Martha stopped at an open door, which bore the name *Sharon Baehr.* "But I'll let Sharon tell you about that." She put her head through the door. "Hi, Sharon. May I interrupt you? I've brought China to meet you."

"Oh, hello, Ms. Edmond," Sharon replied brightly, getting up from her desk. "It's so good to see you again! And guess what! Your workshops are full and there's a waiting list."

"I'm glad," Martha said, pleased. "Even the herb walk?" She turned to me. "People love strolling through the gardens, looking at herbs. But it's sometimes a little difficult to lure them into the woods, where they might meet a snake."

"Yes, even the herb walk," Sharon said. She was a trim woman with light gray hair and very blue eyes behind gold-framed glasses. She held out her hand. "Hello, Ms. Bayles. Welcome to Mount Zion. We're so glad to have you here." Her enthusiasm was a pleasant contrast to Jane Gillette's unfriendly restraint and Rachel Hart's phony friendliness.

"I was telling China about some of your programs." Martha smiled. "I'd just got to the point of saying, 'And too many more to mention.'"

Sharon laughed, a bright, tinkling laugh, and waved her hand toward the large list on the wall. "Tell me about it," she said. "Just look at the things we're offering." She sobered. "Although Larry Foley will no longer be giving his art classes, I'm sorry to say."

"Oh?" Martha frowned. "Why?"

"You haven't heard? Saturday night, somebody broke into the studio in the Brothers' Shop and completely trashed out some very nice paintings Mr. Foley was storing there for his next show. Vandalized his canvases and supplies, too." She went back to her desk. "Maybe you don't remember, but there was another problem early in the spring—some of Mr. Foley's things were stolen. He says he can't afford to teach here any longer."

"Oh, no!" Martha exclaimed. "Who would have done such a horrible thing? Poor Larry!" To me, she said, "The Foleys were our neighbors when I was growing up. Larry and I went to school together."

"It's a serious loss," Sharon said, "in more ways than one. Mr. Foley's classes always attracted people who might not have come here otherwise. He liked to teach three- and four-day workshops, so his students would stay overnight, as well. We're going to miss him." She gave her head a gloomy shake. "When word gets around—as I'm sure it will—it may be hard to find a replacement. Local artists won't want to risk losing their stuff."

Mentally, I added the vandalism to my list of dirty tricks. "Was the break-in reported to the police?"

Sharon gave me a questioning look. "I suppose Ms. Hart took care of that. Nobody came around asking me questions, though," she added. "No police, I mean." To Martha, she said, "Do you have everything you need for your programs?"

"I've brought a few things," Martha said. "And China and I will spend some time in the garden, gathering the herbs we need. Anything else?"

"Only that the weather has been iffy this week, and the forecast for the next five or six days doesn't look good. The usual spring storms, you know—lots of lightning and thunder, especially in the afternoons. It might be a good idea to be prepared to work indoors."

"We will if we have to."

Sharon frowned. "It seems like there was something else I'm supposed to—" She snapped her fingers. "Oh, now I remember. Ms. Chatham wanted me to tell you to stop by Accounting for a few minutes this afternoon."

"We were already planning to do that." Martha smiled at me. "You'll like Allie, China. She's . . . well, she's earthy."

Sharon chuckled. "Earthy is right. Ms. Hart is always trying to get her to clean up her language." She glanced up at the clock, which showed ten minutes to five. "Actually, she sounded kind of urgent about seeing you. If you want to catch her, you might want to hurry."

Chapter Seven

Sister Charity Edmond

June 3, 1912

Virgin's Bower (*Clematis virginiana*), also known as Travellers' Joy, Clematis. Leaves: stimulant. Nervine. Used in severe headache, in cancerous ulcers, and as ointment in itches.

Shaker Medicinal Herbs
Amy Bess Miller

Virgin's bower, or clematis, had several contradictory meanings. The ancient Romans believed that, grown on the walls of their houses, it would protect against thunderstorms. On the other hand, people in Northern Europe believed that the same plant attracted lightning. The purity of its white blossoms gave it the name "Virgin's bower," but in France, beggars applied the crushed leaves to their faces and arms in order to create sores and attract alms. Hence, in the Victorian language of flowers, clematis became a symbol of artifice, trickery, and deceit.

As the brothers began to heap the dirt into Sister Sally's grave, Charity Edmond left her mother with Eldress Olive and went to talk with her cousin Suzanne, who was waiting beside the buggy. Charity had been glad to see her mother and Suzanne. It was always nice to visit with them and hear about everything that was going on at home. But it was even nicer to be able to stay safely and quietly here in the village, while everyone else went back to the World. *Their* world, not hers. Not any longer.

Suzanne, of course, never stopped trying to get her to go back. She was only a year older than Charity and very proud of her buxom figure and shiny red curls. She could never understand why her cousin would want to wear those plain Shaker dresses, twist up her hair under a silly white cap, and live in such a boring place.

"I wish you'd come back home where you belong!" she said almost fiercely, as they stood beside the buggy that Charity's mother had driven to the funeral. "Just think of all the good times you're missin', Charity! Why, last Saturday, Carl an' Sandy an' me drove all the way to Lexington to see the horse races. And there was fireworks, too, and a merry-go-round! It'ud been such fun if you'd been along." She slipped her arm around Charity's waist and whispered into her ear, "Sandy hisself said so. He told me to tell you he wants to see you again. Wants to see you real bad."

Charity felt her insides clench in a hot, hard knot. Sandy—Suzanne's brother's friend, who was rude and bullheaded and couldn't keep his ugly hands to himself—was one of the reasons she was here in the village, and not in the World. The thought of those hands on her made her sick, almost as sick as the thought of her father's groping hands, and all that came after.

Suzanne's arm tightened. "Why don't you come with us next Saturday, Charity? One day away from this ol' place surely wouldn't send you to hell, would it? I'll give you a dress to wear an' fix your hair an'—"

"Nay, Suzanne," Charity interrupted her, making her voice light and level. "We have good times here, too. Last week, we had a picnic at the river. And we went berry picking and—"

"Oh, bosh!" Suzanne rolled her eyes. "Berry pickin'! Good lands,

Charity—there's a whole world out there! An' you're stuck in this ol' place, pickin' berries with a bunch o' ol' fuddy-duddy *saints*!"

"That's just how I want it, Suzanne," Charity said staunchly. There was no point in trying to tell Suzanne how deeply she craved the sanctity of the Shaker life, how it satisfied her deepest need to be clean, to be spotless and virginal, to be cleansed of every impurity. "I'll never, ever leave. And that's that."

Suzanne shook her head disgustedly. "Well, then, just be an old maid, you foolish girl. You'll be sorry some day, when you're so dry an' shriveled up that no man'll have anything to do with you. As for leavin'—why, this place'll be gone soon, an' then what'll you do? You won't have no husband to take care of you, no babies, no nothin'."

"Gone?" Charity felt a flutter of uneasiness. "What are you talking about?"

Suzanne snickered unpleasantly. "You oughtta wake up and see what's goin' on around you, girl. This village ain't got no more'n a few years left. All the old folks'll soon be dead, and there won't be nobody here to do the work." She folded her arms across her generous bosom. "And when the Shakers' lease on that min'ral spring runs out next year, Will Ayers is gonna take it over and build hisself a hotel. You'll likely find yourself waitin' tables and changin' beds, and then you won't be so blessed uppity to folks who just want to see you happy."

Charity blinked, not believing what she had just heard. Of course, the old people were dying. She didn't like to count the number of funerals she had attended in the last few months. But there would always be Shakers. Wasn't that what Mother Ann had taught? "The hands may drop off, but the body goes on working." They would all go on working, for working was prayer, and prayer was salvation.

This business with the spring, though—that was something else, and worrisome. She'd heard in family meetings that there was some sort of problem with the ownership. It seemed that the spring was only leased, rather than being theirs outright, and that Will Ayers wanted it back. But Elder Aaron had said he thought they could get it straightened out. He hadn't said anything about—

"Where'd you hear this nonsense about a hotel?" she demanded sharply.

"It ain't no nonsense." Suzanne looked wise. "Sandy's been workin' for Will Ayers this last year. He told me all about it. In fact, he says Will is gonna let him run the horse barn at the hotel, when it gets built." She leaned closer, her eyes gleaming wickedly. "Maybe your elders an' trustees are keepin' the news to themselves. Maybe they figger that if the word gets out, all the able-bodied folk'll just up an' leave."

"Nay," Charity said between clenched teeth. "Of course they won't. Nothing is going to happen to Mount Zion."

Suzanne laughed unpleasantly. "Well, don't come cryin' to me when you've got to find someplace to live."

Charity's mother came up just then, and the conversation was over. Rhoda kissed her daughter, got into the buggy, and picked up the reins. Without so much as a good-bye wave, Suzanne climbed in beside her, and they drove off.

Sister Ruth, with whom Charity shared a retiring room, came up at that moment. "Your cousin?" she asked, as Charity watched the buggy pull away, the black horse kicking up puffs of dust in the lane. "She's a pretty girl."

Charity nodded. "When we were little, Suzanne and I played together all the time. Went to school together, too. She seems to be bent on sowing her wild oats, though. And there's nothing anybody can do to stop her." She was about to ask if Ruth had heard anything about Will Ayers taking over the spring and building a hotel, but bit back the words just in time. Suzanne enjoyed making mischief. She'd probably told the tale just to make her cousin feel bad.

"Wild oats?" Something flickered in Ruth's brown eyes, and she said gravely, "Well, sometimes people just have to do that."

"You're right about that, for sure." Charity smiled at Ruth, for whom she had begun to feel a strong affection. When she first came to the village, Charity had lived in the North Family Dwelling, where she shared a retiring room with Sister Nora, who sometimes fell into trances and was visited by heavenly spirits bearing gifts of drawings. It was a little disconcerting to be awakened in the middle of the night when Sister Nora was visited by one of her spirits and began singing in an incomprehensible language, or when she lit the lamp at midnight to work on one of the drawings she'd been given. When Sister Nora had gone home to Mother, Charity had found it easier to sleep.

But after a while, so many in the North Family had died or departed that there were soon not enough left to keep the work, and the members had been reassigned to other families. Now, Charity and Ruth shared a retiring room in the East Family Dwelling. Ruth was a modest young woman, quiet and reserved. And pretty, too, with a slimness of figure and a delicate fragility very different from Charity's own rawboned sturdiness. When she looked at Ruth lying asleep, her hand cupped under her cheek, her golden brown hair spilled loose over the pillow, Charity couldn't help smiling tenderly. She always had the feeling that Ruth ought to be protected. That she should be treated with care, so she wouldn't be bruised.

"I guess I just mostly feel sorry for Suzanne," Charity said with a sigh. "If I could only make her understand how quiet it is here, how peaceful, how *safe*, she might stop trying to get me to move back home."

A wagon filled with people from town drove slowly past them, the passengers staring curiously, just as they had during the funeral service. A little girl waved, but her mother caught her hand and yanked it down, bending over to scold the child. Charity waved back anyway, and the little girl stuck her tongue out and crossed her eyes. Charity was seized with the impulse to do the same, but resisted. She was too old for such silliness. Anyway, the little girl was only doing what she saw the grownup World's People doing: making fun of the Shakers. If only they could understand what a perfect heaven the village was, they'd never make fun. They'd all flock to become Shakers themselves.

"So you're happy here, Charity?" Ruth asked, as they began to walk along the path toward the East Family Dwelling. Among the Shakers, the use of first names was not a sign of disrespect, but a traditional mark of humility. "You've never wanted to . . . well, go away? Someplace where people wouldn't keep telling you what to do?"

"Go away?" The question made her squirm, coming as it did so soon after what Suzanne had said. But she could answer it honestly, for in the two years since she'd signed the Covenant, she had never once thought of leaving.

"Nay, never," she replied fervently. "Where would I go? What would I do?" She looked around at the houses, the dear dwellings and sweet gardens overflowing with flowers and herbs, all surrounded by the green wilderness, like an infant cradled in a mother's loving arms. "I can't imagine living anywhere else but in this blessed place. Can you?"

There was a silence. After a moment, Charity, puzzled and a little unsure, repeated her question. "Can you?"

Ruth shrugged. "My mother brought me here when I was four years old. Don't you think it's only natural to wonder what life is like outside the village?" She put her head on one side. "Of course, you lived in the World until just a few years ago. Maybe you already know all about it."

"Not all about it," Charity said stoutly, "but enough to know that I don't want to know any more. Bad things happen there." She thought of Sandy's hands and her father's brutal thrustings and shivered. There was so much unhappiness in the World, so much unbridled passion and anger and evil—and danger, too. Why would anyone want to live there when they could live in Eden, instead?

"But sometimes bad things happen here," Ruth pointed out in a reasonable tone. "It's not always the paradise people think it is. Look at what happened the other night, for instance. When Sister Hannah's former husband—that Jake Chandler—came to get his son."

"That was terrible," Charity agreed with a shiver, not entirely of fear, for the whole thing had been really very dramatic, and the lingering excitement had kept her awake for half the night. "I felt awfully sorry for Hannah, crying and carrying on the way she did. I'm just glad that Elder Aaron and Brother Alfred were able to handle that ugly man. I don't think they could have managed if Brother Charles hadn't stepped in, though. Charles is strong as an ox. Jake Chandler didn't have a chance."

Charity was so intent on what she was saying that she didn't notice the color that had flooded into Ruth's cheeks at the mention of Charles McBride's name, or hear the little catch in her breath.

"But don't you see, Ruth?" she hurried on. "That bad thing—it came from *outside* the village, not from one of us. Jake Chandler brought it with him. The World is full of that kind of passion. It's like a sickness. It infects everybody."

Ruth was silent for a moment. At last, she said, very quietly, "But does passion always have to be evil? Love is a passion, isn't it? And we're supposed to love, aren't we?"

That stumped Charity. But only for a moment, until she thought of Mother Ann's teachings, and cried, "Aye, but that's different, Ruth. Love is a *pure* passion! We are to manifest it every day, in everything we do. We're to love our neighbors—love our brethren and sisters—exactly as we do ourselves. Love is needful, don't you think?"

Ruth's smile transformed her face. "Yes," she said. "Love is needful." They had almost reached the Sisters' Shop now, and she paused and glanced around. "Oh, look where we are," she said, as if she had just recognized the spot. "I think I'll just go in and finish up the piece on the loom. Thank you for your company, Charity. I'll see you at supper."

"I'd be glad to come in and help," Charity offered. Elder Aaron had given them a free hour to spend privately, and she had intended to go to the herb garden and finish weeding the rows of sage—pleasant, prayerful work. But it would be even more pleasant to work with Ruth.

"Thank you, but I have a bit of a headache. I think I'd rather be by myself." Ruth put her hand on Charity's arm. "I'd like to think about Sister Sally and just be quiet. I'm sure you understand."

Charity pulled in her breath, astonished. She and Ruth had lived together for some six months now, but this was the first time they had ever touched. It was electrifying.

"Of . . . of course I understand," she stammered, feeling herself suffused by a surge of warm, pulsing joy, the kind of great, wild happiness she sometimes felt when she was dancing during Sabbathday worship. "I'll see you at supper, then."

If Charity had lingered for a moment, she might have seen Brother Charles step out from behind the maple tree and go quickly up the side stairs into the Sisters' Shop. But she had already turned and gone on along the path to the herb garden, mystified by the strength of her feeling.

What did it mean, this tingling at Ruth's touch? This joy?

Well, she needn't look far for the answer. It was love, a manifestation of exactly what they'd been talking about! The chaste and needful passion of love. She and Ruth were joined together in the kind of love that Mother Ann described: love that washed through you in a sweet, untainted tide of passion, cleansing every part of you, body and soul, washing you whiter than white, purer than pure. Virginal love.

And suddenly Charity felt such pity for Suzanne and her mother and the staring people in the wagon that the tears started to her eyes. They would never feel this pure, sweet, chaste love that she felt for Ruth, that Ruth felt for her. How could they? They weren't Believers.

Charity was still thinking these ecstatic thoughts when she turned the fence corner in front of the Meeting House and bumped squarely into Brother Joshua, who had charge of the boys who lived in the Children's Dwelling. "Oh!" she exclaimed, righting herself. "Sorry."

"Sister Charity," Brother Joshua said distractedly. He straightened his straw hat and adjusted his steel-rimmed glasses, which had been nearly knocked off in the collision. "Have you seen the little Chandler boy? Seth Chandler? He seems to have . . . wandered off."

"How could he just wander off?" Charity asked, and was immediately sorry for it. Brother Joshua, in his early sixties and a schoolmaster for decades, was conscientious to a fault. Between their schoolwork and their chores, the children were very well supervised. "When did you see him last?"

Sister Pearl, one of the East Family's Negro sisters and an inspired singer and dancer, came up just then. "Somebody lost?" she asked curiously. "Who y'all lookin' for?"

"Little Seth Chandler," Charity told her. "He's wandered off."

"I saw him at the noon meal," Joshua said thinly. "But he didn't appear for afternoon classes, and none of the boys could say where he'd gone. There's been so much commotion, with the funeral and all, and so many of the World's People in and out of the village. I'm afraid—" He broke off.

"Afeerd o' what?" Pearl asked, leaning forward. She was a bulky woman, her white cap sitting crookedly on her wiry gray hair.

"I'm afraid," he said in a lower voice, "that the boy's father may have taken him. I'm on my way to tell Elder Aaron."

"May have taken him?" Charity asked incredulously. "You mean, *kidnapped*? Oh, surely not!"

"It's happened," Sister Pearl said in an ominous tone. "Afore yore time, Charity. The Dyers, Frank an' Mary, lived with us, oh, three, four years. Then Mary Dyer set herse'f on leavin'. Said she was gwine t' take her two boys. O' course, Brother Frank wanted 'em here and the boys theirselves begged to stay, so Elder Aaron told her she had to leave without 'em. But the next week, Mary snuck in here wi' two o' her nachural brothers an' snatched the boys when they was on their way to the field to cut hay. Them men, they had shotguns." She gave her head a grim shake, remembering. "T'rrible. Jes' t'rrible."

"How awful." Charity pulled in her breath. "But let's hope Seth has just run off for the afternoon. Boys do that," she added, remembering her own brothers, who had never been subjected to anything like the discipline the Shaker children received. Seth hadn't been here long—maybe he had just rebelled. "Where have you looked?" she asked Joshua, and then thought about the most obvious. "The spring? Maybe he's gone swimming."

"I shore hope not," Pearl said, blowing out her breath. "That pool is deep. No place for a chile alone."

Brother Joshua's lips thinned. "I doubt he'd do that, Sister Charity. We take the boys in a group sometimes, to bathe. But they're strictly forbidden to go there by themselves. And I know for a fact that Seth can't swim."

"Still, it's worth a look," Charity replied, knowing how sorely she had been tempted on hot, sticky days to jump into that pool. She could imagine that a twelve-year-old boy—even one who couldn't swim—might find it impossible to resist, especially when it was forbidden. Like Adam and the apple. Tell him not to eat it, and he was more likely than not to take a big bite.

"I'll come wit' you," Pearl offered helpfully.

"Thank you," Charity said, and without waiting for Brother Joshua to say yea or nay, she picked up her skirts and began to run as fast as she could in the direction of the mineral spring, Sister Pearl panting along behind her.

Chapter Eight

Fern, Maidenhair. *Adiantum pedatum*. Carminative, refrigerant, expectorant, tonic, sudorific, astringent, pectoral, stomachic. Valuable in cough, asthma, hoarseness, influenza, pleurisy, jaundice, febrile diseases, and erysipelas. A decoction of the plant is cooling and of benefit in coughs resulting from colds, nasal congestion, catarrh, and hoarseness. It can be used freely.

Shaker Medicinal Herbs
Amy Bess Miller

In the Victorian language of flowers, maidenhair fern symbolized discretion.

Flora's Dictionary: The Victorian Language of Herbs and Flowers
Kathleen Gips

Allie Chatham was just closing her office door behind her as we clattered down the steps to the basement, where her office was located. She was about Martha's age, thick-set and cheerful-looking, with graying hair and gold-rimmed bifocals. She wore a white blouse and a loose denim jumper and carried a leather portfolio under her arm. She grinned when she saw us.

"Well, by damn, it's Martha," she said in a husky smoker's voice. "I was wondering whether you'd gotten lost on the way here. Or maybe stopped at the spring for a swim."

Martha gave her a warm hug. "We've been making the tour. You know—Rachel, Jane, and Sharon. When we got to Sharon, she told us you wanted us to drop in. But of course, we were already headed this way." She put her hand on my arm. "This is my friend China Bayles. China, this is Allie. She and I used to swim in the mineral spring when we were girls." She giggled. "We've even been known to go skinny dipping when nobody was around to peek at us. Imagine that."

"Weren't we a pair?" Allie looked down at her swollen ankles. "Nobody would bother peeking these days," she said ruefully, "in bathing suits or in the skinny. You're still trim, Martha, but I'm just a stout old granny."

"We are a pair of tough, well-seasoned old broads," Martha corrected her with a grin. To me, she added, "Don't let Allie fool you, China. She's no granny. She's the one who makes sure that there's always enough money in the bank to pay the bills."

"Sometimes a challenge," Allie conceded.

"So," Martha said, "what does one tough, well-seasoned old broad have to say to another, Allie? What was it you wanted to tell me?"

Allie gave me a quizzical glance.

"It's fine," Martha said quickly. "I've been talking to China about—well, about pretty much everything. She's a lawyer," she added in a meaningful tone. "And a friend. I've known her mother for years."

"I see." Allie narrowed her eyes at me. "Well, I sure as hell hope you're a lawyer who can be trusted. I've met a few of the other kind. Sons of bitches'll steal your damn shirt while they're admiring your shoes."

I laughed. I liked this lady already. "I've run into some of those myself."

"China can be trusted," Martha said firmly. "If she gives us any trouble, I'll take it up with her mother." She shook her head reprovingly. "You know, your mouth is as foul as ever, Allie. You'll never change."

"You better damn well hope not. I call 'em the way I see 'em." Allie linked her arm in Martha's. "Hey," she said confidentially, "I'm on my way to my cottage. Come with me. You can join me for a drink and we can have us a cozy little sit-down talk. It's been too long. Anyway, I don't want to talk here."

"Cottage?" Martha asked in surprise, as the two of them went up the stairs ahead of me. "You're staying here in the village?"

"Yup. After I divorced Pete, I sold the house and bought a condo, so I wouldn't have as much yard to deal with. But the damn builder can't get his act together, and the new place won't be ready until September. Rachel offered to let me spend the summer, rent-free, in one of the cottages. Not exactly five stars, more like maybe one and a half. But what the hell, the price is right."

Martha pushed the door open. "Rachel? Free rent? I thought she didn't like you all that much."

"She doesn't, not since I did that audit and she had to change her spending habits." Allie chuckled. "I told her she couldn't use the foundation's bank account as if it were her own personal mad money fund."

"You told her that," Martha said disbelievingly, "and she still offered you the cottage?"

"Maybe she felt sorry for me." She drew her friend closer. "So tell me, Martha. What's new in your life? Met any interesting men lately?"

Martha hooted. "Don't I wish!" Then she grinned. "Maybe I don't."

THE cottages were fifty yards beyond the conference center, tucked into the side of the hill above the mineral spring. The spring itself spilled out of a towering limestone cliff some thirty feet above the water, cascading in a frothy waterfall into a rocky pool—Zion's Pool—about the size of a tennis court. The water was turquoise, shading off to green at one end, and the pool was overhung with trees and surrounded by ferns.

"I bring people here on our herb walk, to look at ferns," Martha told me as we stood on the ledge above the spring. "Most of them don't know that ferns were used medicinally for centuries, and that the Shakers gathered, dried, and sold them."

"Ferns for medicine?" Allie asked skeptically. "You're kidding."

"No, I'm not," Martha replied. "Both male fern and polypody fern were used for the same purpose as wormwood, to expel intestinal worms. Maidenhair fern—there's some right over there—was used to treat lung ailments, coughs, and the like. And because maidenhair was diuretic, it was used in cases of kidney stones and bladder infections. It was quite a popular remedy." Martha looked around, her voice softening. "No matter how often I come here, I'm always impressed by how beautiful this place is."

"The pool looks deep," I said.

"At that end, it is," Martha replied, pointing to the left. "The bottom shelves off fast, down to some thirty feet. There have been several drownings here over the years." She hesitated. "Remember Brother Joshua? The Shaker ghost I told you about? People say that he comes here to the mineral spring, with his lantern, looking for that lost child."

"I've seen him," Allie said, unexpectedly. "Twice, since I've been here." She looked at me. "Don't laugh, China. The Shakers were very big on spirits. Saw 'em all the time, particularly during their worship services, when they were dancing and twirling and shaking off their sins. The sight of a spirit was supposed to be a gift from heaven." She grinned mischievously. "So if I can see Brother Joshua, maybe I'm not as sinful as I think I am."

"What did he look like?" I asked half skeptically.

"Oh, the usual. Fella with a lantern and a Shaker hat."

Martha was frowning. "What happened to the safety rope across the pool?"

"It disappeared a couple of days ago," Allie said. "The pool isn't in use this season, so I guess somebody figured the rope wasn't necessary."

I stood, listening. "It's so quiet," I marveled. I could hear the water splashing. Somewhere nearby a thrush sang.

Allie made a face. "Won't be quiet for long, if Rachel gets her way. Construction is supposed to start in a month or so. This time next year, there'll be a fancy spa building here, glass and concrete, like the conference center. It'll completely enclose the spring." She gave Martha a meaningful glance. "You can forget about those ferns."

"But the board hasn't voted on the project yet," Martha objected.

"Rachel intends to see that it does. She also intends that the vote goes her way." Allie lifted her chin. "But it ain't over 'til the fat lady sings. Come on, guys. I'm ready for a drink."

We followed Allie around the pool, over a narrow wooden footbridge, and up a steep, rocky slope. Near the top of the hill stood a small frame cabin, painted green, one of a trio of cabins built close together. The cabin on the left was overgrown with vines and was obviously not in use. The cabin on the right looked like it was in the process of being demolished. One side was smashed, the roof had caved in, and ugly tire tracks scythed through the brush and trees, as if heavy equipment had been at work.

"They're tearing down the cabins already?" Martha asked in surprise.

Allie lifted a flowerpot on the small porch, took out a key, and unlocked the door. "That's no tear-down. That's the cabin the truck plowed into. Huge crash. Sounded like all hell was breaking loose."

Martha gasped, her eyes wide. "You were actually here when it happened? You heard it?"

"You bet your twinkies I was here." Allie dropped her leather portfolio onto the coffee table. "It was the middle of the night, wasn't it? I was tucked into my little beddie-bye, right there in the bedroom." She pointed.

"That was close," Martha said in a half whisper. The two cabins weren't more than twenty feet apart, and it was the side nearest Allie's cabin that had been wrecked.

"Damn right it was close. Wouldn't have taken much for that truck to swerve and come straight through my wall." With a gravelly laugh, Allie added, "I figured maybe it was Pete. He wasn't too happy about the divorce. He's always been a hothead, and age hasn't improved his temper." She turned down her mouth. "Could be he got soused and thought he'd teach me a lesson. He used to be a heavy-equipment operator, you know."

I frowned. "Did they ever find out how the driver lost control?"

Allie laughed grittily. "Hell, they never even found the driver. Seriously, they never figured out who took the truck from the equipment shed or why he was driving it on the road at the top of the hill. Nobody ever goes up there."

"Brother Joshua, maybe?" Martha hazarded, with a lopsided smile.

"Yeah, sure." Allie went across the room and opened a cupboard. "And since our good brother doesn't know how to drive, it's no wonder he crashed. Martha, I laid in a supply of that red wine you like so much. I'm having Scotch. China, what'll it be for you? Wine? Something harder?"

"Martha's red is fine with me," I said. I stepped to the window. We were some fifty feet above the spring. The pool looked like a huge turquoise set in a filigree of rocks and ferns. It seemed a shame to spoil the natural beauty with something man-made and artificial.

Allie poured wine into two plastic glasses. "Sorry, no fancy stemware," she said, and handed us our glasses. "We're roughing it."

"Not a problem," I said, looking around. The cottage was small and dark and smelled of tobacco smoke. It was furnished like any other vacation cottage, with a sofa slipcovered in frayed pink and red chintz and a pair of dark green overstuffed chairs. A wooden coffee table held a stack of old magazines and a beanbag ashtray overflowing with cigarette butts—Allie's, I presumed, unless she kept company with somebody who smoked. A cheap wooden dining table and chair—not Shaker—stood under the chintz-draped window. Through one open door, I could see a small kitchen, through another, on the side nearest the wrecked cottage, a tiny bedroom. A narrow bed covered with a white chenille bedspread was pushed against the wall.

"Spartan," Martha observed. "Couldn't Rachel have found a television set for you?"

"She didn't offer," Allie said. "She hasn't hooked up the phone yet, either, although I've been asking. At first I was teed off about it, but now I kinda like it. I can use the phone at work all I want. If I don't have one here, Pete can't call and threaten me."

"Is he in the habit of doing that?" Martha asked uneasily.

"He calls at work sometimes, just to harass me. And when I was still in the house, he'd show up—drunk—in the evenings. But it's no big deal. I can handle Pete." Supplied with a hefty slug of Scotch, neat, Allie dropped into one of the overstuffed chairs, kicked off her shoes, and propped her feet up on the coffee table. "Have a seat," she invited, and lit a cigarette, inhaling, as we sat down.

"You're still smoking," Martha said disapprovingly.

"Don't you start, Martha, old girl. You know I'll never quit." Allie sucked in and breathed out an appreciative breath. "There. That's better. Rachel won't let me smoke at work or around the village. Might destroy the image of saintly Shaker perfection." She ran her fingers through her hair, loosening it. "Such a crock. The Shakers weren't any different from the rest of us sinners."

I grinned, suspecting that she was right.

Martha took a sip of her wine and put her glass down. "Now," she said, being serious, "tell us what all this is about, Allie."

"What? The business with Pete? We're finished. Kaput. History. Nothing much else to tell."

Martha shook her head, frowning. "No, what you mentioned to me on the phone. What you wanted to talk to me about when I got here."

"Oh, that." Allie gave her a wicked grin. "Is that what this is all about?"

"Partly." Martha paused, pursing her lips. "Well? Is it money?"

Allie pulled on her cigarette. "Of course it's money. What the hell else?"

"I thought it might be," Martha said, "so I went over the operating expense report that was included with the agenda for the trustees' meeting. The bottom line isn't all that healthy, but it seems okay. More or less what I expected, anyway."

"The problem isn't in the operating report," Allie replied. "It's in the endowment funds report. Actually, it's not *in* the report—not yet. It's still in my working papers." She nodded to the portfolio on the coffee table. "I thought I ought to give you a heads-up, Martha."

"A heads-up? About what?"

"There are assets missing from the endowment."

Uh-oh, I thought.

Martha sucked in her breath. "That sounds bad."

"You bet," Allie replied succinctly. "If what I'm thinking is right, it is very bad. Very, very bad. The trustees are not going to like what they hear."

Martha sighed and sat back in her chair. "Okay, Allie. So tell."

Allie tapped her cigarette into the ashtray. "As you probably remember, Ernest's will set up an endowment fund for the Mount Zion Foundation. When Lottie died, she left a substantial amount of additional assets to be added to the endowment. So it now consists of a portfolio of blue chip stocks."

"When was it last inventoried?" I asked. "Officially, that is."

Allie gave me an appraising look. "Good question. At the time of Lottie's death, four years ago."

"How much was it worth then?" I asked.

Allie blew out smoke. "Some three million dollars.

"The dividends are paid into the endowment fund at the bank, and the monthly statements come to me. The quarterly dividend reports go to Rachel—I don't normally see them. The totals vary, of course, with the performance of the market. Sometimes the stocks do well, sometimes they don't. Generally, though, they do."

"And who is your portfolio manager?" I asked.

Martha leaned forward. "Portfolio manager? I don't think—"

"The board doesn't have a portfolio manager," Allie said, drawing on her cigarette. "I know, I know, damn it. A fund that size, somebody ought to be keeping an eye on it. But Ernest Ayers made all the family's financial decisions. Lottie didn't have much of a head for money management."

"That's putting it mildly," Martha said wryly. "That's why we have a conference center that doesn't pay its way."

"Yeah, right," Allie said. "Anyway, Lottie thought that Ernest's stock choices were just fine, and that there was no point in hiring an expensive funds manager who might end up costing the foundation more money than he brought in. And as I said, the stocks are all blue chips or what were blue chips at the time—IBM, Exxon, American Express, Microsoft. So the certificates went into a safe deposit box in the bank in Lexington and that's where they've stayed. Mount Zion operates out of the dividends, plus the program income."

"We haven't touched the principal," Martha put in.

"The board hasn't," Allie said in a cautionary tone. "Yet." She gave me a level look. "So the bottom line is that we don't have a portfolio manager, China. Or, to put it a different way, the trustees manage the portfolio very conservatively—by leaving it strictly alone."

I sat back. Some nonprofit boards operate this way, reasoning that whatever extra yield a portfolio manager might be able to get would be offset by the management fees. But times change, companies change, and once a blue chip isn't always a blue chip. In my opinion, it would be a good idea for the trustees of Mount Zion to hire a financial manager. But I only said, "Sorry for the interruption. Please go on."

"There's not much more to tell," Allie said with a little shrug. "For a number of months, as the dividend reports have come in, I've had the feeling that something isn't right. The totals are lower than they ought to be. So one night last week, I let myself into Rachel's office and—"

"If you got caught, she'd fire you for that, Allie," Martha put in.

"You're damn right," Allie growled, "*if* I got caught. But I didn't get caught, did I? I was very discreet."

"And what did you find?" I asked.

"The latest dividend reports. I made copies and double-checked the numbers against the stock inventory—the one that was made when Lottie died. It's tough to tell without a detailed audit, but it looks to me like some of the stocks are missing."

"Missing?" Martha asked, frowning.

"As in stolen, old dear," Allie said. "We was robbed." She stubbed out her cigarette.

Martha gulped. "Oh, heavens," she said helplessly. "Oh, my stars!"

"You said that the stock certificates are kept in a bank safe deposit box," I said. "Who has the *official* copy of the certificate inventory? The one that was made when Mrs. Ayers' will was probated."

"It's in the safe deposit box with the certificates." She paused and added in a meaningful tone, "Or at least that's where it *was*."

I understood. If somebody had taken the stock certificates, they'd likely have taken the inventory as well, so a comparison couldn't be easily made.

"But as I said," she went on, "I have my own inventory. I made it when I drew up the list of stocks for probate. Nobody knows I have it."

What she had might be proof of embezzlement. "Who has access to the safe deposit box?"

Allie gave me a long, hard look. "Rachel Hart. She has both keys."

"How about the foundation's financial officer?" I asked, surprised. "Doesn't he—or she—have a key?"

"You mean, the treasurer?" Martha asked uncertainly. "That would be Laurie Perkins. Since the beginning of the year."

Allie rolled her eyes.

"Inexperienced?" I hazarded.

"Inexperienced, inattentive, and Rachel Hart's bosom buddy," Allie replied in an acid tone. "Laurie can't even read a balance sheet. But I'm sure that her name is on the signature card at the bank, if that's what you're asking."

"Allie is right," Martha said. "If there's a problem with the endowment fund, Laurie won't have a clue. She wouldn't even know where to look for a clue—unless Rachel tells her, that is."

"Who was the financial officer before Laurie Perkins got the nod?" I asked.

"Karen Sanders." Allie snorted. "Another of Rachel's dearest friends."

This was going from bad to worse. It was obvious that the Mount Zion Foundation was either the victim of criminally negligent management, or criminal mismanagement, or maybe both. "If you don't mind my saying so," I said quietly, "it looks like your board has a problem. A serious problem."

"You bet," Allie said.

"I told you there was trouble," Martha said. "Of course, I only knew about the other problems. Not about this one." To Allie, she added, "The barn, I mean. And the greenhouse, and the truck that demolished the cottage—although I didn't know the cottage was right next door to the one you're staying in." She paused. "Oh, and Sharon just told us that somebody broke into the Brothers' Shop and vandalized Larry Foley's art supplies and paintings."

"Yeah," Allie replied. "Larry was royally pissed off. Can't say I blame him for feeling that way—although he does bring these things on himself. Still, there's far too much bad stuff going on around here. If you ask me, we're way past coincidence or poltergeists or even Brother Joshua. Somebody has it in for Mount Zion. Somebody wants the village to go under. Or go belly-up, depending on how you look at it."

"Do you have any idea who?" I asked.

She regarded me thoughtfully. "Yeah, I might. But I need to stew about it for a while."

Don't stew about it for too long, I wanted to say, but Martha beat me to it. "Why don't you stew about it until dinnertime, and then join us at the restaurant?" She put down her glass and stood up.

Allie brightened. "Best idea I've heard all day." She tossed back the rest of her Scotch and got up to pour herself another. "What time?"

Martha glanced at the clock on the shelf. It was nearly six. "Seven thirty?"

"That'll work," Allie said, "although I might be a little late. I need to crunch some more numbers." She gave Martha a straight look. "I'm going on the record with this at the trustees' meeting, Martha. I'm recommending a formal audit by an outside accounting firm. And I'm not saying a word to Rachel about it beforehand."

Martha pressed her lips together. "This will not be fun."

"Tell me about it. Rachel will probably direct the trustees to fire me—but if that's what happens, that's okay." She gave me a crooked grin. "Hell's bells. At least I know a good lawyer."

"I won't let the trustees fire you," Martha said stoutly.

Allie made a sharp noise. "Don't know how the hell you could stop them, Martha, if that's what Rachel wants 'em to do."

Martha looked at her anxiously. "There's no way to get around this? You couldn't speak to Rachel ahead of time? Alert her to what you're planning?"

"I don't think that's a good idea," I said quietly.

"Not a good idea at all," Allie agreed. "Rachel hates it when somebody throws a monkey wrench into her works. If she knew what I had up my sleeve, she'd make damn sure I didn't attend that board meeting." With a cheerful grin, she added, "Remember what Lottie always said, Martha? 'A girl's gotta do what a girl's gotta do.' And I gotta do this."

"I suppose," Martha replied reluctantly. "We'll see you at dinner, then."

"Yeah. See you at dinner. If you get there first, order me a salad and today's soup."

As we left, it occurred to me that if I were Allie and knew that somebody was stealing from the foundation's endowment fund, I might want to be a little careful. The thief wouldn't be too happy to learn that somebody was on to him—or her.

Later, I was going to wish I'd said something about it. But by that time, it was too late.

Chapter Nine

Sister Charity Edmond

The intensely bitter, tonic and stimulant qualities have caused Wormwood not only to be an ingredient in medicinal preparations, but also to be used in various liqueurs, of which absinthe is the chief, the basis of absinthe being absinthol, extracted from Wormwood. Wormwood, as employed in making this liqueur, bears also the name "Wermuth"—preserver of the mind—from its medicinal virtues as a nervine and mental restorative. If not taken habitually, it soothes spinal irritability and gives tone to persons of a highly nervous temperament.

A Modern Herbal
Mrs. M. Grieve

By the time she reached the spring, Charity was hot and sweaty, her cap was hanging by its strings, and her hair had come unpinned. Sister Pearl, who was unexpectedly fleet-footed for her bulk, had caught up with her, and the two of them arrived at the same moment on the rocky ledge above the spring. Zion's Pool was occupied by several Recuperants. Three women were paddling lazily in the shallow end, their hair done up in white turbans, their voluminous blue bathing costumes ballooning up around them. Two men in swimming trunks, both pale and ill-looking, sat in the shade in wooden deck chairs. One was reading; one was lying back with his eyes closed.

"Don't look to me like the child's here," Pearl said, gazing down at the blue-green pool, its surface ruffled by a cooling breeze and the motion of the women. She raised her voice. "Any you folks seen a little boy 'round here?"

The man looked up from his book, frowned, and shook his head.

Pearl threw back her head, laughed, and clapped her hands. "That's purely a relief. Lord sakes, I would'a hated to see that little boy afloatin' facedown in that beautiful water."

"Oh, aye," Charity said with a shudder. She wiped her forehead with her sleeve, realizing just how anxious and afraid she had been. "The brethren will be mounting a search party. We need to let them know that they don't have to look here."

They could go more slowly now, on the way back—in fact, Charity had to. She had a stitch in her side that forced her to slow down and breathe deeply. Sister Pearl, however, was unfazed by her exertion.

"You young folks." She chuckled. "Y'all need a little strengthenin'. You oughtta eat more, girl. Get a little more fat on you."

Sister Pearl was almost a legend in the East Family. She had sought refuge at Mount Zion as a little girl at the end of the War, as had other freed slaves. They needed a place to call home, and the Shakers had need of their willing labor, so for some at least, it was a good match. Pearl's gift, it had turned out, was for cookery, and she'd had full charge of the East Family's meals for the last fifteen years. Charity mostly worked in the herb garden and the herb shop, but when her rotation took her to the kitchen, she went with a willing enthusiasm. She especially admired Pearl's almost magical touch with desserts and pies, her endless patience, and her energetic, enthusiastic cheeriness.

Now Charity was grateful for this interlude. There weren't many in the family she could talk to about what Suzanne had said, but Pearl was one of them. "Sister Pearl," she said carefully, "I wonder if you know anything about Will Ayers and the mineral spring."

Pearl's leathery forehead creased. "Why you askin'?" she said darkly.

"My cousin told me that Mr. Ayers says it's his, and he's taking it back. He's going to build a hotel."

Pearl rounded on her, eyes slitted. "Yore cousin! You talkin' Suzanne? How'd that lit'l twit of a girl come to know 'bout this?"

"A friend of her brother's works for Will Ayers. He says Mr. Ayers promised him he could run the horse barn at the hotel, when it's built." Charity frowned. "You're saying that it's true?"

"True 'nuff," Pearl said heavily. "An' I am sad to hear that some in the World know 'bout it."

"But I thought the spring was ours!" Charity exclaimed. "How can Mr. Ayers just take it?"

Pearl's laugh was sour. "Us'ns thought it was our'n, too. Turns out that the brother who donated it to the Society—Ezekiel Ballard—didn't have no true title. His daddy had the spring on a fifty-year lease, from Will Ayers' daddy. Will Ayers' daddy's dead this past six months, and now Will Ayers says he owns the lease."

"A fifty-year lease! I never heard of such a thing."

"Well, you has now. All paid for in advance, it was, right an' proper, and nobody never knew a thing about it. But then Will Ayers found out, an' he wants it back, the spring an' the cabins, all of it."

"Can he get it?" Charity asked, bewildered. "Can he take it away from us?"

"Cain't see how us'ns can stop him," Pearl said softly. "If 'twas somebody other'n Will Ayers, Elder Aaron might could get another lease. But not Will Ayers. He's a mean man, a real mean man." She shot a narrow-eyed warning look at Charity. "You keep away from him, you hear, Sister?

He's right bad wit' the girls. He been told not to come 'round the village no more."

Bad with the girls. Charity shuddered. She didn't have to ask what Pearl meant. The words brought back the vivid image of her father in his flour-sack nightshirt beside her bed and the rasp of his eager panting. "But Mr. Ayers wouldn't bother a Shaker sister, surely. He knows we don't . . . that we abstain. That we're celibate."

"Sure he knows. But some men, they takes that as a challenge." Pearl faced her squarely, her dusky face serious, her large dark eyes intent. "'Fore you came, Charity, that man Will Ayers was the cause o' Sister Anna White leavin' the Society. She was havin' his baby, and him a married man with his own babes at home."

Charity cringed. "What . . . What became of her?"

"We never heard. Guess she was jes' too sad an' shamed to write an' tell us where she was. But I'll tell you what became o' him. His wife up an' left him an' took his babes, that's what happened. An' just last week, I saw him hangin' 'round the Sisters' Shop—'spite o' being told to stay away." She wagged her finger in Charity's face. "So you take care, y'hear? You stay out of his way."

"Thank you," Charity said. "I will certainly take care. And I'll mention it to Ruth. She works in the Sisters' Shop most of the time." She swallowed. "You say we can't stop him from taking back the spring. Does that mean we'll lose that income?"

The five Recuperants who were at the pool just now—she knew that each of them was paying nearly two dollars a day for the privilege of sleeping in a nearby cottage, bathing in the pool, and taking their meals in a separate dining room in the East Family Dwelling. Ten dollars! And on weekends, there were even more people. If the Shakers lost that money— Charity shuddered.

"That's what that means," Pearl said ominously. "If I warn't such a good Shaker an' a Christian, I'd say somebody oughtta smack that buzzard upside the head. Might jes' do it myself, if'n I catch him in our lane some real dark night."

Charity couldn't help laughing, although of course she knew that Pearl would never do such a thing.

By the time Charity and Sister Pearl got back, Elder Aaron had organized all the brethren to look for the missing boy. They were out for the rest of the afternoon and evening, coming in to eat their suppers but going right back out to search until it was too dark to see. Most came home to sleep, although the next morning it was said that Brother Joshua, sick with guilt for losing a child who was in his charge, had stayed out the whole night with his lantern, looking and calling. When he returned for a bite of breakfast, he had a ghastly, haunted look. By that time, most of the Shakers assumed that Jake Chandler had stolen his son away.

Meanwhile, Hannah, the boy's mother, was taking it very hard. She had become hysterical, crying, screaming, fainting. At last, Eldress Olive administered a restorative, a glass of herbal liqueur from the stock she had brought from Mount Lebanon, which distilled many such products. The eldress sat with Hannah all night, in case she wakened and needed anything. The next morning, she appeared at breakfast haggard, hollow-eyed, wretched, unable to eat. Charity felt an immediate pity for her. Seth was her only son, a strong, beautiful boy that any mother would be proud of. The idea that the child's father would actually steal him made Charity feel sick.

But there was nothing she could do to ease Hannah's pain, and her own anxieties were always comforted by work. So she went out to the sunshiny garden, picked up a hoe, and attacked the weeds that had dared to invade the orderly green rows of wormwood and sage. She assailed them as savagely as if they had been the wicked Jake Chandler himself, trying to work away the feeling of impending doom that seemed to hang over her like a dark cloud.

Was it true what Suzanne had said, that the village had only a few more years of life left? Charity had to admit that things were difficult. It was undeniably true that the older Shakers were dying, and that it was almost impossible to find enough people to do the work. If Will Ayers was successful in taking the spring away from them—

Charity shuddered, feeling chilly and gloomy in spite of the cheerful warmth of the sun on her shoulders. The gloom stayed with her for the rest of the day, until black clouds gathered in the afternoon and a fierce storm, with hard winds, cold rain, and thunder, forced her to retreat to the Drying Shed. Since Brother Joseph had been killed by a lightning bolt in the herb garden three years before, everyone was careful to seek shelter during a storm. She always loved the Drying Shed anyway, for it was filled with wonderful herbs—lavender for headaches and easy sleep, peppermint to flavor medicines, Johnswort for urinary afflictions and wounds, dock for purifying the blood. The sisters and some of the young girls had been wild-gathering in the woods and fields, and the bundles of elder flowers and life everlasting they had gathered were hung on the walls, while goldenseal roots were laid out in trays to dry.

Charity joined the two sisters working there, taking down the boneset that had been hanging from pegs high on the wall and settling herself to the satisfying business of pounding the dried leaves into powder. Normally, the sisters used a large crushing mill to grind dried herbs, but the gear was broken, and Brother Charles, who had charge of the Herb Department, had not yet gotten around to fixing it. Today, Charity was glad the mill was broken. She pounded the dried leaves so hard that her shoulders ached, while the storm growled and snapped and rattled the windows like a savage animal wanting to get in. But the work eased her spirit, and when she went to supper, she was almost cheerful.

The brothers and sisters often returned to work for an hour or two after supper, before prayers and bedtime. But tonight was the weekly Union meeting, which brought the East Family together for an hour of social exchange. Union meetings were meant to satisfy any need people might feel for conversation between the sexes, supervised, of course, by Elder Aaron and Eldress Olive, who made sure that the exchanges were all appropriate. The meeting was held in the family's upstairs Meeting Room, the women and men seating themselves in two long, facing rows of ladder-back chairs, arranged on either side of a woven mat laid down the middle of the room. The mat was wide enough so that there was no danger that a brother's knee might inadvertently brush against a sister's, although so many of the brothers were elderly that it hardly seemed to be a necessary precaution. Elderly and few, for the sisters now outnumbered the brothers two to one. The brothers' chairs were spaced so that their row didn't look so short.

When she entered the lamplit room, Charity saw an empty chair between Ruth and Sister Pearl and immediately made for it, glad for any opportunity to talk to Ruth. They slept in the same room, yes, but Ruth preferred to write in her journal before they went to bed, so their conversation was more limited than Charity would have liked. Lately, they had not talked at all, for Ruth, always quiet and thoughtful, seemed to want to be left alone. And tonight, Charity wanted the comfort of a real conversation, something that could take her mind off her anxious thoughts about the future welfare of the Society.

But just as she sat down and turned to say hello, Charles McBride slipped into the seat directly opposite Ruth, putting both hands on his knees and fixing his gaze on her face. Ruth herself did not so much as glance at Charity, who felt as if she had suddenly become invisible.

"Good evening, Sister Ruth," Charles said, his voice low and deep. His eyes were on Ruth, hungrily, as if he were feasting on her.

"Good evening, Brother Charles," Ruth replied primly, and Charity thought that she lingered over the name.

From then on, the two spoke very little to each other, but neither did they speak to anyone else. Indeed, looking at their faces, it seemed to Charity that, as far as Ruth and Charles were concerned, all the rest of the brethren and sisters had completely vanished, and they were completely alone in the room. There was no pretense, no effort at concealment, nor could there be because what they felt was impossible to conceal. Their bodies strained toward each other as if Charles were a compelling magnet and Ruth a willing piece of iron, separated by some force that neither could or wanted to break, and their undisguised desire was a kind of nakedness. They said little to each other because there was nothing they could say that would not set the room on fire, or bring down the walls and the ceiling and the wrath of Mother Ann and the angels upon all their heads.

Charity felt as if she had taken a savage blow to the stomach. She knew beyond the shadow of a doubt that Ruth and Charles had entered into a forbidden carnal relationship, and the knowledge brought back the shuddering memory of her father's grunts and of Sandy's grasping hands. She closed her eyes against hot tears. She could still vividly recall Ruth's hand on her arm the day before, and the electrical jolt that had run through her body at the touch. She had thought that she and Ruth had a special relationship, that they were somehow joined in the purest, the most chaste love. But now, cleaved nearly in half by a pain as sharp

110

as one of the knives in Sister Pearl's kitchen, Charity knew that Ruth had already given herself to Charles, whether in the flesh or only in the imaginings of her heart. She felt betrayed, as if she were Ruth's rejected lover, thrown over for someone stronger, more attractive, more desirable. The pain rose to her throat, tightening like a noose so that she could scarcely breathe.

Charity fished in her pocket for her handkerchief, and with a show of blowing her nose, managed to surreptitiously wipe her eyes. She glanced around to see if anyone else had noticed her distress, but the others were intent on their own quiet conversations. Shakers were used to keeping their voices down, except in worship, when they could sing to the skies, to the angels, to Mother Ann, sing and shout and stamp and shake, shake off their sins and sinful desires.

But tonight, they were more subdued than usual. The evening storm had rumbled off into the distance, but everyone seemed to feel its effects, and the conversations lacked the energetic spiritual uplifting and enfolding they all craved. Little Seth Chandler had not been found, and Eldress Olive had excused Hannah, who had missed both dinner and supper, from the meeting. Brother Joshua was absent also, for he had gone out once again on his search.

As the end of the hour neared, Elder Aaron stood to make a few announcements. He said nothing about the mineral spring or Will Ayers. When he concluded, Sister Pearl was given the gift of a new song, mournful and slow and in an oddly pitched key, in a tongue that none of them understood. Usually, Charity loved to listen to Pearl's gift songs, but she was glad when this one was finished, for it made her shiver. Elder Aaron said a prayer, asking Mother to watch over the lost child. Eldress Olive gave them a blessing, and they all picked up their chairs and hung them on the wall pegs, so that the room could be easily swept clean.

111

As if all she had seen and felt were not yet hurtful enough, Charity was witness to one more painful thing. As Charles hung up his chair and turned, his hand brushed Ruth's and he passed her a note. And then they filed out, the brethren through one door, the sisters through the other. They reached their retiring rooms just as another storm descended on them with a frightening vengeance, as if the hosts of heaven were pouring out a furious anger upon the earth.

In the room she shared with Ruth, Charity undressed behind her curtain, then pulled it back to see Ruth sitting beside the lamp, writing in her journal. She still wore the day's blue work dress, but she had taken off her cap, and her loose golden brown hair, the color of light molasses, rippled down her back. Charles' note lay unfolded on the table beside her.

There was nothing to be said, Charity knew, nothing that *could* be said without forever breaking whatever fragile bond connected them. So she lay down on her bed, pulling the sheet to her chin, lying very still and staring at the ceiling. After a time, Ruth blew out the lamp and lay down on her bed. But when the clock struck midnight, Charity heard the hallway door open. Ruth crept out and did not come back until after three.

Brother Joshua found Seth Chandler the next morning. The boy had fallen from a rock cliff along the stream some hundred yards below the mineral spring. He had been dead for several days.

His mother was inconsolable.

Chapter Ten

Mugwort (*Artemisia vulgaris*). In folklore it is said this herb causes the dreamer to remember his or her dreams. It does seem to increase clarity, while also encouraging relaxation.

Mugwort is the only artemisia that I know to be useful in dream blends. It has been claimed for centuries to help people remember their dreams but other artemisias can cause nightmares and headaches. Mugwort is a strong growing perennial and you can grow it easily in your garden, although it may become invasive. Place it at the back of a perennial border where its frilly, gray-green leaves and height will serve as a beautiful backdrop to colorful blooming plants.

Making Herbal Dream Pillows
Jim Long

Our rooms in the East Family Dwelling were on the third floor, on the side of the building where the Shaker sisters had lived. We reached them by the pair of double staircases—one for brothers, the other for sisters—that ascended through the whole house, from the first floor to the attic. The oak stair treads were polished by many feet, the newel posts were carved with a stunning simplicity, and the oak banisters swept upward, starkly beautiful. If I had been a Shaker, I might have imagined this as the stairway to heaven.

My room—Sister Hannah Chandler's Retiring Room, according to the nameplate on the door—was furnished with a Shaker ladder-back rocking chair, a tall cupboard, a bed table, and bed, all reproductions, I was sure, but lovely. The faint scent of lavender sweetened the air, and the white plaster walls, white linen-weave drapes at the window, white chenille bedspread, and pale blue-and-gray braided rug on the plank floor gave the room a fresh but traditional Shaker look.

It wasn't all vintage Shaker, though. An adjacent private bathroom gleamed with contemporary plumbing and plush white towels. A cupboard concealed a television set. An electric coffeemaker and tea service waited on a shelf, and there was a fan in the ceiling and a phone beside the bed. I looked for a high-speed Internet connection but didn't see one, which was just as well, because I deliberately hadn't brought my laptop. If Ruby needed me, she'd leave a message on my cell phone, and I'd be talking to McQuaid at least once a day. I wouldn't be gone all that long—I could live without email.

I washed my face, combed my hair, and put away the few things I had brought with me—a denim skirt for dress-up (denim is about as dressed up as I get), jeans and shirts, two pairs of khaki shorts. Then I lay down on the bed, thinking about the woman who had once lived in this room. Who was she? How long had she lived here? What would she have made of the telephone on the table, of the electric fan, the electric light? Would the television set have seemed an invention of the devil?

I closed my eyes and tried to conjure an image of Sister Hannah in her plain blue Shaker dress and white apron and kerchief, her simple black shoes, her hair tucked up under her white cotton cap. Was she tall and thin or short and dumpy? Plain or pretty? Why had she come to the village? Was she happy in her chosen Shaker life?

Ruby would probably have been pretty good at this conjuring business, but I wasn't getting anywhere. I'm too left-brained for this kind of thing, she always says. I need to do more work on my intuition. In fact, the bed was deliciously comfortable (this was no Shaker husk pallet) and I was mostly getting drowsy—it had already been a long day. For a few moments I fought to stay awake, but the room was warm, the lavender was comforting, and I found myself drifting into an uneasy sleep, and into a dream.

In my dream, I had slept through the night and it was now early morning, so early that the sun was not yet up. Somewhere, a bell was ringing, and I knew—the way you know things in dreams that you've never known in waking life—that this was the Rising Bell, and that it was time to be about the day's work. I got out of bed, splashed water from a white earthenware pitcher into an enamel basin, washed my face, and combed my hair. There was an ankle-length blue cotton dress hanging in the tall cupboard by the window. I pulled it over my head and tied on a fresh white kerchief, crossing the ends over the front of my dress and pinning them, a little surprised at my own expertness. I added a white apron and a cap and pulled on a pair of sturdy black leather shoes that felt like old friends. Then I opened the door and stepped out.

And then there was one of those odd discontinuities that come in dreams, for I didn't step into the hallway in the East Family Dwelling, but onto the path to the mineral spring. The hem of my dress was already wet with dew, and the early-morning chill in the air made me shiver. I passed the Shaker graveyard, passed the site of the modern conference center, all glass and angular concrete. But if it was there, I couldn't see it, for a gauzy mist veiled the landscape around me, thinning and thickening and twisting through the green trees like a troubled throng of half-transparent ghosts. In the distance, a mourning dove called, its voice trailing off eerily into the misty gray air.

Then I was on the downhill path that corkscrewed through the woods toward Zion's Pool and the Recuperants' cottages. Coming around a rocky outcropping, I saw a woman some twenty paces in front of me, disappearing into the fog. Like me, she was wearing a blue Shaker dress and white apron but her thick dark hair, instead of being bundled neatly into a white cap as it should have been, was flowing loosely down her back, gypsylike, and her apron strings were untied. She was rushing, almost running down the path, with an urgency that seemed at once quite calm and determined and at the same time almost frantic.

I quickened my pace to keep up with her, sensing that some passion compelled her and curious—no, surprisingly anxious—to know what it was. So far as I knew, the path went only to one place: to the spring. But why would this woman be going to the spring at this hour of the morning? And why was she in such a hurry?

I came out of the woods onto the rock ledge above the pool, where Martha and Allie and I had stood, admiring the ferns and the clear blue-green water. The woman had reached the ledge before me, and she stood on the edge just as we had, her hands folded at her waist, her head bowed, as if in prayer. And then, with a suddenness that took me completely by surprise, she jumped, feet first and fully clothed, into the deepest part of the pool.

"No!" I cried horrified. "Don't! You mustn't!" But it was too late. Her blue skirts ballooned around her, her hair skeined loosely upward, and she was sinking to the bottom of the pool. Without pausing to consider that I, too, was fully clothed, I kicked off my clumsy shoes and jumped in after her. I'm a strong swimmer. I've had lifesaving training. I could rescue her, could pull her out, could—

She was gone. The water was clear, as clear and transparent and temperate as air, and under the surface, I could see in all directions. But there was nothing, absolutely nothing to see. The woman had vanished.

Frantically, I swam to the surface, gulped air, and kicked my way down to the bottom again. But the pool was empty. When I surfaced again, I thought I saw her, lying facedown at the far edge of the pool. But there was something wrong. Instead of wearing a blue dress, she was wearing a yellow raincoat.

"CHINA! China! Wake up!"

I gasped as a hand shook my shoulder. "What—"

"Wake up." It was Martha, shaking my shoulder. "Wake up!" She frowned down at my blouse. "My gracious, China, you're all *wet.*"

"Of course I'm wet," I said groggily. "I've been—" Feeling suddenly foolish, I bit back the words *in the water.* "I guess I've been dreaming," I said, pushing myself up. My dreams are usually fairly sedate, but this one had had an unaccountable vividness. An image of the blue-green, empty water rose up in my mind, closing over my head, and I shivered.

"Yes, I guess you have been dreaming," Martha said emphatically. She was dressed for dinner in neat black slacks, white blouse, and red quilted vest. "And shouting."

"Shouting what?" I asked, thinking I knew.

"Something like, 'No, don't.'"

"I'd better change." I stood, looking down at myself. For dinner, I'd planned to wear the same khaki wraparound skirt and plaid blouse I'd worn all day, but now it looked like . . . well, like I'd been sleeping in it. I got a clean shirt and my denim skirt and—still disturbed by my dream—went to the bathroom to change. On the way, I glanced out the window. The blue sky had turned gray and clouds were racing from west to east, their edges curling and swirling.

"Looks like rain," I said.

"There's lightning off to the west," Martha replied apprehensively.

"We'll have to hurry. I don't like being out in a storm. When I was a girl, my friend's mother was struck by lightning not very far from here." She paused. "Did you bring a raincoat?"

"I have a poncho," I said. As I went into the bathroom, there was a thunderclap loud enough to make us both jump.

I was combing my hair when Martha said, through the door, "Oh, I meant to tell you, China. Missy Thatcher will be joining us for dinner, too. I phoned her office on the chance she might be working late, and she was. I made reservations for four."

I opened the bathroom door and came out. "Missy's the person who's writing the Society's history?" Maybe she could tell me something about Sister Hannah.

Martha nodded. "Another one of Lottie's hires, and a good one. She works part-time here and at the library in Georgetown. But I thought you and I would go to the kitchen first, before we meet Missy and Allie for dinner. I want to introduce you to Jackie Slade, our restaurant manager."

I straightened my blouse. "She's not related to Maxine, I hope."

"Don't be sarcastic," Martha said.

I looked up. "Well, is she?"

Martha laughed. "Not so far as I know. And I don't have any reason to think she might be involved with any of the things that have been going on. But you'll want to meet her, and the kitchen staff, as well. I'm acquainted with all of them, because I'm the restaurant's official consultant on herbs."

I stepped into my sneakers, feeling their lightness on my feet, nothing like the stiff sturdiness of my dream shoes. "Jackie Slade. Do you like her?"

She considered. "Yes, although—" She paused, sighed, and said, "Well, here's what happened. Not long before she died, Lottie hired Jackie to replace the guy who originally opened the restaurant here. He was very well liked. The staff loved him, in fact. It's a little harder to like Jackie. She's inclined to play favorites. Once you're on her bad side, you stay there."

"Lottie hired her? How do she and Rachel get along?"

"They don't. After Lottie died, they feuded for a while. One thing led to another, and there was a huge fight."

We went out into the hallway. I closed the door and locked it, dropping the key into my fanny pack. "A fight about what?" As we walked down the hallway, our steps echoed on the uncarpeted wooden floor.

She frowned. "I don't think I ever heard, exactly. Whatever the disagreement, it was pretty serious. Jackie quit, or was fired, depending on who's telling the story. She got a job managing a restaurant in Lexington. But Rachel had trouble finding a replacement, and for all her problems, Jackie knows her stuff. Finally, Rachel went back to Jackie with an offer of more money and a promise—or so I heard—not to meddle in the management of the restaurant. So this is Jackie's second tour of duty at Mount Zion."

"And she and Rachel are on better terms?"

"Not exactly. I think they just try to stay out of each other's way." Martha chuckled grimly as we went down the stairs. "To tell the truth, I try to stay out of Jackie's way when she's angry, too. She can be pretty explosive."

THE rain held off long enough for us to reach the Trustees' Office, the large building where the restaurant was located on the main floor. Bypassing the half-filled waiting area, we went down a long hall to the modern kitchen in the basement—a makeover, Martha told me, of the original Office Kitchen.

In Shaker times, the Office Kitchen had cooked food for the guests, the hired laborers, and the Believers who worked in the Trustees' Office—men and women who held positions of financial trust. Now it was busy with white-aproned workers, five or six of them, and three or four young women and men—waitpersons—in Shaker costume, came and went with trays. Martha stopped at an open office door and greeted a woman sitting behind a desk doing paperwork.

"Hi, Jackie," she said. "I promised I'd bring my friend in to meet you. This is China Bayles—she owns an herb shop and a tearoom in Texas. She's the person who wrote the book I gave you. The *China Bayles' Book of Days.*"

"Oh, sure," Jackie exclaimed, getting to her feet. She was attractively slim, in her early forties, with reddish blond hair in loose curls around her face. She was wearing a white cook's coat over street clothes. She put out her hand. "I really enjoyed the book, China. Lots of information about herbs."

"I'm glad you liked it," I said. "The book was fun, but it sure took a lot of work." That was an understatement. Still, writing *Days* had been a great deal more satisfying than writing the dry, stuffy legal briefs I'd done when I was practicing law. "I love having it for sale in the herb shop. We sell a couple of copies every day."

Jackie smiled thinly. "I could write a book about my experience running a restaurant in a Shaker village—but maybe that wouldn't be such a good idea." Her laugh sounded brittle. "People wouldn't believe what goes on behind the scenes around here."

Martha saw that as an opening and plunged right in. "China and I have been talking about some of the weird things that have happened here lately. I told her about the walk-in freezer."

"Oh, that." Jackie made a wry face. "That wasn't just weird, it was a catastrophe. The food loss amounted to something like three thousand dollars. It was damned disruptive, too. We had to close the restaurant while we cleaned up and restocked, so we lost that revenue, as well. Very unhealthy for the bottom line."

"Too bad," I said sympathetically. "You never found out what happened?"

"Sure, we did." She looked grim. "Somebody raised the setting on the thermostat. But if you mean, did we find out who did it, the answer is no. It was most likely an accident. Somebody changed the setting inadvertently and was too scared to 'fess up."

"Somebody?" I asked. "You mean, one of the kitchen staff?"

"Probably. When we're busy, it's chaos. Of course, it's organized chaos," she corrected herself with a covert glance at Martha, who—as a board member—was one of her bosses. "But there's easy access. Lots of people come and go. If somebody put on a Shaker costume and walked through here, we probably wouldn't notice he didn't belong. Or she."

It was true. Shaker garb was intentionally designed to erase the differences among people and make everyone look pretty much alike. "Somebody who doesn't work in the restaurant, you mean," I said.

"Yes, although I don't know why they'd want to cause so much trouble. Still—" She frowned and rubbed one hand along her shoulder, as if she were trying to massage a tight muscle. Her voice was edged with irritation. "You may not have heard about this, Martha, but there was another incident just last week. Not the same thing, thank God. But serious enough."

Martha shot a glance at me. "No, I haven't heard," she said, concerned. "What happened?"

"It wasn't Brother Joshua, was it?" I asked lightly.

Jackie was not amused. "Not unless the good brother has traded his lantern for a telephone. Somebody called in a tip to the county food service

121

inspector, claiming that there were cockroaches and mice in our food storage pantry." Her eyes had darkened.

"Oh, dear," Martha said.

"Yeah, really. The inspector made a surprise visit the next day. Went straight to the pantry." She snorted sarcastically. "Guess what he found. A mouse corpse in the flour bin and a half dozen dead cockroaches in the corner. The waste bin lid was missing and there was a goopy spill of syrup. A gallon can had been tipped over and the lid loosened. It had dripped all over the floor." She smiled with grim satisfaction. "I fired the boy who cleans that area. He should have spotted that syrup."

"How do you know it was a tip-off?" I asked.

Jackie gave me a you-should-know look. "Because the inspector told me—*after* he gave us a failing score. We've always scored close to perfect on our inspections, you see." She smiled thinly. "The Shakers believed that cleanliness was without a doubt the next best thing to godliness, and we've tried to maintain that standard. The inspector said he was a little surprised at the mouse and the roaches, but that didn't stop him from giving us twenty points off."

"I imagine he's been through this before," I said. "It's not unusual for a disgruntled employee to set his employer up for something like this."

"Set up?" Martha asked, her eyes widening.

"Sure. That's what happened to the two gals who run the restaurant across the street from my shop in Pecan Springs. They fired a cook. The next week, the Adams County Health Inspector showed up, on a tip, and they failed. Failed twice, as a matter of fact. After that, they changed the locks." I turned to Jackie. "Have you disciplined anybody lately? Besides the boy you fired, I mean."

She looked at me for a moment, pursing her lips. "As a matter of fact, I have," she said finally. "We had a problem with one of our waitpersons not long ago. People skills are important in this business, and Gretel's left something to be desired. She couldn't keep her attitude under wraps. After a couple of incidents, I finally had to let her go. Jane took her on over at Housekeeping, I understand." She frowned. "I wonder why I didn't think of her as a possibility."

Martha looked at her watch. "We need to go. Missy and Allie will be waiting for us." To Jackie, she added, "If it's okay, I'd like to introduce China to your kitchen staff."

"Sure, go ahead," Jackie said. "Say, did you know about Missy's recipe research? She's been going through the Kitchen Sisters' diaries and has found some really interesting recipes." She turned back to her desk and pulled a card from a card box. "Here's one of my favorites. Sister Pearl's vinegar pie. Tell me what you think."

I read the recipe with interest. "It looks as if the vinegar was a substitute for lemon juice, as in a lemon meringue pie. There must have been lots of times when the Shakers couldn't get lemons." I handed the recipe back. "It would be fun to try it with one of the lemon herbs—fresh lemon balm, maybe."

"Now, there's an idea," Jackie said. "We've got plenty of lemon balm. In fact, Martha came up with a sorrel soup recipe with lemon balm that we prepare for her wild-gathering class."

"And people really like it, too," Martha said, "especially after they've gathered the sorrel and lemon balm themselves." She grinned. "But I'm not sure you could interest customers in something called Vinegar Pie, Jackie. Doesn't sound very appetizing."

"You might call it Lemon Balm Pie," I said with a laugh, "and put a quotation from Nicholas Culpeper on your menu. He said, 'Lemon balm causeth the mind and heart to grow merry.'"

"That's what we need," Jackie agreed. "Guests with merry minds and hearts. And big appetites. The servers would be happy if they were big tippers, too." She put the recipe back in the file. "Interesting, but not for our menu, I guess."

The six women in the kitchen were skilled workers who had been there since the restaurant opened, and if any of them had any animosity toward Jackie or one another, it wasn't immediately evident. Martha knew two of the women and they chatted for a few minutes while I looked around, making mental notes—but not about the people. Thyme and Seasons is a smaller operation but all kitchens are basically alike, and (I confess) I was especially interested in the layout of the salad prep area. Cass has been wanting us to expand our salads, but we need more room. Or rather, that was what I thought until I saw the way this area was laid out. We don't need more room; we just need better organization.

Martha and I were halfway down the hall, headed in the direction of the dining room, when one of the kitchen staff, a teenager with dark brown hair and large brown eyes, caught up with us. "I'm sorry to bother you, Ms. Edmond," she said to Martha in a low voice, "but I couldn't say anything in front of the others. You're a member of the board of trustees, aren't you?"

"I am," Martha said pleasantly. "How can I help you, Ms.—"

"Trevor. Jenny Trevor." The girl, who was probably seventeen or eighteen, glanced nervously over her shoulder. "I told them I was going to the bathroom. I don't want people to see me talking to you. Is there a way I can reach you?"

Martha frowned. "I suppose I could give you my cell phone number." She took a card out of her purse and scribbled something on it. "What's this about, Jenny?"

The girl snatched the card. "I'll call you," she said, and fled.

"My stars," Martha said, gazing after her. "What in the world—?"

"If you want my guess," I said, "she's going to tattle. On her boss, probably."

"On Jackie? But why doesn't she talk to Jane? She's the assistant director. Or even to Rachel?"

"Maybe the girl just likes your looks." I laughed. "Face it, Martha. Freezer failure, phony tips to the food police, and now mysterious hints in the hallway. Something is definitely fishy in your kitchen."

Martha scowled. "It's not funny, China."

"I know it's not. But what are you going to do? Cry? Stamp your feet and tear out your hair?" I put my arm around her shoulders. "Come on, Martha. You'll find out what Jenny Trevor has to say soon enough. Meanwhile, Allie and Missy are waiting. And I haven't had anything to eat since lunch. I'm hungry."

Chapter Eleven

We cheerfully submit to every invalid and his family physician . . . the ingredients used in the preparation of this great purifying and strengthening medicine [Shaker's Sarsaparilla], which are the roots of Sarsaparilla, Dandelion, Yellow Dock, Mandrake, Black Cohosh, Garget, Indian Hemp, and the Berries of Juniper and Cubeb, united with Iodide of Potassium [and] made by our Society, because we know them to be the best in the vegetable kingdom, and because we carefully select every one according to its power.

Shaker advertisement,
reprinted in *Mary Whitcher's Shaker House-Keeper*

But Allie hadn't arrived yet. It was only Missy Thatcher who was waiting, her hair glistening with a few raindrops. By this time, it was seven thirty (no wonder I was hungry!) and the dining room crowd had thinned out. A pert, pretty, dark-haired woman with glasses, Missy had already snagged a table in a corner.

Martha introduced me as an herbalist who had come to help with the workshops. "China is also a lawyer," she added casually. "She's helping me look into a couple of issues related to the board."

Missy gave me a searching look—troubled, I thought—but said nothing. Over the next few minutes, I learned that she was a librarian and archivist by training and an avid local historian. A single mom with a couple of young children, she was enjoying her work at the research center, especially the village history she was writing. And right now, she was into recipes, among other things.

"Jackie Slade just showed us one of the recipes you found," I said. "Sister Pearl's vinegar pie. Looks interesting."

"Pearl herself is a really interesting character," Missy said. "She kept her journal faithfully, so I'm finding out quite a bit about her. She and her mother and three sisters—they had all been slaves—arrived in the village in 1864, while the war was still going on. The Shakers taught her to read and write and she was proud of being able to write her own recipes. Her sisters eventually went back into the World, but Pearl signed the Covenant and stayed on for nearly sixty years. She died here in 1922, just before Mount Zion closed." She smiled. "I love the old-fashioned terms she uses in her recipes. 'Pie coffin' for a pastry shell, and 'searce the sugar,' which meant sieving out all the lumps. Oh, and a 'gang of calves' feet'—all four of the feet, apparently. They were cooked to make calves'-foot jelly. Gelatin. It was used in dishes for invalids."

Martha picked up the menu. "We are not having calves' feet tonight," she said firmly. "I recommend the herbed chicken—baked, with rosemary, thyme, and garlic. That's what I'm ordering."

"I think I'll just have a salad," Missy said. "I haven't been feeling up to par lately. Too much running around." She sounded dispirited. "I feel like I could go to bed and sleep for a week."

Martha giggled. "What you need is some of that all-purpose Shaker's Sarsaparilla," she said. "Back in the old days, everybody swore by the stuff. It was the closest thing they had to a heal-all."

"I'll have the herbed chicken," I said to our waiter, who was costumed as a Shaker brother, down to the flat-crowned, broad-brimmed straw hat. "But what about Allie? Shouldn't we wait until she gets here?"

Martha shook her head. "I'll order for her." To the waiter, she said, "Our other guest will have a Caesar salad," she said, "and a bowl of broccoli soup. And I'll have the chicken, as well."

Missy dittoed Allie's order, and we settled on a bottle of white wine, which was served with big chunks of hot, satisfying multigrain bread, in a Shaker basket with a stoneware crock of herb butter.

"So you're writing a history of the village," I said to Missy, as I buttered a chunk of bread. "The research sounds like fun."

"It is." Missy poured wine for the four of us. "I'm just about finished with the short version, which we're going to print as a pamphlet and sell in the gift shop. The longer version will eventually turn into a book. I've already talked to the University of Kentucky Press about it, and they're interested."

Martha glanced up. "Have you looked at Aunt Charity's journal yet? My great-aunt," she corrected herself. "My grandmother's sister, on my father's side. She's the one who introduced me to herbs."

"Haven't gotten to her yet. I'm cataloging Aaron Babbitt's papers right now. He was an elder in the East Family in the early 1900s. All the Shakers kept journals, although some of them only jotted a few notes about the weather or the work they did. But Aaron Babbitt was the elder of the East Family—the village's last surviving family—and he took his journal seriously. It's a treasure trove. Journal entries, clippings, newspaper articles, all kinds of stuff. Fascinating reading." She picked up her wineglass and turned the stem in her fingers. "You know, everybody thinks that the Shakers lived a peaceful, totally Utopian existence, but that's not true at all. They were continually running into trouble, not the least of which was the challenge of getting along together."

"I don't know how they did it," Martha said, sipping her wine.

"Hundreds of people, all with different skills, different temperaments, different motives for becoming Believers—and everybody working together, with a common goal. They must have been saints."

Missy hooted. "That's what you think! If you want the inside story, read Elder Babbitt's journal. You'll see just how saintly they were—or weren't."

"I'm staying in Sister Hannah Chandler's room in the East Family Dwelling," I said. "I'm curious—do you know anything about her?"

"Hannah Chandler." Missy sipped her wine, frowning. "She came in 1912. At least, that's what I've read in Elder Babbitt's journal. I'll look her up and see what I can find out." She turned to Martha. "I did discover something very interesting about Zion's Spring, though. In early 1912, Elder Babbitt was really concerned about its ownership."

"But why?" Martha asked blankly. "The spring belonged to the Shakers, didn't it?"

"Well, yes and no. Mostly no, I guess. Around the time of the Civil War, Ezekiel Ballard, a local property owner, joined the Shakers here. He donated a large farm to the Society—the Outer Farm, they called it—and the mineral spring. That was the practice, you see. When people signed the Covenant, they turned over all their property to the Shakers."

Martha turned to me. "That was one reason the Society managed to survive into the twentieth century, China. Some of the villages owned enormous amounts of property, most of it given by members. If the village closed, the property was sold and the money sent to the Central Ministry at Mount Lebanon, in New York."

"An interesting arrangement," I said. "What happened if somebody donated some property and then left the Society?"

"He—or she—got the property back," Martha said, "or an equivalent sum. The Shakers really tried to play fair." She passed the bread basket around again. "I hope you like the bread. It's made from a Shaker recipe, and the butter is flavored with herbs grown here at Mount Zion."

I took another piece. "It's luscious. So what about the mineral spring, Missy?"

"In 1912, Elder Babbitt learned that the village didn't own the spring. It was leased."

"Leased?" Martha looked surprised.

"Right," Missy replied. "The lease was a long one, fifty years, and maybe the Shaker trustees and elders understood at the time they took it over that they didn't actually own the property. But over the years, that information got lost. So poor Elder Babbitt was totally stunned when the real owner showed up—with a deed. A legitimate deed."

"You can't argue with that," I said.

Martha regarded Missy, waiting. After a moment, she said, "Well? Aren't you going to tell us who the real owner was?"

Missy tilted her head. "You mean, you don't know?"

"I haven't a clue," Martha said. "Should I?"

"Well, I thought you would. It was William Ayers."

"Ayers? And this happened in 1912? Why, William Ayers must have been Ernest Ayers' grandfather!"

"His father."

"That's very strange," Martha muttered. "Lottie and Ernest acquired the spring when they bought the village, you know, back in the 1960s. But if Ernest's father already owned it, why would they have to buy it?"

"Maybe I'll be able to tell you when I finish reading Elder Babbitt's journal," Missy replied. "I've only gotten as far as May 1912. At that point, he was worried sick about the situation because the spring was a major source of village revenue. The Shakers relied on the room and board payments from the Recuperants—that's what they called the people who

131

came here to take mineral baths and recover from various illnesses. So losing the spring would have been a real blow."

"I thought their herb sales were their major revenue," I said.

"Not by that time," Martha replied. "The Shakers' medicinal herb business began declining toward the end of the century, not just here, but in all the Societies. The practice of medicine was changing, you see. Doctors were prescribing other types of medicines. Just one example: aspirin had been invented, and people were using it instead of willow bark. And the 'snake-oil' marketing of herbs had put a lot of doctors off. The Shakers didn't do a lot of that kind of promotion—not very often, anyway." She grinned. "Although they certainly made all kinds of claims for that Sarsaparilla Syrup of theirs. But other herb vendors were much more aggressive. The reputation of medicinal herbs suffered, and the Shakers' herb business wasn't profitable any longer."

"Their broom manufacturing folded, too," Missy put in, "and there wasn't any market for hand-woven straw hats. At the same time, the village population really began to fall off, particularly among the brothers, so there were fewer and fewer to do all the physical work—plowing, harvesting, tending the cows. Reading their actual documents, I'm amazed that they held out as long as they did."

"When did Mount Zion close?" I asked.

"In 1923," Martha said. "Eldress Olive died that year. At the end, she was the one who held things together. When she went home to Mother— that's the way they always put it—the village was empty until Ernest and Lottie Ayers came along and bought it as a restoration project." She chuckled. "You know, it would really be ironic if Ernest's father had title to the spring all along. Ernest wouldn't have had to buy it."

"When William Ayers died, his family didn't claim the spring?" I asked curiously.

"Apparently not," Missy said. "Ayers' wife—that would have been Ernest Ayers' mother—left him in 1910 and moved to Louisville with Ernest and his sister. She might not have known about the spring. Or maybe she didn't care."

Martha frowned. "Lottie may have known about this—and Rachel, too. I'll have to ask her."

"There's Rachel, over there." Missy tilted her head toward a table in the corner. "She's having dinner with her brother. Why don't you ask her right now?"

Martha glanced in that direction. "By golly, you're right. China, you were asking about Bruce. Well, there he is. See for yourself."

I peered through the candlelit gloom. Bruce was a handsome, classically featured man, blond and solidly muscular. He was wearing a black T-shirt and blue Adidas running jacket with black stripes down the sleeves, like the one I'd given McQuaid for Christmas last year. He and his dark-haired sister didn't resemble each other much, I thought. They didn't like each other, either. Both were staring down at their plates, and when they looked up, they didn't look at each other. I could practically read estrangement written on their faces.

"Not a particularly happy family," I remarked.

"I like Bruce," Missy said in an offhand way. "He's always struck me as a straight shooter." She didn't say so, but her tone implied that she didn't think Rachel always shot straight, which seemed to be a nearly unanimous opinion.

"Let's all go over and say hello," Martha suggested. "China, I'll introduce you to Bruce."

"You go," Missy said. She bent over and picked up her purse. "If you'll excuse me, I'll visit the girls' room before our entrees arrive."

Martha pushed back her chair and stood up. "Come on, then, China."

The introduction was quick. Bruce clambered to his feet, his smile warm and friendly, his glance direct, his handshake firm. Rachel, who was dressed casually in black jeans and a burgundy-and-black knit top, was clearly uncomfortable at the sight of us. She seemed to hope we wouldn't linger, but Martha wasn't about to be put off.

"Missy Thatcher has just been telling China and me something interesting about Will Ayers," she said brightly.

"Will Ayers?" Bruce asked. He had a deep, rich voice, a baritone. "Oh, yes, one of our forefathers." He frowned. "Missy Thatcher? Don't think I've met her. Who is she?"

"The curator in our research library," Rachel told him. "She's trained as an archivist and is doing some background research for a history of Mount Zion." To Martha, she said, "Will Ayers was our great-grandfather. Granddad Ernest's father."

Bruce looked interested. "Oh, right. I've seen pictures of the old guy. Bearded, gaunt, typical Kentuckian. Had himself a whiskey-brewing business over in Georgetown, as I recall. But the family got split up— divorce or something. I don't think Ernest ever knew his father." He put his hands in his jacket pockets and gave Martha a curious look. "So what about him?"

"Missy was reading one of the Shaker journals, and came across the information that your great-grandfather had a deed to Zion's Spring," Martha replied. "That was in 1912. Did you ever hear anything about that?"

Rachel looked genuinely surprised. "Why, no," she said. "If Lottie and Ernest knew about it, they never mentioned it to me."

"First I've heard of it, too," Bruce said. "Far as I know, the spring always belonged to the Shakers. They used to rent out cottages and rooms to people who came to dunk themselves in the water. It's supposed to be healing or something." He frowned. "But if old Will owned it back in 1912, how come Granddad Ernest had to buy it again in the 1960s? How come he didn't just inherit it?"

"Your grandfather might have ended up selling or giving it to the Shakers," I suggested. "Missy hasn't finished reading the journal yet."

Bruce gave a dry cough. "Maybe you'd better tell her to stop where she is," he said to Rachel. "If she keeps poking around, there's no telling how many skeletons she might dig up. Those old Shakers—they weren't all the saints they were made out to be, you know."

Was it my imagination, or was there a barb hidden in that innocuous remark? Martha and I laughed, but Rachel was definitely not amused. She lifted her chin and gave her brother a frigid stare.

"I hardly think Missy's job is any business of yours, Bruce," she said in a low voice. "You're not a part of this organization, you know. So you can keep your opinions to yourself."

Bruce looked down, saying nothing. I remembered Martha saying that Lottie had left her grandson out of her will, and it was obvious that Rachel didn't want him involved with the management of Mount Zion. Sounded to me like Rachel had control issues with just about everybody, although her brother seemed to be a special case. I also wondered about the source of the animosity, but I know from experience that old family feuds can live on for a long time in our hearts. Sometimes the smallest unkind cut can fester into an open sore that never quite heals.

Over my shoulder, I saw our Shaker waitperson arriving with our food and elbowed Martha. We said good-bye and went back to our table just as Missy returned.

As we sat down, I looked at the plate of salad and bowl of soup waiting to be eaten. "Shouldn't Allie be here by now, Martha? Maybe we ought to give her a call." The words were just out of my mouth when I remembered. "Scratch that. We can't call. There's no phone in the cottage."

Missy shook out her napkin. "You know, I don't understand why Allie didn't insist on having the phone connected when Rachel offered her the cottage. I sure wouldn't have wanted to stay out there by myself without a phone, especially after that truck came roaring down the hill and crashed into the cottage next door." She looked at me. "You heard about that, China?"

"I heard," I said. "About that, and about the barn burning down, and the problems in the kitchen. And the vandalism in the artist's studio. Sounds like a lot of trouble for a small village."

Missy looked as if she might be about to say something but thought better of it. Instead, she picked up her fork and began on her salad. When she looked up, she said, "Maybe Allie decided not to come because of the rain. And since she doesn't have a cell phone, she couldn't call and let us know."

"Or maybe she got involved with that work she was doing and forgot about us," Martha said in a tart tone.

"Does that happen often?" I asked, picking up my fork.

"Oh, you bet," Martha replied. "Allie loves numbers. She can get so caught up that she even forgets what day it is. Anyway, I'm going to enjoy my dinner and worry about her afterward."

I agreed. And sniffing the chicken, I found I was very hungry.

Chapter Twelve

Elder Aaron Babbitt

[At Pleasant Hill Shaker Village, Kentucky] the elder who embezzled family funds was expelled . . . At South Union [Kentucky] a new member got away with a team, a wagon, and $100 worth of brooms. He was caught and imprisoned. Another who collected $1,000 on a seed trip never returned to the village.

The Kentucky Shakers
Julia Neal

Document 1.1912.06.09. Text of letter copied into journal.

Mount Zion
June 9, 1912

To his dear Sister in Mother's Love & in the Flesh, Priscilla, from her brother Aaron

Your letter of May 20th was received, for which I thank you heartily, Sister, and for the Syrrup, which seems efficacious. My health is not improved, however. I will be consulting Dr. Barnard again soon and will write again when I know more. But my Spirit is more sorely distressed than my Body, for we have endured many bitter Afflictions here and worse to come.

You inquire about the ownership of the Spring, but I fear I cannot ease your concern. There is much labor & anxiety among ourselves in the Ministry regarding this Matter. Will Ayers has submitted to us a copy not only of the Lease but also of the Deed, both of which look to be in good order. Elder Benjamin of the South Family and I undertook a search of Bro Ezekiel Ballard's papers (those few that have been preserved) for a later Document which might record a Purchase, but to no avail, although Benjamin thinks other papers may yet be found in the attic of the Trustees' Office. Will Ayers says that he means to repossess the Spring and all the Improvements (that is, the Recuperants' cabins) six months hence, at the expiration of the lease. He has been making a great Annoyance here these past days, coming and going as if he owned the Place, and when he comes, he is not always sober. He encountered Sister Ruth on the path to the Sisters' Shop and made a lewd Advance against her, which was repelled by Bro Charles who near broke Ayers' arm. Elder Benjamin and I have decided to consult Lawyer Howard Barnes about a legal Bar to Ayers' visits.

But even sadder to relate, young Seth Chandler wandered off by himself on the day of Sister Sally's funeral and fell from a rock ledge not far below Zion's Pool and was killed. It was at first thought that he might have been stolen by his Father, who came here threatening to take the child. Indeed, the Brethren gave up the search after two days, thinking that this must be the case. Brother Joshua, who had charge of the boy, continued to look, however, often going out at night with his Lantern. He found the dead child and is now heavy with Grief, blaming himself. The boy's mother, Hannah, is inconsolable.

My pen trembles and would stop there, but must relate yet an-

other Matter, sorely troubling. You will remember Brother Charles (above mentioned), who has been in charge of the Herb Department since coming some three Years ago. He is an eager and zealous Worker, but I have been attempting to reconcile the Herb account which appears to be out of balance by something over three Thousand Dollars. At first I thought it was simply a matter of muddle, for the Account was considerably confused. But after much Study I believe that the muddle is deliberate, carefully designed to obscure what must be named for what it is: an Embezzlement. O wretched sin, bitter as Wormwood. O greedy, sinful man!

I was obliged to share this painful Discovery with Eldress Olive and Sister Lillian (our Trustee Sister). We had agreed that Charles must return the Money and be required to leave the Society, but have not decided on Prosecution. We would prefer not to involve the Police, if he will return the money and depart.

But of other matters, there is thankfully much Good to be written. The Season's work is upon us, in the gardens and the Fields. The sisters have been gathering Fern, Mint, and Lobelia and have trimmed Wormwood, Thyme & Tansy. They filled an order of tins (marjoram) for Dodge & Co. and have another order of dried sage to complete, for which we are grateful, since there have not been many orders of late. We have a plenty of mulberries & blackberries & etc, thanking God for the abundance.

I trust this finds you well. Eldress Olive bids me copy out for you her recipe for Pectoral Syrrup, which she recommends as excellent comfort for Sister Eliza's cough. To which fervent Plea I add my own and remain

Yrs faithfully in Mother's Love
Elder Aaron Babbitt

HANDWRITTEN RECIPE FOUND WITH LETTER

Document 2.1912.06.09

Pectoral Syrrup

2 tablespoons Wa-a-hoo bark

1 tablespoon Boneset

1 tablespoon Waterpepper

1 tablespoon Princes pine

1 tablespoon Bittersweet bark

1 tablespoon Black cohosh

To be boiled in an iron kettle with soft water, when the strength is out, to be strained off, then boiled down to the consistency of thin Molasses, to which add one fourth West India Molasses. This should be scalded an hour over a slow fire and it is fit for use.

Dose: a tablespoon full to be taken three or four times a day before eating. To be used in consumption, Coughs, affections of the liver, spleen, etc.

NEWSPAPER CLIPPINGS FOUND
IN AARON BABBITT'S JOURNAL

Document 3.1912.06.09

Lexington Leader
June 6, 1912

CHILD KILLED IN FALL

It was reported yesterday that Seth Chandler, 12, was killed in a fall from a cliff at the Shaker village of Mount Zion. The boy is survived by his grieving parents. His mother, Mrs. Hannah Chandler, is currently in residence with the Mount Zion Society of Shakers. His father, Mr. Jake Chandler, resides in Evansville, Indiana. The child has been buried at Mount Zion.

Document 4.1912.06.09

Georgetown Graphic
June 11, 1912

MR. AYERS ANNOUNCES PROPERTY DEVELOPMENT

Mr. William Ayers, long of this city, has notified Georgetown city leaders of the establishment of a consortium of investors to develop property owned by Mr. Ayers in the vicinity of Zion's Spring. According to Mr. Ayers, who is in the distilling business, a group of seven men from Louisville and Lexington have joined together to provide funds for the building of a resort hotel and a paved road, so that automobiles might have access to the site. He anticipates that construction will commence in the summer of 1913, with the hotel being opened in 1914. City leaders responded with enthusiasm to Mr. Ayers' report, noting that Zion's Spring (currently in the possession of the United Society of Shakers at Mount Zion) has the potential to attract a considerable number of people to the area.

Document 5.1912.06.09

SHAKERS' SARSAPARILLA

The Great Purifier of the Blood and other
Fluids of the Body
By reason of their intimate knowledge of medicinal
plants the Shakers are enabled to excel in the
preparation of a purely vegetable medicine.

SHAKERS' SARSAPARILLA

Beyond all doubt the most powerful Blood Purifier, Liver and
Kidney Remedy and General Tonic. It is prepared from roots, herbs
and berries grown, selected and discovered by the Shakers.

For Diseases of the Kidneys, Liver, Bladder, Skin and Blood, Scrofula or
King's Evil, Swellings or Sores, Cancerous Ulcers, Syphilitic Humors, Erysipelas, Dropsy, Scurvy, Gout, Gravel, Rheumatism, Neuralgia, Palpitations of the Heart, Female Weakness, Loss of Appetite, Nervousness and
Emaciation.

SHAKERS' SARSAPARILLA

is prepared by the Society of Shakers, Mount Zion, Kentucky
Price, $1 per Bottle; 6 Bottles for $5
Sold by Druggists. Inquire by name, avoid imitations.
Wholesale Agents, Baum & Weeks, 255 Jefferson St.,
Lexington, Kentucky

Chapter Thirteen

In St. John's vision of the end of the world (Revelation 8:11), after the opening of the Seventh Seal, a star fell from heaven. "The name of the star is Wormwood," St. John wrote. "A third of the waters became wormwood, and many died from the water, because it was made bitter."

Mugwort (*Artemisia vulgaris*), one of the wormwoods, was carried by travelers as a charm against lightning, rainstorms, and all perils of travel, including being set upon by robbers and drowning.

The thunderstorm was reduced to a misty drizzle by the time Martha, Missy, and I finished dinner. "I'd love to show you the collection, China," Missy said as we left the dining room. "I'll be in at nine tomorrow. Why don't you drop by?"

Martha had stopped at the restroom, and it didn't sound as if the invitation included her. I wondered whether that was intentional.

Testing, I said, "Sure. I'll ask Martha what would be a good time for her, and we'll let you know."

"Oh, don't bother Martha," Missy replied carelessly. "She's already seen the stuff I want to show you. Just come by yourself."

Now, what was that about? I didn't think it was my magnetic personality or my irresistibly attractive appearance. We settled on nine thirty and, when Martha came up, said our good nights. As Missy drove off,

Martha turned to me. She was holding a plastic sack containing Allie's soup and salad, boxed to go.

"Room service," she said. "I'm taking Allie's supper up to the cottage. But you don't have to come," she added, glancing down at my canvas sneakers. "Your shoes will get soaked."

"So will yours," I pointed out as I shrugged into my poncho. "We'll need a flashlight. There's one in my car. And an umbrella, if you want it."

"A flashlight would be good," Martha said. She pulled the hood of her raincoat over her head, glancing up. "I don't think we'll need the umbrella, though. It's barely misting. And look—there's the moon, just peeking through the clouds. We won't be completely in the dark."

I found a forgotten brown sweater-vest in the trunk of the car and put it on under my poncho. The combination of sweater, poncho, and the fanny pack I was wearing was not terribly chic but what the heck. It was dark, and nobody was going to see me. I also found a small torch and stuck it into my fanny pack, handing the larger flashlight to Martha.

The two of us trekked along the gravel lane toward the conference center, Martha leading the way with the flashlight, I skirting puddles and keeping an eye out for wildlife. A possum hurriedly crossed the road, not wanting anything to do with us, and two pairs of yellow-green eyes—raccoons?—watched us from the shadows. As we passed the old graveyard, an owl hooted deep in the dark woods and I shivered, remembering the Shakers' belief that their spirits lingered at Mount Zion until Judgment Day. That was a long time to hang around, I thought. What if they got bored? They'd worked their whole lives—they'd probably get restless just lying in the ground with nothing to do. And judging from the large number of markers, there might be quite a few restless spirits. The owl hooted again and I remembered the dream that had brought me along this very path. I pushed that thought away, though, as fast as it came. The dream had left me soaking wet and gasping for breath. It had been all too real. I'd just as soon not go there again.

To disguise my uneasiness, I cleared my throat and asked, "Seen anything of Brother Joshua this trip?" My voice sounded too loud in the quiet night air.

"Not yet," Martha replied over her shoulder. "But then, we just got here this afternoon." Her giggle sounded nervous. "The evening is yet young. And maybe he doesn't like to go out in a storm. Might get struck by lightning."

"Yeah, right," I muttered, glancing at my watch. It wasn't even nine thirty yet. There was still plenty of time before the witching hour— midnight, when ghosts were supposed to rise and roam. Thinking of witches made me think of Ruby. If she were here, she'd probably pitch a tent and camp out all night right here at the graveyard, on the chance of getting a glimpse of the itinerant Brother Joshua and his lantern.

But thinking of my favorite spiritualist made me feel more than a little homesick, and I couldn't help wishing I was back home with Mc-Quaid and Brian and Ruby and the rest of the Pecan Springs gang. Why had I consented to this idea of Martha's, this so-called investigation? Allie might be on to something serious, but I was too far out of the loop to be of any help with an investigation into a theft of securities. What the trustees needed was a forensic accountant. On the other matters, the dirty tricks, Allie and Martha were smart, motivated, and they knew where to look. If they put their heads together, they could figure out who dunnit. Really. If I learned anything about what was going on here, it would be entirely by accident. I was wasting my time, and Martha's.

Martha's flashlight beam bounced from side to side, highlighting rain-wet grass and trailing shrubs. We had passed the cemetery now and were on the path that angled off through the woods to Zion's Pool. The marbled moon flickered in and out of the clouds, the shadows making walking difficult, and the wind had picked up again, bearing a bouquet of earthy fragrances. To the west, I heard the rumble of thunder, and forked-tongue lightning stabbed out of the darkness on the far horizon.

Should have brought the umbrella, I thought gloomily. We were in for yet another storm. I hoped we could deliver Allie's supper and get back to our rooms before it hit. And as we walked back, I would tell Martha that, while I understood her concerns, there wasn't much I could do to help. I was going to enjoy myself, snag some pleasant R & R, and let her and Allie take care of the rest.

We reached the top of the bluff, where the path began twisting down the side of the hill to the pool. The cottages were on the other side, partway up the opposite hill. I peered through the trees, wondering if there was a light on in Allie's cabin, but if there was, I couldn't see it through the thick foliage. Martha started down and I followed, both of us slipping on the muddy path, grabbing at bushes to keep from tobogganing all the way to the bottom.

"If Rachel intends to build an upscale spa here, she's going to have to do something about this approach," I grumbled to myself, halfway down. But of course, she would. She'd cut the trees, landscape the hill, and build a real road, a parking lot, and an easy concrete ramp for the handicapped. But would people drive all the way to Mount Zion just to use a spa? The village wasn't exactly on the beaten track, and while the East Family Dwelling served as a pleasant inn for overnight tourists, the rooms weren't five-star-hotel quality.

We reached the foot of the path and were standing on the ledge above the pool. Beneath us, the water was liquid ebony shot with silver wind-stirred ripples that caught and reflected the fugitive moon. I shivered. It was the same ledge where I had stood in my dream and watched the Shaker sister jump into the pool.

Martha peered anxiously across the pool. We could see the outline of the cottage on the hill above the pool, but it was dark. And we hadn't met Allie on the path. Where was she?

"No light." Martha gave a frustrated sigh. "Well, come on. We'll go across the footbridge and—"

I reached for her arm. I'd caught a glimpse of something at the shallow end, in the water, a yellow bundle of— I thought of my dream and felt a sudden, bewildering disconnect. Was it *then*? Was it *now*? Was I dreaming? My heart gave an erratic bounce. "Martha, swing the flashlight over there. To the right."

"What?" she asked, startled, but did as I asked. Then the beam of the flashlight hit it. We were looking at a still figure in a yellow raincoat, floating facedown in the water a few feet from the edge of the pool. The water rippled and lapped over it. The raincoat cocooned a bubble of air, buoying the body up.

A yellow raincoat. I gasped and blinked, feeling suddenly dizzy. This couldn't be real. I must be imagining it.

But Martha saw the figure, too. She shrieked and dropped the flashlight. Still lit, it bounced on the rocks and splashed into the water not far from the body, bobbing like a phosphorescent fish. The moon disappeared and on the ledge, we were engulfed in darkness so thick and heavy I could almost taste it. I fished in my fanny pack for the small torch, switched it on, and scrambled across the slippery rocks, down the hill to the pool. Martha followed me, still clutching the bag of Allie's take-out food, stumbling, whimpering when she cracked her ankle against a rock. I remembered briefly that she was my mother's age and hoped she'd be okay.

I thought I knew what we were looking at. If I was right, this wasn't going to be easy.

We reached the edge of the pool, near enough to the waterfall that I could feel its mist on my cheek. My heart had stopped ricocheting around in my chest and settled for a ruthless hammering. I handed the small torch to Martha. Ignoring the chilly water that soaked my sneakers and dragged at the hem of my skirt, I waded out and snagged the floating flashlight and aimed it at the raincoated figure.

"Who is it?" Martha quavered, on the shore. "Can you see?"

Yes, I could see. I could see enough of her face, pale and composed in death, to recognize her. When I leaned closer to check the pulse at her neck and caught a faint whiff of the alcohol, I thought I knew what had happened. I felt a surge of sadness and pity that threatened to overwhelm me.

I straightened. "I'm sorry, Martha," I said painfully. "It's Allie. She's dead." The body was cold to the touch. She had been in the water for too long. There was no point in trying CPR.

"Allie!" Martha cried out in anguish, dropping the dinner bag. Her raincoat flapping, she splashed out into the knee-deep water to cradle Allie's limp body in her arms. "Oh, Allie, Allie," she whispered, anguished. "How did this happen? How?"

How? Wasn't it obvious? Allie was already pouring her second Scotch when we said good-bye around six o'clock. If she'd had a stiff one while she worked and another before she left for the restaurant, she could've stumbled on that steep, wet path, tumbled down the hill, and ended up unconscious in the water, where she drowned. And somewhere en route, she had banged her head on a sharp rock, which would account for the deep, bloody depression I could see at the back of her skull.

On the other hand . . .

* * *

I've never been a fan of cell phones—I was probably the last person in Pecan Springs to get one—but I have to admit that the blasted thing makes life a lot easier. If mine hadn't been in my fanny pack just then, I would have had to run all the way back to the East Family Dwelling to find a phone to call nine-one-one.

I made the call after Martha and I dragged Allie's body out of the water and onto the rocky shore and I retrieved the flashlight, waterproof, still functioning. Then, still sobbing, Martha searched her shoulder bag for the number for Mount Zion security. The officer on duty was a boy named Hank, who sounded as if he might be nineteen or twenty. He'd obviously never been closer to death than a video game, and he found the prospect breathlessly "awesome." But he promised to get here as fast as he could and even had enough wit to find the phone number of Rachel's apartment. She lived in the village, on the second floor of the Children's Dwelling.

"I'll call her," Martha volunteered brokenly, wiping her eyes with her sleeve.

I was thinking my on-the-other-hand thoughts. "I can do it," I said. I punched in the number. The phone rang five times and the answering machine picked up, but halfway into the recorded message, Rachel herself came on the line. She sounded annoyed, as if she'd been summoned from something she'd rather be doing. Or maybe it was just late, and she was getting ready for bed, or—

"It's China Bayles," I said. "I'm sorry to have to tell you this, but Allie Chatham is dead." I could have told her where and how, but I thought it might be useful just to leave it there, and listen for her reaction.

There was a gasp, followed by a silence that stretched out for two beats, three, four, five. Then, "Are you joking?" Her tone wary, guarded. The cliché might have been a way to buy time.

I gave her an equally clichéd reply. "Nobody would joke about a thing like this."

She made a half-strangled sound. "Where are you? How did she . . . How did she die? Who—" She bit it off.

Who? Who what? Who found her? Who killed her? I wished she'd finished her sentence, but she was going on.

"Where are you?" she repeated harshly.

"Martha Edmond and I are at Zion's Pool." The pool I had plunged into in my dream, trying to save a suicide. The pool where I'd seen, in my dream, a figure in a yellow raincoat, rising eerily from the depths. I shook my head, trying to clear it.

"Zion's Pool?" She processed that, silently, and came up with, "I'll call Security. Wait there—someone will be with you in a few minutes. I'm on my way, too. I don't want you to leave until—"

"I've already called Security," I said. "And nine-one-one."

Another pause, longer. Her toned turned chilly. "You should have called me first. I'm responsible for everything that goes on in this village."

I didn't reply, but I doubted that she meant to claim responsibility for Allie's death. Briefly, I wondered why she hadn't wanted me to call nine-one-one. For the same reason she hadn't reported Maxine's theft? But you can't keep a drowning under wraps—at least, not for long. There are certain legal niceties that have to be observed when a fatality occurs.

She must have thought better of her remark. "Poor, poor Allie." Her tone was less chilly. "How did she die?"

I'd let her worry about this. "I think you should come," I replied. I clicked off the phone. To Martha, I said, "Rachel's on her way. She says we should have called her first."

"I'm not surprised," Martha said. She looked at me. "I don't think this was an accident, China. Do you?"

"I don't know," I said honestly. "If the path on Allie's side of the hill is as slippery as the path we just came down, she could have fallen. And she'd been drinking. Wouldn't take much to miss her footing and end up in the water."

"But her head!" Martha's wail was anguished. "It looks like somebody smashed her head in with a rock!"

"Or that she smashed her head on a rock when she fell," I replied matter-of-factly. "We'll have a better idea when the autopsy report comes back." I stopped. Back home, I could pull a few strings in the police department and get a look at the autopsy report. Here, I was stringless. Rachel might see that report, but I doubted that Martha or I would.

But there was something I could do, and I'd better do it now, before the place got crowded. I pushed away the nagging uneasiness of my dream and got down to business. "Will you be okay if I leave you here for a few minutes, Martha? I want to go up to Allie's cottage, and I'd prefer to get back here before Rachel shows up—or the cops."

Martha looked down at Allie's raincoat-clad body. One shoe was missing, I noticed—a loafer. Was it in the pool? If so, finding it would have to wait until tomorrow.

"I'll be okay," she said sadly. "Nothing can happen that could be any worse than this." She looked back up, frowning. "Why are you going to the cottage, China?" She hesitated. "You're not thinking—"

"I'm not thinking anything," I interrupted. I handed her the smaller torch and took the flashlight. "I just want to have a look."

I started off around the pool to the footbridge and the path up the hill. Mindful that I might be walking across a crime scene, I made my way carefully, shielding the flashlight and using it to check the path as I went. I was looking for a couple of things. For Allie's shoe. For any spot where she might have caught a heel or stubbed a toe on a rock, or where she had grabbed at a bush or a tree to keep from falling. Or where somebody might have stepped out behind her and given her a hard shove. I made a mental note of a couple of possible places to look at on the way back down. At one spot, I picked up the unmistakable scent of fresh mint, although I couldn't see any mint bordering the path.

But I didn't linger. I had something important to do, and I wanted to do it before anybody arrived. I didn't want to have to explain.

The key was under the flowerpot, where it had been earlier, when I watched Allie unlock the door. That made me feel a little easier. I wasn't exactly crazy about the idea of going in through a window. Inside, the air was heavy with Allie's cigarette smoke, and dark, and I wondered why she hadn't left a light burning when she went out. There was no sound and the place had the feel of an empty house, but I checked the kitchen and bedroom just to make sure. I didn't turn on the lights. I didn't want to call attention to my presence, just in case somebody was out there—hanging out in the woods or on the road above—and curious. I went to the living room window and closed the drapes, then shone the flashlight around the room.

The leather portfolio Allie had brought home with her was not on the coffee table, where I'd seen it last. I frowned. Where was it? If I were Allie, where would I put something like that to hide it from curious eyes? I found it in the first place I looked, in the bedroom, under the mattress. I wasn't exactly thrilled. If I had located it this easily and quickly, somebody else could have beaten me to it and lifted the contents.

That hadn't happened. I put the portfolio on the bed, opened it, and shone my light on the contents, feeling like Caitlin when she hit her home run. There they were, five or six letter-sized pages of computer printout, a couple of pages of what looked like a photocopied securities inventory, and two pages of handwritten notes, presumably Allie's. It was the material for the report she'd been working on, the report that she'd intended to use to request an outside audit of the endowment fund. It didn't take a Sherlock Holmes to deduce that—if Allie had been hit on the head and shoved into the pool—these pages might hold the motive. But one way or another, they ought to be in a safe place. I was willing to bet that my mattress was safer than Allie's. At the moment, anyway.

Without stopping to examine the material in detail, I folded the pages once and then again, creasing them into a tight package that I tucked into the back of my fanny pack, where I keep my credit cards when I'm traveling. The slight bulge wasn't noticeable when the pack was on my hip again. Then I closed the leather portfolio, found the paper towels in the kitchen, and gave it a thorough wiping. There was a legitimate reason for my prints being in the house—I'd been there earlier that evening with Martha—but not on this particular item. Using a paper towel, I carried the portfolio to the closet, where I leaned it against the back wall, among the shoes. There, it wouldn't call attention to itself, the way it would if it was found, empty, under Allie's mattress.

That done, I made one more trip through the kitchen and bedroom, looking for any signs of disarray and checking the back door and the windows. Everything was neat and orderly, the door and windows locked, no sign of a struggle. It looked to me like whatever happened to Allie had happened after she left the cottage. And if someone had made it happen, he—or she—had not come to the cottage to search for the papers. Yet.

Why not? Well, I could think of a couple of reasons. For one thing, it was entirely possible that the killer (if there was one) didn't know that Allie had brought the materials home with her. It might be more logical to look for them in her office.

For another, while pushing a woman down a slick hill and into the water might sound like a piece of cake, it isn't, even if you've konked her a good one on the head. She's more likely to be stunned, rather than out. And even a stunned woman can struggle and kick and scream and hang on to whatever she can grab. If you're the pusher and she's the screamer, you're probably in a hurry to have it over and done with. If there's any searching to be done, you'll come back later and do it.

I went out, closing the door behind me and leaving the key, wiped clean, where I had found it. I looked down the hill toward the pool. No lights, no voices, so I had a few moments. Heading back down, I checked the path carefully, trying to see everything the police would see when they searched the scene, but without leaving any clues that I had been there first.

I was halfway down when I encountered that fresh, clean scent of mint again. Peppermint. It hung in the air, distinctly comforting and pleasantly familiar, about a dozen yards above the rocky ledge that jutted out over the pool. I found it off to the right of the path, under the tree, a small patch of thickly growing mint, crushed as if someone had crouched there, concealed, waiting. There was a bent branch, a couple of broken twigs, and on the path itself, a long, muddy scrape, as if someone had fallen.

And more: just off the path, on the left, I spotted Allie's missing shoe. There was no sign of the rock that had damaged her skull, but if there was one, the police—if they did their jobs—would find it. I straightened. It was beginning to rain again.

I left the shoe where I'd found it and hurried back down to Martha. When I got there, she sniffed.

"Peppermint?"

"You have a good sense of smell. It must be on my shoes. I found a patch on the hill, beside the path. Looks like somebody might've been waiting there." I knelt down beside Allie's body, lifted her raincoat, and felt in the pockets of the knitted green sweater she was wearing, now dark and heavy with the weight of water.

"The person who killed her?"

"Whoa," I said, going to the other pocket. "We don't know she was killed. Not yet."

"She was killed." Martha frowned, bending over to see what I was doing. "What are you looking for?"

"Keys," I said, as my fingers closed over them.

The security guard arrived just about the same time as the heavens opened and the rain poured down. Hank was a slim kid with a concave chest and jug-handle ears. He stood hunched over Allie's body, hands in his pockets, chewing gum and muttering a repeated litany of *awesomes*, punctuated by an occasional prayerful *jeez* or *omigawd*. The only other thing he managed to say was that he sure didn't want to have to carry her *up* that gol-blasted hill.

Hank was followed almost immediately by Rachel, wearing the same black jeans she had worn to dinner and wrapped in a neon green rain poncho. She was carrying a flashlight, and exhibiting a state of tightly suppressed hysteria. She looked down at Allie's body.

"Are you sure she's dead?" Her voice was shaking.

"Yes," I said shortly. I didn't think the matter needed any further explanation, but if it did, I didn't get a chance to offer it, for Rachel clapped her hand over her mouth, scooted behind a bush, and threw up loudly. Martha gave me an inquiring glance. *No*, I mouthed. It was better to let Rachel deal with it herself.

In a few minutes she returned, wiping her chin with her sleeve. The hood of her poncho had fallen back and her wet hair was patent-leather slick. Her mascara was running in rivulets against her pale skin, and her lipstick was smeared. She looked as if she'd been dunked, wrung out, and hung up to dry.

But she was still game, and still teed off at me for denying her the privilege of calling nine-one-one. "I don't understand how you happened to find her," she said accusingly, as if finding the body was itself a crime. "What were you doing here at this time of night, in the rain?"

Martha lifted her chin. "We were bringing Allie's dinner," she replied with great dignity, pointing to the plastic sack that sat on the shore. "She was supposed to meet us. When she didn't show up, we started out for the cottage. We found her in the water and pulled her out. She was already dead." She narrowed her eyes. "If there'd been a phone in the cottage, we would have tried to call her. Damn it, Rachel! It wasn't smart to let Allie stay up there without a phone—especially after that truck came down the hill."

Rachel's expression changed and she looked away. Maybe she didn't want people asking questions about her refusal to install a phone—or her invitation to Allie to stay in the cottage in the first place. I had taken a deep sniff when she showed up, testing for the scent of mint. The scent would probably have disappeared by that time, of course, or she could have changed shoes. Or maybe that hadn't been her hiding in the mint patch on that hillside, waiting for Allie to come down the path. It's always a good idea to entertain all the options.

Two sheriff's deputies arrived about five minutes later, talking loudly as they flatfooted it down the hill, grabbing at whatever they could reach to keep from sliding. Martha and I told our stories, but we had to repeat everything fifteen minutes later when Sheriff Franklin showed up, corpulent, flushed, and so winded that he barely had enough breath to ask our names. By this time it was raining steadily, and he was deeply annoyed at being called away from his television set to officiate at the death of somebody who'd been careless enough to fall into Zion's Pool and drown.

Meanwhile, the deputies were beating the bushes along the path up the hill to the cottage, destroying the evidence and failing to find Allie's missing shoe. I was glad I'd had the time to do my own investigation, whatever it was worth. I'd give that path another look in daylight, when the deputies weren't around. There might be some small piece of evidence they had managed not to step on.

The sheriff had dismissed Rachel and Hank almost immediately. Hank, still muttering his *awesomes*, was happy to be released. Rachel left peevishly. I couldn't tell whether she was offended at not being considered important enough to stay around, or whether she wanted to listen in on the story that Martha and I told the police. We finished giving our statements just as the EMS team arrived, bringing a stretcher down the hill.

"I'm finished with you," Sheriff Franklin growled—ominously, I thought, although he gave us his card and told us to call him if we remembered anything else. Martha knelt briefly beside Allie's body, touched her face, and stood. There was nothing else we could do, so we headed back in the direction of the East Family Dwelling.

I was silent, ensnared in the mystery of my dream. I've never been terribly prescient—as Ruby keeps reminding me, I'm too left-brained, too logical, too rational. I've never understood Ruby's adventures with the Ouija board or the Tarot or astrology. How was it I could manage to dream, this afternoon, something like what had happened tonight?

Martha was silent, too, her head down, her hands shoved into her pockets. I understood. She and Allie had been friends for a long time, and she had to deal with her grief. But when she said, between her teeth,

"I'm going to *get* whoever did this, China," I understood. It wasn't grief. It was fury.

"We don't know that anybody did this," I reminded her gently. "It could have been an accident."

"It was no accident." She clenched her fist and puffed out her cheeks. "I'm going to get her."

"Wait a minute," I said. "Aren't you jumping to conclusions?"

"No, I am *not* jumping to conclusions." She made a gritty noise. "Didn't you see the way Rachel looked at us, China? She was fuming. If it hadn't been for us, Allie wouldn't have been missed until she didn't show up for work. And with this rain, any evidence would be washed away."

"I don't disagree," I said, "although maybe Rachel was angry simply because Allie's death is going to make things difficult. Is there anybody in the financial office who can fill in?"

"Hazel Lowery is Allie's assistant. She's pretty sharp, although she doesn't have Allie's experience." She went back to her train of thought— Rachel's supposed guilt. "There's also the fact that Rachel was so anxious for Allie to have that cottage, China. And that she refused to connect the phone. Don't you think that's suspicious?"

"Could be," I said offhandedly, not wanting to encourage her speculations.

Martha aimed a narrow glance at me. "So what were you looking for in the cottage?"

"Remember the portfolio Allie had with her earlier this evening?"

She nodded. "The one with the—" Her eyes widened. "So that's it! Rachel murdered her because—"

"We don't even know *whether* she was murdered, Martha," I said patiently. "And if she was, we have no idea why, let alone who. For all we know, maybe her ex came around to talk to her and they got into an argument and—"

"Pete!" Martha pursed her lips. "I didn't think of him. But I suppose that's a possibility. He's hotheaded, and he's a drinker. That's why she divorced him. She loved him, but she just couldn't take his drinking anymore." She paused, going back to the subject. "Well? Did you find the portfolio?"

"Yep."

"What did you do with it?"

"Left it in Allie's closet. But to be on the safe side—" I patted my fanny pack. "I thought it was prudent to make sure that those work papers were safe."

"Good. Terrific." Martha puffed out a relieved breath. "I wonder," she said after a moment, "if there's only one copy of that stuff. The copy you have."

"Might be," I said. "Or might not. Maybe we should—"

"There's a copy machine in Allie's office," Martha interrupted. "We could do it tonight. Make copies, I mean." She glanced at me. "Isn't that what you were thinking?"

"Actually, it was." I grinned. "Are you adding mind-reading to your list of accomplishments?"

"Well, it seems logical. Especially since we just happen to have Allie's keys. That's why you took them out of her pocket, isn't it?"

"I'm not exactly sure why I took them," I confessed. Which was true. It just seemed like a good idea at the time. But now that we had them, we might as well use them.

So that was how we ended up in Allie's basement office in the Children's Dwelling, where the administrative offices were housed. One key had let us into the building's side door, another into the office. The old wooden door was solid and there were curtains at the window, which was set high in the wall, but I didn't feel comfortable advertising our presence by switching on the lights. Instead, I held the flashlight while Martha made two copies of each of the pages I'd taken from the portfolio.

"Two?" I asked.

"Two," Martha said firmly. "I'm mailing a set to myself, back home. Just in case."

"Good insurance," I said approvingly. In the stillness of the old building, the copy machine was loud. Hank didn't strike me as the kind of security officer who would be diligent about making the rounds, but I'd be glad when we were—

"Done," Martha said, and switched off the machine. She collated the pages, handed the originals back to me, and put the copies into a manila envelope she found in Allie's desk. She tucked the envelope under her arm and looked around, her eyes filling with tears. Resting her hand on the back of Allie's desk chair, she said, "We had so many good times together, over the years. I can't believe she's never coming back."

I flicked off the flashlight and opened the curtains partway, leaving them as we had found them. "I'll feel better when we're out of here," I growled. Ruby likes to play at being Nancy Drew, but entering a dark office with a key that belongs to a dead woman to copy a handful of her work papers is not at the top of my must-do-before-I-die list. "If we're finished, let's go."

The hallway was dark, but the Exit sign at the end of the hall gave a dull red glow, enough to see by. Then, just before we reached the stairs, I heard a sharp *click-click*—footsteps, coming down the stairs at the other end of the hall. I turned and saw the gleam of a flashlight bouncing through the dark.

"Damn." I grabbed Martha's arm, pulling her into an alcove. She started to say something, but I shushed her into silence and we both stood very still, listening to heels tapping lightly, swiftly, the steps of someone familiar with the hallway, someone who had a definite destination. The steps paused partway down the hall and I risked a glance around the corner of the alcove. A slender figure stood in front of Allie's door, a flashlight in one hand and a ring of keys in the other.

"It's Rachel," I whispered. "She's unlocking the door. She's going into Allie's office."

"This is too much," Martha said angrily, pushing past me. "I'm going to find out what she's doing there."

"Not that way," I said urgently. I seized her by the arm and propelled her up the stairs and out the side door. "We don't want her to know she's been spotted. Let's see if we can get a look through the window."

The basement window was set into a brick-lined well. Crouching, we could see down and into the room through the curtains I had conveniently left half open. It was dark out here and Rachel had turned on the desk lamp in there. What's more, she was fully occupied and not likely to look up and see us.

As we watched, Rachel sat down in Allie's chair and began methodically going through the drawers, one after another. She obviously knew what she was looking for. When she didn't find it in the desk, she got up and went to the file cabinet in the corner. She must have felt secure and unobserved in her task, for she wasn't trying to be quiet. We could hear her banging the drawers shut, one after another.

"Not a happy camper," Martha whispered gleefully.

I agreed. But there was no point in hanging around, watching Rachel hunt fruitlessly for what we already had in our possession. Besides, I was sweating under my poncho. And the drizzle had started again. It was time to get out of here.

But just as I was straightening up, Rachel's frenetic searching came to an end. She got to her feet, shaking her head. Clearly frustrated, she gave one more look around the office. A moment later, she turned off the desk lamp and left, closing the door behind her.

"Bet I know what she was looking for," Martha said grimly.

"Bet I do, too." I tugged at the sleeve of Martha's raincoat. "Come on. I'm getting wet. Let's go to my room and brew ourselves a cup of tea."

Chapter Fourteen

Sister Charity

The Shakers were among the first people in this country to gather wild herbs and roots for sale. In the earliest days of the Shakers, as was true of all rural dwellings, it was necessary to do something to earn some money, for not quite every necessity could be produced on the farm. What could have been more logical than to search the woods and fields for the herbs that everyone used for medicine and to develop those not found growing wild? Would that you might have seen the Marigolds [calendula, or pot marigold], Poppies, Foxgloves, Feverfew, Lobelia, Yellowdock and other plants growing in this garden . . .

Sister Marguerite Frost
quoted in *The Shaker Cookbook*,
Caroline B. Piercy

Most of the time, Charity was assigned to work in the garden and the Herb House, which made her very happy. She loved using her physical strength to do the needful spading, planting, raking, and hoeing, while she delighted in the warmth of the sun on her back and the playful touch of the cooling wind against her cheek. But Mother Ann's dictum, "Hands to work and hearts to God," meant that every Believer (including the elders and trustees) was expected to do every kind of labor, from cleaning the privies to working in the laundry, the dairy, and the kitchen. Charity did her turns with all the others.

This morning was the first of Charity's two-week rotation to the East Family kitchen, which she enjoyed almost as much as the garden and certainly more than the dreaded laundry, which was stifling in the summer. For one thing, being a Kitchen Sister allowed her to work with Sister Pearl and Sister Lillian, who were funny and smart. For another, it gave her a chance to learn more about what was going on in the Society, for both Lillian and Pearl always knew the latest bits of gossip and were inclined to discuss them from every angle. Suzanne's disquieting remark about the future of the village still lingered in Charity's mind, and she hoped to find out as much as she could. As well, there was another little piece of tittle-tattle she'd heard the sisters in the herb shop murmuring, which she couldn't really make sense of but which was all the more ominous for that.

So Charity was glad to be back in the kitchen, which was managed by Sister Pearl, ably abetted by Sister Lillian. Lillian was all of seventy, a brisk, excitable woman with steel gray hair and glasses. When they got together, Lillian and Pearl were talkers, like Charity's mother, who couldn't work with her hands without keeping time with her mouth. As Charity went about her own kitchen work, she listened. Indeed, she said so little and worked so quietly that the two older Kitchen Sisters often forgot she was there, and talked as if they were alone.

The kitchen—a large one—was in the basement of the East Family Dwelling. In the 1840s and '50s, it fed nearly a hundred family members, three times a day. Then, the food preparation area had been extensive and well organized, like all the other spaces the Shakers created. There was a huge cellar where food was stored in neat rows of cupboards, standing shelves, and ceiling-hung shelves screened against mice and other invaders. Great joints of cured meat, smoked in the family's own smokehouse, hung from iron hooks overhead, and the corners were filled with bins of potatoes, turnips, and carrots. Now, with fewer than thirty people living in the house, only a small portion of the storage cellar was used, but it was every bit as neat and orderly as it had been in the past.

Just outside the storage cellar stood the kitchen's wood-fired oven, built on the model of the famous oven at Canterbury Village in New Hampshire, but smaller. It was brick, with heavy cast-iron doors and revolving shelves turned by the Baking Sisters so that every pie or loaf of bread baked evenly. The oven consumed a very great deal of stove wood, so it was now fired up only once a week, when the South and East Families did their weekly baking together. The oven in the huge wood-fired kitchen range was used for the daily biscuits and other family baking.

The kitchen work began shortly after five each morning, so that the breakfast could be served on time in the two dining rooms: the large one where the brethren and sisters of the family ate in silence; the smaller one where the Recuperants took their meals. Most mornings, Charity had no difficulty climbing out of bed at the first peal of the Rising Bell. This morning, though, it had been hard to get up. Ruth had crept out the night before and was gone for two hours, and Charity had lain anxiously awake the whole time, praying for her friend's safety and trying to screw up the courage to reason with Ruth about what she was doing. But when Ruth came in, Charity found that she couldn't say a word. Long after her friend had gone to sleep, she was still awake, scolding herself for her cowardice. She was glad that mirrors were not allowed, for a mirror would have shown pale cheeks and dark circles under her eyes.

When she came into the kitchen, late, pushing her rebellious hair under her cap and adjusting her modesty kerchief, Sister Pearl gave her a long, searching look. "Get yourse'f a cup of hot coffee 'fore you start on them biscuits," she instructed, and Charity gratefully obeyed. She poured a hefty dollop of fresh cream into the cup and gulped down the burning coffee. Then she put on her kitchen smock, rolled up the sleeves of her blue work dress, and set herself to measuring flour into the large enamel basin in which the biscuits were mixed.

Pearl returned to the slices of thick bacon she was frying on a cast-iron griddle at the kitchen range. "Ruth get back to bed all right, did she?" she asked over her shoulder. "Midnight's a mite late to be goin' out for a walk, I'd say."

"How—" Charity looked up, startled. "How did you know?"

"Seed her from my winder," Pearl said. She cocked her head knowingly. "Seed that feller o' hers, too. Hope it warn't that bad man, that Will Ayers."

"Of course it wasn't," Charity said indignantly. Ruth wouldn't have anything to do with a man like Ayers. "It was Brother Charles." Then she colored and bit her lip. Charles was Ruth's secret, not hers.

"Well, that's good," Pearl said, deftly flipping bacon.

"Good!" Charity was shocked. "How can you say that?"

"Well, if it's Brother Charles—" Pearl shrugged philosophically. She still wasn't looking at Charity. "Not all B'lievers is cut out to be B'lievers, Charity. Some folks jes' gotta listen to the song o' the blood." She chuckled softly, as if to herself. "Sings purty loud, y'know. Sings purty sweet. Heard it my own self, when I was Ruth's age. You shouldn't oughtta take it to heart, girl."

"But what's going to become of her?" Charity cried, feeling hopeless. "If they're caught, they'll be made to leave! They'll be driven out!"

Pearl nodded wisely. "Like Adam and Eve, I reckon. But if Eve didn't go off with Adam, where would us be? That's how us'ns came on this ol' earth, ain't it? Adam 'n' Eve."

"But what they're doing is sinful," Charity moaned.

Pearl turned to face Charity directly. "Some folks jes' cain't stay in the garden, girl. If Ruth be bent on leavin', you give her your blessin' and let her leave."

"But I don't want her to leave," Charity blurted helplessly. "I . . . love her. I want her to stay." The tears welled up and trickled down her cheeks and a sob choked her throat.

Pearl abandoned her bacon. In two strides, she had enveloped Charity in a vast, warm embrace. " 'Course you does," she said in a comforting tone, her rough cheek against Charity's forehead. " 'Course you loves her. But sometimes when we loves somebody, the bes' thing we can do for 'em is to let 'em do what they gots to do."

Charity thought of Charles, his urgency, the hunger in his eyes, and in her mind, he was all mixed up with her father, with Sandy. "But what if she doesn't really love him?" she whispered bleakly. "What if he's . . . he's seducing her? Or forcing her? What if she leaves and then wants to come back?"

"Why, then, she'll be took back, won't she?" Pearl said in a reasonable tone. "Mount Zion ain't like the ol' Garden of Eden. Onct you's out of that, you's out to stay, an' that ol' wormwood grows up like a hedge to keep you out. B'lievers'll take anybody back if they truly wants t' come. Mother teaches that true repentance is a sign of grace. Ain't that right?"

Charity wanted to say that even if Ruth repented and came back, she would be changed. She would be . . . blemished. Soiled. But somehow she couldn't give words to the thought. And anyway, she knew it wasn't right. As a Christian, as a Shaker, she had to forgive.

Pearl gave Charity a hard squeeze and released her. "Ruth an' Charles, they gwine to do what they gwine do anyway, y'know." She laughed richly and tipped up Charity's chin. "Now, ain't they? You ever try to keep a young bull away from a heifer, girl? Human nature ain't much diff'rent. Sometimes it jes' cain't be denied."

With a last comforting squeeze, Pearl returned to her bacon, and Charity, feeling sadly confused, wiped her eyes, blew her nose, and returned to her biscuits. She wanted to accept what Pearl said. She wanted to let Ruth go with her blessing, if Ruth felt she loved Charles so much she could not live without him. But surely a warning should come before the blessing, shouldn't it? She loved Ruth—shouldn't she shout out the danger to Ruth's immortal soul?

These anxious questions were churning in Charity's insides as she rolled out a large sheet of dough and began cutting circles. She was transferring the biscuits to a baking pan when the door was flung open and Sister Lillian rushed in—not unusual, for even though Lillian was getting quite elderly, she had never gotten into the Shaker way of moving with deliberate speed. It wasn't strange, either, that her steel-rimmed glasses had slid down to the tip of her short nose, or that her white cotton cap was slightly askew. What was unusual was the worry on her face. Lillian was a bright-side person who cheerfully elbowed her way through every crisis. But this morning, she looked as anxious as Charity felt.

"Where's Hannah?" she cried.

"Good question." Pearl pointed her spoon at the list of names on the wall, where Charity's and Hannah's names appeared together next to today's date. "I've been wonderin' myself what's 'come o' that gal. She's s'posed to be in here, peelin' potatoes." Potatoes, sliced thin and fried with onion in bacon grease, were a staple on the breakfast menu.

Lillian only just managed not to wring her hands. "Hannah's room is just down the hall from mine. Her lamp was burning late in the night. I saw the light under the door when I got up to shut the window at the end of the hall. This morning, as I was going past, the door swung open. She was gone, but her bed wasn't made. The covers were all tossed about, half on the floor."

Charity frowned. Mother's teachings stressed personal neatness and cleanliness. Failing to make your bed was a sin. You did it the minute you got up, even before you began getting dressed. And when you were dressed, you swept the floor. *Then* you could leave to carry out the rest of your day's work.

Pearl shook her head darkly. "Hannah been grievin' sore over that chile. But grievin' ain't good. What that gal needs is to turn her hand to work. That's what'll ease her soul."

"Ruth is sweeping the stairs," Lillian said. "I'll send her to help with the potatoes. And I'll give Hannah your message, when I find her." She darted out of the room.

But it was Brother Lawrence who found Hannah.

Dressed in her blue work dress and white apron and still wearing her shoes, she was floating facedown at the shallow end of Zion's Pool. It could only be concluded that she had drowned herself.

AND then, if Hannah's suicide weren't enough, the South Family barn burned.

It happened that same night. Awakened just past three by the frantic pealing of the bell, Charity and Ruth hurried into their clothes and raced down the stairs. To the south, the sky was lit by the infernal glow of fire. Outdoors, Charity could see the red fingers of flames reaching up into the heavens and hear people shouting, cows bawling, and the bell urgently ringing, as if to summon the dead.

But by the time Charity and Ruth reached the barn and joined the bucket brigade that the brethren had already set up, there was little that could be done. The roof collapsed with an enormous crash, a spurt of flame, and a fountain of sparks that threatened the nearby wood-framed Dairy, with its cedar-shingled roof. The sisters raced to move the cheeses, butter, and eggs to another shed, in case the Dairy couldn't be saved.

Charity picked up a heavy crock of butter. "Were there any animals in the barn?" she asked Sister Deborah, a South Family sister with whom she had worked in the herb garden.

Sister Deborah's face was streaked with ash and her arms were laden with wrapped cheese, but she managed a thin smile. "We got the cows out, thank heavens, all of them." Then the smile faded. "But we'd just got a new wagon. That was burned, and some plows and harrows. Pray that we don't lose the Dairy."

But prayer didn't help. The wind came up, a nearby tree caught fire, and spouts of flame engulfed the Dairy. In what seemed like only an instant, that was gone, too, and they went back to their rooms, downcast and grimy, to wash and change into fresh clothes. There was no time for sleep, for the early-morning chores would have to be done and breakfast eaten before Hannah's funeral.

The graveside rites were attended only by Shakers, some of whom still had not changed their clothes after the fire. Charity had heard that Popists would not allow suicides to be buried in their cemeteries, but the Mount Zion Believers had no such qualms. Several doubted whether Hannah had gone home to Mother, but she was still buried beside her son, in a quiet corner of the graveyard, with the fresh bloom of wild-flowers all around.

Their farewells said, the brethren and sisters tried to go back to their work as if nothing had happened, although of course it had. The somber cloud of Seth's accidental death and his mother's suicide hung over them all, darkened by the shadow of the fire. It was like that for several days, a week, and nobody seemed to be able to shake it.

Charity continued her work in the kitchen, which she found comforting, with all its familiar smells, the fresh, rough textures of the vegetables, the rich heartiness of the meat. One morning, she was working there alone, while a fragrant pot of corned beef, carrots, and turnips simmered on the back of the range. With the addition of boiled potatoes and cooked cabbage, they would serve it for their midday dinner, the biggest meal of the day. She was sitting in the corner opposite the cast-iron range, with a knife, a large bowl, and a lapful of potatoes, when Pearl and Lillian came into the room. Lillian was not her usual buoyant, sprightly self, and even Pearl, determinedly cheerful, looked sad and worn down.

"I brewed a pot of tea," Charity pointed out, having already poured a cup for herself. "I put some lemon balm in it."

"Good girl," Lillian said, and slumped into a chair. "Lemon balm'll cheer us up." She sighed heavily. "It was the barn fire that done it. And Hannah's drownin'."

"Amen," Pearl agreed, pouring two more cups of tea. "Wish Hannah'd spent more time in the kitchen. She might've worked her way out o' some o' her heartache."

Lillian gave her a pretend scowl. "You think a good pie and a batch of biscuits is the answer to every spiritual dilemma, Pearl."

"Ain't that the truth," Pearl said with determined cheerfulness. "What's more, I bet if'n you'd asked Mother straight out, she'd say the same thing." She took out a plate of cookies. "Have some of these, Lillian. Eatin' 'em is jes' about as good for the soul as cookin' 'em."

"I wish it were as easy as that, Pearl," Lillian said. "It's not just the fire, you know. Or the funeral, as if that weren't enough. There's a certain

Believer I'd have in here right now, cooking *and* eating. And some good old-fashioned down-on-his-knees repentance, while he's at it."

Charity finished peeling a potato and dropped it into the pot, reaching for another one. The Kitchen Sisters had forgotten all about her, and she wasn't going to remind them.

"Brother Charles is who you're talkin' about, I reckon," Pearl said.

Lillian's sigh was heavier. "You heard about the Herb Department accounts, then? I don't know what it is these days, Pearl. I swear I don't. It almost feels like the place is infected. What we need is a good old-fashioned Sweepin' Gift. That'd get rid of it."

The Sweeping Gift, Charity knew, was something the Shakers used to do in the old days, back when the spirit filled everyone, not just a few. The sisters and brothers would arm themselves with imaginary brooms and brush out the filth of anger, lust, and greed. But what was wrong with the Herb Department accounts? She knew that Charles was in charge of keeping the records and handling whatever money came in—was there something amiss?

Pearl grunted. "We got us a problem there, I reckon."

"An ugly problem, as it turns out," Lillian replied sadly. "Elder Aaron found it when he was going over Brother Charles' account books. You know how careful Aaron is, such a stickler for getting the sums down to the exact penny." She rolled her eyes. "Which I certainly can't fault him for, although I've got so I dread it when he looks at my Housekeeping accounts, since he always seems to find something wrong and always points it out, even the littlest jot or tittle." She sipped her tea. "Not to speak ill, but I think he likes to find fault."

"Sometimes you gots to know when to stop lookin'," Pearl remarked wisely. "But that ain't Aaron's way."

"No, it's not," Lillian agreed. "But Aaron was sick last year and didn't do all his regular audits, and this is only the third year that Charles has been in charge of the Herb Department."

"So it's the first chance he's had to give Charles' books a good goin'-over," Pearl said.

Lillian nodded. "At first he thought it was just that Charles wasn't a very good bookkeeper. The invoices were all mixed up and the billings weren't in the proper order, and the payments didn't seem to match." She chuckled dourly. "If it'd been me right then, I might just've let it go, instead of trying to get everything to balance."

"Me, too," Pearl said. "I ain't much of a head for figgers."

Charity found herself agreeing. Columns of numbers gave her a headache.

"But Aaron is clever that way," Lillian said. "After he'd been through the account book several times, he said he began to see a pattern, so he set himself to working it out, like a puzzle. When he'd got it figured out, he said he could see that there was about three thousand dollars missing."

"Lord sakes a'mighty!" Pearl threw her hands up in the air. "Why, what on the good Lord's earth could a mortal man do with three thousand dollars? Where is it?"

Charity stifled a gasp. The knife fell from her hand and clattered onto the floor. Hastily, she retrieved it, but the sisters hadn't seemed to notice. Three thousand dollars was a fortune! Charles could never spend that kind of money at Mount Zion. He must be planning to leave the Society and take it with him. The minute the thought came to her, she was glad. If Charles left, Ruth would be out of danger.

"Where is it?" Lillian shook her head sadly. "I'm sure he's got it holed away somewhere. Who knows? Anyway, Aaron is going to talk to him today."

"And then what?"

"Depends, I s'pose. If Charles gives it back, he'll be free to go and that'll be the end of it. If he doesn't—" Lillian looked bleak. "Aaron says he'll have to face prosecution."

"What some folks'll get up to," Pearl said heavily. She glanced quickly at Charity, then turned back to Sister Lillian, lowering her voice. "An' what about Ruth?"

"Ruth?" Lillian blinked. "What about her?"

Charity felt a sudden icy chill. What if Charles didn't go alone? What if he insisted that she go with him? And what if Ruth knew nothing about the stolen money?

Pearl glanced up at the clock on the wall. "Land sakes, jes' look at that time!" she exclaimed, pushing herself to her feet. "We gots to start makin' dinner, Lillian." She opened a drawer, and took out a clean kitchen smock. "Gots to feed the fam'ly. An' they'll be hungry, after a good mornin's work."

Lillian put down her cup and stood, too, businesslike. "I'll cut up the cabbage and onions. And grate some horseradish, too, to go with the corned beef. Ask me, there's nothing like fresh-grated horseradish mixed with a little cream." She went to the range and lifted a lid on a pan. "Green beans," she said appreciatively. "And there's beets left from yesterday. What's for dessert?"

"I put a pot of Indian pudding in the oven afore breakfast." Pearl shook out her smock and slipped it on. "Be done by the time they's ready for it."

"Indian pudding," Lillian said approvingly. "That'll be tasty."

"Maybe it'll win a soul or two," Pearl said with a grin. To Charity, she said, "If you're done with them potatoes, girl, you can shell the rest of them fresh peas."

Charity stood. Her mind was in a whirl, her thoughts were muddled, her stomach was tied in a knot. But she tried to pretend that she had heard nothing of what Lillian and Pearl had said, and turned to her work with a determinedly steady calm.

After the noon-hour dinner there were dishes to wash, the kitchen to clean, and vegetables and fruit—strawberries, at this time of year—to gather for the next day's dinner. And then there was supper to prepare, a lighter meal, especially in the summer, when the days were longer. Following supper, there would be several hours of light left and the temperatures would be cooler, so people often went back to work. For Charity, there would be the supper dishes to do, and the preparation for the next morning's breakfast. By the time she finished, it would be nearly dark.

Sometimes, in the evening, there were meetings—the weekly Union meeting, discussions of work plans, Family meetings. Other times, Charity loved to walk to Zion's Pool through the gathering dusk, with the rich, sweet scents of the earth rising up around her and the sleepy songs of the birds settling in for the night, the softness of the twilight breeze like a benediction. Sometimes she would stop at the edge of the herb garden, where the rose petals seemed to glow in the dusk and the tiny lights of the fireflies, like happy sprites, danced in the darkening air.

But tonight, Charity didn't go to Zion's Pool or linger along the edge of the herb garden. She had thought it all through while she washed the dishes and helped Sister Pearl set a bread sponge to rise for the morning and skimmed the cream for coffee and checked to see whether they needed some fresh pints of jam. She had considered everything, everything she knew and had heard, as logically and dispassionately as she could. By the time her last chore was finished, she had made up her mind what to do.

She would tell Ruth that Elder Aaron intended to confront Charles with the fact that he had stolen three thousand dollars, which of course Ruth did not know. Three thousand dollars! It was an unthinkable amount. Charles would have to return the money, but even so, he'd be expelled from the Society, in complete disgrace. And if Charles didn't return the money? Well, then, Elder Aaron would turn him over to the sheriff. He would be prosecuted to the full extent of the law, as he rightly should be, for stealing from the Society. He would be branded publicly as a thief. And since Shakers liked their gossip as much as the World's People (even though they weren't supposed to, of course), this horrible thing was bound to be on everybody's tongue as soon as it happened. Ruth had to be warned. She had to know what was coming, so she wouldn't be dragged down into the filthy mire Charles had created for himself.

So as soon as her kitchen duties were finished, Charity took the path to the Sisters' Shop, where she knew Ruth would be working late at her loom, as she did most evenings. For the first time in several weeks, she felt her anxieties and fears flying away, like summer's leaves blown from the trees by a crisp autumn breeze. She felt bold and courageous, and as light and happy as a bird, so full of joy that she found herself actually skipping along the gravel path, for it had become clear to her that this horrible thing that Charles had done was really and truly a blessing in disguise. Perhaps it was even a gift sent by Mother Ann to free Ruth from the entangling snares of the tempter's seduction! When Ruth understood that Charles had stolen from the Society, which was the same thing as stealing from Mother Ann and from Jesus Christ, she would gladly give him up. And not only would she give him up, but she would be grateful to Charity for saving her from herself, and from him.

And then the two of them, Ruth and Charity, Charity and Ruth, would be as they had been, dearest sisters, just the two of them, just two, together. Together for always and always, safe in the peace and serene sanctity of Mount Zion.

Charity couldn't help smiling.

Chapter Fifteen

Rue lends second sight. If you carry a bundle of it, mixed with maidenhair, agrimony, wormwood, and ground-ivy, you'll be able to see into a person's heart and know whether he or she has committed a crime.

Medieval folklore

Rue is probably the most bitter plant known, but wormwood comes a close second. This is due to a compound called absinthin . . . which has a bitterness detectable at one part in 70,000. Pliny records that after Roman chariot races the victor would be given a wormwood drink, as a reminder that even victory has its bitter side.

The Book of Absinthe
Phil Baker

Before we separated on Thursday night, Martha and I spent a half hour going through Allie's working papers: six pages of computer printout, a couple of pages of what looked like a photocopied securities inventory, and two pages of handwritten notes. The securities inventory was a copy of the 706—the IRS' estate tax form that has to be filed for the estate of any decedent whose gross worth is more than a couple of million dollars. The computer printouts were copies of the latest dividend statements. The notes detailed what she had found, and the implications—talking points, I thought, for what she was planning to say at the board meeting. Allie had told us that it would be tough to know what was going on without a full-scale audit, but she felt sure that some of the stocks were missing. After a quick comparison of the inventory and the statements, I agreed. Yes, it looked like some were missing. And yes, without a full-scale audit, including a current inventory of the stock certificates in the safe deposit box, it would be difficult to know the full extent of the damage.

Martha, already numb with grief and anger over Allie's death, threw the papers down on the floor beside the rocking chair where she was sitting, her feet propped up on a small Shaker stool. She leaned her head against the rocker's back. "We're looking at a crime here, aren't we?" she asked wearily. "Apart from murder, I mean."

"Murder, we don't know about," I reminded her. "But this stuff—" I gestured to the papers on the floor and the bed, where I was lying. "I'd say yes, pending an audit."

"Pending an audit." She rubbed her hands through her short white hair, standing it on end. "Always the lawyer, aren't you?"

I frowned. I'm a great believer in keeping an option open until the door slams shut. There's no point in closing out benign explanations. "There could be other reasons for these numbers."

"Such as?"

"Careless reporting, mistakes in the original inventory, changes in valuation, incomplete paperwork, etcetera etcetera. Allie thought there was theft involved, but even she wasn't prepared to say for sure. That's what the audit is designed to show."

"So what do we do now?"

I swung my legs off the bed and sat up. I'd hung up my blouse and skirt to drip dry and was wearing one of McQuaid's T-shirts, the one I love to sleep in. "Get an audit. That's what Allie intended to recommend to the trustees."

"And now Allie's dead, murdered. Maybe." Martha regarded me warily. "Are you saying that I should make the recommendation to the trustees, in her place?"

"When's the trustees' meeting?"

"Next Wednesday. All day. We start at nine in the Trustees' Office building—there's a boardroom there. We break for lunch in the restaurant, and we're usually finished by three."

Wednesday. And today was Thursday, so we had some time to prepare. I thought about Rachel, on her knees in front of the file cabinet in Allie's office. And then I thought some more about Rachel, about how she had appointed her friends to the board, friends who would support her "change of direction" without asking questions. About how she was wearing two hats at once—a trustee's hat and a director's hat—which gave her a great deal of power. About the fact that Rachel had both keys to the safe deposit box, as well as having the foundation's financial officer in her pocket. About her interest in turning the mineral spring into an upscale spa. About—

"Yes," I said quietly. "I think you should do what Allie intended to do. Go on the record at the board meeting with the facts as we have them now, and demand a full-scale forensic audit of the stock holdings." I paused. "But I think you should talk to Rachel first. Tell her what you intend." This was a dangerous strategy—it would give Rachel time to figure out what to do. But to my mind, it beat going into the board meeting blind. This way, we'd know a lot more about what Rachel knew. And that was important.

Distractedly, Martha ran her fingers through her hair again. "Can't I just take it directly to the board? That's how Allie must have intended to do it. She was counting on Rachel being so startled that the cat would be out of the bag before anybody could stop her."

"And she was counting on having you to back her up. But if I read the players' roster right, you won't have anybody to back *you* up. I won't be there to help—I'm sure the board rules don't permit casual visitors. And everybody else sitting around that table will presumably be loyal to Rachel. They'll follow her lead. She'll quash you and there won't be anybody to say nay."

"That's certainly true." Martha looked worried. "But I don't see what's to be gained by tipping her off."

"It's dicey," I agreed. I leaned forward. "Here's my idea, Martha. The two of us will go to see Rachel. We'll tell her what Allie suspected—not the details, and we certainly won't give her any of Allie's material. You demand that she ask the board to initiate an audit. How she reacts will tell us a lot about her involvement. If she had nothing to do with filching the stocks, she'll agree, without hesitation. If she's had her hands in the foundation's cookie jar, she'll refuse."

"What do we do if she refuses?"

"We tell her that she can expect a lawsuit."

She thought about that. "What kind of lawsuit?"

"A civil suit against Rachel and the trustees, requiring an audit of the foundation's assets. The suit would also request a review of other practices of the foundation's management. And since this is a nonprofit foundation, the Feds will likely be involved. They don't look kindly on embezzlement from a nonprofit." I paused. "Usually, such a suit wouldn't be filed until a forensic accountant has examined the records. But given Allie's death—"

"Allie's murder, you mean," Martha muttered.

"Given Allie's death, and the preliminary evidence that Allie has compiled, I think it would be prudent to move swiftly. Hence the threat of a suit."

Martha slanted a look at me. "Do you think Rachel might say something that would tell us she murdered Allie?"

"She might," I said. "*If* Allie was murdered. *If* Rachel murdered her."

Martha considered this. "Then we could take our suspicions to the police."

"We could. But we'd have to have some pretty strong evidence to impress that sheriff." I stretched, glancing at the clock. Not quite midnight, but it seemed like the middle of the night. "So what's on our agenda tomorrow? Want to call Rachel and set up a time to see her?"

"There's nothing scheduled for tomorrow, thankfully. I'll arrange something with Rachel. And I'd like to go through the herb garden and maybe take a walk in the woods. The first workshop is on Monday, which gives us plenty of time. I usually plan my presentation around what's currently available for people to see and smell." She smiled. "And touch. People always enjoy petting the lambs' ears." Her smile faded. "But of course, there's Allie. Will her body be released tomorrow?"

"Not a chance. I don't know what the county's arrangements for autopsies are, but tomorrow is Friday, and then there's the weekend. It's likely that the body won't be released until next Tuesday or Wednesday." I paused. "Relatives?"

"There's just Pete. Allie's parents are dead, and she and Pete didn't have any children." Martha looked thoughtful. "I suppose the police will have notified him. I'll call him in the morning and see what he thinks we should do about a memorial service. Maybe we should have it here, in the Meeting House. Allie would like that, I think."

"Allie mentioned that her ex-husband sometimes called the office to harass her. Was there bad blood between them?"

Martha shrugged. "I wouldn't have called it murderously bad blood.

And I don't think he'd deliberately harm her. But Pete definitely has a temper problem. If they got into an argument, I suppose he might give her a shove." She frowned. "If he had something in his hand, he might even hit her with it."

"Sounds pretty murderous to me," I remarked. "If you talk to him, you might see if you can find out what he was doing last night. Just casually. Don't tip him off."

She brightened. "Oh, you mean an alibi? Sure, I can do that. I've known Pete since we were kids."

"Then it's something you should do on your own. Anyway, I have a date with Missy tomorrow morning, to look at some of the old journals. We're getting together pretty early."

If Martha had wanted to ask whether she was invited, she didn't get the chance. At that moment, her cell phone gave a couple of imperative chirps. With a frown, she reached for her bag and took out her phone. "Hello," she said. Then, "Who? Oh, yes, Jenny Trevor." She looked at me. "Yes, of course I remember. We spoke earlier this evening."

I recognized the name. It was the teenager who had left the kitchen and followed us into the hall. Martha motioned to me to come closer and held the phone out from her ear so I could hear.

"I'm really sorry for calling so late, Ms. Edmond," Jenny was saying apologetically. "I couldn't get away any earlier. I just finished my kitchen shift." She paused. "I hope you weren't asleep."

"Asleep?" Martha rolled her eyes at me. "No, I wasn't. What's on your mind, Jenny?"

The young woman's voice became guarded. "Could we talk? I mean, get together. Not talk on the phone. Like, maybe tomorrow."

"I suppose we could," Martha said carefully. "But I need to know what this is about, Jenny."

"Can't that wait until we get together?" Jenny asked. I could hear the anxiety in her voice. "I really don't want to—"

"I am not going to meet you until I know what you want to see me about," Martha said firmly.

There was a moment's silence. "It's about . . . It's about the barn," Jenny said reluctantly.

Martha was startled. "The barn that burned?"

"Yes, ma'am." Jenny cleared her throat. "Really, I don't want to talk about it on the phone."

Martha gave me an inquiring look, and I nodded. It might be important—or it might be nothing at all. But Jenny Trevor sounded as if she thought it was important. I wanted to know what she had to say.

"Where would you like to meet?" Martha said into the phone. "When?"

"Besides working in the kitchen, I'm an interpreter," Jenny said. "And a weaver. I'll be demonstrating in the Sisters' Shop tomorrow. I usually break for lunch at one. If you came then, I could hang the Closed sign on the door and we could talk without being interrupted."

I put my hand on Martha's arm and pointed to myself. "Me, too," I mouthed, silently.

"I'll be there," Martha said, and added, "I'm bringing my friend China, the woman who was with me tonight."

That brought a hasty exclamation. "Oh, but I don't want anybody else to—"

"China is helping me try to figure out what's going on here in the village."

185

"I still don't think—"

Martha was very firm. "If she can't be included, I can't see you."

The reply, when it came, was sullen. "I guess I don't have a choice, do I?"

"Good," Martha said. "We'll see you tomorrow, then, about one o'clock." She clicked off the phone and held it, frowning. "What do you suppose—?"

"I suppose we'll find out tomorrow," I said, and yawned hugely.

Martha took the hint. "Gosh, I'm tired, too." She pushed herself out of the chair, shaking her head bleakly. "Poor Allie. Poor, sweet Allie. Who would've believed, when we started the day so cheerfully, that we'd end it with her murder."

I held up my hand, cautioning. "Let's not jump to conclusions."

She gave me a fierce look. "Allie was murdered," she said between clenched teeth. "She was murdered, and you know it."

"Murdered?" McQuaid asked sharply, when I got him on the phone a few minutes after Martha had gone across the hall to her own room.

"That's what it looks like to me," I said, and outlined the situation— enough of it, anyway, to give him an idea of what was going on.

"What do the cops say?"

"They don't. The sheriff would have preferred to have stayed indoors, out of the rain, and the deputies got right to work muddying up the crime scene."

McQuaid sighed. "Typical." He knows investigations aren't always done the way he would do them, if he were the detective in charge.

"Yes," I said. "However, I was able to get my hands on what Martha and I think might be the motive."

I could almost hear him frowning. "Just how did you manage that?"

I thought swiftly. McQuaid still thinks like a cop. If I told him I had searched Allie's cottage, he'd come down on me like a ton of bricks for trespassing on a crime scene. For obstructing justice. So I fudged.

"Allie left her working papers where she knew I'd find them," I said. Which was true. Otherwise, how could I have known to look under her mattress? "When Lottie's estate filed its 706, she made a copy of the securities inventory. Plus, she obtained copies of the current dividend reports. The two don't match up."

"Ah," McQuaid said, and came to the same conclusion I had. "Somebody's been dipping into the till. Naughty-naughty." He paused. "Speaking of naughty," he said in his sexiest voice, "are you naked?"

I giggled. "My, how you talk."

"I can do better, wife."

"I know you can, my love. I really wish you were here." It was true. If I had insisted to Martha that McQuaid come along, he'd have the mystery of Allie's death solved in no time. And he'd have Rachel nailed before you could say— I made myself stop. I'd already cautioned Martha at leaping to conclusions.

"I wish I were there, too." His voice deepened. "I'd lick you all over. And over. And over."

"Ah," I said, and we were both quiet for a moment, contemplating this pleasure.

"But I'm not there," he said regretfully, and his tone changed again. Now it was his cop's voice. Tough and hard. "Listen, China, whatever you think about that sheriff and his deputies, I want you to leave this investigation to them. You hear? And if you have anything relating to their case—as in motive, for instance—you need to hand it over."

"I don't think you understand," I said. "Those cops would never in a million years be able to deal with this stuff. It's going to take a forensic accountant to sort it out."

"So get a forensic accountant," McQuaid said. "But tell the cops, too."

"I'll take it under advisement," I replied evenly.

"You heard me," McQuaid said. Then, relenting, added, "Now can I tell you my news?"

"Sure. What?"

"Caitlin's here."

"Caitlin?" I was surprised. "For how long?"

"Until Marcia gets out of the hospital."

"Oh, gosh," I breathed. I knew that she hadn't been well, and that Miles' death had set her back. But beyond that, I was clueless. "Has Marcia told you what's wrong?"

"No. Tests, she told me. Just tests. I didn't want to be nosy."

"I wish she'd said something about this before I left," I said, annoyed. "I wouldn't have come."

"Maybe that's why she didn't," McQuaid remarked dryly. "Or maybe she didn't know this was going to happen. Anyway, Caitlin didn't have anywhere else to go, so I volunteered. She's sleeping in the guest room, and she and Brian and I are doing stuff together."

"What kind of stuff?"

"Today we went tubing on the San Marcos River. Tonight we had a barbecue. Tomorrow night we're going to Sheila's for a neighborhood picnic. That kind of stuff."

"Maybe I should come back," I said, thinking of Caitlin.

"What? You think I can't handle a girl-child?" McQuaid laughed. "I raised Brian, you know. Single-handed, until you came along. Damn good job, too."

It was true. McQuaid and Sally, his first wife, were divorced when Brian was in preschool, and McQuaid got custody. He's done a great job with the boy. I knew that he might have wanted more children, too—but for me, having babies wasn't an option. I lucked out with Brian, who came to me already raised, as it were. But being a mom still bewilders me, and the idea of joining the Diaper Brigade when I was forty (my age when I married McQuaid) held absolutely no appeal.

"You did a wonderful job with Brian," I said. "I'm eternally grateful for the way you raised him. So yes, I know you can handle Caitlin. It's just that . . . well, she's my problem, not yours. I'm sorry she's been imposed on you. Sorry I'm not there to help out."

"Forget that," McQuaid said gruffly. "She's a good kid who's been dealt a very bad hand. I'm glad to help." He paused. "But do me a favor, huh? Get your workshops over with, enjoy yourself, and come home. And don't play cops and robbers. This isn't your affair. It could be dangerous."

"Yes, sir," I said meekly.

"You'll do it?"

"No, sir," I said. "But thanks all the same. I appreciate your concern."

"Sometimes I don't know how we stay married," he growled.

"It's all that good sex," I replied wisely. "You can't get enough of my body."

"You've got a point there." He laughed, and with that, we said good night.

My next thought was of Ruby, but all I got was her answering machine. "Hi," I said, in reply to her recorded message. "Hey, Ruby, it's me. I've had a dream and it's bothering me, big-time. I thought maybe my favorite dream interpreter could tell me what it means. I'll give you a call tomorrow. I'm ready for bed now."

I was tired, but my mind was full of a confusion of whirling images, and sleep was a long time coming. I kept seeing Allie, brusque and confi-dent, sure she was on to some financial monkey business—and Allie, facedown in Zion's Pool, the figure in the yellow raincoat I'd glimpsed in that inexplicable dream.

I did finally sleep. But when I dreamed, it was a gentler, sweeter dream. I was wearing that blue Shaker dress and a white apron and cap, but now I was exhilarated, ecstatic, victorious. I was walking—no, skipping, so light on my feet that I fairly flew—through a summer evening, dark fall-ing over a garden lit by fireflies, on my way to see someone I loved.

I had a message for her, a very important message, but for the life of me, I couldn't remember what it was.

Chapter Sixteen

Eldress Olive

Among the herbs we grow [at Mount Lebanon Shaker Village, New York], hyoscyamus [henbane], bella donna, tarazacum [dandelion], aconite, poppies, lettuce, sage, summer savory, marjoram, dock, burdock, valerian, wormwood, and horehound occupy a large portion of the ground; and about fifty minor varieties are cultivated in addition, as rue, borage, carduus (*Benedictus*), hyssop, marsh-mallow, feverfew, pennyroyal, etc. Of indigenous plants we collect about two hundred varieties . . .

American Journal of Pharmacy, 1852

Hannah Chandler's burial had been very difficult for Olive. The young woman's suicide, coming so swiftly after the sad death of little Seth, seemed the crowning tragedy in an endless procession of tragedies, and she felt a heavy burden of guilt. Olive knew in her heart that she should have seen it coming, should have been aware of the potential danger. She might have counseled Hannah, set a watch over her, perhaps even brought her into her own retiring room to sleep.

"You mustn't feel this way," Elder Aaron told her bleakly, when she confessed her guilt to him in the small first-floor office where the two of them met several times a week to talk over family problems—"labor over" them, as Aaron put it, since spiritual direction was as true and sacred a labor as any labor the Shakers turned their hands to. Like all the other rooms in the East Family Dwelling, the office was very plain, containing nothing but a table for the elders' papers and writing supplies and the two chairs they had taken down from the wall pegs and placed at right angles to each other, close enough to make conversation easy, far enough apart so that there would be no accidental touching.

"If anyone is at fault, Olive, it is I," he went on sadly. "Hannah came to me for study and spiritual guidance, in preparation for signing the Covenant. I knew she was in distress. I should have provided sufficient comfort for her to weather the storm in her soul. I failed her." He rested his elbows on his knees and dropped his face into his hands.

Olive regarded him with concern, seeing him with some shock, as if for the first time. She had known Aaron Babbitt since he came to Mount Zion in the prime of his life, a vital, energetic man, firm in his faith and constant and unstinting in his care for others. He was no more than five or six years her senior, but now he seemed terribly old. His face was lined and gray, his shoulders were slumped, and his hands trembled. His clothing hung loose on his frame, and she realized that he had been losing weight for some time. Suddenly, she was frightened. Everyone at Mount Zion depended on him for leadership. And in spite of the fact that she sometimes resisted his conservative inclinations—old-fashioned, she often thought him, backward-looking—she depended on him even more than the others.

Impulsively, Olive put out her hand and rested it lightly on his arm, feeling the warmth of his flesh through the cotton of his sleeve. They had long since called each other by their given names when they met in private, for the formal mode of address was cumbersome. But in the two decades they had worked closely together—five years as elder and eldress, fifteen years as the family's trustees—this was the first time she had ever deliberately touched him. Against the Society's rules or not, she knew how urgently he was in need of comfort.

"Don't berate yourself, please, Aaron," she said in a low voice. "There was nothing you could do for her." Hearing the words, she knew they were true—and true for her, as well. Hannah Chandler, lovely, eager young Hannah, had been mistress of her own fate. No matter how truly she had been counseled, how carefully she had been watched, she could not have been restrained from taking her life, if that was what she was bent on doing.

There was a long pause. Olive saw that tears were trickling down Aaron's lined cheeks. To her great surprise, he placed one work-worn hand over hers. For precious moments they sat this way, as Olive felt herself enveloped in an astonishing cloak of love and closeness—the kind of intimacy, it seemed to her, that long-married couples must share in times of sorrow. Then Aaron removed his hand from hers, and looked her full in the face.

"Thank you, Olive," he said somberly. "I suppose you are right." He wiped his eyes with his sleeve and bowed his head, as if in prayer. After a moment, he lifted his head, cleared his throat, and made an obvious effort to return to business as usual. "There are several other urgent matters we must discuss. I spent a few moments before breakfast with Elder Benjamin. The sheriff has ruled that the fire at the barn was deliberately set."

"Oh, no," Olive exclaimed in dismay. "Oh, Aaron, that's terrible! Who could have done such a thing?"

It wouldn't be the first time that village buildings had been set afire. In the early days, when the people in the area resented their coming, such things happened often. Barns and other outbuildings had been lost, and dwellings and animals had been destroyed. But times change and people change, and the Believers had long been accepted as helpful, productive neighbors. What made this worse, of course, was the fact that the barn, which was much too large, was only a few years old. Both the barn and the Dairy had been built with the money old Elder Thomas had borrowed so ill-advisedly from the bank. Elder Thomas was dead and now the buildings were gone, too. But the loan still had to be repaid.

Aaron got up from his chair and went to stand by the window, looking out at the herb garden, at the blooming roses along the fence. Olive's question—"Who could have done such a thing?"—hung in the air between them, but he didn't answer it, not directly. Instead, after a long moment, he said over his shoulder, "I encountered Will Ayers yesterday. At Zion's Pool."

Will Ayers. Olive frowned. Was Aaron suggesting, without actually saying so, that he was the one who set fire to the barn? Aloud, she said, "I thought Will Ayers was supposed to stay away from the village! After what he did to Sister—"

"He says he does not consider the spring to be a part of the village," Aaron said somberly. "He considers it to be his property, which by rights, I suppose, it is. Or will be, in a few months." He shoved his hands into his pockets, and Olive noticed the slump in his shoulders. "He was looking over the cottages. They will be razed when he builds his hotel—at least, that's what he says."

Olive lifted her chin. She had finally forced herself to accept the fact of the lease and the inevitability of losing the spring. But she still could not believe that Will Ayers would build a hotel, so far from town and so close to the village.

"That's all a lot of empty talk," she scoffed. "That man doesn't have the money to build a hotel, or the business sense to run one. It's only a scheme, Aaron, just pie in the sky. Nothing is going to come of it." She didn't say so, but she was hoping that after a period of time, when Will Ayers' foolish dreams had played themselves out, he'd be willing to lease the spring back to them.

"He says he has backers, Olive." Aaron did not turn around. "Investors—a banker in Lexington, and some others—who are willing to put up whatever it costs. They're going to manage it, too. The papers have already been signed."

Investors! Olive bit her lip. She had not imagined that Will Ayers would be able to sell his idea to anyone else. But surely, when his investors found out just how far the property was from town, they would change their minds. City folks might talk on telephones and drive automobiles instead of horses and switch on electric lights at night. But Mount Zion had neither telephones nor electric lights, and ten miles of unimproved road lay between them and the nearest paved highway. They were still remote. And that remoteness might be their best defense.

She laughed lightly. "I don't think we have anything to be concerned about, Aaron. The spring is too far off the highway, and the road is bad. What's more, hotel guests will expect electricity and a telephone. Surely the investors will realize that."

Wearily grim, Aaron turned to face her. "Ayers says that the power and telephone companies have already agreed to install their lines, and the investors are planning to build a macadam road from the highway. He expects that people will drive over from Lexington to spend the day, as well as stay for several days at the hotel." He paused, and when he spoke again, his voice was lower, and trembling. "He says that lots of people will come just to see the Shaker village."

Olive stared at him, hardly able to believe her ears. A road? A paved road? If that happened, not only would they lose the spring and its sustaining revenue, but they would be forced to endure an endless parade of noisy, smoky, smelly automobiles. And worse, for the automobiles would be filled with curious passengers who wanted to see for themselves how those crazy Shakers lived. Even the Recuperants, few as they were, often made nuisances of themselves, asking nosy questions, peering into windows, intruding into the privacy of the dwellings.

But if Will Ayers built the hotel and if a road made access easy, there wouldn't be just a few nosy Unbelievers poking around. There would be hordes of them. The village would be invaded, overrun. And if they built fences and posted guards, the effort to keep people out would quickly become a regular preoccupation, then an obsession. One way or another, their lives would be taken over. There would be no more peace at Mount Zion.

Aaron was obviously thinking the same thing, for he made a low sound in his throat, almost a growl. "It will be a circus, Olive. And we will be the center ring."

Olive clenched her hands into fists. "There must be some way to keep this from happening," she said fiercely.

"If there is, I haven't been able to think of it," Aaron said. "But there is another alternative for us."

"What?"

"We can sell."

"Sell?" She repeated the word stupidly, sure she hadn't heard correctly.

Aaron pulled in his breath and let it out in one long exhale. "Ayers says that his investors are prepared to make an offer for the village."

Olive rose from her chair and took two steps toward him, uncomprehending. Surely she hadn't heard what she thought she had heard. "You can't be saying that we should sell Mount Zion!"

"He has made a fair offer. A hundred and thirty dollars an acre for the land."

Olive's eyes widened. "A hundred and thirty—" Breathing heavily, she retreated to her chair again. She had not imagined that their land was worth so much. But still—

"Plus eight hundred for each of the larger buildings." Aaron's chuckle was ironic. "Of course, now that the barn is gone, that's eight hundred dollars less Ayers would have to pay."

"You're not suggesting that the fire was related to . . . to this offer, are you?"

"No, but it might have been. The offer is fair, but Ayers himself is not a fair man, nor good, as we know to our sorrow. I believe him fully capable of setting fire to the barn, as a warning of what might happen if we don't sell." He paused. "If we accept, the funds will be payable when we leave the village, which we could delay for up to a year. But the offer is good for only two weeks. After that, it will be withdrawn." His mouth tightened. "Or so Ayers says. He promises to tender it in writing early next week. The money will be put in escrow at the bank."

Olive gave her head a violent shake. "It doesn't matter what is offered, Aaron. Mount Zion is our home, and more. We cannot—"

"We cannot ignore the fact that the world is changing around us, Olive," Aaron said with heavy regret. He came back to his chair and sat down wearily. Folding his arms across his chest, he said, "As you know, the Society at Pleasant Hill closed two years ago. The members had grown so old and so few that it was impossible to go on."

Olive didn't need to be reminded. She heard regularly from Sister Mary Settles, one of the dozen elderly Shakers who were living at Pleasant Hill when it closed. They had sold off their land and deeded what was

197

left—some 1,800 acres—to a man who lived at Harrodsburg, in return for the promise that he would take care of them for the rest of their lives. It was a risk, but so far, at least, the man had honored the agreement.

"Of course I know about Pleasant Hill," she said. "And I know that our numbers are declining here at Mount Zion. But we are far more viable than the Pleasant Hill Society, Aaron. We have several energetic, dedicated younger members, like Sister Charity and Sister Ruth."

"And Brother Charles?" Aaron put in wryly. "He will not be with us long."

Olive's mouth tightened. Of course Brother Charles would have to go, but that was not the point. "We don't have to make a decision now, do we? We have more years to—"

"Union Village in Ohio has closed, and the Society at Shirley, Massachusetts," Aaron interrupted, his voice firm and hard. "And yesterday, I received a letter from the Ministry at Mount Lebanon. If we wish to close our Society here at Mount Zion, they will extend a warm welcome to all who care to live out the rest of their days with them." He smiled wearily. "My sister Priscilla tells me that they would be especially happy to welcome you, Olive."

Olive turned her head away, feeling almost breathless. Mount Lebanon—New Lebanon, it had been called in the old days—was the home of the Shakers' Central Ministry, the heart of the United Society of Believers. She had lived and worked there for three years when she was a young woman, learning how to grow herbs and helping with the extensive catalog that advertised the Shaker herbs and medicines. She had loved the sweet order of the gardens and orchards, the prosperity and abundance of the vineyards and fields, the neatness and cleanliness of the streets and well-maintained buildings. In her mind, Mount Lebanon was a paradise on earth. Priscilla's invitation was a powerful temptation.

But if she accepted now, she would be abandoning older Believers, like faithful Pearl and Lillian. And younger ones, like Charity and Ruth, who might one day make important contributions to the Society as a whole. She turned to face Aaron. "But surely, surely we are not yet at a point where this decision must be made," she argued. "Our family is nearly thirty, and the South Family—"

"The South Family lost three yesterday," Aaron said. "They are now just thirteen. Elder Benjamin proposes that the South Family Dwelling be closed and the remaining family members be moved here. And after the barn burning, I have to agree. For everyone's welfare, it must be so."

"Yes, of course," Olive hastened to say. It only made sense. The North Family had closed some time before, so there were only the two families left. Their dwellings were large and difficult to heat in the winter. The laundries had already been consolidated some time ago, and it would be much more efficient to manage a single large kitchen, rather than two smaller ones. Sister Pearl, for one, would be glad to have a larger family to cook for. And perhaps the consolidation would buy them a few more years here at Mount Zion.

But Aaron shook his head. As if he were reading her mind, he said, "Bringing the families together in one dwelling does not solve our central problem, Olive." His voice was softer and more gentle than she could remember. "Besides the possibility of selling our land at an advantageous price and avoiding the threat of the Unbelievers who would besiege us when the hotel is built, there is something else. I have been reluctant to tell you this, but I cannot delay any longer."

Struck with apprehension, Olive leaned forward. "What is it, Aaron?"

His intent gaze held hers. "I have been consulting with Dr. Barnard. There is a cancer in my stomach. The good doctor cannot tell me how much longer I will be able to continue in my work, but speaks of months, rather than years."

"A . . . a cancer!" Olive gasped. "Months?" She pulled in her breath, feeling the room tilt around her, as if they were in the midst of an earthquake. "Oh, Aaron!"

He took her hand. "I do not fear death, Olive. Speaking for myself alone, I am ready to go to Mother, contentedly, even joyfully. But there is the urgent question of leadership. Benjamin is nearly eighty and has not the strength to carry his present load, let alone take on the village. I had hoped that Brother Charles would grow to fill my place, but—" His eyes darkened. "You know the story there. I have spoken to Charles, and one way or the other, he will be leaving us soon. Brother Alfred is not a leader, nor are any of the other brethren. Of the sisters, there is only yourself, Olive. When I have gone home to Mother, you will have to carry on here alone. Are you ready to face that prospect, given the complications of the loss of income from the spring and the likelihood that the hotel will bring hordes of the World's People to the village—as well as our declining membership?"

Olive stared hopelessly at him, unable to comprehend so much, coming all at once. It would all be on her shoulders, the whole heavy load. What could she say? What could she do?

"You must not answer now," Aaron said. "You must pray about this, as shall I. But even a bad man can accomplish some good. The money we receive from him could be used to repay the note to the bank. What is left—and the amount would be substantial—could be divided among us, as has been done elsewhere. Those who wished—you, Charity, Ruth, Pearl, Lillian, and others—could go to Mount Lebanon. And people who wanted to return to the World would have enough for a new start."

Olive still could not speak. It was utterly unthinkable. But so was the alternative. A hotel at the spring. A road along the edge of the village. Automobiles and endless noise and prying, peering people of the World. But much worse, unimaginably worse: Mount Zion without Aaron.

At last she said, "How long . . . How long did you say that we have to decide about selling?" She took a deep breath. "Perhaps if we wait, Ayers' investors will think better of the idea. Perhaps he will not be able to get the money to build his hotel, or the road. Perhaps—"

"Perhaps the Resurrection will come," Aaron said with a small smile. "But I fear that we cannot hope for such a happy release, Olive. We must be realistic. With or without the spring, with or without Ayers' hotel, our options are limited by our age and declining numbers." He paused. "We have two weeks to decide whether to take the offer. If we do, we have a year to sort out arrangements and settle things. *You* have a year," he added with a brutal emphasis. His implication, *I may not have that long*, echoed silently between them.

Suddenly, it was all too much. Olive jumped out of her chair, the red-hot rage inside her boiling so close to the surface that she feared it would explode.

"I hate this!" she cried. "I don't want to hear another word!" She bolted from the room, leaving Aaron sitting in his chair, as stunned by her outburst as if she had slapped him hard across the face.

Out in the empty, silent hallway, Olive leaned her forehead against the wall and let the burning tears erupt. She didn't want Aaron to see her cry, for none of this was his fault. He couldn't help getting old and infirm, no more than she could. He couldn't help dying and leaving her to struggle through the cold, bleak future alone, faced with the impossible task of trying to keep everyone together here at Mount Zion or letting herself take the easy way out: give up their home, break up their family, and go back to Mount Lebanon. The easy way out, but the road to defeat.

It's all Will Ayers' doing, she thought furiously, and pounded her fists against the wall in a storm of helpless frustration. Will Ayers, that evil, immoral man, the personification of evil, the serpent in the Garden. It's a good thing he was somewhere else at the moment, for if he were here, Olive would take down the nearest chair from its pegs and break it over his wicked, wretched head. She would beat him with the pieces until he cried for mercy.

Shaker teaching forbade the laying on of hands in anger, and Olive had never struck another person in her life.

But even Mother would forgive her if she broke the rule and smashed Will Ayers in his ugly face.

Chapter Seventeen

Entries from the East House Family Journal

Pleasant Hill Shaker Village, Kentucky
1848–1850

June 24, 1848. Went after elder flowers.

Sept. 7, 1848. Went to the cliff pasture after life everlasting, found lobelia there very unexpectedly.

October 24, 1848. Produce for sale, 529 pounds of herbs.

July 25, 1849. Gathered sage and other herbs in the garden. The largest cutting ever known.

Sept. 29, 1849. Gathered hops, grapes and walnut roots for dye. Went after herb roots with Joel and three sisters and all the boys, but got none.

May 1, 1850. Trimmed off the thyme and tanzy in John's garden. Cut herbs, burned caterpillars, gathered hoarhound, tanzy, bugleweed in the hen lot, cleaned herb house and press house.

June 16–19. Gathered and shipped off catnep, gathered sage, thyme and other garden herbs.

Quoted in *Shaker Medicinal Herbs*
Amy Bess Miller

Breakfast began at eight, Martha had told me, so we planned to meet in the restaurant at eight fifteen. She'd invited me to go for an early walk with her, but I had something else to do, and I intended to do it by the dawn's early light, when nobody else was around. I slept well, and the only dream I could remember was a happy dream of skipping down a pretty green path—thankfully, there were no more dreams of drownings. I was awakened by the insistent chirping of a noisy robin in the tree outside my window, and when I rolled over and peered at the clock, it was five forty-five. The sun wasn't yet up, but the predawn sky was light. Light enough for what I needed to do.

I got up, splashed water on my face, ran a comb through my hair, and pulled on a pair of jeans, a T-shirt and the brown sweater-vest, and sneakers. Quietly opening my door, I slipped out into the hall. There had to be at least a few guests sleeping behind the closed doors, but the large, dim building had an eerie feeling of emptiness as I crept silently down the stairs. The walls were pure white, the woodwork and floors gleamed softly, the banisters swept in the graceful curve of an angel's wing down three flights of stairs. I had to admire the serene simplicity, the symmetrical flow of space, the subtlety of fine details. Surely the many members of the East Family who had lived and worked in this huge house would not have wanted to leave here when they died. I could almost feel the force of their longing spirits. I pushed that thought out of my mind. I wasn't anxious to meet a Shaker ghost.

Outside, the morning air was cool and sweet, washed by the night's rain, and the early-morning stillness lay across the landscape like a blessing. The roses beside the path filled the air with a sweetly seductive scent. Everything was so peaceful, I thought. It was easy to believe that nothing disquieting, nothing alarming, nothing evil had ever happened here.

And yet Martha's friend Allie had died the night before, murdered, perhaps, to keep her from revealing the theft of a considerable amount of stock from the foundation's endowment fund. The killer? Well, I wouldn't go so far as to name names, but after what I had seen in Allie's office, I certainly had my suspicions.

And what had happened last night only reminded me, in case I had forgotten, that the Utopian serenity around me was somewhere between truth and lies. It was a carefully planned illusion, designed to create the impression of Shaker harmony, peace, and goodwill—the impression of a long-dead past. But there's a difference between appearance and reality. Mount Zion was a reconstruction, a museum, a tourist destination, like Williamsburg or the Alamo. While it might be more to my liking than, say, Disneyland, what I saw around me was more like a theme park than it was like the original Shaker village. The "Shakers" were costumed employees or volunteers; most of the furniture was reproduction.

And behind the scenes was something dark, ominous, and evil. Last night it had reached out and killed a woman. I might have my suspicions, but that wasn't good enough. I needed to know why and who.

I pulled in a breath of sweet, clean air and picked up my pace, walking fast, with purpose. I passed the conference center, remembering that I had a date to visit Missy Thatcher there later this morning. I passed the Shaker graveyard (did Brother Joshua go abroad during the day, or just at night?), and in a few moments I was following the corkscrew path down to Zion's Pool, where the water was so clear and blue and transparently innocent that it was difficult to imagine that Allie had died there last night. Like everything else in the village, what you saw was deceptive. You couldn't trust it.

But there was the cops' yellow crime-scene tape, declaring the pool off-limits and giving reality to what might have seemed like a bad dream. The path up the hill to the cottage was not cordoned off, however, which made me think that the police were operating under the theory that Allie's death was an accident. I shook my head, imagining what McQuaid would say about this kind of sloppy investigation. No doubt he'd tell me to stay off the hill and away from the cottage and give the police time to come back and make another, more thorough search. But McQuaid wasn't here, and I was. And there was something I needed to do.

I crossed the footbridge and headed up the path on the other side of the pool, stopping first at the place where I had spotted Allie's loafer the night before. Yep, there was the shoe, half hidden under a fern. Not surprisingly, the cops had missed it when they were blundering around in the dark. I left it where it was and moved to the other side of the path, to the patch of crushed mint that had attracted my attention the previous night. I knelt down among the leaves to make a careful search, going over the ground inch by inch, finding absolutely nothing but the usual litter of pebbles, twigs, rotting leaves, and a variety of ants, snails, and scurrying beetles.

But after a few moments I began to be aware of more. Of the pale green light filtering through the foliage canopy overhead. Of the enveloping silence, broken only by the flutelike whistles and high, liquid trill of a wood thrush. Of the imperative *rat-a-tat-tat* of a woodpecker, the fruity scent of mint, and the rich, peaty smell of damp earth and decaying leaves. Of the crystalline glitter of a fragile cobweb, catching the light as if it were a dream. Of trillium and plantain and wild lobelia, with its pale blue bloom. And goldenseal and winter fern and wild ginger, and even the magical white wand of devil's bit—valuable herbs that would have been gathered and used by the Shakers for ointments, salves, and poultices, among other things. I was crouched in the center of a charmed circle of rich and fruitful beauty.

Well. If I hadn't found anything else but these lovely plants, there was enough here to reward me for the effort of coming. I reached out to brush the tiny white flowers of the devil's bit, so called because the root looks like something—or someone—bit it nearly in half. And then I got lucky.

On top of the leaves lay a thin metal strip a quarter-inch wide and about three-quarters of an inch long, blue. It was tapered, with openings at both ends, one wide, one narrow. The wider opening was empty. The narrower had a two-inch piece of blue cord looped through it. I recognized it immediately, and you would, too, if you'd seen it. A zipper tab. The thingy you pull when you zip your jacket. The thingy that sometimes comes loose in your hand, or falls off when you're not noticing, which means that your zipper is hard to pull up and down.

And then I got even luckier, for a few inches away from the zipper tab I found a cigarette butt. It was wet from the rain and smoked almost down to the filter, but not quite far enough to burn away the brand name. Pall Mall. Ugly, yes. Disgusting, yes (at least, to this nonsmoker). But the sight of it made me very happy, for where there is a cigarette butt, there is also and inevitably DNA—usable DNA, too. The courts have concluded that when you abandon your DNA, as on an envelope you've licked or a cup you've thrown in the trash or a cigarette you've tossed aside, it's free booty to anybody who wants it, including the cops.

But then I remembered that Allie was a smoker, and I felt a little less lucky. It was entirely possible that the butt was hers, and that she'd carelessly flicked it into the woods on her way to or from work.

But maybe not. Maybe it had been dropped by the killer. And now I was hung on the horns of an uncomfortable dilemma, suspended by something called a chain of custody. If I took possession of what I'd found—the zipper pull-tab and the cigarette butt—it would never be of use in a prosecution. Heck, it couldn't even be introduced into evidence.

If I didn't take it, and instead told the cops where it could be found, the defense attorney—oh, that wily, diabolical bastard—would argue that it could have been planted there to incriminate his client.

I contemplated this distasteful catch-22 for a moment. I made a mental note of the spot where the cigarette lay (three inches to the left of the zipper tab, at the foot of the devil's bit), and turned my back on it. I'd have to trust that the prosecutor's case, if there ever was one, would be strong enough to stave off the arguments of that wily defense attorney. Feeling heartened by my find and virtuous for having let it lie, I searched for another few minutes. When nothing turned up, I quit and headed up the path toward the cottage.

The key was still under the flowerpot, so I let myself in and spent the next thirty minutes (being careful to leave no prints) going through the cottage once more. If there was anything important to find—anything that might shed some light on the identity of Allie's killer—I failed to spot it. But in some circumstances, even the things you don't find have significance. There were no blue jackets—with or without their zipper tabs—in her closet. And when I checked the butts in the ashtray on the coffee table, I discovered that Allie smoked Marlboro Lights. The cigarette butt awaiting discovery by the local county mounties had not belonged to her.

Locking the door behind me, I headed down the hill and across the bridge, in the general direction of breakfast. I was empty-handed, but I wasn't downhearted. It was three minutes after eight, and I could reasonably expect that a county official would be in his office, no matter how late he'd worked the night before. So I fished my cell phone and Sheriff Franklin's card out of my fanny pack and punched in his number.

After a brief delay, the sheriff himself came on the line. I identified myself and reported, in a factual way, what I had found on the hill above the pool.

"Oh, yeah?" he growled. "If that stuff was there last night, how come the deputies didn't find it? I sent 'em up there to search."

Tactfully, I didn't answer.

After a moment, and to his credit, the sheriff gave a gruff chuckle. "Yeah, well, it was a rotten night. Rain and dark and all. I wouldn't be surprised if something got missed. I'll come out myself and take a look. But we've got a situation here, and I can't get away for another couple of hours. Can you meet me there, say, eleven?"

"Works for me," I said, and clicked off the phone, thinking better of him.

THERE were only a few people in the dining room when we arrived, but as the hour went on, they came straggling in for the abundant and attractive breakfast buffet. By the time Martha and I were finished eating, the room was nearly half full of people who had stayed overnight at Mount Zion, evidence that the inn business was meeting with some success. I didn't say anything to Martha about my finds or my date with Sheriff Franklin. I thought it would be easier for her to learn the outcome, rather than get a progress report.

It wasn't an entirely comfortable breakfast. Martha was in a somber mood, obviously thinking about her friend's death and the encounter with Rachel that lay ahead. I had the sheriff on my mind, and my visit with Missy Thatcher. And later today, Martha and I were supposed to talk to Jenny Trevor, who might or might not have something interesting to tell us.

But the food was good and we managed to keep the conversation going. After breakfast, Martha suggested that we take a look at the herb garden. "I don't think I'll find any surprises," she said, "but I always like to check. And I'd prefer to do it now, before the tourists are out and about."

So we went outside and walked along the street until we reached the square fenced garden, which lay near the Sisters' Shop. It was simple, orderly, and beautifully cared for. Four raised beds were arranged around a trellised climbing rose, with neatly clipped grass paths between the beds. Each bed contained herbs used for a particular purpose: medicinal herbs, tea herbs, culinary herbs, and fragrance herbs. In the tea bed, I spotted lemon balm, lavender, catmint, spearmint, and strawberries. The medicinal bed contained foxglove, feverfew, wormwood, and boneset. Lavender, rosemary, dill, and lemon balm grew in the fragrance bed, around a clump of peonies. And the culinary bed was lush and green with familiar cooking herbs: parsley, sage, thyme, basil, oregano, summer and winter savories, and garlic, most of which the Shakers would have used as medicinal herbs. The corners of the garden were filled with rhubarb's green and red foliage, the large, floppy leaves of comfrey, and the fuzzy green rosettes of mullein, which wouldn't push up their distinctive bloom stalks for another couple of months. There were several artemisias: wormwood, mugwort, tarragon, and southernwood—lad's love, it's sometimes called, a name I find charming. But there wasn't a weed in sight.

I thought ruefully of the weeds in my gardens back home. "What I need is a Shaker-trained gardener," I grumbled. "Look at this. No weeds, and everything is beautifully trimmed. I am so envious."

"What you need is a team of volunteers," Martha said wisely. "You could trade herb lessons and workshop fees, and maybe even plants, for help in the garden—that's what we do here. Why don't you talk to Jane?

She's the one who manages our volunteers. She'll be glad to tell you how she handles it."

"Good idea," I said. "You may have just solved a very big problem." Not only a big problem, but a problem that was growing bigger by the minute. Weeds have a tendency to do that, especially when my back is turned. "This is your demonstration garden?"

Martha nodded. "The Shakers grew their cash crops—lavender, sage, mustard, horseradish, and so on—in the fields behind the West Family Dwelling." She paused. "Actually, the Kentucky Believers never got quite as involved with herb production as the Shakers at Canterbury and Mount Lebanon. They did grow quite a bit, and of course they wild-gathered, as well. I've been reading Amy Beth Miller's book on Shaker herbs. She quotes some entries from a journal that was kept at Pleasant Hill in the late 1840s. It's amazing, the herbs those folks grew or gathered. At one point, they had more than five hundred pounds of dried plant material for sale. Can you imagine harvesting and processing that much? The labor that went into it must have been colossal."

I surveyed the garden. "Looks to me like you've got everything you could possibly need for Monday's workshop."

"More than I need, really. In fact, this part of the workshop is embarrassingly easy. The herbs are right here in front of us, and all the people have to do is walk along, take notes, and ask questions. We'll show them which herbs to gather for the afternoon session, and they'll do all the work. After lunch, we'll go to the Herb House and do a few make-it-take-it projects. A potpourri, a simple salve, a tincture. That's where you come in. It'll be so much easier with you there to help with the hands-on stuff."

"Sounds simple," I said. "What about the workshop on wild herbs? When is it?"

"On Tuesday. That's a little more challenging. Maybe you and I can walk through the woods today and see what we can find."

I was about to tell her that I knew where she could locate some lobelia, red trillium, goldenseal, and devil's bit—all together in the same place—but I thought better of it. After the sheriff and a deputy or two finished going over that area, the plants might be trampled to the ground. At least, that was what could happen if the sheriff took my finds as seriously as I hoped.

"I've done this workshop for the past three years now," Martha was saying, "so I've made a sketch-map to remind myself of the locations of some of the more important wild herbs. We don't pick or dig anything, we just look and take photos, so the plants tend to stay put from year to year. But sometimes a clump of something dies out." She glanced at her watch. "Want to go and take a look?"

Trying not to sound as awkward as I felt, I said, "Could we put it off until after lunch? I've got a date with Missy Thatcher at nine thirty."

"Oh, yes. You mentioned that last night." She regarded me thoughtfully. "Missy asked you to come?"

I nodded.

"By yourself?"

I nodded again, uncomfortably. "I hope you don't mind."

"No, of course not," she said. She put her hands in the pockets of her khaki pants. "I'm just wondering why I wasn't invited, that's all."

"I wondered that, too," I confessed. "Is something going on between you and Missy?"

"No, of course not," Martha said. "We're probably making too much of this, China. I've been through the museum and the library a hundred times. Most likely, Missy just wants to spare me the repetition." A bleak look came into her eyes. "You'll have to tell her about Allie."

"I hate to be the one, Martha. You don't think she's already heard?"

"Not unless it was on the local radio news this morning, and she happened to hear it while she was driving to work. So, yes, I think you have to be the one." She squared her shoulders. "Since you're busy this morning, would it be okay if I borrowed your car? I need to see Pete about the memorial service, so I might as well get that out of the way." She eyed me. "I also want to find out what he was doing last night."

"You can take the car, of course." I regarded her, frowning. "But maybe I'd better come along."

"And do what?" She raised both eyebrows. "Ride shotgun? I've never been afraid of Pete Chatham. Not even when I was twelve and he shoved me off a merry-go-round on the school playground. That was the last time he ever tried anything like that." She smiled crookedly. "I warned Allie when she married him, but she didn't listen."

"Sounds like a reckless kind of guy, Martha." I frowned. "Maybe it's not a good idea for you to start asking questions about his whereabouts when his ex-wife died. He might take offense."

"If he does, I'll handle it the same way I handled that business on the merry-go-round," she said staunchly, and I thought she could. Martha is the kind of woman who can take care of herself—in most situations, anyway. She added, "I also thought I might ask him if Allie ever said anything to him about being worried. Or afraid. Or suspicious."

I cocked my head. "Would she have mentioned the missing stocks to him?"

"I doubt it. But I'll see what I can find out."

I took my car keys out of my fanny pack and handed them to her. "Well, be careful. Not with the car," I added hastily. "With this guy. You never know what he might have up his sleeve. And you said yourself that he was hot-tempered."

213

She looked a little worried. "You're right. I'll be careful."

And on that note, we went our separate ways.

MARTHA had told me that Lottie Ayers had gone on a "spending spree" when she built the conference center, which included a research library to house the Shaker documents and journals she had collected over the years, as well as a small museum. As I approached the building, I saw what Martha meant. The conference center was a long, low building, modern and architecturally sleek, with lots of windows, an interior courtyard, even an atrium, not the sort of thing you'd expect to find in this out-of-the-way place. Lottie Ayers had big plans for it. She had expected the building to pay for itself with conference fees.

But according to Martha, that hadn't happened, and the trustees might have to start dipping into the endowment to make the note payment. I wondered what they would do if they ran out of endowment funds, which might happen if the embezzler carried on with the dirty work. I wondered, too, if that was where Rachel Hart planned to find the money to build her spa. But if she had looted the endowment, what did she use the money for? And how could she expect to have enough left to build the spa? This didn't make sense to me. But there were a lot of things about this place that didn't make sense.

The parking lot, large and nicely landscaped, was empty, except for Missy's car. The building was open, but it seemed empty, too—not a soul around. I pushed open the glass door and went in.

Just inside the door, on the right, was a gallery of old photographs, beautifully displayed, of Mount Zion Shaker sisters at work in their herb garden, at their looms and spinning wheels, and in a large dairy, with dozens of cheeses lined up on the shelves behind them. Other photographs pictured a large, imposing barn, a Shaker brother standing in front of it with a cow and her calf.

Missy had come up to stand beside me. "Good morning, China," she said cordially. "I'm glad you could come. What do you think of the photographs?"

"They make the place seem very real," I said. I paused, studying a close-up of a tall, sturdy young woman, plain-faced and with something of an ungainly awkwardness about her, as if she were not quite comfortable in her body. But her gaze was straightforward and direct, and her eyes met mine without evasion or apology. Beside her was an older woman, much shorter and thin-cheeked, almost gaunt, with gold-rimmed glasses, her hands clasped at her waist. The plainness of the two women's faces was emphasized by the austerity of their Shaker dress, but both were somehow quite beautiful. "The photos of the actual people give Mount Zion a different kind of authenticity," I added. "As it is, this place doesn't seem quite . . . well, real."

Missy laughed. "I know. I have exactly the same problem when I visit Williamsburg or the Alamo—places like that. No matter how realistic the reconstruction, I'm always aware that I'm in a museum and that the people wearing period costumes are reenactors. When it's time to quit, they get in their SUVs and go home to their kids and TV sets and day jobs."

"But these people lived here twenty-four-seven," I said, looking back at the photos. "Without TV and SUVs."

"That's why we have their photos here, just inside the door. These people believed in this place and what it stood for, and they gave everything they had to keep it going."

"Who are they?"

She pointed. "The young woman—that's Martha's great-aunt. Sister Charity. The other one is Eldress Olive."

"Really!" I exclaimed, leaning for a closer look. "Charity is the one who left the village so abruptly—in 1912, I think it was. Martha says her family never understood the reason. She'd love to know."

"Is that right?" Missy said. "Well, maybe there's something in Elder Babbitt's journal about her leaving. I'm reading his 1912 entries now. Maybe you'd like to have a look. You might find it interesting."

"I would," I said. I looked at the photograph of the barn. "That's a pretty impressive barn. It's gone now? I don't remember seeing it."

"Yes. It burned to the ground, along with the dairy, in 1912. They suspected arson, but it was never proved."

"So barn burnings aren't a recent phenomenon," I said wryly. "Mount Zion had its problems along that line, even in the old days."

"You're thinking of the recent event, are you?"

I nodded. "Martha told me that the sheriff suspected that it was torched."

"Right." Missy sighed. "But arson was always a problem for the Shakers. Every village seems to have lost a couple of barns, and sometimes even a dwelling or a Meeting House. If one of the neighbors had a grudge, arson was an easy, no-risk way to get even." Missy looked back at the photo and added, in a musing tone, "In fact, that was the barn that caused poor Eldress Olive so much grief."

"Caused her grief when it burned, you mean?"

"After that. The barn was built with a loan from the bank and wasn't insured. Eldress Olive had to come up with the money to repay the note, even though the barn no longer existed and the Society was out of cash." She shook her head. "It was a stupid idea to build it in the first place—it was too large and cost way too much. But that was typical of what was happening in a lot of the Shaker communities toward the end of the nineteenth century. The leadership was past its prime, some of them in their eighties and nineties, and they made some really stupid business decisions. One old elder, down at Pleasant Hill, bought a lot of worthless Nevada gold-mining stock. His bad investment wound up costing Pleasant Hill nearly fifty thousand dollars. In those days, that was a bundle."

"It's still a bundle," I said. But she was right. Fifty thousand dollars in 1880 was probably equivalent to a couple of million today.

Missy pointed down the hall. "I've made coffee. Want a cup?"

"Wonderful." I fell into step beside her as we walked down a hall with closed doors on either side—conference rooms, I supposed, or offices. But there were no names on the doors. Where was the staff? Was Missy the only person who worked in this huge building?

It didn't seem politic to ask—anyway, I could find out later, from Martha. Instead, I said, "If the Shaker leaders were past their prime, why didn't they just appoint new ones?"

"Because there wasn't anybody else to choose from," Missy replied. "After 1900, the Believers were on their way out. Young folks were going to the cities for jobs, for fun, for excitement, even for sex." She grinned ruefully. "The celibate Shakers just couldn't compete. There were only five when Mount Zion closed in 1923."

"Was Eldress Olive one of them?"

"You bet. She held on until the bitter end." She opened a glass door at the end of the hall. "This is our library."

We walked into a large, open area lit by skylights. Narrow shelves along the wall were partially filled with books, and wider shelves for archival material held what looked to be boxes and manila envelopes—research material, no doubt.

"Very nice," I said, glancing around.

"Yes, indeed," Missy said. "I count myself very lucky to be able to work in such a beautiful place." She laughed a little sadly. "But I'm afraid

217

the library, and the conference center itself, is rather like that ridiculous barn that was such a burden to Eldress Olive. Bigger than we need, hard to pay for. Lottie Ayers had some great ideas, but her enthusiasms sometimes ran ahead of her common sense."

I was going to ask Missy what she thought of Rachel Hart's idea for turning the mineral spring into an upscale spa, but decided against it. Judging from what I had heard at dinner the night before, Missy wasn't one of Rachel's fans. I could guess her opinion. And now that I'd seen the conference center, it was my personal opinion that the board should take care of that debt before it took on another.

We spent the next few moments going around the room, looking at various collections, boxes of documents, framed photographs on the wall, and so on. Lottie Ayers had collected all sorts of material, including some beautiful pieces of Shaker furniture, on display in an adjacent room.

"You've done an extraordinary job," I said, admiring the displays.

"There's more furniture in the Trustees' Office," Missy said. "I'd like to get it over here, where at least we have an alarm system. The Trustees' Office doesn't. But Rachel isn't in a mood to part with the stuff—yet." She brightened. "I'm going over this morning to pick up a few other things, though."

"The gift drawings?"

She slanted me a look. "You know about those?"

"I saw them yesterday, in Rachel's office. They're quite remarkable."

"They'll be safer here, away from the light. Now, how about that coffee?"

The coffee service was set out on the counter in a small but beautifully equipped stainless-steel kitchen. Missy poured a cup for me and one for herself, and we carried them out to the library, to a long table piled with books and other material.

"Last night, you asked about Hannah Chandler," Missy said as we put down our cups. "I found something this morning that I think you'll find interesting. Sad, but interesting."

I sat down across the table from her. I'd been dreading this moment since I walked in the building, and I couldn't put it off any longer. "Before we get started with that," I said soberly, "I have some bad news. Something happened last night, after Martha and I left you."

Hearing the grimness in my voice, she looked at me, startled. "What? What happened?"

"I'm sorry to be the one to tell you this, Missy. Allie Chatham is dead."

"Allie?" She blinked confusedly at me, not quite taking it in. "But she can't be! She wasn't sick. She's the healthiest woman I know!" Her face crumpled. She pushed her glasses up on her forehead and put a hand over her eyes.

After a long moment, she replaced her glasses and looked up, wiping her eyes with the back of her hand. "Poor Allie. What was it? A stroke? An accident?"

"That's not clear," I said, and told her.

Her eyes opened wide. "Oh, my God," she whispered. "So that's why she didn't come to dinner last night. And while we were having fun and laughing and eating, she was—" She gulped painfully. "Do you think . . ." she whispered after a moment. "Do you think somebody *pushed* her?"

"I don't know." I gave her a steady look. "The police don't know yet, either. There'll be an autopsy, but it may not tell us anything." I paused. "Missy, what made you ask if somebody pushed her?"

"Well, because." She took off her glasses, wiped her eyes with the back of her hand, and put her glasses back on again. "Because she knew something." She picked up her cup and took a gulp of coffee. "Something about the foundation's finances."

Ah. A break. "What about the finances?"

"I don't know. She wouldn't come right out and tell me." Her cup rattled when she set it down. "She was just hinting. Fishing, actually."

"Fishing?"

"She was trying to find out if I knew something. Which I didn't." She pulled a tissue out of her pocket and blew her nose.

"What was she fishing for, do you think?"

"I don't know. Something to do with money. Something crooked. At least, that's what Allie thought. She said that if a certain person knew what she knew, the you-know-what would hit the fan."

"How many other people did Allie talk to about her suspicions?"

Missy went back to her coffee. After a sip, she said, "Well, there was one, at least. Jane Gillette. I know, because Jane asked me about it. She was puzzled. And concerned. Jane said she got the impression that Allie had talked to others as well, or meant to. Jackie Slade, for one."

"Did Jane say whether Allie mentioned who the 'certain person' was?"

Missy's face darkened. "No. But she did say that Allie was playing a dangerous game. And I agreed."

"What do you mean?" I thought I knew, but I wanted to hear Missy say it.

"Allie had somebody in her sights. She was trying to get whoever it was to come out in the open. Kind of like baiting a trap. Or setting a lure." She gave me a look. "That's why she was telling people, figuring that one way or another, her target would hear about it."

Dangerous, I thought. People who played games like that could wind up dead. And she had.

Missy eyed me. "You're a lawyer. Martha said you were helping her with some board-related stuff. Maybe I should ask you. Is . . . Is there someone I should tell about this? About what Allie was doing, I mean."

"Yes. I'm seeing Sheriff Franklin later this morning. I'll let him know what you told me, if that's okay. He'll probably want to talk to you." I would, if I were Sheriff Franklin. What Missy had told me definitely went to motive. What's more, this information would take him in the direction I hoped he'd go—investigating the financial angle. This would put some additional pressure on Rachel Hart, all to the good, as far as I was concerned.

"Thank you. I'll wait to hear from him." Missy pulled the tissue out of her pocket again, blew her nose, and straightened her shoulders as if she wanted to move on, away from the bad news. "Last night, you asked about Sister Hannah. I came in early this morning to work on Elder Babbitt's journal, and I discovered what happened to her. It turns out that Hannah Chandler was never 'Sister' Hannah at all, because she wasn't here at Mount Zion long enough to sign the Covenant. She came in the spring of 1912, she and her son, Seth, who was twelve. It was all very sad, though. A double tragedy."

"What happened?"

"Seth disappeared. At first, people thought that Hannah's ex-husband had sneaked into the village and carried the boy off. He and Hannah were recently divorced and she had legal custody, but he objected to the boy's living with the Shakers. Reading the old records, I've seen that sort of thing happening a lot. Mothers, or sometimes fathers, would come to the Shakers and bring their children, and the other parent would try to get the kids back. In fact, if Jake Chandler had gone to a judge, he'd probably have gotten custody of his son. The Kentucky courts didn't look favorably on the Shakers."

"But he kidnapped the boy instead?"

"No, as it turns out. Brother Joshua, the village schoolmaster, found him. He had fallen from a cliff. He was dead."

Twelve years old. Just a little older than Caitlin. Had he been killed instantly, or had he lain there for days, suffering? It was a horrible thought.

"And then I guess his mother just sort of went out of her mind," Missy said. "A few days later, she drowned herself in Zion's Pool."

I gasped.

"That's why Hannah didn't live in the village long enough to sign the Covenant," Missy went on. "So, strictly speaking, we shouldn't call her 'Sister Hannah.'" She paused and added thoughtfully, "But she's probably still here, you know. She and the boy must be buried in the Shaker—" She broke off, staring at me. "What's wrong, China?"

"Nothing." I picked up my coffee cup and took a steadying sip. "It's a sad story, that's all. And to think I've been sleeping in her room."

What else could I tell her? That I had dreamed of Hannah Chandler's suicide? That I had followed Hannah and tried to rescue her? That I had failed, and Hannah had vanished, and I had seen something else, a figure in a yellow raincoat? That last night, I had found Allie in that same pool, wearing a yellow raincoat?

I could tell Ruby these things—she would understand them. Ruby would probably tell me I'd plugged into some sort of universal stream-of-consciousness that gave me access to both the past and the future, to Hannah's 1912 suicide and to Allie's impending death. Ruby would tell me that this was all perfectly natural, and that instead of being frightened, I ought to feel pleased. I'd been initiated into the mystical Inner Circle.

But Missy was a rational woman, and these things were utterly irrational. I didn't understand them, either, and I certainly didn't want to belong to any Inner Circle, mystical or otherwise. If I told Missy about the dream, she'd think I was crazy. I cleared my throat and went to a safer subject.

"You said you had something to show me."

Missy gave me a thoughtful look, as though she suspected that I was withholding something, but she only said, "Elder Babbitt's journal." She gestured toward a worn, leather-bound book that lay open on the table. "This volume covers the years between 1907 and 1912. It's so incredibly detailed—a wonderful inside look into what went on in the village. If you'd like to spend some time reading it, you're certainly welcome. I've put a marker in the page where Elder Babbitt tells Hannah's story." She pushed back her chair. "As I said, I'm going over to the Trustees' Office to pick up the gift drawings from Rachel. I won't be long."

"I'd love to look through the journal," I said, glancing at my watch. There was still plenty of time before my meeting with Sheriff Franklin. I shifted the subject again. "Just out of curiosity—was there a reason you didn't ask Martha to stop in this morning with me?"

Missy paused in the act of rising. "Why, no," she said, surprised. "I mean, no real reason. Martha has seen the collection and the museum a dozen times, and you haven't. I thought it might give you some perspective on the village, that's all." She frowned. "I certainly hope I didn't offend Martha."

"No, of course not," I said, feeling foolish. "Just wondering, that's all." So much for my suspicions. Sometimes it doesn't pay to read too much into people's random remarks.

"Good." She went to a box and took out a pair of white latex gloves. "Please put these on before you read. The pages are fragile. The oil from our hands can damage the paper."

And that was how I came to spend the next hour turning the pages of Elder Babbitt's century-old journal, stopping to read here and there. Someone—Missy, I suppose—had encased the newspaper clippings in acetate envelopes and labeled them with document numbers, for easy reference, and I found myself envying her the primary source materials. If she ever got around to writing the history of the village, it was going to be extremely interesting, and not at all what people might expect.

From Elder Babbitt's journal, it was clear that Mount Zion had never been a peaceful, serene refuge from the storms and tempests of the World beyond its borders.

There were plenty of storms right here.

Chapter Eighteen

Elder Aaron Babbitt

Entry in a journal by Elder Dunlavy, of Pleasant Hill:

December 5, 1883. Marion and Henry Scarball who have been living in the Centre Family some years past got Denica Perkins & Sally Monday in a Family way between them this summer. This is the kind of Shakers we have now days. When asked to leave, they refused to go unless they received cash, Henry asking fifty dollars and Marion seventy. This is awful.

The Kentucky Shakers
Julia Neal

Document 1.1912.06.15. Text of letter copied into journal.

Mount Zion
June 15, 1912

To his dear Sister in spiritual Love & earthly Relationship, Priscilla, from her brother Aaron,
This is a painful Letter to write, for I must give you some unfortunate news about my Health, which I have suspected for some time. Dr. Barnard tells me I have a cancer in my Stomach, and that he

cannot prescribe a Cure. I am conscious of the Worry & Sadness this will cause you, but beg you to be mindful of the Glory that awaits when I am gathered home to our beloved Mother Ann, which I know will bring your Soul the greatest Comfort. So do not fret, dear Sister, but be of joy and cheerful Contentment.

There is other News. Since I last wrote, there have been some new Developments in the matter of Zion's Spring, for Will Ayers tells us that he proposes to build not only a Resort Hotel, but also a Road from the nearest Highway, which will undoubtedly result in a great deal of automobile Traffic, hardly conducive to a concentration on Work & Worship.

But far more importantly, Mr. Ayers has proposed also to purchase the Village. He has quoted a fair Price and given us a deadline to accept or reject it. His offer comes at a time when the burning of our Barn & Dairy greatly impairs our ability to continue the Cheese production. Together with the loss of the Recuperants' income, this will make it impossible to repay the outstanding debt on the Barn. I am sadly cognizant of this, and of our declining Numbers, my worsening physical Health, & the heavy burden all this must necessarily place on the Shoulders of our dear Eldress Olive. I believe that the best course of Action is to dissolve our Society and remove to Mt. Lebanon, at the invitation of our sisters and brothers there. Brave soul that she is, Eldress Olive is not ready to agree to this Plan. But I believe that she must of necessity heed my counsel and reconsider. I pray that she does.

The Matter of Bro. Charles' embezzlement of the Herb Account is moving toward resolution. I cannot give you an Account of all that has passed between us, but I continue to find him re-calcitrant and impenitent, arguing that he has invested of his Labor & Attention far beyond what is required of a Brother and that what he has taken is his Due. I have given him until this af-ternoon to bring me the Money (some three Thousand Dollars), after which he will be expelled from the Society. If the Money is not returned, we will be forced to call in the Police and he will be prosecuted to the fullest extent of the Law. As old Elder Dunlavy at Pleasant Hill was wont to lament, this is the kind of Shakers we have now days.

And there is yet more Sadness to narrate. I believe I wrote to you of the accidental Death of young Seth Chandler. Now, I must tell you that his poor bewildered Mother, her Wits completely addled by sorrow, has drowned herself in Zion's Pool. We buried Hannah Chandler beside her son and pray that she may at last Rest in Peace.

As I relate these Matters, I fear that they must sound a mourn-ful Litany. But all Burdens are lightened by our constant Faith and Trust, and we accept all as a Gift in the truest Humility, knowing that these are meant as Tests & Purifications. As for myself, I take great comfort in the ordinary Work & Prayer of every day. The bounty of the early Summer is joyfully and ex-travagantly upon us, and we daily labor in the Gardens and Fields. Please remember me to all my Brothers & Sisters amongst the Believers and share with them as much of this News as you deem of value.

Yrs in the truest of brotherly Love,
Elder Aaron Babbitt

NEWSPAPER CLIPPINGS FOUND
IN AARON BABBITT'S JOURNAL

Document 2.1912.06.15

Georgetown Graphic
June 13, 1912

CONTRACT LET

A contract for road development to the site of the planned resort hotel at Zion's Spring has been let to R & R Construction, of Georgetown, by Mr. William Ayers, also of Georgetown. Recently, Mr. Ayers formed a consortium of persons from Louisville and Lexington to secure funds for the project. Road construction is anticipated to commence shortly. Hotel construction will begin in the summer of 1913, with the hotel being opened in 1914. Mr. W. H. Stickney, Mayor of Georgetown, applauds the new venture—both the road and the hotel—as highly advantageous for our fair City.

Document 3.1912.06.15

Georgetown Graphic
June 14, 1912

SOCIETY OF BELIEVERS' BARN BURNED

The Mount Zion Shaker Village sustained a considerable loss on the night of June 12, it was learned today, when their large barn burned, along with the dairy building and a number of locust trees that were growing beside. Elder Aaron Babbitt says that, happily, no one was injured in the blaze and the livestock were successfully removed from the burning building. Arson is suspected, although Sheriff A. W. Lowe has not yet released a report of the incident. The barn, recently built, was the largest and best equipped in the county.

Document 4.1912.06.15

SHAKERS' RADICAL CURE FOR CATARRH

The great American Balsamic Distillation of Witch Hazel, American Pine, Canada Fir, Marigold, Clover Blossoms, etc., for the immediate relief and permanent cure of every form of Catarrh, from a simple Head Cold or Influenza to the loss of Smell, Taste, and Hearing, Cough, Bronchitis, and Incipient Consumption. Purely Balsamic & Vegetable, sweet, wholesome, economical, safe.

SHAKERS' RADICAL CURE

is prepared by the Society of Shakers, Mount Zion, Kentucky
Price, $1 per Bottle; 6 Bottles for $5
Sold by Druggists. Inquire by name, avoid imitations.
Wholesale Agents, Baum & Weeks, 255 Jefferson St.,
Lexington, Kentucky

Document 5.1912.06.15

HANDWRITTEN RECIPE FOUND
IN AARON BABBITT'S JOURNAL

Bro. Benjamin's Pain King

20 gal. water. 10 lbs. Witch Hazel bark, stir well every-day for one week. 20 gal. strong alcohol—oils Spruce, Sassafras, Peppermint, Camphor gum, dissolve in separate portions of alcohol and mix all together. Add tincture of Opium, reduce to a miscible condition with warm water and Masher till all parts are accessible to alcohol and water, after the former mixture has been put together and well stirred. Then mix with the rest.

Chapter Nineteen

But among his so many prosperous, pleasant, and lucky affairs, fortune mingled some seeds of wormwood and corrupted his pure grain with the malignant seeds of cocklebur.

Decades of the New World, 1555
Richard Eden

Elder Babbitt's faded script was not easy to read, but I kept at it, turning the pages carefully, reading forward and back through the large volume, pausing to study the clippings and handwritten recipes and notes. I was still reading when Missy came back, carrying a wide, flat box.

"You were right," I said excitedly, looking up. "This is fascinating stuff. Those Shakers—they had a wonderful vision of peace and tranquility, and they worked so hard to bring it to life. But they had an extraordinarily hard time of it, didn't they?" I shook my head. "Barn burning, the threat of development, accidental death, suicide, embezzlement. Elder Babbitt's journal reads like a suspense novel."

"Truly," Missy said, putting the box on the table. "The more I read, the more I'm amazed by their determination, especially in the later years. They could see the end coming—some of them could, anyway—but they weren't about to give up."

"So what finally happened?" I closed the journal and peeled off my gloves. "Did they sell the village to Will Ayers? Did Eldress Olive decide to throw in the towel and go to Mount Lebanon? Did Brother Charles hand back the money he stole, or did they have to call the cops?"

"I'll know more after I've finished studying the journal," Missy said. "I have an idea of the general outline, but not the details. In the meantime— *ta-da!*" She took the lid off the box. "You've seen these drawings?"

I stood to get a better look. "Yesterday, on the wall of Rachel's office," I replied. Only yesterday? It felt like a decade ago. "They're amazing, aren't they?"

"I've looked at quite a few gift drawings in other museums. These are very special." Missy took out a framed drawing and peeled off the protective Bubble Wrap around it. "This is the one drawn by Martha's aunt— Sister Charity. It's the only drawing of hers that we have—probably the only one in existence. Martha said it was found among her possessions after she died. It was in this frame." She put it on the table. "The Shakers were opposed to decorations of all kinds, so they never displayed the gift drawings. I plan to take these out of their frames, remove the mats, photograph them, and store them in archivally safe folders."

I leaned closer, resting my hands on the table. The drawing was cheaply framed and matted, but that didn't detract from its beauty. Sister Charity had a real skill—a gift, as the Shakers would have said. In the center—drawn in pen and ink and carefully tinted with watercolors— was a Tree of Life, its many branches reaching upward, embellished with bright birds and fanciful fruit. Around the tree was a circlet of green herbs. Rue and wormwood, I thought, looking closely. I frowned. Rue and wormwood? Wormwood represented bitterness, pain, loss. Rue represented the consciousness of sin, remorse for wrongs done, repentance, self-reproach. An odd combination, I would have thought, but there it was. Rue and wormwood.

Like the other gift drawings I'd seen in Rachel's office, this one was constructed with a strong sense of symmetry. In addition to the tree in the center, surrounded by a circlet of herbs, the empty spaces in the drawing were filled by many delicate scrolled lines, embellished with tiny, elegant decorations. Below the tree, centered, there was the all-seeing eye of God inside a triangle, the same thing that's on the reverse of a one-dollar bill. And in each of the four corners, there were small, carefully executed drawings of people. In the top left corner, two Shaker sisters were singing from a sheet of music. Top right, a Shaker sister at her loom, a brother with a hoe. Bottom right, a man approaching a building that bore the tiny sign, Sisters' Shop. Bottom left—

I blinked and looked closer. There were two figures, a woman standing, a man lying on the ground in front of her. The woman had something in her hand. What were they doing? I took another look, not quite sure what I was seeing. Was it—?

I straightened. "Missy, do you have a magnifying glass?"

"Sure," she said, unwrapping another of the framed drawings. "It's over there, in that plastic tray on the shelf in the corner. Can you get it? I've got my hands full."

I was searching for the magnifying glass when the library door opened and someone came in. I heard a man's voice, deep and rich, a baritone. "Oh, hey, there you are, darlin'," he said warmly. "I checked your office, but—"

I turned. It was Bruce Hart. Missy was looking at him, startled, her eyes wide. Then she glanced at me, the flame rising from her throat to her cheeks. She cleared her throat, then asked, in a businesslike tone, "You're looking for someone, Mr. Hart?"

Bruce turned his head, following the direction of Missy's glance. He stiffened when he saw me, and his eyes narrowed. I knew what he was thinking, for that was in my mind, too. Last night, he'd acted as though he'd never heard of Missy Thatcher. This morning, it was clear that he knew her—in fact, that they knew each other rather well, judging from the warmth of his greeting and the heightened color of Missy's cheeks.

He covered with a cough. "Excuse me," he said. "I think I'm lost. Can somebody tell me how to get to the Brothers' Shop?"

Missy laughed brightly. "I'd say you're lost. You're at the wrong end of the village. You need to go back out the front door and through the parking lot. When you get to the road—"

"I'll show you, Mr. Hart," I said, stepping forward, making a show of looking at my watch. "Gosh, Missy, it's later than I thought. I've got to be on my way."

"It's Ms.—uh, Rails, isn't it?" he asked, frowning. "We met last night, in the restaurant. You were with one of Rachel's board members."

"Bayles," I said. "China Bayles." I turned to Missy. "Would it be okay if I came back later for a closer look at that drawing? It's really interesting."

"Oh, sure," Missy said, with great carelessness. "I'll be here all day. Come anytime." Her show of easy nonchalance belied by her still-crimson cheeks, she went back to the work of unwrapping the framed drawings, as Bruce Hart and I walked out of the library and down the hall.

I might have asked him why he'd pretended not to know Missy Thatcher the previous evening, but I wouldn't get a straight answer, so there wasn't any point in bothering. I gave him a surreptitious glance. He was looking from side to side with great interest, pretending that he'd never been in this building before, which suggested to me that he'd been here rather often. To see darlin' Missy? They were having a fling?

Well, so what if they were? Missy was a single mom. Rachel's brother was married, or so I'd been told, but maybe he and his wife were separated. I had to admit that he was certainly a good-looking guy. If Missy was attracted to him, I could see why. The blue of his jacket was a good match for the startling blue of his eyes, and his blond hair, neatly combed, a little long in the back, gave him a Scandinavian look.

"Martha Edmond tells me that you're in real estate," I said.

"Yes, I'm a broker. Hart and Associates. Commercial properties, office buildings, hotels, restaurants." He was smiling at me, turning on the charm. "You in the market, maybe?" He remembered, and the smile faded a tad. "I remember now—you're from Texas. Up here for a visit?"

"Helping Martha with a couple of workshops," I said. We had reached the parking lot. "To get where you're going, you need to follow this road back to the village. The Brothers' Shop is just past the Trustees' Office. You can't miss it."

"Hey, thanks," he said, and sauntered off, hands in his pockets. I watched him go, then turned in the opposite direction. I hadn't lied to Missy. It was time to meet Sheriff Franklin. And when I saw the brown-and-white county car parked at the end of the lane, I knew he was waiting.

TEN minutes later, the uniformed, white-hatted, gun-totin' sheriff and I were standing in the path that led up the hill to the cottage where Allie had been living—and back down the hill to the pool where she had died. I pointed out Allie's loafer, lying where I had found it, and he grunted disgustedly.

"The boys shoulda seen that," he muttered. Perspiring from the walk, he pushed back his cowboy hat and wiped his forehead with his sleeve. In addition to being some thirty pounds over his ideal weight, he was nearly bald.

"It was dark last night, sir," I said. "And raining. I'm sure they did their best." A few "sirs" now and then never hurt anybody. And sometimes they go a long way toward establishing a relationship.

"Yeah." He was cool, but thawing. "So. How come you were up here so early this morning, Miz Bayles? You called me eight on the dot."

"Because I couldn't sleep last night," I lied. Given the circumstances, I'd slept pretty well. "The thing is," I went on diffidently, "I don't believe Allie fell into that pool by herself. I think she had help." I gave him a lopsided grin. "I'm married to a policeman, you see. An ex–homicide detective, that is. Some of it has probably rubbed off on me."

His glance became more kindly. I wasn't a member of the cop fraternity. But I was related by marriage. Made me a member of the family, sort of.

"I thought you might need a little help," I went on, in the deferential tone I'd learned to use with some judges. "My husband says that most departments are understaffed. And since I know the lay of the land—a little, anyway—I thought I'd have a look. It wasn't taped off," I added, in my own defense.

"Shoulda been," he said gruffly.

I agreed, but it wouldn't be tactful to say so. "Oh, and I noticed something else besides the shoe, Sheriff Franklin. A couple of things, actually. Of course, I don't know whether they have any relation to the crime. That is, if this is a crime. But—" I shrugged artlessly. "I thought you might like to take a look."

He was interested now, but trying not to show it. "Well, seein's I'm here, might as well. Where'd you spot this stuff?"

I gestured toward the opposite side of the path. "Over there, in the weeds." I didn't think "wild mint" would mean much to him. "I'll show you, sir."

He was remarkably agile and light-footed for a man of his bulk. He followed me to the place where the cigarette butt and the zipper tab lay, and bent over, examining the area closely. In a moment, he straightened up, took a small digital camera out of his shirt pocket, and clicked a photo.

He turned back to me. "You didn't touch this stuff?"

"Oh, no," I said truthfully, although I had pushed the cigarette butt with a twig so I could read the brand label. "My husband's always talking about chain of custody and things like that. He'd really bawl me out if he thought I'd messed up your crime scene."

A smile glimmered across his mouth and his eyes crinkled. "Good thing you listen to him. Can't say my wife always listens to me." He chuckled, signaling that the opposite was true.

"I doubt that, sir." I paused. "There . . . There's something else, although I don't know if it means anything."

He smiled. "Why don't you just tell me, and let me be the judge of what it means." He didn't call me "pretty lady," but he was all but chucking me under the chin.

"Well, I was talking to Missy Thatcher this morning. She's the curator and archivist here. She told me that Allie—the victim—happened to mention something to her about a problem with the foundation's finances." I glanced at him. "I'm sure you know that Allie runs the accounting office here."

His eyes slitted. That little bit of information hadn't zipped across his radar screen yet. "The foundation's finances, huh? What kind of problem?"

"Allie wouldn't say. But Missy got the idea that she suspected somebody was stealing money or something. Missy said she might've been fishing—or setting a trap."

"Oh, yeah?" He eyed me narrowly. "For a lady who just got here, you've been digging up a lot of stuff."

I gave him my best smile. "Golly, Sheriff Franklin, that's really nice of you. Can I tell my husband you said that?"

That got another chuckle. "This Missy Thatcher. Where's she work?"

"In the conference center, near where you parked your car."

He fished a couple of evidence bags out of his pocket and bagged the cigarette butt and the zipper tab. As he did, I noticed the tab again, and some thought, some idea, nibbled at the back of my mind. What was it? But whatever it was, it had slipped away before I could latch on to it.

The sheriff moved over to the path, photographed, and bagged the shoe. "You been up to the cottage?" He jerked his head. "That's where Ms. Chatham lived, I understand."

"I was up there yesterday," I said. "Martha Edmond and I walked home with Allie after work." I paused. "If you want to check it out, the key's under the flowerpot. At least, that's where Allie got it yesterday afternoon." Someday I will probably have to account for all my egregious sins of omission, but not today, I hoped. I wasn't going to tell him that I had gone up there by myself and that I had helped myself to what was likely to prove some very pertinent information.

"Thanks. You'll be around for a few more days?"

"Yes. My cell number's in the statement I made last night. I'm staying in the East Family Dwelling." I paused. "By the way," I said, "I suppose I ought to tell you that I'm a lawyer." I gave him a shamefaced grin. "Just in case it happens to come up sometime."

"I shoulda reckoned," he said. "Too smart by half. But I guess a few years in law school didn't hurt you none." He tipped his hat and grinned briefly. "You tell that hubby of yours he's trained you right."

* * *

THE temperatures had climbed and the air had grown humid as the morning wore on, and by the time I left the sheriff, the sky was beginning to look stormy. I was walking toward the Trustees' Office when Martha drove my car into the parking lot and got out. It was nearly time for lunch, so we walked to the restaurant while she told me about her morning's session with Pete, Allie's former husband. The police had just left, and Pete was distraught. After he calmed down a little, he'd agreed that it would be best to hold a memorial service in the Meeting House, if that could be arranged. When Martha had asked him whether Allie had talked to him about the foundation's financial situation, he shook his head.

"She never told me anything about her job. Far as I know, she might've been working on the moon." Then he'd looked up. "But she was a good wife," he'd said sadly. "Allie was always a good wife to me, right up to the end. Everything that happened between us was my fault. All my fault, damn it. She deserved better."

That had made Martha tear up, and the two of them had cried together. After that, she found it harder to ask him where he'd been the night before, but it finally emerged that he was now working nights at the Toyota plant in Georgetown. Martha hadn't pressed further.

"I don't think he had anything to do with Allie's death," she said, as we went into the restaurant. Only about half of the tables were full, so we got a table immediately.

I had heard the hesitation in her voice. "What about the truck that crashed into the cottage next door?" I asked as we sat down.

She made a face. "That's a different matter. That was Pete, all right. He got roaring drunk one night and drove out here. He took the truck from the equipment lot—found the gate unlocked and the keys in it, would you believe? Then he drove up the old road above the cottages and 'just let 'er rip.' His words. He said he never meant to hurt Allie. He just wanted to give her something to think about."

I snorted. "That would give *me* plenty to think about. Are you sure you want to cross that jerk off our list?"

"He didn't kill her, China. I'm sure of it." Martha picked up her menu. "Chilled potato soup today. That's good. And I'll have a salad."

We ordered, and I made my confession. "I went up to the path above the pool this morning, and found a couple of things I thought the sheriff ought to see." I filled her in briefly on my discoveries and my conversation with the sheriff. "I also reported to him something that Missy told me," I added, and relayed that, as well. I thought Martha might be annoyed that I had gone up there without telling her about it, but she was more interested in what Missy had said.

"Setting a trap!" She rolled her eyes. "Oh, God, China, that is so like Allie. She must have thought she could draw Rachel out of hiding by spreading the word that she was on to something. But Rachel heard what she was up to, and that's why Allie is dead."

"You really think it's Rachel, then?"

"Who else could it be?" she asked, and began ticking items off on her fingers. "Rachel has the key to the safe deposit box. Rachel has the stock inventory. Rachel searched Allie's office last night. And Rachel smokes." She held up four fingers. "It all adds up, China. It's got to be Rachel."

"What brand?"

"Brand?" She frowned. "I don't know. But we can find out when we go to her office to talk to her."

"When are we doing that?"

"I set it up for two or two thirty this afternoon. She asked me what it was about, and I said that Pete and I were thinking about a memorial service for Allie. I didn't want to put her on her guard." She glanced at her watch. "Don't forget that we're seeing Jenny Trevor after lunch." She frowned. "I wonder what that's about."

"It'll be interesting to find out," I said. I thought for a moment of telling her about Missy Thatcher and Bruce Hart, but decided against it. Bruce Hart had nothing to do with any of this, so there was no point in my spilling the beans on a private relationship. And just as I thought this, there he was, just entering the restaurant. Again, something clicked at the back of my mind, but I didn't reach for it fast enough. Whatever it was, I'd missed it.

He gave us a quick wave and went to a table in a corner. Returning his wave with a smile, Martha leaned toward me. "I've always wondered why Lottie left her grandson out of her will. Excluded him from the foundation, too. It's never seemed fair to me, or even very smart. He has so many good connections in Lexington. He could be useful to the foundation as a fund-raiser, if nothing else."

"He certainly has good people skills," I said. "Too bad he can't help out here."

Martha sighed. "Especially given the situation with Rachel. She has such a hard time getting along with everyone."

It was nearly one by the time we finished eating. Outside, the sky had turned dark and threatening again, with blue-black clouds piled up against the western horizon. We were in for another round of storms. We set off for the Sisters' Shop, located in a white-painted two-story frame building a couple of hundred yards from the East Family Dwelling, near the herb garden. It was called the Sisters' Shop, Martha told me, because it was the place where the Shaker women worked, mostly on fiber crafts, spinning, weaving, dyeing. On the way, she pointed out the foundations of a large barn and what remained of a wood-frame building—the dairy, she said.

"There are some photographs of those buildings in the conference center," I said. "Missy has put up a really interesting display." I looked at the ruined foundation. "The barn was huge. They must have had a lot of cows."

"They did indeed. At one time, Aunt Charity told me, the Mount Zion dairy herd was the largest and best in this part of Kentucky. The Shakers supplied milk, butter, and cheese to the whole area. In her day, though, they only kept enough cows for their own use. She watched the barn burn and helped get some of the cheeses out. It was something she never forgot."

We went up the steps to the front door of the Sisters' Shop. The neatly lettered sign on the door read "Open. Kindly step inside." We entered a sizable room that contained a large floor loom and a couple of spinning wheels. The place had a cozy, yarn-shop feel, with skeins of colored hand-spun yarn hanging on the walls and from lines across the ceiling, and rolls of carded wool piled in baskets beside the spinning wheels.

Jenny Trevor was bending over the back of the loom, adjusting the warp. She was wearing a blue Shaker dress and white apron and her hair was tucked into a Shaker cap. In this room, with the loom and the yarn and the unspun fiber, she looked startlingly authentic.

"Hello, Jenny," Martha said, and Jenny turned.

"Oh!" she exclaimed. "I didn't hear you come in." Her eyes went to me, and a nervous furrow appeared between her eyes. "I'm sorry, Ms. Edmond. I've changed my mind. I don't want to talk about—"

"That's not going to work, Jenny," Martha said. "Something happened last night, something very serious. If you have any information at all about what's been going on here, you'll have to share it."

Good for you, Martha, I said silently.

Jenny pulled in her breath, and I could see how young she was, and how vulnerable. And frightened. "What . . . What happened?"

"After we left the restaurant last night, China and I found Mrs. Chatham's body. In Zion's Pool."

The girl paled. "Mrs. Chatham?" she whispered. "The lady from Accounting? Somebody killed her?"

"Yes, that's the one." Martha pressed her lips together. "We don't know exactly how she died. But the sheriff is treating it as a suspicious death. China spent the morning at the scene, talking with the sheriff about it." She paused. "I'm sure you can see why it's important that you tell us whatever you know."

Martha might not have intended to imply that I had some official connection with law enforcement, but that was how Jenny seemed to take it. She sat down heavily on a stool beside one of the spinning wheels. "I really want to talk to you," she said, with a helpless glance at me. "It's just that . . . well, I could lose my job over this."

"Over what?" Martha asked insistently.

Jenny frowned. "I told you. It's about the barn."

For an instant, I felt muddled, and then it fell into place. Jenny was talking about the barn that had recently burned, with two of Bruce Hart's horses in it. Not the one whose foundation we had just looked at, the one that had burned in 1912.

As Martha asked, "Do you have some information about the fire?" I stepped to the door, flipped the sign to "Closed. Kindly return later," and shut it.

Jenny nodded reluctantly. "I . . . I saw something that night. I thought I ought to tell somebody."

Martha gave me a pointed look and I stepped forward. "Did the police interview you?" I asked. "Either that night, or later?"

Jenny transferred her nervous glance to me. "No. I . . . I was sort of waiting for them, but they didn't. I guess they figured it wasn't worth the trouble to talk to everybody on the staff. Or maybe they didn't have the time."

"You're probably right on both counts," I said. Of course, she could have volunteered, but most kids have a hard time dealing with the cops. I wasn't surprised that she hadn't taken the initiative. I leaned against a heavy wooden table, using the calm, quiet tone I always reserved for nervous witnesses. "Why don't you tell us what you saw, Jenny? Maybe we can help you decide what should be done with the information."

"If your job is in jeopardy, I'll do whatever I can for you, Jenny," Martha put in. "I promise."

Jenny thought about this for a moment, pressing her lips together. "Well, okay. Anyway, maybe I'm making too big a deal about this, you know?"

"Sometimes it's hard to figure out whether something's important enough to bother the police with. What was it you saw?"

She fidgeted. "Well, Carl and me—Carl and I—we were out for a walk that evening."

"Carl?" I asked.

"Carl Dickey. My boyfriend."

"What time that evening?"

"It was a couple of hours after our shift, so it was maybe ten o'clock. We'd been swimming at Zion's Pool." She colored prettily, and I got the picture. Skinny dipping. And more, no doubt. The Shakers would be scandalized. "We were coming back through the woods. It was dark and we didn't have a flashlight, but the moon was out and we know the way. We were coming along the path behind the barn—it's a shortcut to the parking lot. Anyway, we saw somebody."

Somebody. "A man? A woman?"

"A guy. Like, he was messing around at the back corner of the barn."

Messing around. I gave an internal sigh. "What exactly was he doing?"

She shifted. "Well, we couldn't really see, but it looked like he was dumping something along the wall of the barn."

"Did you recognize him?"

She shook her head. "No. I didn't—that is, not right then. But Carl did. He's a server in the restaurant, and he'd seen the guy a couple of times, having meals." She grinned briefly. "Carl said he always remembered a big tipper, and Mr. Hart tipped pretty good."

Martha made a startled sound. "Mr. Hart?"

"Yes. After Carl said who it was, I recognized him, too. I'd seen him around, here and there. I just didn't know his name. He keeps a couple of horses here." The corners of her mouth turned down. "That is, he did. Until they died. In the fire."

"Ah," I said.

Her mouth twisted. "You know, that's what I really don't get. I mean, why would somebody burn a barn when they knew there were horses inside? And they were *his* horses! That's not just cruel and inhumane, it's stupid! What reason could he have?"

Insurance was the word that came first to mind. But we hadn't established that Bruce Hart—if that was who it was—was actually preparing to torch the barn.

"You saw this person dumping something," I said. "Was it a solid, a liquid? What was he dumping it out of? A can? A bottle? A bucket?"

"It was liquid. Out of a bucket." She frowned. "A little bucket."

"Not a gasoline can?"

A head shake.

"Did you smell anything?"

Another head shake.

"He had horses in the barn," I said. "Maybe he was dumping water. Or something he was using to clean the horses."

She lifted her chin defensively. "You're saying Mr. Hart had nothing to do with the fire?"

"I'm saying it's pretty hard to be sure—just based on what you saw." I didn't say that a clever defense attorney would gobble you alive on the stand, honey, and wouldn't even burp. "So what happened after you saw Mr. Hart dumping something?" If that was who it was.

"Well, we didn't think much of it, you know. We went on to the parking lot and sat in Carl's car for a while." There was that color again. "He drove back to Georgetown. I went to my room—I stay in the East Family Dwelling during the summer, when I'm working full-time. Anyway, I went to sleep. An hour or so later, the fire sirens woke me up. The next morning, somebody said it was the barn. And the horses were dead." She shuddered. "Burned alive. I can't get over it."

"At the time, did you think of talking to the police?"

"Of course," she said vehemently. "I called Carl and told him about the fire, and that we should talk to the police. But Carl—he was afraid of getting fired. He made me promise I wouldn't say anything."

"Why are you telling us now, then?"

She ducked her head. "Because . . . Because Carl and I broke up. He left a couple of days ago. He's taking summer classes at the university."

So now that her reluctant boyfriend was out of the picture, I thought wryly, Jenny felt free to tell her story. Or maybe she had some other reason.

Martha leaned forward with another pertinent question. "Why did you decide to tell *me*?"

"Because you're not the cops." Jenny's lips twitched. "And because one of the ladies in the kitchen said you're the only person on the board who isn't in Ms. Hart's pocket."

Martha smiled. "Whatever the reason, Jenny," she said gently, "we very much appreciate your telling us this."

Jenny returned the smile, tightly. "You promised I wouldn't get into trouble."

"You won't," Martha said in a reassuring tone. "I always keep my promises."

"We'll let Sheriff Franklin know that you have some information," I said. "He'll want to talk with you. But it's okay," I added, as she looked alarmed. "He'll keep it confidential, as long as he can." If she heard the qualifier, it didn't seem to register.

The sound of voices came from outside, and Jenny wrinkled her nose. "I guess I'd better get back to work." She glanced from me to Martha. "I'm glad I told you." She scrunched up her mouth. "I just kept thinking about those poor horses. It makes me sick."

"I'm glad you told us, too," Martha said. She took Jenny's hand and squeezed it. "Please keep all this under your hat for now, dear."

"Are you kidding?" Jenny asked. "I wouldn't dare tell anybody else. Mr. Hart might come after me!"

I frowned. "You said that one of the ladies in the kitchen suggested talking to Ms. Edmond. Did you tell her what you and Carl saw at the barn?"

"Well—" Jenny was putting her cap back on, tucking in her hair. "Well, maybe I did. But she's somebody I can trust." She slid me a glance that suggested that she wasn't so sure about me.

"I hope so," I said. "What about Carl? Did he tell anybody?"

"He might've," she said slowly. "He was friends with one of the guys who worked in the stable."

Just like a pair of kids, I thought. They'd tell their friends what they saw, but they wouldn't tell the police.

She gave me a nervous look. "You don't think there's a problem, do you?"

I thought of Allie, facedown in Zion's Pool, the back of her head battered and bloody. Of course there's a problem, I wanted to say. Somebody's killing people, and it wouldn't be cool if you turned up dead. But I only smiled and patted her arm. "I'll talk to the sheriff right away. In the meantime, be a little careful. Okay?"

She might have thought of Allie, too, for she looked troubled. "Yes," she said, in a small voice. "Yes, I will."

I hoped so.

Chapter Twenty

Sister Charity

His Physicke must be Rue (ev'n Rue for Sinne).
George Wither, 1628

Why, what a ruthlesse thing is this . . . to take away . . . the life of
a man . . .

Measure for Measure
Shakespeare

As Charity hurried through the growing dark along the path to the Sisters' Shop, she felt happier than she had in weeks. She had realized that Charles' terrible transgression—his theft from the Herb Department accounts—was a miraculous gift, sent by dear Mother Ann to unshackle Ruth from the deadly entanglements of temptation and sin. Charles would be sent away in disgrace, perhaps even prosecuted. And Charity was confident that once Ruth learned who Charles really was and what he had done, she would reject him entirely, even eagerly. Of course, she would be terribly distressed. She might be even a little angry at Charity for bearing such a message. But eventually, she would forget all that. She would be grateful, and they could go on living together and loving each other. Charity tried to keep her feet from skipping but she could not, and she felt herself nearly flying, so light and happy she was, flying to Ruth with this liberating message.

By the time she reached the Sisters' Shop, Charity was almost dizzy with anticipation. The front door was open, as well as the door at the back, which brought in a fresh breeze and the scent of roses from the nearby herb garden. She had thought to find Ruth alone, but when she opened the screen door and went in, Sister Annabelle and Sister Maureen were there, finishing up the day's work.

The oil lamps had been lit in their sconces on the wall, warming the room with their soft golden glow. Old Sister Annabelle was carding wool with a pair of large hand-carders—wooden paddles with wire teeth that separated and straightened the wool fibers so they could be easily spun. She was stooped and so nearly blind that she had to feel her way around the shop, but she had carded wool from the Believers' flocks for such a long time that she knew by the feel of the fiber when it was ready for spinning.

Sister Maureen—not quite so old as Sister Annabelle but as deaf as Annabelle was blind—was spinning at the large wooden wheel in the corner, the wheel turning in a blur, her gnarled fingers drawing the fiber out of a handful of the wool Sister Annabelle had carded.

The Shakers had long since reduced the size of the flock of sheep. The sisters had stopped carding and spinning and had given up home-spun wool in favor of the mill-spun fiber that Ruth used in her loom. So the work of Annabelle and Maureen was for nothing, in the end. But Charity thought that perhaps it wasn't, after all, for work was prayer, which made all work good work, whether it was entirely useful or not. Anyway, the carding made Annabelle feel useful and Maureen said the spinning kept her fingers limber and helped her to remember the old times, when the village was inspired with spiritual ecstasy, when spinning at her wheel was like dancing the worship dances in the Meeting House.

Ruth looked up from her weaving, nodded, and went back to her work. Impatient, Charity resigned herself to waiting. Of course, she could talk to Ruth when they went back to their retiring room, but that was never very satisfactory, because Ruth always went straight to her journal or was too tired for serious conversation. Just at that moment, though, Sister Annabelle laid her carders aside, pushed herself out of her chair, and announced in a creaky voice that it was time to end her work for today. With a scratchy laugh, she added that if Charity had come to talk with Ruth, she might as well do some carding while she was there. "Hands to work, hearts to God," she said.

Charity stared at her, wondering if Sister Annabelle was not quite as blind as everyone thought. "I've never been any good at carding," she protested halfheartedly.

"All you need is practice," Sister Annabelle said, and began feeling her way to the door. Sister Maureen, seeing her go, stopped her wheel and stood. "I'll go with her," she said, and followed Sister Annabelle into the darkening evening.

Feeling suddenly shy and at a loss for words, Charity picked up a carder and a handful of wool, and made a clumsy attempt at brushing the wool against the carder, so that the fibers caught the teeth. Then she picked up the other carder and began to brush. But the teeth caught and the fibers bunched. Charity's strong hands felt huge and awkward.

Ruth turned her head. "Sister Annabelle's gone," she said wryly. "You can stop now."

"It wouldn't do any good for me to keep going, anyway," Charity said, laying the carders aside. "My hands are too big. I'd just make a mess of it. I'm better with a hoe." She got up and went to stand beside the loom, where she could see Ruth's face. "I'm glad Sister Annabelle left," she said, feeling breathless. "I need to talk to you, Ruth."

"Well, talk, then," Ruth said, her hands and feet busy with her weaving. She didn't look at Charity, and her voice was wary. "Although of course, it depends on what you want to talk about."

Charity felt her heart fail her. She hadn't anticipated the guarded, almost hostile look. "It's about Brother Charles," she blurted, before she could lose quite all her courage.

Ruth's hands paused briefly, then went on about their work. "I don't want to talk about Charles," she said, over the *slap-slap* of the loom. "It's none of your business, Charity."

"I know it isn't," Charity said, reaching out desperately. "And I wouldn't say anything, honestly, I wouldn't. Except that— Except that there's something you need to know, Ruth."

"I know all I need to know." Ruth's voice was coldly defiant. "And anyway, you're just a girl. Wait until you grow up. You'll see things differently."

"This isn't about you and Charles," Charity said, wishing she had given more thought to just how she was going to do this. They were already off to a bad start. "It's about . . . Charles. There's something I have to tell you, Ruth."

Ruth's hands and feet were moving again, deftly, swiftly, the shuttle shooting across the warp, the sheds lifting and dropping in an angry rhythm. Her face had closed down and her mouth was tight. "No," she said. "Go away, Charity. Just go away."

Charity leaned forward urgently. "Please listen," she begged. "Charles took some money, a lot of money, from the Herb Department accounts. Elder Babbitt is going to send him away. Unless he returns the money— three thousand dollars—he'll be prosecuted. He'll go to jail, Ruth! Either way, he'll never be allowed to come back to the village." At the thought of such a frightening exile, Charity felt herself choking.

"Oh, pooh—is that all?" Ruth asked lightly, derisively. She made a brushing gesture with her hand, as if she were waving away a fly. "Charity, you are such a child. Go say your prayers. It's nearly bedtime."

"But Ruth!" Charity cried, her heart filling up with despair. "Oh, Ruth, Ruth! Don't you understand? Charles is leaving the village! You will have to renounce him and confess and ask forgiveness and make your peace!" She threw out her hands. "But I'll be with you. I promise I will. I'll be with you every inch of the way."

Ruth stopped the loom with her hands and her feet and swung her legs over the bench, speaking with a cruel ferocity. "Now, you listen to me, Charity Edmond. I have just about had enough of your silly pieties. The money that Charles took is money that is owed him—owed to the both of us, come to that. We have worked our fingers to the bone for that money. We've earned it. It's ours. And I'm leaving with him."

Charity stared at her. There was a roaring in her ears and such a tumble in her insides that she put her hand over her mouth to keep from being sick. "Leaving . . . with him?" she whispered through her fingers. "No!"

"Yes," Ruth hissed. "We're going back to the World as soon as all the arrangements are complete. So you can go away. Now, and quickly. I'm expecting a visitor."

In a flash, Charity saw everything quite clearly. Ruth's long evenings in the Sisters' Shop, her late returnings to their room, none of it had anything at all to do with work or prayer. It was all to do with Brother Charles and their plan to run away, to abscond with the money. Charity had been a fool, a complete fool.

But still— Whatever Ruth had done, how could she bear it if she went away? How could she *bear* it?

"It doesn't matter about the money," she heard herself saying. "But please say you're not going away." She sank to her knees, her skirts billowing out around her. "Please!"

"Do hush, you silly child," Ruth said impatiently. She took Charity by the arm and pulled her to her feet. "I told you, I'm expecting a visitor. I want you to go straight to our room and don't say a word to anyone." She looked into Charity's face, and the lines around her mouth seemed to soften. "And if you love me, little Charity, truly love me, you will not tell a soul about this. Not a single soul."

"Oh, I do love you!" Charity burst out recklessly. "I love you more than—"

Ruth put her finger on Charity's lips, silencing her. "Good," she said in a softer voice, "because I love you." She paused. "I'm sorry I spoke harshly, Charity. But I need you to go away. Now."

"You love me!" Charity exclaimed triumphantly, grasping eagerly at Ruth's hand. "You do love me, then, Ruth?" If that were true, if Ruth loved her, that would make everything else all right. She wasn't sure how, exactly, but she knew it would. Mother said that love healed all, encompassed all, understood all. And if Ruth loved her, she couldn't really mean to leave with Charles, could she? That would make no sense at all.

"Yes, of course I love you, you silly thing." Ruth took her hand, turned it over, and kissed the palm, a gesture so easy and natural that Charity felt that it could only be heartfelt. "There. You see?" She put her hand on Charity's cheek, gently smoothing away the tears as a mother might ease a fretful little girl. "But I need to do some important business this evening, and I can't do it as long as you're here. You must go. Will you?"

Charity found herself wanting more, aching for another kiss on her palm, another sweet touch to the cheek. But Ruth loved her. There would be more kisses, more touches. Later. "Yes. If that's what you want. I'll do anything for you, Ruth. Anything!"

"Good again." Ruth put her hands on Charity's arms, squeezing hard. "I promise I'll tell you all about it later tonight, my dear." Her lips curved into a smile, although there was something in her eyes that Charity couldn't read. "When you hear all about what has happened and what's to be done, you'll understand and agree that it's all for the best." She paused for emphasis. "That is, if you love me the way I love you. If you really mean it when you say you'll do anything for me."

Charity gazed into Ruth's beloved face, into her dear dark eyes, feeling the lingering fear washed away by a rushing relief. Ruth wasn't shutting her out at all. Ruth loved her—she *loved* her! And if she loved her, she couldn't mean to go away. Whatever this was about, Charity knew, it would all come out right in the end. They would be together.

"Now, go!" Ruth commanded, and softened her sternness with a smile that nearly melted Charity's bones. "We'll talk tonight. Wait up for me, won't you? I'll explain everything and then you'll see. You'll see."

Ruth guided her toward the back door and, when Charity hesitated, gave her a push that almost sent her headfirst down the stairs and into the dark.

But Charity couldn't go very far. She meant to obey Ruth's command, but her legs failed her when she reached the herb garden, where the rich scent of the red damask roses almost smothered her and the ivory blossoms of the white roses floated like vagrant ghosts in the shadowed darkness. The full moon was just beginning to rise over the trees to the east, and in its light, Charity sank to her knees beside a bed of wormwood and rue, pressing her face to the earth, giving way to the great, wrenching sobs that tore up out of her belly and shook her whole body.

She could not have said whether they were tears of misery or tears of joy, for it was all mixed together: an abysmal despair over Ruth's claim that she already knew about Charles' theft and meant to leave with him; an ecstatic joy at her confession of love for Charity. What could it all mean? If Ruth left—oh, but surely, surely not! How could she leave, and leave Charity behind? But if Ruth left, how could she survive?

Charity had no idea how long she knelt there, her shoulders heaving, her wet cheek against the forgiving earth, still warm from the day's sun. The fireflies flitted around and above her, among the scented blossoms. The moon rose higher into the velvety sky, its beams reaching to earth as if they were a silver ladder, lowered so that she could climb aloft to the angels and to Mother, in the distant and beautiful heaven. Somewhere nearby, frogs sang their throbbing night song, and even closer, there was a rustling under the earth, the burrowing of a rabbit, the slow push of a mole. She could feel it in her bones, that pushing, the urgent tunneling, could hear the frogs' singing ringing in her ears, could breathe deeply of the healing, sweetening scent of the roses. Ruth loved her and that was enough, more than enough. And surely, if Ruth loved her, she would not leave. She could not leave.

After a time, Charity pushed herself upright, sitting, her arms cradling her bent legs, her cheek resting on her knees. The glow of the oil lamps in the Sisters' Shop spilled out into the darkness of the night. Through the window, she could see that Ruth had seated herself at her loom again and was weaving with a rhythmic serenity, as if nothing unsettling had ever happened. She had pulled her cap back and the pins had fallen out of her hair, flowing in waves down her back. Watching the rise and fall of her shoulders, the moving fingers, the fluttering kiss of light across her hair, Charity was struck by a longing so wrenchingly physical that it almost felled her.

She took a deep breath and wiped her eyes with the back of her hand. It would not do to sit out here in the moonlit dark until Charles came—he might see her and tell Ruth, and Ruth would think she did not trust her. Charles? Of course, Ruth was waiting for Charles. Who else? She would do as Ruth said—return to their room. And when Ruth came, they would talk it all out.

Charity was just getting to her feet when she saw the shadow under the window. A slowly moving shadow, silent, deliberate, hunched over in a crouch. For an instant, she thought it was Charles, but the moment that thought came, it was pushed away by another, by the sure conviction that it was not. Charles had a long, swinging gait; he moved easily, confidently, displaying himself—it was one of the things Charity didn't like about him. This ominous hunching shadow was some other person, some other man, and Charity knew in a flash of intuitive certainty that whoever it was, he did not wish Ruth well. He had come to harm her.

Charity's mouth went dry and it was hard to get her breath. Suddenly aware that her white cap was visible in the moonlight, she hastily pulled it off and thrust it in her pocket. Intent on the shadow, she crept forward for a better look.

The man crouched under the window was no brother. He was thin, dressed in tight-fitting pants and a jacket. A bowler hat—nothing like the broad-brimmed, flat-crowned straw hats of the brothers—was pulled low over his eyes. He raised his head to peer through the window into the room, then ducked back down again hurriedly. Then he turned, glancing around. The moonlight caught his face, and Charity stifled a scream.

The man was Will Ayers. "The baddest man on God's earth," Sister Pearl had called him. The man who had defiled Sister Anna White. Who had caused her to be turned out of Mount Zion, carrying his child.

Charity's blood chilled. Will Ayers was outside the window, and Ruth was all alone in the Sisters' Shop, waiting for Charles. Charles! Where was he? Why didn't he come? Had he already been sent away from the village?

But however things stood with Charles, Ruth was all alone and easy prey to Ayers. In a moment, he'd be inside the room. He would take Ruth by surprise and overpower her. And Charity knew very well what would happen after that. If Charles didn't come to keep Ruth safe, Ayers would rape her.

At the thought, Charity was swept by a searing pain, her own pain, and the bitter shame and humiliation her father had inflicted on her. She couldn't let Ruth suffer as she had suffered. She had to do something to stop it. What?

And just as she asked the question, the answer came into her hand with all the stunning grace of a gift. In front of her was the neatly piled stack of stove wood, dried and split and ready to fire the two small stoves that warmed the Sisters' Shop. And beside it a careless brother had left the long-handled ax that he had been using to split wood, wedged into a piece of firewood. The blade glinted; the wooden handle gleamed and beckoned. It was a gift, surely—oh, surely, a gift from Mother, a blessed weapon to save Ruth!

Charity could not refuse Mother's gift, nor the obligation it imposed. Not daring to think, she grasped the handle and silently wrenched the ax free. Eyes narrowed, her chest so tight she could not breathe, she crept closer and closer to Will Ayers, who had once again raised his head and was staring hungrily into the room where Ruth was working at her loom. He was so intent on her that he seemed to have lost all sense of what was around him.

Charity moved silently. One step, two steps, three steps, closer and closer. After a year, a century of silent movement, she was close enough to smell his whiskey-sodden jacket. She raised the ax over her head with both hands. Deliberately, with all her strength, she brought it down on Will Ayers' head, just behind his right ear.

What happened next seemed to happen in slow motion, each smallest movement drawn out to an unbearable length. Ayers grunted, lifting his right hand to his head. Then he grunted again—a sharp exhalation of sour, alcoholic breath—and half turned, half lurched toward her, reaching out for her, grabbing the front of her dress and the camisole she wore under it, holding on as the fabric ripped, exposing her breasts. He bent at the knees then, as if he were kneeling in fervent prayer, hands scrabbling at her breasts, eyes rolling up in their sockets until nothing could be seen but the terrifying whites. He fell forward against her, knocking her backward, smearing her with his spouting blood.

Struggling to keep her feet, Charity gave a strangled cry, dropped the ax, and clapped both hands to her mouth. Will Ayers lay facedown on the ground in front of her. His arms and feet jerked horribly for a moment, the way a chicken did when she wrung its neck. Then he lay still.

Ruth appeared in the lighted doorway, her face white, her eyes staring. She grasped the doorframe for support, looking from Charity to the man on the ground at her feet to the bloody ax. But instead of the gratitude and relief that Charity might have expected, there was a sudden, violent anger.

"You stupid, stupid girl!" Ruth cried. "You've ruined everything!"

Chapter Twenty-one

And the LORD saith, Because they have forsaken my law which I set before them, and have not obeyed my voice, neither walked therein; but have walked after the imagination of their own heart . . . thus saith the LORD of hosts, the God of Israel, Behold, I will feed them, even this people, with wormwood, and give them water of gall to drink.

Jeremiah 9:13–15

Martha and I left the Sisters' Shop as a group of tourists, led by one of the Shaker interpreters, crowded into the small weaving room. Jenny Trevor gave us a tiny wave and went back to her loom.

"Bruce Hart torched the barn?" Martha exclaimed incredulously, the minute we were outside and alone. "I don't believe it, China! Why? What reason could he possibly have?"

"Insurance, maybe," I said. "It's been known to happen." I looked up at the sky. It had grown even darker, and the air was very still, but I didn't hear any thunder or see any lightning. I dipped into my fanny pack for my cell phone. I've read that the jury is still out on whether cell phones attract lightning, but I'm not about to take any chances.

I flipped my phone open, noticing that I'd missed a call from Ruby, no doubt wanting to interpret my dream. But I skipped that and speed-dialed McQuaid. I caught him in his office at the house, working at his computer, and gave him my request.

"Hey," he said urgently. "I thought I told you to stay out of that business."

"I know you did," I said in a conciliatory tone. "But this is important. I'm not doing anything dangerous. I promise. I had a good conversation with the local sheriff this morning. He considers me one of the family. He'll look out for me."

He made a noise low in his throat.

"Please?" I said. "Will you do it?"

After a moment, he sighed. "Oh, all right. I don't suppose there's anything I can do to stop you from meddling in police business. Is there?"

"I love you," I said sweetly, and clicked off. To Martha, I said, "McQuaid's going to make some calls and find out how much—if anything—Bruce Hart collected for the death of those horses. Shouldn't take him too long." I grinned at her raised eyebrows. "Remember? I told you a good P.I. could solve your dirty-tricks case in nothing flat."

Martha frowned. "You know, after what happened to Allie, I'd almost forgotten about the barn." She hesitated. "You don't really think Jenny Trevor is in danger, do you?"

"Of losing her job?"

"Or . . . anything else."

"There's no way of knowing," I said honestly. "I doubt it." Of course, collecting insurance for a pair of dead horses (if that was what had happened) didn't constitute proof that Bruce Hart had torched the barn, although taken together with Jenny Trevor's testimony, it might constitute enough of a case to warrant prosecution. But there wasn't any connection—at least, none that I could see—between the barn burning that took place a month ago and what had happened last night. Like the truck crashing into the cottage—Pete's doing—and the vandalism at the Brothers' Shop, it was likely an unrelated incident.

Still, there was something I wanted to confirm. I'd hesitated to mention this at lunch, but now it seemed that it might be relevant. "Last night, when we talked to Rachel and her brother at the restaurant, was it your impression that Bruce Hart had never heard of Missy Thatcher?"

Martha wrinkled her nose, thinking. "Seems to me I remember his asking Rachel who Missy was and what she was doing. Rachel was a little huffy about it—told him it was none of his business. So I guess the answer is yes." She regarded me. "Why do you ask?"

"Because when I was at the conference center this morning, Bruce Hart walked in, looking for Missy. He didn't see me right away. From the way he spoke to her—and from her reaction—I'd say that their relationship is . . . romantic."

"Romantic!" Martha looked shocked. "But—but Bruce Hart is married!"

"It happens." Out of curiosity, I added, "Do you know his wife?"

"We've been introduced. She's quite a horsewoman, and occasionally comes to ride with Bruce. Linda, her name is. She manages a bank in Lexington, I understand, and is active in the arts community. She's beautiful, in a stylish way, but older than Bruce, by several years." She tilted her head. "And Missy's younger, which is the appeal, I suppose. Oh, dear. I'm sorry to think that Missy might be involved in a difficult relationship. But I'm positive that she doesn't know anything about the barn burning, if that's what you're suggesting. She was as shocked as we all were when it happened."

"I'm not suggesting she does," I said. I thought back to my conversation with Missy this morning about the barn that had burned in 1912—and the barn that burned recently. "We talked about the barn," I added, "and Missy didn't give me any reason to think that she has any idea who torched it."

A pair of fresh-faced girls wearing blue Shaker dresses, carrying baskets of herbs, came toward us along the path. They greeted us pleasantly and went on. In the distance, I heard the rumble of thunder.

"Isn't it time we paid Rachel a visit?" I asked.

Martha glanced at her watch. "You're right. Let's go." As we set off, she added, "How much of what we know are we going to tell her?"

We spent the rest of the walk strategizing.

WE ducked into the Trustees' Office just as it began to rain. Jane Gillette met us on the steps, looking worried. "The weather service has posted severe thunderstorm warnings for our area—wind and dangerous lightning. I'm on my way to notify the interpreters and the staff at the gift shop, so they can encourage people to stay indoors as much as possible. Please pass the word. Oh, and the warning siren is working. We tested it a couple of days ago."

Martha nodded. To me, she added, "Last year, there was a tornado a couple of miles away. The board decided to install a siren to let visitors know they should head for one of the basements."

I glanced outside. The wind was beginning to pick up, whipping leaves across the grass. "Let's hope it blows over," I said. Back in Texas, I've seen what tornadoes can do. I'm not eager to get up close and personal with one of them.

When we stepped into Rachel's office, she was hanging a framed photograph on the wall where the gift drawings had hung. I thought briefly of that tiny detail I'd noticed in the drawing by Martha's great-aunt and wished I could go back to the conference center and see if I'd really seen what I thought I had. It was pretty remarkable.

But that would have to wait. Right now, Martha and I had some urgent business with Rachel Hart, and I wasn't looking forward to it. But first, the usual chitchat.

"The wall looks a little empty," I said after our hellos.

Rachel was dressed in black slacks and a slim black sleeveless top. I wondered if the outfit was meant to be a token of mourning for Allie's death. She put down her hammer and went to her desk.

"I miss those drawings already. But I've asked Missy to bring over some more photographs to fill the empty space." She gave a dispirited gesture at the two empty chairs in front of her desk. "Have a seat, won't you? Martha, I know I said I'd be free all afternoon, but that's changed. My brother will be stopping by in about an hour. So—"

"That's okay," Martha said. "This won't take long."

Rachel sat down at her desk and we took the chairs. Behind her, through the window, I could see the sky growing darker. Inside, the room was gloomy and shadowed. Rachel flicked on the desk lamp and opened a drawer, taking out a pack of cigarettes. Pall Malls, I saw, which answered one of my questions. Martha saw them, too, and shot a quick glance at me, her mouth tightening. Pall Malls. Proof.

Rachel had no way of knowing that she had just been tried and convicted. She picked up a slim silver lighter and lit her cigarette, inhaling deeply. "I sent a note to the staff, letting people know about Allie's death. We're all in shock." She exhaled a puff of blue smoke. "I didn't get much sleep last night, thinking about it." That was obvious. Half of her face was lit, half shadowed, but the dark circles under her eyes couldn't be disguised by makeup and her face was so pale that her red lipstick was a garish slash. "I just can't believe it," she said, catching her lower lip in her teeth. "Such a horrible accident."

A horrible accident. The phrase sounded utterly phony, something made up to deflect suspicion. Martha's face was calm, but there was a tic at the corner of her mouth and her fingers, white-knuckled, were clenched in her lap. Silently, I urged her to ignore the remark and the brand of Rachel's cigarette and stick to the script we'd agreed to. She did, bless her.

"I spoke to Pete Chatham this morning—Allie's ex-husband," she said in a thin, stretched voice that betrayed the difficulty of controlling her feelings. "We'd like to hold a memorial service in the Meeting House, early next week. Is there a problem with that?"

"Of course not. It will provide some closure for all of us." Rachel picked up a pen and jotted a note on a pad in front of her. "Just tell me when you want to do it, and I'll make the arrangements. We should invite the whole staff, of course." She made another note, frowning in concentration. "Perhaps a light meal in the Gathering Room afterward. No charge, of course. It's the least we can do."

"Thank you," Martha said with only a trace of sarcasm, and sat back in her chair, slipping a glance at me. It was time to put our strategy into operation.

I leaned forward. "Has Sheriff Franklin stopped by to see you yet, Rachel?"

The question took her by surprise. Her eyes widened, but she tried to hide her fright behind a show of unconcern. She pursed her lips and exhaled again. "Sheriff Franklin? Why, no. Why should he?"

"He's investigating Allie's death as a possible homicide."

She looked as if I had slapped her. "A . . . a homicide?" she faltered.

"Yes," I said. "I found several pieces of evidence on the path below the cottage, and notified him. He met me at Zion's Pool this morning. Thought I'd give you a heads-up. He wants to speak with you."

She tapped her cigarette into an ashtray on her desk. There were two other butts, both of them smoked down to the same place, just above the brand label. "Evidence?" Her voice sounded tinny and she seemed to be hunching down, as if against an attack. "What kind of evidence?"

"I'll let the sheriff fill you in on that."

"Really." She took a deep breath, pulling herself together. "I don't see why he'd want to talk to me. I wasn't there when it happened. I wasn't the one who found her." Her gaze settled on Martha, almost accusingly. "You were. *You* were there."

"That's right," Martha said. "China and I were the ones who found her. We were the ones who phoned nine-one-one and Security, even though you didn't want us to." She put her hands on the arms of her chair. Her voice was tense and I could see her gathering her muscles, as if she were about to spring at Rachel. "And *you* were the one who went into her office last night, Rachel. You searched it pretty thoroughly, didn't you?"

"Went into—" Rachel paled.

"We saw you," Martha said flatly. "China and I. You were looking for Allie's notes and work papers."

Outside, there was a low, ominous roll of thunder. Rachel swallowed. "Well, I had to, didn't I?" She checked her breathing, making sure it was under control. "She's the foundation's accountant, and there's a trustees' meeting next week. I needed—"

"You needed the papers Allie was working on." I gave her a hard look. "But you couldn't find them, because we have them."

That caught her by surprise, and she flinched. "You . . . have them?" she managed weakly.

"We have them," Martha said. "The copies of the stock inventory at the time of Lottie's death. Copies of the recent dividend reports."

Rachel pulled at her cigarette, trying to steady herself. "I don't see where you're going with this. It has nothing to do with—"

Martha went on as though Rachel hadn't spoken. "We also have Allie's notes comparing the inventory and the dividend reports. Allie figured out that somebody stole some of the foundation's stock certificates. And since the opportunity to get into the safe deposit box is limited to the one person who has the keys, she had a pretty good idea of the identity of the thief."

Rachel opened her mouth, but nothing came out. Martha went on, drilling her with her glance.

"Allie planned to take her concerns to the trustees at their next meeting. She asked me to make a motion that the board hire an outside forensic auditor to examine the foundation's current holdings and determine how much is missing." Martha's expression was grim. "I am putting you on notice, Rachel. I intend to make this motion."

"No!" Rachel cried desperately. "No, you can't!"

"Yes, I can. I already have." Martha gave her a bleak smile. "I put my motion into writing and sent it to each of the trustees this morning, along with a background statement. I didn't name any names or assign any guilt. I just stated the facts."

I turned to look at her, surprised. This wasn't part of the script, and we hadn't discussed it. But it was a good move. A very good move.

"You had no right to do that, Martha," Rachel flared. "You've exceeded your authority. You—"

"Read the bylaws, Rachel," Martha said savagely. "Each trustee has the power to place an item on the agenda. All we have to do is send it out in advance of the meeting. That was Lottie's way of guaranteeing that nobody would try to put a lid on discussion."

"But *why*?" Rachel wailed. "Why couldn't you have waited and talked it over with me? We could have worked it out. Instead you had to go and mail this . . . this *accusation* to everybody. They'll all think it was *me*!"

Martha's gaze was fixed on Rachel, her eyes steely. "I did it because I felt that the more people knew about my intentions, the less likely I was to end up like Allie."

Rachel grew even paler. After a moment, she said, "What if I refuse to put your item on the agenda?"

"That's easy," I said pleasantly. "You can expect a civil suit. My client will demand an audit of the stock certificates and a review of the foundation's management."

Stunned, Rachel looked from Martha to me. "You can't—you couldn't—"

Martha smiled.

"You watch," I said, and chuckled.

When Rachel finally spoke, her voice was dull and flat. She had a cornered look, like an animal backed against a wall. "Well, then, I suppose I'll have to tell you. I don't have any choice, do I?"

"Tell us the truth, I hope," Martha said.

"I'll tell you what happened to the stocks." Rachel stubbed out her cigarette and sat back in the chair, resting both hands on the arms. She was silent for a long time. She looked infinitely weary.

"What happened to them, Rachel?" I spoke gently, thinking that a harsh word might crumple her.

She took a deep breath and fastened her eyes on me. I could sense, rather than see, the tightening of her muscles. "My brother took them."

There was a long silence. In my mind, something jiggled, joggled, and fell into place.

"Your brother?" Martha's tone was both disbelieving and scornful, as though Rachel's attempt to shift the blame was beneath contempt. "Oh, come now, Rachel."

But Rachel was speaking directly to me. "Bruce has had a gambling addiction since he was a teenager." She took a deep breath, held it, let it out. "He's a compulsive gambler."

Outside, twin slashes of lightning forked across the sky. Martha was staring, almost uncomprehending. "A compulsive gambler?"

"Horse racing. He's lost hundreds of thousands of dollars to the bookies. Could be a million or more, for all I know. Lottie bailed him out until she reached the end of her tether." Rachel's voice became bitter. "He never paid back a penny, of course."

"That's why your grandmother left him out of her will?" I asked.

"Yes. Lottie loved him—she loved him dearly, obsessively." Her mouth twisted. "She tried everything, even paying for treatment. But nothing worked. He kept on gambling. Sometimes he'd win big, but that only gave him more to lose. Finally, she gave up. She didn't leave him anything in her will because she said he'd already gotten his inheritance, all those thousands and thousands of dollars he'd borrowed and gambled away. She also made sure Bruce would never have anything to do with the foundation. She was afraid that if he was involved with it, he'd find a way to siphon off money to support his habit."

Martha pressed her lips together. "This is very hard to believe."

"How could I make it up, Martha?" Rachel asked wearily. "If you don't believe me, ask Linda. She knows all about it." To me, she added, "Linda is Bruce's wife. Her parents loaned him money, too, a lot of it."

"Did they know about the gambling?" I asked.

She shook her head. "They thought it was a business loan. Business— that's a laugh," she said harshly. "Bruce doesn't have a business anymore, not a viable one, anyway. He's sucked his real-estate firm dry. He's even taken money from escrow accounts."

Stealing escrow funds. That will land you in jail faster than you can say *stupid*. But maybe Bruce figured that jail was preferable to what would happen when the bookies caught up with him. "Did you loan him money?"

She nodded bleakly. "All I had."

"Has he paid it back?" Martha asked.

"Not a red cent." Rachel put her hand to her eyes. "This gambling—it's such a horrible disease. Like alcoholism, but worse. Alcohol doesn't necessarily ruin an entire family the way gambling does."

I grew up with an alcoholic—my mother. I know about addiction and the way addicts can turn everybody in the family into enablers, helping them get their fix. I could sympathize with Rachel, who—if she was telling the truth—had certainly been victimized by her brother. But she wasn't off the hook yet. She might have been coerced, but she had to take responsibility for what she had done.

I gave her a hard look. "When did you give him access to the safe deposit box?"

"I didn't!" she cried. She dropped her hand, stiffening. "It wasn't me, I swear it! I didn't even know what had happened until the dividend reports came."

"But you have the keys," Martha said accusingly.

"Bruce took my key."

"But he's not on the list of people who have access to that box," Martha said. "As I understand it, only you and the foundation's treasurer are on the signature card."

"Linda overlooked that," Rachel said bleakly. "She manages the bank where the stock certificates are held."

"Linda!" Martha gasped. "But that's a violation of bank regulations. She wouldn't do that."

But it's happened. I thought of an investigation I'd read about not long ago. A bank employee had been charged with the theft of nearly a million dollars in jewelry and coins from several safe deposit boxes at a California bank. But claims against banks are tricky. Some victims don't document the contents of their boxes, so they can't prove what, if anything, was stolen. Others are reluctant to go to the cops for fear that the IRS will be curious about whether they've paid taxes on whatever they've squirreled away. In the foundation's case, however, there was an official inventory, a regular dividend report, and—presumably—a tax record. No lack of documentation. If the bank's manager was involved—

"Yes, Linda," Rachel said heavily. "But not the way you think. Bruce lied to her. He told her I'd given him my permission to look through the box. It used to belong to our grandparents. She didn't see it as a big deal."

Martha made a strangled noise.

"No big deal?" I laughed shortly. "The bank considers that kind of thing a firing offense." What's more, she's an accomplice to felony theft, both before and after the fact. Her best bet would be to rat him out in exchange for the best deal the D.A. would give her.

Rachel pressed her lips together as if she were in pain. "Linda said she had no idea what was in the box. She thought it was just old family papers or something. When I saw from the dividend reports that some of the stocks were missing, I went to her and she told me what had happened. She feels terrible about it." She cleared her throat. "She's filed for divorce. She says Bruce has ruined her life."

I couldn't blame her. If all this was true, the guy was a solid gold loser. "Did you confront your brother about the theft?"

Rachel's eyes were on her hands, the fingers woven tightly together in her lap. "Yes," she said, very quietly.

"When?"

"Right after I talked to Linda. A month or so ago."

"What did he say?"

Her lipsticked mouth twisted painfully. "The same thing he always says, of course. He'll pay it back. He's working on a big deal, a really big deal. There's enough money in it to take care of everything." Her head came up and she gave a hard laugh. "I've heard that story so many times before. Wouldn't you think I'd get smarter? But I fell for it again. Like a damned fool. Only this time, it seemed—" She stopped.

"It seemed—what?" I asked.

She made a face. "It seemed like he might finally be able to help *me* for a change, instead of me always helping him."

"How?"

"He said he could line up some . . ." Her voice failed her. She cleared her throat. "Some investors who'd be interested in putting money into the spa. A joint venture, a partnership, something."

"So *that's* where the money was going to come from!" Martha said in surprise.

"That's why I had the plans drawn up—so the investors could take a look at them. But the deal's fallen through. Bruce says the investors aren't interested. If there ever were any in the first place," she added bitterly. "He was probably lying to me to keep me quiet."

I was thinking. A compulsive gambler can get himself into very serious trouble. Bookies connected with organized crime are inclined to play rough with people who owe them money, twisting arms and shooting guns and the like. Which can cause the people who owe the money to do some pretty stupid and dangerous things.

"When did you find out that Allie had discovered the securities theft?" I asked.

"About a week ago, when I realized that she'd made copies of the dividend reports. I knew that she had the inventories. The only reason she'd want the reports was to compare the two."

"And when did you tell your brother what Allie knew?"

Martha swiveled to look at me, her eyes wide and dark. "You can't think that Bruce—"

"When?" I interrupted sharply.

"Yesterday afternoon, after you were here," Rachel whispered. Her hands went up and she dropped her face into them, rocking back and forth. "Oh, God," she whispered. "Oh, God."

"Yesterday afternoon," I repeated brutally. "And yesterday evening, Allie was killed." Without a pause, I added, "What kind of cigarettes does your brother smoke?"

Rachel dropped her hands and looked at me, her eyes like round dark holes punched in her white face. "Cigarettes? Why, Pall Mall. We've both smoked them for years. Why are you asking?" Then she got it. "You're saying that you found—" She couldn't finish the sentence.

That tied it up, as far as I was concerned—that, and the blue zipper tab I had discovered near the cigarette butt. That was what had been nibbling and nudging at the back of my mind: the tab I found was the same color blue as Bruce's Adidas jacket. I'd bet dollars to doughnuts that the tab on his jacket was missing.

Martha pushed herself out of her chair. "So that's why you went to Allie's office last night! You had to find her papers. Her notes. Because you thought—you *knew*, even then—that your brother had killed her. You were trying to cover up for him. Weren't you? *Weren't you?*"

By this time Martha was screaming. I stood and put my hands on her shoulders, pulling her back, forcing her into her chair. "We're not going to solve this by yelling," I said quietly. "Let Rachel tell us herself." I sat down again, looking hard at Rachel. "What were you looking for in Allie's office?"

"I was . . ." She gulped. "You're right. I was looking for the copies of the inventory. And the dividend reports."

"Because you knew those papers might be the motive for her murder?"

She stared at me wordlessly.

"You suspected your brother of killing her?"

Her lips were pressed tightly together. She was silent.

I leaned forward. "You're in way over your head, Rachel. Allie suspected *you* of taking those stocks. In fact, she was convinced of it. You could just as easily be the killer, couldn't you? You could have killed her to allow your brother more time to round up those investors. Couldn't you?"

She gasped. "Oh, no! No, of course not! I wouldn't—"

"Where were you between six thirty and seven thirty?"

"I was . . . I was in my apartment, taking a nap. Then I went to the restaurant to meet Bruce."

"You were alone?"

"Of course I was alone," she flared. "You don't take a nap when you've got company. But if you mean, can I prove it, no. I . . . I can't."

I sat back. "And after Allie was dead, you went to her office, looking for her papers. The threat had been taken care of. All you had to do was get rid of those papers and you'd be safe. You and Bruce. Right?"

Rachel shrank back into her chair. She looked limp and washed-out and empty, like a rag doll with all the stuffing knocked out of it.

"Let's try this again," I said. "You suspected your brother of killing Allie?"

Hopeless now, eyes filling with tears, she nodded. "I . . . I thought of it the minute you called. That's why I didn't want you to call the police. It was stupid, but I couldn't . . ." Her voice failed.

"Then you went to Allie's office, hoping to recover the papers. To cover your brother's tracks."

She nodded again.

"Do you see the position you've put yourself into? Can you see where this is likely to lead—for both you and your brother?"

Another nod, slow, reluctant.

"Well, then," I said, very gently, "don't you think it's time to end it?"

"Yes," she whispered. She closed her eyes. "Yes, it's time. It's past time. But I don't know how." She opened her eyes. The tears were running down her cheeks. "Tell me how, please!"

It was the answer I was waiting for.

Chapter Twenty-two

Seek the LORD, and ye shall live; lest he break out like fire . . .
and there be none to quench it . . . Ye who turn judgment to
wormwood, and leave off righteousness in the earth.

Amos 5:6–7

It took longer than I would have liked to get everything lined
up, especially since the clock was ticking and Bruce Hart would
be showing up in Rachel's office in something like half an hour.

I started with Sheriff Franklin, who was out of the office but reach-
able. While I was waiting for him to return my call, I used Martha's cell
phone to check in with McQuaid. He had just gotten off the phone with
a former buddy, now a Kentucky private detective, and had turned up
some useful information. According to his source, Bruce Hart's gambling was an open secret, at least among those who hung around the
track. He had collected a sizable chunk of insurance change from the
deaths of his horses in the barn fire. The whole wad, it was rumored, had
gone to pay off a bookie who was notorious for his connections to organized crime. Which meant that somebody had been leaning hard on Mr.
Hart, very, very hard.

McQuaid had heard enough to make him nervous. "I want you to
drop this *now*, China," he said in his sternest cop voice. "Arson, gambling,

organized crime—there's no telling what else is involved with this. Murder, maybe."

"I *am* dropping it," I said. "Into the lap of the law. In fact, I'm waiting for a call from Sheriff Franklin right now."

"Good girl," McQuaid said warmly, and spoiled it immediately by saying, "You're finally showing some sense."

"I'll let you know what happens," I said and clicked off, just in time to field Sheriff Franklin's call. I explained the situation as economically as I could, including what I had just learned from McQuaid, giving credit where credit was due. He listened without comment and when I was finished, grunted shortly.

"You say Hart's still at Mount Zion?"

"I assume so. He's supposed to see his sister in"—I checked my watch—"about twenty minutes."

"I'll get over there as soon as I can. But it'll be the better part of an hour, maybe more. I'm at a three-car pileup on the far side of the county, and I've got two deputies out sick."

I'd already thought of an alternative plan, in case he couldn't make it by the time things got rolling. "Is Kentucky a one- or a two-party state, Sheriff?"

He gave an amused chuckle. "I take it that you're not asking whether we're all Republicans."

I returned the chuckle. "No. I'm sure there must be one or two Democrats around someplace." We both knew what I was asking: whether Kentucky state law required that both parties to a conversation had to consent to being audio taped, or whether a taping was legal if only one party agreed. Texas is a one-party state. There's an obvious advantage.

"We're a one-party state, I'm glad to say." The sheriff was cautious.

"Just what've you got in mind, Ms. Bayles? And remember that we're dealing with somethin' pretty serious. I won't have any monkey business."

When I told him, there was a short silence. "I don't much like it," he said quietly. "Any way this could wait until I get there?"

"I don't see how, sir. Not without making Hart suspicious. For all we know, he has a plane ticket in his pocket. And it might take a while to extradite him, depending on his destination. This is a chance I'd rather not pass up."

He grunted. "You're a lawyer. You know the downside."

I did. People sometimes tape-record conversations with the idea that the tape might come in handy as evidence. But even if the recording has been lawfully made, there are bound to be challenges to its evidentiary use from one side or the other—from the defense, in this case. A smart defense attorney would make a blizzard of motions in an effort to keep it out. But in this instance, there would also be witnesses. And any tape of the conversation between Rachel and her brother would be better than no tape at all, in my opinion.

"I don't much like it, either, Sheriff. But we don't have many options."

"Well, then, watch yourself. I'll get there quick as I can." I could hear the thunder rumbling. "Quick as this storm allows," he amended. "Pourin' buckets where I am."

"No sirens," I cautioned.

"No sirens," he agreed.

RACHEL was a nervous wreck by the time her brother arrived, but I doubted that he was expecting her to be anything else. Martha and I, almost as nervous as Rachel, were uncomfortably crouched in a stuffy cloakroom adjacent to Rachel's office, the door open a crack so we could hear. The sky outside the high, narrow window at the end of the room had grown so dark that there was barely enough light to see my watch. I heard the rap on the door of Rachel's office and felt my stomach muscles tense. I hoped to hell that the sheriff could get here before this was over.

"Come in." Rachel's voice was thin and reedy.

A door opened, a chair scraped, a jacket rustled. "I've come to say good-bye," Bruce Hart said, without preamble.

"Good-bye!" This obviously took Rachel by surprise. "What . . . What do you mean? Where are you going?"

"It's probably better you don't know," Bruce said. "I'm catching a plane out of Cincinnati in a few hours."

I felt a surge of righteous vindication. I'd been right to go ahead with this.

"Oh, no, Bruce," Rachel mourned.

His voice was stubborn. "I've decided I just can't take it anymore. The divorce, the debts, the pressure, everything. I've got to get away."

"But you can't leave!" Rachel spoke with a barely restrained hysteria. "You've got to put back the money you stole from the foundation!"

"I'll put it back, I promise. But I can't do it now, sis." He was asking for pity. "Come on, Rachel," he wheedled. "Give me a break. I've got to get some clear space around me. Some breathing space. I'll be back as soon as I've got my head together."

Rachel wasn't in a pitying mood. "It's all about you, isn't it, Bruce?" she said harshly. "It's always about you, you, you. Can't you see what you've done to *me*? After all the ways I've helped you, year after year?"

"Done to you? What are you talking about, Rachel? I haven't done anything to you."

Outside, the purplish sky was torn by three sharp fingers of lightning. Thunder *rip-rapped* through the clouds like the wrath of God. I glanced nervously at the window, hoping the sheriff wouldn't be slowed up by the storm.

"You self-centered bastard!" Rachel cried. "Yesterday afternoon I told you that our accountant figured out that the stock was gone. That she thought I did it."

"So?" There was the sound of a lighter clicking, a long, slow drag of breath. "You're safe, sis."

"Because she's dead. Because you killed her."

Outdoors, there was the sound of rushing wind. Beside me, Martha sucked in her breath. In the other room, there was a long silence.

"Well, hell, Rachel," Bruce said finally. "There wasn't any other way." The chair squeaked as he settled back in it, and I pictured him crossing one leg over his knee. "Anyway, with her out of the picture, you're off the hook. And I've got some breathing room. We've bought some time."

I felt my stomach muscles tighten. Beside me in the gloom, Martha raised clenched fists in jubilant triumph. It was as clear an admission of guilt as we could have expected. If a jury got to hear it, they would undoubtedly agree. *If.* If the tape recorder in Rachel's desk drawer was working. *If* the defense motion to exclude was overruled. *If if if.*

"I'm off the hook?" Rachel asked heavily. "Hardly, I'm afraid. One of the board members—Martha Edmond—found the accountant's working papers. She figured out what you did. She has moved to hire an auditor, Bruce. He'll go through everything. The records, the stock inventory, the foundation's financial holdings. It'll all come out. Every penny you've taken."

"A motion? That's easy." Bruce gave a confident laugh. "All you have to do is quash it. Don't allow her to bring it up. You control the agenda, don't you?" His voice became bitter. "You've always controlled everything, and everyone else—including Grandma Lottie. Remember? You're the reason she left me out of her will. You poisoned her mind against me."

"Oh, shut up," Rachel said wearily. "Lottie just got sick of constantly giving you money to throw after the horses. And no, there's nothing I can do about Martha Edmond. She's already mailed the motion to every trustee."

"You didn't try to stop her?"

"She's got a lawyer," Rachel went on, as if he hadn't spoken. "If the trustees don't approve the motion, Edmond will file a lawsuit. Against me, against the board. And now you've killed somebody—oh, God, Bruce! What are we going to do?"

She was weeping now. If this was an act, I thought, it was heart-breakingly authentic. But I didn't think it was an act. The years of giving money to her brother, of being used and manipulated to help him cover his addiction, of worrying and hoping and praying—it had all come to a climax in these last few moments.

Lightning flared against the window. Thunder cracked. I looked at my watch. The sheriff ought to be here by now. Maybe he was waiting outside for Bruce to come out of the building. Or standing in the hallway with his ear to the office door. Cooped up in this cloakroom, I had no way of knowing.

The chair scraped back. "Shut up, Rachel," Bruce said angrily. "I've had just about all I can take. I'm getting out of here."

Martha flinched and I tensed. Damn. I should have anticipated that things might turn violent. I looked around for something I could use as a weapon. A Shaker chair was hanging on a peg high on the wall—in a pinch, it would have to do.

"I won't shut up!" Rachel cried desperately. "I can't! Because it's not just about the money now. Because you and I are the only ones who had any reason to want Allie Chatham dead!"

Bruce growled something ominous. I stood and reached for the chair.

"I know I didn't kill her," Rachel sobbed, "but Sheriff Franklin doesn't know that, not yet. All he knows is that somebody who smokes our brand of cigarettes was waiting by the path near Allie's cottage. How could you be so stupid as to *smoke*, Bruce?"

"Oh, hell," Bruce spat out. There was a long silence. "Has he questioned you yet?"

I sat back down again and let out my breath silently.

"Not yet, but he will. It's not just the cigarette, Bruce." There was a short, accusing silence. "It's the zipper tab from your jacket. The sheriff found that, too."

I could imagine Bruce looking down at his jacket, the terrible light suddenly dawning. "Shit," he said explosively. A chair fell over with a bang. "Listen, Rachel, I've got to go. I've got a plane to catch. When they do the DNA on the cigarette, they'll know it wasn't you, so you're clear. Just don't tell them I was here. Just—"

"But the money, Bruce! The stocks you stole from the foundation! What'll I tell the trustees?"

"You'll think of something." I could hear his footsteps crossing the floor. "You'll take care of it, sis. You've always taken care of everything." The door opened. "I'll be in touch."

Rachel gave a long wail. The door closed.

Martha lurched to her feet. "My God," she whispered. "Do you suppose the sheriff is here?"

"I hope so." I was already on my way into Rachel's office. "Did the recorder work okay? Did you get it all?"

"So far as I know," Rachel said. She was sitting in her office chair, so limp that she looked almost boneless. She closed her eyes. "If I'd known it was going to be so hard—"

I left Rachel to Martha's tender mercies and went into the hall. The back door, standing open, was suddenly slammed shut by the wind. I raced toward it, reached it, flung it wide, and stood on the steps, searching the green space in front of me. Rain was lashing down, the trees were bending, and neither the sheriff nor his auto were in sight.

But there was Bruce, running across the grass in the direction of the parking lot. He stopped for a moment in the shelter of a tall sycamore tree, zipping up his blue jacket. He reached for his cell phone hooked to his belt. Shoulder to the tree, he punched in a number, held the phone to his ear, and—

There was a blinding blue flash, a deafening clap of thunder, a spurt of flame, a puff of smoke, and a splintering crack.

I blinked. The sycamore tree was slowly, agonizingly splitting, the two pieces falling, falling, one across a flower bed, the other, wreathed in flame, across the roof of a small shed.

And Bruce Hart was sprawled on the grass, unmoving, some fifteen feet away, as if hurled there by divine vengeance.

Chapter Twenty-three

You may wear your rue with a difference.

Shakespeare
Hamlet IV.5

Conscience, anticipating time,
Already rues the enacted crime.

Sir Walter Scott
"Rokeby"

The storm passed on quickly and after a while the afternoon sky took on the color of a freshly laundered Shaker dress. An emergency services crew removed Bruce Hart's body, his face and right shoulder charred from the lightning's strike, while the tourists came out of the buildings to huddle in frightened groups. I could hear them whispering among themselves that they couldn't imagine something so horrible happening in such a place—as if God should turn off the lightning because Shakers had once worshipped here. A deputy took statements from Martha and me, while Sheriff Franklin, having confiscated the tape, began his interrogation of Rachel.

Now that Bruce Hart was dead, the tape was moot, at least as evidence in a criminal trial. But it cleared Rachel of both the theft and Allie's murder. I doubted if the trustees, her friends, would take any action against her for failing to report her brother's raid on the foundation's cookie jar—although it was certainly true that if she had reported the theft when she discovered it, Allie would be alive today. It was the same mistake she had made when Maxine stole the money from the gift shop. There's a lesson here about unintended consequences. I could only hope that Rachel had finally learned it.

Since there was nothing more we could do to help the sheriff, Martha and I headed for the conference center and Missy Thatcher's office. We had a chore, unpleasant but necessary.

It took only a moment to relate what had happened. "Bruce is dead?" Missy Thatcher looked from Martha to me, uncomprehending. "But he can't be! I just saw him this afternoon. He just left—"

Her face crumpled. She sagged into a chair, Martha's arm around her, and began to cry.

Tactfully, I left Missy's office and went down the hall in the direction of the library, leaving Martha to comfort her friend in private. I didn't know how much of the truth about Bruce's crimes Martha was going to tell Missy. Actually, there was no need to tell her anything until the sheriff concluded his investigation into Allie's murder, or the truth about the stock theft came out, or Rachel made some announcement to the staff. And as far as Missy was concerned, I couldn't help feeling that Bruce's death was for the best. She might be temporarily devastated, but she'd get over it. And she didn't need the kind of havoc that a man like that would inevitably wreak on her life. Nobody needed that.

Now all that was left was to pick up the pieces. I wondered how Bruce's wife would cope with the wreckage he had left behind, and what Rachel would say to the trustees, and whether Mount Zion would survive this latest round of misfortune. Which reminded me of what I had read in Elder Babbitt's journal, and the curious thing I had seen—or thought I had seen—in Sister Charity's gift drawing. I picked up my pace.

The magnifying glass was on the table where I had left it, and so were the drawings. I guessed that Bruce Hart had come back here after lunch and Missy had been too busy to put things away. I picked up the glass, settled myself at the table, and went back to studying the complexities of Charity's drawing.

And again it struck me, that odd combination of rue and wormwood in the circlet of herbs that surrounded the delicately colored Tree of Life in the center of the symmetrical drawing. Rue and wormwood: remorse for wrongs done, guilt, sorrowing repentance, twined with bitterness, pain, loss. Hardly the herbal bouquet I would have expected in a drawing that was thought to be a gift of heavenly spirits, meant to convey the mystical bliss to be experienced in the hereafter. Why not rosemary for remembrance, almond flowers for hope, amaranth for immortality, bay for glory, a white lily for purity of heart? There was a wealth of plants to choose from.

Why wormwood and rue?

Still puzzling over that, I studied the small, carefully executed drawings of people in each of the four corners. They were done in pen, ink, and watercolor, their clothing and surroundings—gardens, trees, Shaker buildings—painted in rich blues and purples, bright yellow and scarlet, and several shades of green. In the top left corner were the two Shaker sisters, singing from a sheet of music. Looking more closely with the magnifying glass, I saw that the drawing was surrounded by a pen-and-ink scroll that looked like a series of elaborate curlicues but was really two cleverly disguised names—Sister Charity and Sister Ruth—repeated over and over.

Ah! I thought with pleased surprise. Here was more confirmation that this was Charity's work, and that it had some unique personal significance. I moved to the top right drawing. A Shaker sister at her loom, a brother with his hoe, two names repeated in the same way around the drawing. But these names were Sister Ruth and Brother Charles, disguised with scrolls and loops and coils. The bottom right drawing pictured a man—not a Shaker, judging from his bowler hat, jacket, and tight pants—bent over under the window of a building labeled *Sisters' Shop*. Inside the window, minutely drawn, I could see the woman at her loom. Must be Sister Ruth, I thought. Curled and coiled around the picture was the name Will Ayers.

Will Ayers, I thought in surprise. Rachel and Bruce's grandfather! The man who owned Zion's Spring and who had given poor, beleaguered Elder Babbitt no end of grief, at least according to the elder's journal, because he planned to build a resort hotel at the spring. The man who had offered to buy the entire village of Mount Zion.

I frowned. Obviously, the purchase had never taken place. Ditto the hotel. What had happened?

Eagerly, I swung the glass to the next picture, and the whole story came into sudden focus. The man—Will Ayers—was lying facedown on the ground, a pool of red blood under his head. Over him stood a woman in Shaker dress, a bloodied ax in her hand. In the doorway of the Sisters' Shop stood Ruth, her mouth a perfect *O* of horror. Around the picture, only one name: Charity. And Charity had to be the one with the bloody ax.

I sat back, startled. So that was what had happened to Will Ayers. Charity Edmond had whacked him with an ax!

Why? I looked at the drawing again. I was only guessing, of course, but it looked to me like Charity was defending Ruth from Ayers. Hadn't I read something in Elder Babbitt's journal about Ayers making free with the Shaker ladies? Maybe that was it. Maybe Ayers was trying to sneak up on Ruth, alone in the Sisters' Shop, and rape her, and Charity had killed him, rather than let her friend be harmed. It made sense.

And then I saw that what I had originally taken as ornamented curlicues and spirals and loops and flourishes was really an intricate maze of minuscule script. Under the magnifying glass, I could begin to make it out. There were two Bible verses.

And the LORD saith, Because they have forsaken my law which I set before them, and have not obeyed my voice, neither walked therein; But have walked after the imagination of their own heart . . . Therefore thus saith the LORD of hosts, the God of Israel; Behold, I will feed them, even this people, with wormwood, and give them water of gall to drink. Jeremiah 9: 13–15

Seek the LORD, and ye shall live; lest he break out like fire . . . and there be none to quench it . . . Ye who turn judgment to wormwood, and leave off righteousness in the earth. Amos 5: 6–7

Break forth like a fire, I thought, my eyes lingering on the words. Was that what had happened to Bruce Hart, who thought he could get away with murder? *Turn justice into wormwood*—a pretty good description of what he had hoped to do.

I went back to the drawing and found two similarly hidden lines of non-biblical poetry—Housman, I thought: "With rue my heart is laden, For golden friends I had." And another, from the Renaissance: "His physick must be Rue, even Rue for Sin."

Rue, a powerful medicine, a "physick" for sin. And with that I understood. Charity's gift drawing was the confession of a sorrowful, repentant murderer, whose deed was wormwood in her soul.

I leaned forward, frustrated, wanting to know more, but the drawing seemed to have nothing more to tell me. I pushed it away. What had happened after Charity killed Will Ayers? Was she tried for the murder and convicted? No, surely not, since the family—Martha's family—seemed not to know anything about it. Was she expelled from Mount Zion when the murder came to light? Was *this* the mysterious reason that Charity had been exiled from the life she loved?

I frowned. Too many questions. There had to be more to this story, some sort of documentation, *something*. Surely, such a momentous event as a murder at Mount Zion would not have gone unchronicled. I turned to Elder Babbitt's journal, still open on the table, put on the latex gloves Missy had given me to protect the pages from the oils in my fingers, and began to read.

A half hour later, breathless, I finally closed the book.

"I don't understand," Martha said, puzzled. Sitting across the table from me, with Charity's drawing and Elder Babbitt's journal between us, she spread out her hands. "You're saying that my great-aunt—modest, shy, spiritual Aunt Charity—actually killed a man? Killed Will Ayers?" She shook her head incredulously. "I just can't believe it, China."

"Believe it," I said. "Her confession is in that drawing. She's drawn herself holding the bloody ax. That's Ruth, horrified, in the doorway of the Sisters' Shop, where the murder happened."

Martha bent over to look. "Amazing," she murmured. "I've looked at this drawing any number of times. I never noticed this!"

"That's probably because there's so much in it," I said. "And everything is so tiny. But that's not the only evidence. Charity confessed to Eldress Olive Manning and Elder Babbitt. And the good elder wrote it all down in his journal, in the entry for June 14. You can read it for your-self."

Martha looked bewildered. "But why did she kill him? Honestly, China, that woman was the sweetest lady who ever walked this earth. Everybody in the family thought she was a saint." She looked down at the drawing and shuddered. "Why would she do something so horri-ble?"

"Because she thought he was about to attack and rape Sister Ruth, whom she loved, as the good elder put it, 'beyond all reason, and with an unnatural passion.'"

Martha's eyes grew round. "Oh, dear. You're saying that Aunt Char-ity and Sister Ruth—"

"I'm not saying any such thing," I replied emphatically. "I'm telling you what Babbitt wrote in his journal. I have no idea what the real story was, or how he came to that conclusion. Anyway, Sister Ruth seems to have given her heart to Brother Charles, who had stolen some three thousand dollars from the Herb Department accounts. He argued that it wasn't theft, but a 'proper recompense' for his years of service to the Society."

Martha was shaking her head. "Three thousand dollars was a lot of money in those days. I suppose he was going to use it to buy property or something."

"Or something. Turns out that he'd made an under-the-table deal with Will Ayers."

"A deal? What kind of deal?"

"Well, it seems that Ayers had some pretty big plans. He started out by wanting to build a hotel at Zion's Spring. Then he offered to buy the village. Maybe he thought it would be cheaper to turn one of the dwell-ings into an inn, the way Ernest and Lottie Ayers did much later. Charles planned to invest his stolen money in Ayers' project in return for a share of the profits, plus the livery concession." At Martha's puzzled look, I added, "Charles would manage the stables, which in those days would've been a pretty big deal. He and Ruth figured they'd be set up for life. But with Ayers dead, the deal was off. As they saw it, Charity killed the goose that was about to lay their golden nest egg. They were furious with her."

Martha frowned. "But Aunt Charity was only trying to protect Ruth! How could they be angry about that?"

"Because Charity was wrong. Ayers wasn't there to rape Ruth. He was there to meet Charles, who was going to hand over the money and finalize their deal. Charity said that when Ruth saw Ayers on the ground, and the bloody ax, she said, 'You stupid girl—you've ruined everything!'"

"But Aunt Charity was never charged with murder," Martha pointed out. "If something like that happened, the family would have to know. It couldn't have been hidden, especially back in those days, when everybody knew everybody else."

"They didn't know because she wasn't charged. Except for Ruth and Charles, only Babbitt and Eldress Olive knew about the murder. Babbitt took Ayers off into the woods and buried him. Then Charles and Ruth took off—with the money."

"Elder Babbitt didn't make him pay it back?"

"He tried. He threatened Charles with prosecution. But Charles threatened to tell the sheriff that Charity had murdered Ayers. So Babbitt had to back down. Ayers' disappearance caused a fair amount of consternation locally. But after a while, the hubbub died down and everything went back to normal."

"Unbelievable," Martha was saying. "Incredible."

"Any more incredible than Bruce Hart being struck by lightning?"

"You've got a point there," Martha conceded. "So what happened?"

"Babbitt died the next year—1913. Olive stayed until 1923. At that point, there weren't enough people to keep things going. She closed Mount Zion and went to Mount Lebanon. You know the rest—except that I guess you didn't know that when Lottie and Ernest bought the village, they didn't buy the spring. They didn't have to. It was already in the family."

"Oh, I see," Martha said. She frowned. "But Aunt Charity didn't stay with Olive."

"No. Charity was so remorseful that Babbitt and Olive forgave her. But she seems to have passed judgment on herself. She went into exile, into the World. She had to be cast out of the Garden, she said. She could not stay here and reap the fruit of her sin—a life of worship."

"How sad," Martha said, shaking her head. "And none of us knew. No one in the family, I mean."

"It had to be that way, I suppose. She chose her own punishment. Exile from paradise." I looked at the drawing. Rue and wormwood, wormwood and rue.

And I understood.

THAT wasn't the end of it, of course. The weather cleared up and there were no more thunderstorms to contend with. The village filled up with tourists. Martha conducted her workshops, with my help. The trustees held their meeting, most of which was dedicated (as Martha told me) to Rachel's report of what had happened. By the time it was over, the board had approved Martha's motion to hire an independent auditor, and Rachel had withdrawn her proposal to build the spa. Finances would be tight, but perhaps if they were able to bring in some more new programs and open the convention center to outside organizations, they could at least make the note payments.

The day before we left, a memorial service for Allie was held in the Meeting House, where her friends celebrated her life and said their good-byes. When that was done, Martha and I packed up and headed home, a couple of days early. Neither of us had the heart to swim in Zion's Pool. And both of us were glad to go back to our ordinary lives.

BUT my life, as I discovered when I returned to it, wasn't exactly ordinary.

Caitlin was still staying at our house. And Marcia was very, very sick.

"It's cancer," McQuaid said to me, as we cleared off the table after dinner, my first evening at home. He and the kids had collaborated on pizzas, and we had eaten every scrap. "It turns out that she had breast cancer several years ago. It's metastasized. Spine. And lungs."

I shuddered. "The prognosis?"

He put his arm around me. "They're not saying. But I don't think it's good." He paused. "She's worried, of course. But more about Caitlin than herself."

I wasn't surprised. More than anything else, Marcia had wanted to make a home for Caitlin. It must be torture for her to give up that hope. I took a deep breath and rested my forehead against his shoulder. "Did Marcia ask us to take her to live with us?"

"I didn't wait to be asked. I volunteered."

"You volunteered?" I stepped back, looking up at him. Another child in the house? A girl, not far from her teens? "Are you sure?"

"No." He pressed his lips together. "Yes. Yes, I'm sure. Anyway, we don't have much of a choice, do we? At best, Marcia will be doing chemotherapy all summer. She'll need all the strength she has just to look after herself. And at worst—" He dropped his shoulders. "Caitie has lost her mother and her father, China. With Marcia out of the picture, temporarily or permanently, we're all she has. I know you don't want any more kids, but—"

I came back into his arms. It was true. I'm not a mothering kind of person. And mothering Caitlin was going to be a job and a half. But this wasn't a challenge we could step away from, either one of us.

"Sounds like we have a daughter," I said.

He held me close.

Books About the Shakers

The Believers: A Novel of Shaker Life, by Janice Holt Giles. The University Press of Kentucky, 1957.

The Earth Shall Blossom: Shaker Herbs and Gardening, by Galen Beale and Mary Rose Boswell. The Countryman Press, 1991.

The Kentucky Shakers, by Julia Neal. The University Press of Kentucky, 1982.

Pleasant Hill and Its Shakers, by Thomas D. Clark and F. Gerald Ham. Pleasant Hill Press, 1968, 1983.

The Shaker Cookbook, by Caroline B. Piercy. Gramercy Books, 1953.

Shaker Medicinal Herbs: A Compendium of History, Lore, and Uses, by Amy Bess Miller. Storey Books, 1998.

Simple Gifts: A Memoir of a Shaker Village, by June Sprigg. Alfred A. Knopf, 1988.

Recipes

Cherry Tomatoes with Pecans, Mozzarella, and Cass Wilde's Tarragon Dressing

12 small mozzarella balls (*bocconcini*), halved
1 pound cherry tomatoes, halved
½ cup pecans, toasted and coarsely chopped*

DRESSING
2 tablespoons best-quality Balsamic vinegar
1½ tablespoons Dijon mustard
½ cup olive oil
small bunch tarragon, leaves only, chopped fine
salt
freshly ground pepper

In a small bowl, whisk together the vinegar and mustard. Gradually whisk in oil, a few tablespoons at a time. Stir in the chopped tarragon; taste and adjust for seasoning with salt and pepper.

Pour dressing over mozzarella balls and marinate at room temperature for 1 to 2 hours. Stir in tomatoes. Just before serving, add toasted pecans, and gently stir to combine. Taste and adjust seasoning as desired.

*To toast pecans, preheat oven to 300 F. Spread nuts in a pie pan and roast till they are fragrant and just beginning to darken, shaking occasionally. The pecans will continue to darken as they cool.

China Bayles' Fried Chicken,
with Twelve Herbs and Spices

1 frying chicken, cut up
3 cups sifted flour
2 teaspoons paprika
2 teaspoons garlic salt
2 teaspoons onion salt
1 teaspoon celery salt
1 teaspoon dried oregano
1 teaspoon dried rubbed sage
1 teaspoon dried powdered basil
½ teaspoon dried powdered rosemary
½ teaspoon dried powdered thyme
½ teaspoon dried bay
½ teaspoon allspice
1 teaspoon ground black pepper

Thoroughly combine all ingredients and use to coat chicken pieces for frying.

Sister Charity's Vegetable Bisque

3 tablespoons butter
2 cups coarsely chopped broccoli heads and peeled stems
¾ cup chopped carrots
½ cup chopped celery
1 small potato, peeled and chopped
1 small onion, peeled and chopped
2 cloves garlic, minced
4 cups chicken broth
¼ teaspoon thyme
¼ teaspoon summer savory

2 bay leaves
½ teaspoon salt
⅛ teaspoon pepper
1 egg yolk
1 cup half-and-half
1½ cups shredded Cheddar cheese

In a heavy saucepan, melt butter. Add broccoli, carrots, celery, potato, onion, and garlic and sauté for 3 to 4 minutes, stirring so that the vegetables do not brown. Add broth and bring to a to boil, stirring. Add herbs, salt and pepper. Cover and simmer until vegetables are tender, about 10 to 12 minutes. Remove bay leaves. In a small bowl, beat egg yolk, then add the half-and-half, continuing to beat. Gradually blend in several teaspoons of soup. Return the creamy mixture to the soup and cook, stirring until thickened. Blend in shredded cheese and serve. Serves 6 to 8.

Sister Charity's Raspberry Flummery

⅓ cup sugar
¼ cup cornstarch
¼ teaspoon salt
½ teaspoon nutmeg
3 cups milk
1 egg yolk, beaten
1 tablespoon rosewater
2 cups fresh raspberries, sweetened to taste

Combine sugar, cornstarch, salt, and nutmeg in a saucepan. Stir in milk. Cook and stir over medium heat until thickened and bubbly. Stir a small amount of hot liquid into the egg yolk; add yolk mixture to saucepan. Cook and stir for 2 minutes or until thickened. Remove from heat; stir in rosewater. Pour into individual sherbet dishes, filling each half full. Cool. Fill dishes with fresh raspberries. Serves 8.

Sister Pearl's Vinegar Pie

1 cup sugar
3 heaping tablespoons all-purpose flour
1 cup cold water
3 egg yolks
1 whole egg
2 tablespoons butter
6 tablespoons cider vinegar
1 (9-inch) pie crust, baked

Mix sugar and flour in saucepan. Add water, egg yolks (reserve egg whites for meringue), whole egg, butter, and vinegar. Cook, stirring, until thick. Pour into baked 9-inch pie shell. When cool, cover with meringue.

Meringue: Beat reserved egg whites until stiff. Continue to beat, gradually adding 4 tablespoons sugar. Spread over pie, being careful to seal against the crust. Brown meringue lightly in a 350-degree oven.

Martha Edmond's Fresh Sorrel Soup

1–2 tablespoons butter or margarine
1 onion, thinly sliced
1 small potato, diced
½ cup diced carrots
1 garlic clove, minced

6–8 ounces fresh sorrel (4–6 cups chopped)
1½ cups half-and-half
2 cups water or vegetable stock
¼ teaspoon ground nutmeg
1 teaspoon fresh lemon juice
1 teaspoon salt
½ teaspoon fresh ground black pepper

GARNISH
sour cream or plain yogurt
fresh lemon balm

Over medium heat, melt butter in a medium stainless or enamel pan (do not use cast iron). Cook onion, potato, and carrots until soft, about 10 minutes. Add garlic and cook 3 more minutes. Stir in sorrel and cook over moderate heat, uncovered, about 5 minutes, stirring occasionally. Add half-and-half, water or stock, and nutmeg. Bring to a low boil and remove from heat. Puree in a blender until smooth. Stir in lemon juice, add salt and pepper to taste, and refrigerate at least 4 hours. Serve in cold bowls garnished with sour cream or yogurt and sprigs of fresh lemon balm.

Indian Pudding

Indian Pudding was a favorite dessert in early New England. Colonists had a British fondness for baked and steamed puddings but could not obtain the necessary wheat flour. Instead, they used the native cornmeal and gave the dish the name "Indian" pudding. This is a traditional recipe, adopted by the Shakers.

6 cups milk
½ cup butter
½ cup yellow cornmeal

¼ **cup flour**

1 **teaspoon salt**

½ **cup molasses**

3 **eggs, beaten**

½ **cup granulated sugar**

1 **teaspoon cinnamon**

1 **teaspoon nutmeg**

½ **teaspoon ginger**

1 **cup raisins**

1 **cup cream, whipped with** ½ **teaspoon vanilla**

Scald milk in a large double boiler. Add butter. In a small bowl, mix cornmeal, flour, and salt; stir in molasses. Thin the mixture with about ½ cup of scalded milk, then gradually add the cornmeal mixture to the scalded milk. Cook, stirring until thickened. In another bowl, mix eggs, sugar, and spices. Stir in the milk-cornmeal mixture and mix until smooth. Stir in raisins. Pour into a greased casserole dish. Bake for 2 hours at 275 F. Cool about one hour, or warm if it has been chilled. Serve with whipped cream. Yield: 8 to 10 servings.

Herbs for Shaker Gardens

These are some of the herbs that would have been grown in a Kentucky Shaker garden and would be suitable for your garden, as well. For more information, additional recipes and garden drawings, visit www.abouthyme.com.

A Medicinal Garden

Blue Flag
Boneset
Catmint
Chamomile
Cohosh, Black
Comfrey
Elecampane
Feverfew
Foxglove
Hyssop
Motherwort
Mugwort
Mullein
Oswego Tea, Bee Balm
Peppermint
Queen of the Meadow, or Joe-pye Weed
Roman Wormwood

Rue

Southernwood

Tansy

Thyme, Common

Valerian

Vervain

Wild Carrot, or Queen Anne's Lace

Wood Betony

Yarrow

A Tea Garden

Many Shaker teas were medicinal. They did, however, enjoy the pleasures of peppermint, spearmint, lavender, lemon balm and strawberry teas.

Boneset

Borage

Catmint

Chamomile

Comfrey

Feverfew

Goldenrod, Sweet

Horehound

Lavender

Lemon Balm

Oswego Tea, or Bee Balm

Peppermint

Rhubarb

Sage

Spearmint

Strawberry

Sweet Gale, Sweet Fern
Wood Betony

A Culinary Garden

Until the late nineteenth century, the Shakers grew almost no
herbs exclusively for culinary use. Here are some herbs the later
Shakers might have grown for use in cooking.

Borage
Caraway
Chicory
Coriander
Dill
Fennel
Garlic
Horehound
Horseradish
Lemon Balm
Peppermint
Rosemary
Sage
Savory, Summer
Savory, Winter
Spearmint
Sweet Basil
Sweet Marjoram
Thyme, English or Common